OROONOKO
AND OTHER STORIES

APHRA BEHN

OROONOKO
AND OTHER STORIES

KÖNEMANN

🔔 Notes (on pp. 267 to 272)
are keyed thus in the margin

© 1999 for this edition
Könemann Verlagsgesellschaft mbH
Bonner Straße 126, D–50968 Köln

Series and volume editor: Michael Hulse
Cover design: Peter Feierabend
Layout and typesetting: Birgit Beyer
Printed in Hungary
ISBN 3-8290-0902-X
10 9 8 7 6 5 4 3 2 1

CONTENTS

OROONOKO
OR
THE ROYAL SLAVE

OROONOKO

I do not pretend, in giving you the History of this *ROYAL SLAVE*, to entertain my Reader with the Adventures of a feign'd *Hero*, whose Life and Fortunes Fancy may manage at the Poet's Pleasure; nor in relating the Truth, design to adorn it with any Accidents, but such as arrived in earnest to him: And it shall come simply into the World, recommended by its own proper Merits, and natural Intrigues; there being enough of Reality to support it, and to render it diverting, without the Addition of Invention.

I was myself an Eye-witness to a great Part of what you will find here set down; and what I could not be Witness of, I receiv'd from the Mouth of the chief Actor in this History, the *Hero* himself, who gave us the whole Transactions of his Youth: And I shall omit, for Brevity's Sake, a thousand little Accidents of his Life, which, however pleasant to us, where History was scarce, and Adventures very rare, yet might prove tedious and heavy to my Reader, in a World where he finds Diversions for every Minute, new and strange. But we who were perfectly charm'd with the Character of this great Man, were curious to gather every Circumstance of his Life.

The Scene of the last Part of his Adventures lies in a Colony in *America*, called *Surinam*, in the *West-Indies*.

But before I give you the Story of this *Gallant Slave*, 'tis fit I tell you the Manner of bringing them to these new *Colonies*; those they make Use of there, not being *Natives* of the Place: for those we live with in perfect Amity, without daring to command 'em; but, on the contrary, caress 'em with all the brotherly and friendly Affection in the World; trading with them for their Fish, Venison, Buffaloes Skins, and little Rarities; as *Marmosets*, a sort of Monkey, as big as a Rat or Weasel, but of a marvellous and delicate Shape, having Face and Hands like a Human Creature; and *Cousheries*, a little Beast in the Form and Fashion of a Lion, as big as a Kitten, but so exactly made in all Parts like that Noble Beast, that it is it in *Miniature*: Then for little *Paraketoes*, great *Parrots, Muckaws*, and a thousand other Birds and Beasts of wonderful and surprizing Forms, Shapes, and Colours: For Skins of prodigious Snakes, of which there are some three-score Yards in Length; as is the Skin of one that may be seen at his Majesty's *Antiquary's*; where are also some rare Flies, of amazing Forms and Colours, presented to 'em by myself; some as big as my Fist, some less; and all of various Excellencies, such as Art cannot imitate. Then we trade for Feathers, which they order into all Shapes, make themselves little short Habits of 'em, and glorious Wreaths for their Heads, Necks, Arms and Legs, whose Tinctures are unconceivable. I had a Set of these presented to me, and I gave 'em to the *King's Theatre*; it was the Dress of the *Indian Queen*, infinitely admir'd by Persons of Quality; and was inimitable. Besides these, a thousand little Knacks, and Rarities in Nature; and some of Art, as their Baskets, Weapons, Aprons, &c. We dealt with 'em with Beads of all Colours, Knives, Axes, Pins and Needles, which they us'd only as Tools to drill Holes with in their Ears, Noses and Lips, where they hang a great many little Things; as long Beads, Bits of Tin, Brass or Silver beat thin, and any shining Trinket. The Beads they weave into Aprons about a Quarter of an Ell long, and of the same Breadth; working them very prettily in Flowers of several Colours; which Apron they wear just before 'em, as *Adam* and *Eve* did the Fig-leaves; the Men wearing along Stripe of Linen, which they deal with us for. They thread these Beads also on long Cotton-threads, and make Girdles to tie their Aprons to, which come twenty times, or more, about the Waste, and then cross, like a Shoulderbelt, both Ways, and round their Necks, Arms and Legs. This Adornment, with their long black Hair, and the Face painted in little Specks or Flowers here and there, makes 'em a wonderful Figure to behold. Some of the Beauties, which indeed are finely shap'd, as almost all are, and who have pretty Features, are charming and novel; for they have all that is called Beauty, except the Colour, which is a reddish Yellow; or after a new Oiling, which they often use to themselves, they are of the

Colour of a new Brick, but smooth, soft and sleek. They are extreme modest and bashful, very shy, and nice of being touch'd. And tho' they are all thus naked, if one lives for ever among 'em, there it not to be seen an indecent Action, or Glance: and being continually us'd to see one another so unadorn'd, so like our first Parents before the Fall, it seems as if they had no Wishes, there being nothing to heighten Curiosity: but all you can see, you see at once, and every Moment see; and where there is no Novelty, there can be no Curiosity. Not but I have seen a handsome young *Indian*, dying for Love of a very beautiful young *Indian* Maid; but all his Courtship was, to fold his Arms, pursue her with his Eyes, and Sighs were all his Language: While she, as if no such Lover were present, or rather as if she desired none such, carefully guarded her Eyes from beholding him; and never approach'd him, but she looked down with all the blushing Modesty I have seen in the most Severe and Cautious of our World. And these People represented to me an absolute *Idea* of the first State of Innocence, before Man knew how to sin: And 'tis most evident and plain, that simple Nature is the most harmless, inoffensive and virtuous Mistress. 'Tis she alone, if she were permitted, that better instructs the World, than all the Inventions of Man: Religion would here but destroy that Tranquillity they possess by Ignorance; and Laws would but teach 'em to know Offences, of which now they have no Notion. They once made Mourning and Fasting for the Death of the *English* Governor, who had given his Hand to come on such a Day to 'em, and neither came nor sent; believing, when a Man's Word was past, nothing but Death could or should prevent his keeping it: And when they saw he was not dead, they ask'd him what Name they had for a Man who promis'd a Thing he did not do? The Governor told them, Such a Man was a *Lyar*, which was a Word of Infamy to a Gentleman. Then one of 'em reply'd, *Governor, you are a Lyar, and guilty of that Infamy*. They have a native Justice, which knows no Fraud; and they understand no Vice, or Cunning, but when they are taught by the *White* Men. They have Plurality of Wives; which, when they grow old, serve those that succeed 'em, who are young, but with a Servitude easy and respected; and unless they take Slaves in War, they have no other Attendants.

Those on that *Continent* where I was, had no King; but the oldest War-Captain was obey'd with great Resignation.

A War-Captain is a Man who has led them on to Battle with Conduct and Success; of whom I shall have Occasion to speak more hereafter, and of some other of their Customs and Manners, as they fall in my Way.

With these People, as I said, we live in perfect Tranquillity, and good Understanding, as it behoves us to do; they knowing all the Places where to seek the best Food of the Country, and the Means of getting it; and for very small and unvaluable Trifles, supplying us with what 'tis almost impossible for us to get; for they do not only in the Woods, and over the *Sevana's*, in Hunting, supply the Parts of Hounds, by swiftly scouring thro' those almost impassable Places, and by the mere Activity of their Feet, run down the nimblest Deer, and other eatable Beasts; but in the Water, one would think they were Gods of the Rivers, or Fellow-Citizens of the Deep; so rare an Art they have in swimming, diving, and almost living in Water; by which they command the less swift Inhabitants of the Floods. And then for shooting, what they cannot take, or reach with their Hands, they do with Arrows; and have so admirable an Aim, that they will split almost an Hair, and at any Distance that an Arrow can reach: they will shoot down Oranges, and other Fruit, and only touch the Stalk with the Dart's Point, that they may not hurt the Fruit. So that they being on all Occasions very useful to us, we find it absolutely necessary to caress 'em as Friends, and not to treat 'em as Slaves; nor dare we do otherwise, their Numbers so far surpassing ours in that Continent.

Those then whom we make use of to work in our Plantations of Sugar, are *Negroes*, Black-Slaves altogether, who are transported thither in this Manner.

Those who want Slaves, make a Bargain with a Master, or a Captain of a Ship, and contract to pay him so much apiece, a Matter of twenty Pound a Head, for as many as he agrees for, and to pay for 'em when they shall be deliver'd on such a Plantation: So that when there arrives a Ship laden with Slaves, they who have so contracted, go aboard, and receive their Number by Lot; and perhaps in one Lot that may be for ten, there may happen to be three or four Men, the rest Women and Children. Or be there more or less of either Sex, you are obliged to be contented with your Lot.

Coromantien, a Country of *Blacks* so called, was one of those Places in which they found the most advantageous Trading for these Slaves, and thither most of our great Traders in that Merchandize traffick; for that Nation is very warlike and brave; and having a continual Campaign, being always in Hostility with one neighbouring Prince or other, they had the Fortune to take a great many Captives: for all they took in Battle were sold as Slaves; at least those common Men who could not ransom themselves. Of these Slaves so taken, the General only has all the Profit; and of these Generals our Captains and Masters of Ships buy all their Freights.

The King of *Coramantien* was of himself a Man of an hundred and odd Years old, and had no Son, tho' he had many beautiful Black Wives: for most certainly there are Beauties that can charm of that Colour. In his younger Years he had had many gallant Men to his Sons, thirteen of whom died in Battle, conquering when they fell; and he had only left him for his Successor, one Grand-child, Son to one of these dead Victors, who, as soon as he could bear a Bow in his Hand, and a Quiver at his Back, was sent into the Field, to be train'd up by one of the oldest Generals to War; where, from his natural Inclination to Arms, and the Occasions given him, with the good Conduct of the old General, he became, at the Age of seventeen, one of the most expert Captains, and bravest Soldiers that ever saw the Field of *Mars*: so that he was ador'd as the Wonder of all that World, and the Darling of the Soldiers. Besides, he was adorn'd with a native Beauty, so transcending all those of his gloomy Race, that he struck an Awe and Reverence, even into those that knew not his Quality; as he did into me, who beheld him with Surprize and Wonder, when afterwards he arrived in our World.

He had scarce arrived at his seventeenth Year, when, fighting by his Side, the General was kill'd with an Arrow in his Eye, which the Prince *Oroonoko* (for so was this gallant *Moor* call'd) very narrowly avoided; nor had he, if the General who saw the Arrow shot, and perceiving it aimed at the Prince, had not bow'd his Head between, on Purpose to receive it in his own Body, rather than it should touch that of the Prince, and so saved him.

'Twas then, afflicted as *Oroonoko* was, that he was proclaimed General in the old Man's Place: and then it was, at the finishing of that War, which had continu'd for two Years, that the Prince came to Court, where he had hardly been a Month together, from the Time of his fifth Year to that of seventeen: and 'twas amazing to imagine where it was he learn'd so much Humanity; or to give his Accomplishments a juster Name, where 'twas he got that real Greatness of Soul, those refined Notions of true Honour, that absolute Generosity, and that Softness, that was capable of the highest Passions of Love and Gallantry, whose Objects were almost continually fighting Men, or those mangled or dead, who heard no Sounds but those of War and Groans. Some Part of it we may attribute to the Care of a *Frenchman* of Wit and Learning, who finding it turn to a very good Account to be a sort of Royal Tutor to this young Black, and perceiving him very ready, apt, and quick of Apprehension, took a great Pleasure to teach him Morals, Language and Science; and was for it extremely belov'd and valu'd by him. Another Reason was, he lov'd when he came from War, to see all the *English* Gentlemen that traded thither; and did not only learn their Language, but that of the *Spaniard* also, with whom he traded afterwards for Slaves.

I have often seen and conversed with this Great Man, and been a Witness to many of his mighty Actions; and do assure my Reader, the most illustrious Courts could not have produced a braver Man, both for Greatness of Courage and Mind, a Judgment more solid, a Wit more quick, and a Conversation more sweet and diverting. He knew almost as much as if he had read much: He had heard of and admired the *Romans*: He had heard of the late Civil Wars in *England*, and the deplorable Death of our great Monarch; and would discourse of it with all the Sense and Abhorrence of the Injustice imaginable. He had an extreme good and graceful Mien, and all the Civility of a well-bred Great Man. He had nothing of Barbarity in his Nature, but in all Points address'd himself as if his Education had been in some *European* Court.

This great and just Character of *Oroonoko* gave me an extreme Curiosity to see him, especially when I knew he spoke *French* and *English*, and that I could talk with him. But tho' I had heard so much of him, I was as greatly surprized when I saw him, as if I had heard nothing of him; so beyond all Report I found him. He came into the Room, and addressed himself to me, and some other Women, with the best Grace in the World. He was pretty tall, but of a Shape the most exact that can be fancy'd: The most famous Statuary could not form the Figure of a Man more admirably turn'd from Head to Foot. His Face was not of that brown rusty Black which most of that Nation are, but a perfect Ebony, or polished Jet. His Eyes were the most aweful that could be seen, and very piercing; the White of 'em being like Snow, as were his Teeth. His Nose was rising and *Roman*, instead of *African* and flat: His Mouth the finest shaped that could be seen; far from those great turn'd Lips, which are so natural to the rest of the Negroes. The whole Proportion and Air of his Face was so nobly and exactly form'd, that bating his Colour, there could be nothing in Nature more beautiful, agreeable and handsome. There was no one Grace wanting, that bears the Standard of true Beauty. His Hair came down to his Shoulders, by the Aids of Art, which was by pulling it out with a Quill, and keeping it comb'd; of which he took particular Care. Nor did the Perfections of his Mind come short of those of his Person; for his Discourse was admirable upon almost any Subject: and whoever had heard him speak, would have been convinced of their Errors, that all fine Wit is confined to the white Men, especially to those of Christendom; and would have confess'd that *Oroonoko* was as capable even of reigning well, and of governing as wisely, had as great a Soul, as politick Maxims, and was as sensible of Power, as any Prince civiliz'd in the most refined Schools of Humanity and Learning, or the most illustrious Courts.

This Prince, such as I have describ'd him, whose Soul and Body were so admirably adorned, was (while yet he was in the Court of his Grandfather, as I said) as capable of Love, as 'twas possible for a brave and gallant Man to be; and in saying that, I have named the highest Degree of Love: for sure great Souls are most capable of that Passion.

I have already said, the old General was kill'd by the Shot of an Arrow, by the Side of this Prince, in Battle; and that *Oroonoko* was made General. This old dead Hero had one only Daughter left of his Race, a Beauty, that to describe her truly, one need say only, she was Female to the noble Male; the beautiful Black *Venus* to our young *Mars*; as charming in her Person as he, and of delicate Virtues. I have seen a hundred White Men sighing after her, and making a thousand Vows at her Feet, all in vain and unsuccessful. And she was indeed too great for any but a Prince of her own Nation to adore.

Oroonoko coming from the Wars (which were now ended) after he had made his Court to his Grandfather, he thought in Honour he ought to make a Visit to *Imoinda*, the Daughter of his Foster-father, the dead General; and to make some Excuses to her, because his Preservation was the Occasion of her Father's Death; and to present her with those Slaves that had been taken in this last Battle, as the Trophies of her Father's Victories. When he came, attended by all the young Soldiers of any Merit, he was infinitely surpriz'd at the Beauty of this fair

Queen of Night, whose Face and Person were so exceeding all he had ever beheld, that lovely Modesty with which she receiv'd him, that Softness in her Look and Sighs, upon the melancholy Occasion of this Honour that was done by so great a Man as *Oroonoko*, and a Prince of whom she had heard such admirable Things; the Awfulness wherewith she receiv'd him, and the Sweetness of her Words and Behaviour while he stay'd, gain'd a perfect Conquest over his fierce Heart, and made him feel, the Victor could be subdu'd. So that having made his first Compliments, and presented her an hundred and fifty Slaves in Fetters, he told her with his Eyes, that he was not insensible of her Charms; while *Imoinda*, who wish'd for nothing more than so glorious a Conquest, was pleas'd to believe, she understood that silent Language of new-born Love; and, from that Moment, put on all her Additions to Beauty.

The Prince return'd to Court with quite another Humour than before; and tho' he did not speak much of the fair *Imoinda*, he had the Pleasure to hear all his Followers speak of nothing but the Charms of that Maid, insomuch, that, even in the Presence of the old King, they were extolling her, and heightning, if possible, the Beauties they had found in her: so that nothing else was talk'd of, no other Sound was heard in every Corner where there were Whisperers, but *Imoinda! Imoinda!*

'Twill be imagin'd *Oroonoko* stay'd not long before he made his second Visit; nor, considering his Quality, not much longer before he told her, he ador'd her. I have often heard him say, that he admir'd by what strange Inspiration he came to talk Things so soft, and so passionate, who never knew Love, nor was us'd to the Conversation of Women; but (to use his own Words) he said, "Most happily, some new, and, till then, unknown Power instructed his Heart and Tongue in the Language of Love; and at the same Time, in Favour of him, inspir'd *Imoinda* with a Sense of his Passion." She was touch'd with what he said, and return'd it all in such Answers as went to his very Heart, with a Pleasure unknown before. Nor did he

17

use those Obligations ill, that Love had done him, but turn'd all his happy Moments to the best Advantage; and as he knew no Vice, his Flame aim'd at nothing but Honour, if such a Distinction may be made in Love; and especially in that Country, where Men take to themselves as many as they can maintain; and where the only Crime and Sin against a Woman, is, to turn her off, to abandon her to Want, Shame and Misery: such ill Morals are only practis'd in *Christian* Countries, where they prefer the bare Name of Religion; and, without Virtue or Morality, think that sufficient. But *Oroonoko* was none of those Professors; but as he had right Notions of Honour, so he made her such Propositions as were not only and barely such; but, contrary to the Custom of his Country, he made her Vows, she should be the only Woman he would possess while he liv'd; that no Age or Wrinkles should incline him to change: for her Soul would be always fine, and always young; and he should have an eternal *Idea* in his Mind of the Charms she now bore; and should look into his Heart for that *Idea*, when he could find it no longer in her Face.

After a thousand Assurances of his lasting Flame, and her eternal Empire over him, she condescended to receive him for her Husband; or rather, receive him, as the greatest Honour the Gods could do her.

There is a certain Ceremony in these Cases to be observ'd, which I forgot to ask how 'twas perform'd; but 'twas concluded on both Sides, that in Obedience to him, the Grandfather was to be first made acquainted with the Design: For they pay a most absolute Resignation to the Monarch, especially when he is a Parent also.

On the other Side, the old King, who had many Wives, and many Concubines, wanted not Court-Flatterers to insinuate into his Heart a thousand tender Thoughts for this young Beauty; and who represented her to his Fancy, as the most charming he had ever possess'd in all the long Race of his numerous Years. At this Character, his old Heart, like an extinguish'd Brand, most apt to take Fire, felt new Sparks of

Love, and began to kindle; and now grown to his second Childhood, long'd with Impatience to behold this gay Thing, with whom, alas! he could but innocently play. But how he should be confirm'd she was this *Wonder*, before he us'd his Power to call her to Court, (where Maidens never came, unless for the King's private Use) he was next to consider; and while he was so doing, he had Intelligence brought him, that *Imoinda* was most certainly Mistress to the Prince *Oroonoko*. This gave him some Chagrine: however, it gave him also an Opportunity, one Day, when the Prince was a hunting, to wait on a Man of Quality, as his Slave and Attendant, who should go and make a Present to *Imoinda*, as from the Prince; he should then, unknown, see this fair Maid, and have an Opportunity to hear what Message she would return the Prince for his Present, and from thence gather the State of her Heart, and Degree of her Inclination. This was put in Execution, and the old Monarch saw, and burn'd: He found her all he had heard, and would not delay his Happiness, but found he should have some Obstacle to overcome her Heart; for she express'd her Sense of the Present the Prince had sent her, in Terms so sweet, so soft and pretty, with an Air of Love and Joy that could not be dissembled, insomuch that 'twas past Doubt whether she lov'd *Oroonoko* entirely. This gave the old King some Affliction; but he salv'd it with this, that the Obedience the People pay their King, was not at all inferior to what they paid their Gods; and what Love would not oblige *Imoinda* to do, Duty would compel her to.

He was therefore no sooner got into his Apartment, but he sent the Royal Veil to *Imoinda*; that is the Ceremony of Invitation: He sends the Lady he has a Mind to honour with his Bed, a Veil, with which she is covered, and secur'd for the King's Use; and 'tis Death to disobey; besides, held a most impious Disobedience.

'Tis not to be imagin'd the Surprize and Grief that seiz'd the lovely Maid at this News and Sight. However, as Delays in these Cases are dangerous, and Pleading worse than Treason;

trembling, and almost fainting, she was oblig'd to suffer herself to be cover'd, and led away.

They brought her thus to Court; and the King, who had caus'd a very rich Bath to be prepar'd, was led into it, where he sat under a Canopy, in State, to receive this long'd-for Virgin; whom he having commanded to be brought to him, they (after disrobing her) led her to the Bath, and making fast the Doors, left her to descend. The King, without more Courtship, bad her throw off her Mantle, and come to his Arms. But *Imoinda*, all in Tears, threw herself on the Marble, on the Brink of the Bath, and besought him to hear her. She told him, as she was a Maid, how proud of the Divine Glory she should have been, of having it in her Power to oblige her King: but as by the Laws he could not, and from his Royal Goodness would not take from any Man his wedded Wife; so she believ'd she should be the occasion of making him commit a great Sin, if she did not reveal her State and Condition; and tell him she was another's, and could not be so happy to be his.

The King, enrag'd at this Delay, hastily demanded the Name of the bold Man, that had married a Woman of her Degree, without his Consent. *Imoinda* seeing his Eyes fierce, and his Hands tremble, (whether with Age or Anger, I know not, but she fancy'd the last) almost repented she had said so much, for now she fear'd the Storm would fall on the Prince; she therefore said a thousand Things to appease the raging of his Flame, and to prepare him to hear who it was with Calmness: but before she spoke, he imagin'd who she meant, but would not seem to do so, but commanded her to lay aside her Mantle, and suffer herself to receive his Caresses, or, by his Gods he swore, that happy Man whom she was going to name should die, tho' it was even *Oroonoko* himself. *Therefore* (said he) *deny this Marriage, and swear thyself a Maid. That* (reply'd *Imoinda*) *by all our Powers I do; for I am not yet known to my Husband. 'Tis enough* (said the King) *'tis enough both to satisfy my Conscience and my Heart.* And rising from his Seat, he went and led her into the Bath; it being in vain for her to resist.

In this Time, the Prince, who was return'd from Hunting, went to visit his *Imoinda*, but found her gone; and not only so, but heard she had receiv'd the Royal Veil. This rais'd him to a Storm; and in his Madness, they had much ado to save him from laying violent Hands on himself. Force first prevail'd, and then Reason: They urg'd all to him, that might oppose his Rage; but nothing weigh'd so greatly with him as the King's old Age, uncapable of injuring him with *Imoinda*. He would give Way to that Hope, because it pleas'd him most, and flatter'd best his Heart. Yet this serv'd not altogether to make him cease his different Passions, which sometimes rag'd within him, and soften'd into Showers. 'Twas not enough to appease him, to tell him, his Grandfather was old, and could not that Way injure him, while he retain'd that awful Duty which the young Men are us'd there to pay to their grave Relations. He could not be convinc'd he had no Cause to sigh and mourn for the Loss of a Mistress, he could not with all his Strength and Courage retrieve, and he would often cry, "Oh, my Friends! were she in wall'd Cities, or confin'd from me in Fortifications of the greatest Strength; did Inchantments or Monsters detain her from me; I would venture thro' any Hazard to free her; But here, in the Arms of a feeble old Man, my Youth, my violent Love, my Trade in Arms, and all my vast Desire of Glory, avail me nothing. *Imoinda* is as irrecoverably lost to me, as if she were snatch'd by the cold Arms of Death: Oh! she is never to be retrieved. If I would wait tedious Years; till Fate should bow the old King to his Grave, even that would not leave me *Imoinda* free; but still that Custom that makes it so vile a Crime for a Son to marry his Father's Wives or Mistresses, would hinder my Happiness; unless I would either ignobly set an ill Precedent to my Successors, or abandon my Country, and fly with her to some unknown World who never heard our Story."

But it was objected to him, That his Case was not the same: for *Imoinda* being his lawful Wife by solemn Contract, 'twas he was the injur'd Man, and might, if he so pleas'd, take *Imoinda* back, the Breach of the Law being on his Grandfather's Side;

and that if he could circumvent him, and redeem her from the *Otan*, which is the Palace of the King's Women, a sort of *Seraglio*, it was both just and lawful for him so to do.

This Reasoning had some Force upon him, and he should have been entirely comforted, but for the Thought that she was possess'd by his Grandfather. However, he lov'd her so well, that he was resolv'd to believe what most favour'd his Hope, and to endeavour to learn from *Imoinda's* own Mouth, what only she could satisfy him in, whether she was robb'd of that Blessing which was only due to his Faith and Love. But as it was very hard to get a Sight of the Women, (for no Men ever enter'd into the *Otan*, but when the King went to entertain himself with some one of his Wives or Mistresses; and 'twas Death, at any other Time, for any other to go in) so he knew not how to contrive to get a Sight of her.

While *Oroonoko* felt all the Agonies of Love, and suffer'd under a Torment the most painful in the World, the old King was not exempted from his Share of Affliction. He was troubled, for having been forc'd, by an irresistible Passion, to rob his Son of a Treasure, he knew, could not but be extremely dear to him; since she was the most beautiful that ever had been seen, and had besides, all the Sweetness and Innocence of Youth and Modesty, with a Charm of Wit surpassing all. He found, that however she was forc'd to expose her lovely Person to his wither'd Arms, she could only sigh and weep there, and think of *Oroonoko*; and oftentimes could not forbear speaking of him, tho' her Life were, by Custom, forfeited by owning her Passion. But she spoke not of a Lover only, but of a Prince dear to him to whom she spoke; and of the Praises of a Man, who, 'till now, fill'd the old Man's Soul with Joy at every Recital of his Bravery, or even his Name. And 'twas this Dotage on our young Hero, that gave *Imoinda* a thousand Privileges to speak of him without offending; and this Condescension in the old King, that made her take the Satisfaction of speaking of him so very often.

Besides, he many times enquir'd how the Prince bore himself: And those of whom he ask'd, being entirely Slaves to the Merits and Virtues of the Prince, still answer'd what they they thought couduc'd best to his Service; which was, to make the old King fancy that the Prince had no more Interest in *Imoinda*, and had resign'd her willingly to the Pleasure of the King; that he diverted himself with his Mathematicians, his Fortifications, his Officers, and his Hunting.

This pleas'd the old Lover, who fail'd not to report these Things again to *Imoinda*, that she might, by the Example of her young Lover, withdraw her Heart, and rest better contented in his Arms. But, however she was forc'd to receive this unwelcome News, in all Appearance, with Unconcern and Content; her Heart was bursting within, and she was only happy when she could get alone, to vent her Griefs and Moans with Sighs and Tears.

What Reports of the Prince's Conduct were made to the King, he thought good to justify, as far as possibly he could, by his Actions; and when he appear'd in the Presence of the King, he shew'd a Face not at all betraying his Heart: so that in a little Time, the old Man, being entirely convinc'd that he was no longer a Lover of *Imoinda*, he carry'd him with him in his Train to the *Otan*, often to banquet with his Mistresses. But as soon as he enter'd, one Day, into the Apartment of *Imoinda*, with the King, at the first Glance from her Eyes, notwithstanding all his determined Resolution, he was ready to sink in the Place where he stood; and had certainly done so, but for the Support of *Aboan*, a young Man who was next to him; which, with his Change of Countenance, had betray'd him, had the King chanc'd to look that Way. And I have observ'd, 'tis a very great Error in those who laugh when one says, *A* Negro *can change Colour*: for I have seen 'em as frequently blush, and look pale, and that as visibly as ever I saw in the most beautiful *White*. And 'tis certain, that both these Changes were evident, this Day, in both these Lovers. And *Imoinda*, who saw with some Joy the Change in the Prince's Face, and found it in her own, strove to divert the King from beholding either, by a forc'd Caress, with which she met him; which was a new Wound in the Heart of the poor dying Prince. But as soon as the King was busy'd in looking on some fine Thing of *Imoinda's* making, she had Time to tell the Prince, with her angry, but Love-darting Eyes, that she resented his Coldness, and bemoan'd her own miserable Captivity. Nor were his Eyes silent, but answer'd her's again, as much as Eyes could do, instructed by the most tender and most passionate Heart that ever lov'd: And they spoke so well, and so effectually, as *Imoinda* no longer doubted but she was the only Delight and Darling of that Soul she found pleading in 'em its Right of Love, which none was more willing to resign than she. And 'twas this powerful Language alone that in an Instant convey'd all the Thoughts of their Souls to each other; that they both found there wanted but Opportunity to make them both entirely happy. But when he saw another Door open'd by *Onahal* (a former old Wife of the King's, who now had Charge of *Imoinda*) and saw the Prospect of a Bed of State made ready, with Sweets and Flowers for the Dalliance of the King, who immediately led the trembling Victim from his Sight, into that prepar'd Repose; what Rage! what wild Frenzies seiz'd his Heart! which forcing to keep within Bounds, and to suffer without Noise, it became the more insupportable, and rent his Soul with ten thousand Pains. He was forc'd to retire to vent his Groans, where he fell down on a Carpet, and lay struggling a long Time, and only breathing now and then—Oh *Imoinda*! When *Onahal* had finished her necessary Affair within, shutting the Door, she came forth, to wait till the King called; and hearing some one sighing in the other Room, she pass'd on, and found the Prince in that deplorable Condition, which she thought needed her Aid. She gave him Cordials, but all in vain; till finding the Nature of his Disease, by his Sighs, and naming *Imoinda*, she told him he had not so much Cause as he imagined to afflict himself: for if he knew the King so well as she did, he would not lose a Moment in Jealousy; and that she was confident that *Imoinda* bore, at this Minute, Part in his Affliction. *Aboan* was of the same Opinion, and both together persuaded him to re-assume his Courage; and all sitting down on the Carpet, the Prince said so many obliging Things to *Onahal*, that he half-persuaded her to be of his Party: and she promised him, she would thus far comply with his just Desires, that she would let *Imoinda* know how faithful he was, what he suffer'd, and what he said.

This Discourse lasted till the King called, which gave *Oroonoko* a certain Satisfaction; and with the Hope *Onahal* had made him conceive, he assumed a Look as gay as 'twas possible a Man in his Circumstances could do: and presently after, he was call'd in with the rest who waited without. The King commanded Musick to be brought, and several of his young Wives and Mistresses came all together by his Command, to dance before him; where *Imoinda* perform'd her Part with an Air and Grace so surpassing all the rest, as her Beauty was above 'em, and received the Present ordained as a Prize. The Prince was every Moment more charmed with the new Beauties and Graces he beheld in this Fair-One; and while he gazed, and she danc'd, *Onahal* was retired to a Window with *Aboan*.

This *Onahal*, as I said, was one of the Cast-Mistresses of the old King; and 'twas these (now past their Beauty) that were made Guardians or Governantees to the new and the young ones, and whose Business it was to teach them all those wanton Arts of Love, with which they prevail'd and charm'd heretofore in their Turn; and who now treated the triumphing Happy-ones with all the Severity, as to Liberty and Freedom, that was possible, in Revenge of the Honours they rob them of; envying them those Satisfactions, those Gallantries and Presents, that were once made to themselves, while Youth and Beauty lasted, and which they now saw pass, as it were regardless by, and paid only to the Bloomings. And certainly, nothing is more afflicting to a decay'd Beauty, than to behold in itself declining Charms, that were once ador'd; and to find those Caresses paid to new Beauties, to which once she laid Claim; to hear them whisper, as she passes by, that once was a delicate Woman. Those abandon'd ladies therefore endeavour to revenge all the Despights and Decays of Time, on these flourishing Happy-ones. And 'twas this Severity that gave *Oroonoko* a thousand Fears he should never prevail with *Onahal* to see *Imoinda*. But, as I said, she was now retir'd to a Window with *Aboan*.

This young Man was not only one of the best Quality, but a Man extremely well made, and beautiful; and coming often to attend the King to the *Otan*, he had subdu'd the Heart of the antiquated *Onahal*, which had not forgot how pleasant it was to be in love. And tho' she had some Decays in her Face, she had none in her Sense and Wit; she was there agreeable still, even to *Aboan's* Youth: so that he took Pleasure in entertaining her with Discourses of Love. He knew also, that to make his Court to these She-favourites, was the Way to be great; these being the Persons that do all Affairs and Business at Court. He had also observed, that she had given him Glances more tender and inviting than she had done to others of his Quality. And now, when he saw that her Favour could so absolutely oblige the Prince, he fail'd not to sigh in her Ear, and look with Eyes all soft upon her, and gave her Hope that she had made some Impressions on his Heart. He found her pleas'd at this, and making a thousand Advances to him: but the Ceremony ending, and the King departing, broke up the Company for that Day, and his Conversation.

Aboan fail'd not that Night to tell the Prince of his Success, and how advantageous the Service of *Onahal* might be to his Amour with *Imoinda*. The Prince was overjoy'd with this good News, and besought him, if it were possible, to caress her so, as to engage her entirely, which he could not fail to do, if he comply'd with her Desires: *For then* (said the Prince) *her Life lying at your Mercy, she must grant you the Request you make in my Behalf*. *Aboan* understood him, and assur'd him he would make Love so effectually, that he would defy the most expert Mistress of the Art, to find out whether he dissembled it, or had it really. And 'twas with Impatience they waited the next Opportunity of going to the *Otan*.

The Wars came on, the Time of taking the Field approached; and 'twas impossible for the Prince to delay his going at the Head of his Army to encounter the Enemy; so that every Day seem'd a tedious Year, till he saw his *Imoinda*: for he believed he could not live, if he were forced away without being so happy. 'Twas with Impatience therefore that he expected the next Visit the King would make; and, according to his Wish, it was not long.

The Parley of the Eyes of these two Lovers had not pass'd so secretly, but an old jealous Lover could spy it; or rather, he wanted not Flatterers who told him they observ'd it: so that the Prince was hasten'd to the Camp, and this was the last Visit he found he should make to the *Otan*; he therefore urged *Aboan* to make the best of this last Effort, and to explain himself so to *Onahal*, that she deferring her Enjoyment of her young Lover no longer, might make Way for the Prince to speak to *Imoinda*.

The whole Affair being agreed on between the Prince and *Aboan*, they attended the King, as the Custom was, to the *Otan*; where, while the whole Company was taken up in beholding the Dancing, and Antick Postures the Women-Royal made to divert the King, *Onahal* singled out *Aboan*, whom she found most pliable to her Wish. When she had him where she believed she could not be heard, she sigh'd to him, and softly cry'd, "Ah, *Aboan*! when will you be sensible of my Passion? I confess it with my Mouth, because I would not give my Eyes the Lye; and you have but too much already perceived they have confess'd my Flame: nor would I have you believe, that because I am the abandon'd Mistress of a King, I esteem myself altogether divested of Charms: No, *Aboan*; I have still a Rest of Beauty enough engaging, and have learn'd to please too well, not to be desirable. I can have Lovers still, but will have none but *Aboan*. Madam, (*reply'd the half-feigning Youth*) you have already, by my Eyes, found you can still conquer; and I believe 'tis in pity of me you condescend to this kind Confession. But, Madam, Words are used to be so small a Part of our Country-Courtship, that 'tis rare one can get so happy an Opportunity as to tell one's Heart; and those few Minutes we have, are forced to be snatch'd for more certain Proofs of Love than speaking and sighing: and such I languish for."

He spoke this with such a Tone, that she hoped it true, and could not forbear believing it; and being wholly transported with Joy for having subdued the finest of all the King's Subjects to her Desires, she took from her Ears two large Pearls, and commanded him to wear 'em in his. He would have refused 'em, crying, *Madam these are not the Proofs of our Love that I expect; 'tis Opportunity, 'tis a Lone-Hour only, that can make me happy.* But forcing the Pearls into his Hand, she whisper'd softly to him; *Oh! do not fear a Woman's Invention, when Love sets her a thinking.* And pressing his Hand, she cry'd, *This Night you shall be happy. Come to the Gate of the Orange-Grove, behind the* Otan, *and I will be ready about midnight to receive you.* 'Twas thus agreed, and she left him, that no Notice might be taken of their speaking together.

The Ladies were still dancing, and the King, laid on a Carpet, with a great deal of Pleasure was beholding them, especially *Imoinda*, who that Day appeared more lovely than ever, being enlivened with the good Tidings *Onahal* had brought her, of the constant Passion the Prince had for her. The Prince was laid on another Carpet at the other End of the Room, with his Eyes fixed on the Object of his Soul; and as she turned or moved, so did they; and she alone gave his Eyes and Soul their Motions. Nor did *Imoinda* employ her Eyes to any other use, than in beholding with infinite Pleasure the Joy she produced in those of the Prince. But while she was more regarding him than the Steps she took, she chanced to fall, and so near him, as that leaping with extreme Force from the Carpet, he caught her in his Arms as she fell; and 'twas visible to the whole Presence, the Joy wherewith he received her. He clasped her close to his Bosom, and quite forgot that Reverence that was due to the Mistress of a King, and that Punishment that is the Reward of a Boldness of this Nature. And had not the Presence of Mind of *Imoinda* (fonder of his Safety than her own) befriended him, in making her spring from his Arms, and fall into her Dance again, he had at that Instant met his Death; for the old King, jealous to the last Degree, rose up in Rage, broke all the Diversion, and led *Imoinda* to her Apartment, and sent out Word to the Prince, to go immediately to the Camp; and that if he were found another Night in Court, he should suffer the Death ordained for disobedient Offenders.

You may imagine how welcome this News was to *Oroonoko*, whose unseasonable Transport and Caress of *Imoinda* was blamed by all Men that loved him: and now he perceived his Fault, yet cry'd, *That for such another Moment he would be content to die.*

All the *Otan* was in Disorder about this Accident; and *Onahal* was particularly concern'd, because on the Prince's Stay depended her Happiness; for she could no longer expect that of *Aboan*: So that e'er they departed, they contrived it so, that the Prince and he should both come that Night to the Grove of the *Otan*, which was all of Oranges and Citrons, and that there they would wait her Orders.

They parted thus with Grief enough 'till Night, leaving the King in Possession of the lovely Maid. But nothing could appease the Jealousy of the old Lover; he would not be imposed on, but would have it, that *Imoinda* made a false Step on Purpose to fall into *Oroonoko's* Bosom, and that all things looked like a Design on both Sides; and 'twas in vain she protested her Innocence: He was old and obstinate, and left her, more than half assur'd that his Fear was true.

The King going to his Apartment, sent to know where the Prince was, and if he intended to obey his Command. The Messenger return'd, and told him, he found the Prince pensive, and altogether unprepar'd for the Campaign; that he lay negligently on the Ground, and answer'd very little. This confirmed the Jealousy of the King, and he commanded that they should very narrowly and privately watch his Motions; and that he should not stir from his Apartment, but one Spy or other should be employ'd to watch him: So that the Hour approaching, wherein he was to go to the Citron-Grove; and taking only *Aboan* along with him, he leaves his Apartment, and was watched to the very Gate of the *Otan*; where he was seen to enter, and where they left him, to carry back the Tidings to the King.

Oroonoko and *Aboan* were no sooner enter'd, but *Onahal* led the Prince to the Apartment of *Imoinda*; who, not knowing any thing of her Happiness, was laid in Bed. But *Onahal* only left him in her Chamber, to make the best of his Opportunity, and took her dear *Aboan* to her own; where he shewed the Height of Complaisance for his Prince, when, to give him an Opportunity, he suffered himself to be caressed in Bed by *Onahal*.

The Prince softly waken'd *Imoinda*, who was not a little surpriz'd with Joy to find him there; and yet she trembled with a thousand Fears. I believe he omitted saying nothing to this young Maid, that might persuade her to suffer him to seize his own, and take the Rights of Love. And I believe she was not long resisting those Arms where she so longed to be; and having Opportunity, Night, and Silence, Youth, Love, and Desire, he soon prevail'd, and ravished in a Moment what his old Grandfather had been endeavouring for so many Months.

'Tis not to be imagined the Satisfaction of these two young Lovers; nor the Vows she made him, that she remained a spotless Maid till that Night, and that what she did with his Grandfather had robb'd him of no Part of her Virgin-Honour; the Gods, in Mercy and Justice, having reserved that for her plighted Lord, to whom of Right it belonged. And 'tis impossible to express the Transports he suffer'd, while he listen'd to a Discourse so charming from her loved Lips; and clasped that Body in his Arms, for whom he had so long languished; and nothing now afflicted him, but his sudden Departure from her; for he told her the Necessity, and his Commands, but should depart satisfy'd in this, That since the old King had hitherto not been able to deprive him of those Enjoyments which only belonged to him, he believed for the future he would be less able to injure him; so that, abating the Scandal of the Veil, which was no otherwise so, than that she was Wife to another, he believed her safe, even in the Arms of the King, and innocent; yet would he have ventur'd at the Conquest of the World, and have given it all to have had her avoided that Honour of receiving the *Royal Veil*. 'Twas thus, between a thousand Caresses, that both bemoan'd the hard Fate of Youth and Beauty, so liable to that cruel Promotion: 'Twas a Glory that could well have been spared here, tho' desired and aim'd at by all the young Females of that Kingdom.

But while they were thus fondly employ'd, forgetting how Time ran on, and that the Dawn must conduct him far away from his only Happiness, they heard a great Noise in the *Otan*, and unusual Voices of Men; at which the Prince, starting from the Arms of the frighted *Imoinda*, ran to a little Battle-Ax he used to wear by his Side; and having not so much Leisure as to put on his Habit, he opposed himself against some who were already opening the Door: which they did with so much Violence, that *Oroonoko* was not able to defend it; but was forced to cry out with a commanding Voice, "Whoever ye are that have the Boldness to attempt to approach this Apartment thus rudely; know, that I, the Prince *Oroonoko*, will revenge it with the certain Death of him that first enters: Therefore stand back, and know, this Place is sacred to Love and Me this Night; Tomorrow 'tis the King's."

This he spoke with a Voice so resolv'd and assur'd, that they soon retired from the Door; but cry'd, "'Tis by the King's Command we are come; and being satisfy'd by thy Voice, O Prince, as much as if we had enter'd, we can report to the King the Truth of all his Fears, and leave thee to provide for thy own Safety, as thou art advis'd by thy Friends."

At these Words they departed, and left the Prince to take a short and sad Leave of his *Imoinda*; who, trusting in the Strength of her Charms, believed she should appease the Fury of a jealous King, by saying, she was surprized, and that it was by Force of Arms he got into her Apartment. All her Concern now was for his Life, and therefore she hasten'd him to the Camp, and with much ado prevail'd on him to go. Nor was it she alone that prevail'd; *Aboan* and *Onahal* both pleaded, and both assured him of a Lye that should be well enough contrived to secure *Imoinda*. So that at last, with a Heart sad as Death, dying Eyes, and sighing Soul, *Oroonoko* departed, and took his way to the Camp.

It was not long after, the King in Person came to the *Otan*; where beholding *Imoinda*, with Rage in his Eyes, he upbraided her Wickedness, and Perfidy; and threatning her Royal Lover, she fell on her Face at his Feet, bedewing the Floor with her Tears, and imploring his Pardon for a Fault which she had not with her Will committed; as *Onahal*, who was also prostrate with her, could testify: That, unknown to her, he had broke into her Apartment, and ravished her. She spoke this much against her Conscience; but to save her own Life, 'twas absolutely necessary she should feign this Falsity. She knew it could not injure the Prince, he being fled to an Army that would stand by him, against any Injuries that should assault him. However, this last Thought of *Imoinda's* being ravished, changed the Measures of his Revenge; and whereas before he designed to be himself her Executioner, he now resolved she should not die. But as it is the greatest Crime in Nature amongst them, to touch a Woman after having been possess'd by a Son, a Father, or a Brother, so now he looked on *Imoinda* as a polluted thing wholly unfit for his Embrace; nor would he resign her to his Grandson, because she had received the *Royal Veil*: He therefore removes her from the *Otan*, with *Onahal*; whom he put into safe Hands, with Order they should be both sold off as Slaves to another Country, either *Christian* or *Heathen*, 'twas no Matter where.

This cruel Sentence, worse than Death, they implor'd might be reversed; but their Prayers were vain, and it was put in Execution accordingly, and that with so much Secrecy, that none, either without or within the *Otan*, knew any thing of their Absence, or their Destiny.

The old King nevertheless executed this with a great deal of Reluctancy; but he believed he had made a very great Conquest over himself, when he had once resolved, and had perform'd what he resolved. He believed now, that his Love had been unjust; and that he could not expect the Gods, or *Captain of the Clouds* (as they call the unknown Power) would suffer a better Consequence from so ill a Cause. He now begins to hold *Oroonoko* excused; and to say, he had reason for what he did. And now every body could assure the King how passionately *Imoinda* was beloved by the Prince; even those confess'd it now, who said the contrary before his Flame was not abated. So that the King being old, and not able to defend himself in War, and having no Sons of all his Race remaining alive, but only this, to maintain him on his Throne; and looking on this as a man disobliged, first by the Rape of his Mistress, or rather Wife, and now by depriving him wholly of her, he fear'd, might make him desperate, and do some cruel thing, either to himself or his old Grandfather the Offender, he began to repent him extremely of the Contempt he had, in his Rage, put on *Imoinda*. Besides, he consider'd he ought in Honour to have killed her for this Offence, if it had been one. He ought to have had so much Value and Consideration for a Maid of her Quality, as to have nobly put her to Death, and not to have sold her like a common Slave; the greatest Revenge, and the most disgraceful of any, and to which they a thousand times prefer Death, and implore it; as *Imoinda* did, but could not obtain that Honour. Seeing therefore it was certain that *Oroonoko* would highly resent his Affront, he thought good to make some Excuse for his Rashness to him; and to that End, he sent a Messenger to the Camp, with Orders to treat with him about the Matter, to gain his Pardon, and endeavour to mitigate his Grief: but that by no Means he should tell him she was sold, but secretly put to Death; for he knew he should never obtain his Pardon for the other.

When the Messenger came, he found the Prince upon the Point of engaging with the Enemy; but as soon as he heard of the Arrival of the Messenger, he commanded him to his Tent, where he embraced him, and received him with Joy; which was soon abated by the down-cast Looks of the Messenger, who was instantly demanded the Cause by *Oroonoko*; who, impatient of Delay, ask'd a thousand Questions in a Breath, and all concerning *Imoinda*. But there needed little Return; for he could almost answer himself of all he demanded, from his Sight and Eyes. At last the Messenger casting himself at the Prince's Feet, and kissing them with all the Submission of a Man that had something to implore which he dreaded to utter, besought him to hear with Calmness what he had to deliver to him, and to call up all his noble and heroick Courage, to encounter with his Words, and defend himself against the ungrateful Things he had to relate. *Oroonoko* reply'd, with a deep Sigh, and a languishing Voice,—*I am armed against their worst Efforts—For I know they will tell me*, Imoinda *is no more— And after that, you may spare the rest*. Then, commanding him to rise, he laid himself on a Carpet, under a rich Pavilion, and remained a good while silent, and was hardly heard to sigh. When he was come a little to himself, the Messenger asked him Leave to deliver that Part of his Embassy which the Prince had not yet divin'd: And the Prince cry'd, *I permit thee*—Then he told him the Affliction the old King was in, for the Rashness he had committed in his Cruelty to *Imoinda*; and how he deign'd to ask Pardon for his Offence, and to implore the Prince would not suffer that Loss to touch his Heart too sensibly, which now all the Gods could not restore him, but might recompense him in Glory, which he begged he would pursue; and that Death, that common Revenger of all Injuries, would soon even the Account between him and a feeble old Man.

Oroonoko bad him return his Duty to his Lord and Master; and to assure him, there was no Account of Revenge to be adjudged between them; If there was, he was the Aggressor, and that Death would be just, and, maugre his Age, would see him righted; and he was contented to leave his Share of Glory to Youths more fortunate and worthy of that Favour from the Gods: That henceforth he would never lift a Weapon, or draw a Bow, but abandon the small Remains of his Life to Sighs and Tears, and the continual Thoughts of what his Lord and Grandfather had thought good to send out of the World, with all that Youth, that Innocence and Beauty.

After having spoken this, whatever his greatest Officers and Men of the best Rank could do, they could not raise him from the Carpet, or persuade him to Action, and Resolutions of Life; but commanding all to retire, he shut himself into his Pavilion all that Day, while the Enemy was ready to engage: and wondring at the Delay, the whole Body of the chief of the Army then address'd themselves to him, and to whom they had much ado to get Admittance. They fell on their Faces at the Foot of his Carpet, where they lay, and besought him with earnest Prayers and Tears to lead them forth to Battle, and not let the Enemy take Advantages of them; and implored him to have Regard to his Glory, and to the World, that depended on his Courage and Conduct. But he made no other Reply to all their Supplications than this, That he had now no more Business for Glory; and for the World, it was a Trifle not worth his Care: *Go*, (continued he, sighing) *and divide it amongst you, and reap with Joy what you so vainly prize, and leave me to my more welcome Destiny.*

They then demanded what they should do, and whom he would constitute in his Room, that the Confusion of ambitious Youth and Power might not ruin their Order, and make them a Prey to the Enemy. He reply'd, he would not give himself that Trouble—but wished 'em to chuse the bravest Man amongst 'em, let his Quality or Birth be what it would: "For, Oh my Friends! (says he) it is not Titles make Men Brave or Good; or Birth that bestows Courage and Generosity, or makes the Owner Happy. Believe this, when you behold *Oroonoko* the most wretched, and abandoned by Fortune, of all the Creation of the Gods." So turning himself about, he would make no more Reply to all they could urge or implore.

The Army beholding their Officers return unsuccessful, with sad Faces and ominous Looks, that presaged no good Luck, suffer'd a thousand Fears to take Possession of their Hearts, and the Enemy to come even upon them before they could provide for their Safety by any Defence: and tho'they were assured by some who had a Mind to animate them, that they should be immediately headed by the Prince; and that in the mean time *Aboan* had Orders to command as General; yet they were so dismay'd for want of that great Example of Bravery, that they could make but a very feeble Resistance; and, at last, down-right fled before the Enemy, who pursued 'em to the very Tents, killing 'em: Nor could all *Aboan's* Courage, which that Day gained him immortal Glory, shame 'em into a manly Defence of themselves. The Guards that were left behind about the Prince's Tent, seeing the Soldiers flee before the Enemy, and scatter themselves all over the Plain, in great Disorder, made such Out-cries, as rouz'd the Prince from his amorous Slumber, in which he had remained buried for two Days, without permitting any Sustenance to approach him. But, in Spite of all his Resolutions, he had not the Constancy of Grief to that Degree, as to make him insensible of the Danger of his Army; and in that Instant he leaped from his Couch, and cry'd—"Come, if we must die, let us meet Death the noblest Way; and 'twill be more like *Oroonoko* to encounter him at an Army's Head, opposing the Torrent of a conquering Foe, than lazily on a Couch, to wait his lingering Pleasure, and die every Moment by a thousand racking Thoughts; or be tamely taken by an Enemy, and led a whining, love-sick Slave to adorn the Triumphs of *Jamoan*, that young Victor, who already is enter'd beyond the Limits I have prescrib'd him."

While he was speaking, he suffer'd his People to dress him for the Field; and sallying out of his Pavilion, with more Life and Vigour in his Countenance than ever he shew'd, he appear'd like some Divine Power descended to save his Country from Destruction: And his People had purposely put him on all Things that might make him shine with most Splendor, to strike a reverend Awe into the Beholders. He flew into the thickest of those that were pursuing his Men; and being animated with Despair, he fought as if he came on Purpose to die, and did such Things as will not be believed that human Strength could perform; and such, as soon inspir'd all the rest with new Courage, and new Ardor. And now it was that they began to fight indeed; and so, as if they would not be out-done even by their ador'd Hero; who turning the Tide of the Victory, changing absolutely the Fate of the Day, gain'd an entire Conquest: And *Oroonoko* having the good Fortune to single out *Jamoan*, he took him Prisoner with his own Hand, having wounded him almost to Death.

This *Jamoan* after wards became very dear to him, being a Man very Gallant, and of excellent Graces, and fine Parts; so that he never put him amongst the Rank of Captives as they used to do, without Distinction, for the common Sale, or Market, but kept him in his own Court, where he retain'd nothing of the Prisoner but the Name, and returned no more into his own Country; so great an Affection he took for *Oroonoko*, and by a thousand Tales and Adventures of Love and Gallantry, flatter'd his Disease of Melancholy and Languishment; which I have often heard him say, had certainly kill'd him, but for the Conversation of this Prince and *Aboan*, and the *French* Governor he had from his Childhood, of whom I have spoken before, and who was a Man of admirable Wit, great Ingenuity and Learning; all which he had infused into his young Pupil. This *Frenchman* was banished out of his own Country for some Heretical Notions he held; and tho' he was a Man of very little Religion, yet he had admirable Morals, and a brave Soul.

After the total Defeat of *Jamoan's* Army, which all fled, or were left dead upon the Place, they spent some Time in the Camp; *Oroonoko* chusing rather to remain a While there in his Tents, than to enter into a Palace, or live in a Court where he had so lately suffer'd so great a Loss, the Officers therefore, who saw and knew his Cause of Discontent, invented all sorts of Diversions and Sports to entertain their Prince: So that what with those Amusements abroad, and others at home, that is, within their Tents, with the Persuasions, Arguments, and Care of his Friends and Servants that he more peculiarly priz'd, he wore off in Time a great Part of that Chagrin, and Torture of Despair, which the first Efforts of *Imoinda's* Death had given him; insomuch, as having received a thousand kind Embassies from the King, and Invitation to return to Court, he obey'd, tho' with no little Reluctancy; and when he did so, there was a visible Change in him, and for a long Time he was much more melancholy than before. But Time lessens all Extremes, and reduces 'em to Mediums, and Unconcern; but no Motives of Beauties, tho' all endeavour'd it, could engage him in any sort of Amour, tho' he had all the Invitations to it, both from his own Youth, and other Ambitions and Designs.

Oroonoko was no sooner return'd from this last Conquest, and receiv'd at Court with all the Joy and Magnificence that could be express'd to a young Victor, who was not only return'd Triumphant, but belov'd like a Deity, than there arriv'd in the Port an *English* Ship.

The Master of it had often before been in these Countries, and was very well known to *Oroonoko*, with whom he had traffick'd for Slaves, and had us'd to do the same with his Predecessors.

This Commander was a Man of a finer sort of Address and Conversation, better bred, and more engaging, than most of that sort of Men are; so that he seem'd rather never to have been bred out of a Court, than almost all his Life at Sea. This Captain therefore was always better receiv'd at Court, than most of the Traders to those Countries were; and especially by *Oroonoko*, who was more civiliz'd, according to the *European* Mode, than any other had been, and took more Delight in the *White* Nations; and, above all, Men of Parts and Wit. To this Captain he sold abundance of his Slaves; and for the Favour and Esteem he had for him, made him many Presents, and oblig'd him to stay at Court as long as possibly he could. Which the Captain seem'd to take as a very great Honour done him, entertaining the Prince every Day with Globes and Maps, and

Mathematical Discourses and Instruments; eating, drinking, hunting, and living with him with so much Familiarity, that it was not to be doubted but he had gain'd very greatly upon the Heart of this gallant young Man. And the Captain, in Return of all these mighty Favours, besought the Prince to honour his Vessel with his Presence some Day or other at Dinner, before he should set sail; which he condescended to accept, and appointed his Day. The Captain, on his Part, fail'd not to have all Things in a Readiness, in the most magnificent Order he could possibly: And the Day being come, the Captain, in his Boat, richly adorn'd with Carpets and Velvet Cushions, rowed to the Shore, to receive the Prince; with another Long-boat, where was plac'd all his Musick and Trumpets, with which *Oroonoko* was extremely delighted; who met him on the Shore, attended by his *French* Governor, *Jamoan, Aboan,* and about an Hundred of the noblest of the Youths of the Court: And after they had first carried the Prince on Board, the Boats fetch'd the rest off; where they found a very splendid Treat, with all Sorts of fine Wines; and were as well entertain'd, as 'twas possible in such a Place to be.

The Prince having drank hard of Punch, and several Sorts of Wine, as did all the rest, (for great Care was taken they should want nothing of that Part of the Entertainment) was very merry, and in great Admiration of the Ship, for he had never been in one before; so that he was curious of beholding every Place where he decently might descend. The rest, no less curious, who were not quite overcome with drinking, rambled at their Pleasure *Fore* and *Aft,* as their Fancies guided 'em: So that the Captain, who had well laid his Design before, gave the Word, and seiz'd on all his Guests; they clapping great Irons suddenly on the Prince, when he was leap'd down into the Hold, to view that Part of the Vessel; and locking him fast down, secur'd him. The same Treachery was used to all the rest; and all in one Instant, in several Places of the Ship, were lash'd fast in Irons, and betray'd to Slavery. That great Design over, they set all Hands at Work to hoist Sail; and with as treacherous as fair a Wind they made from the Shore with this innocent and glorious Prize, who thought of nothing less than such an Entertainment.

Some have commended this Act, as brave in the Captain; but I will spare my Sense of it, and leave it to my Reader to judge as he pleases. It may be easily guess'd, in what Manner the Prince resented this Indignity, who may be best resembled to a Lion taken in a Toil; so he raged, so he struggled for Liberty, but all in vain: And they had so wisely managed his Fetters, that he could not use a Hand in his Defence, to quit himself of a Life that would by no Means endure Slavery; nor could he move from the Place where he was ty'd, to any solid Part of the Ship, against which he might have beat his Head, and have finish'd his Disgrace that Way. So that being deprived of all other Means, he resolv'd to perish for want of Food; and pleas'd at last with that Thought, and toil'd and tir'd by Rage and Indignation, he laid himself down, and sullenly resolv'd upon dying, and refused all Things that were brought him.

This did not a little vex the Captain, and the more so, because he found almost all of 'em of the same Humour; so that the Loss of so many brave Slaves, so tall and goodly to behold, would have been very considerable: He therefore order'd one to go from him (for he would not be seen himself) to *Oroonoko*, and to assure him, he was afflicted for having rashly done so unhospitable a Deed, and which could not be now remedied, since they were far from Shore; but since he resented it in so high a Nature, he assur'd him he would revoke his Resolution, and set both him and his Friends ashore on the next Land they should touch at; and of this the Messenger gave him his Oath, provided he would resolve to live. And *Oroonoko*, whose Honour was such, as he never had violated a Word in his Life himself, much less a solemn Asseveration, believ'd in an Instant what this Man said; but reply'd, He expected, for a Confirmation of this, to have his shameful Fetters dismis'd. This Demand was carried to the Captain; who return'd him Answer, That the Offence had been so great

which he had put upon the Prince, that he durst not trust him
with Liberty while he remain'd in the Ship, for fear, lest by a
Valour natural to him, and a Revenge that would animate that
Valour, he might commit some Outrage fatal to himself, and
the King his Master, to whom the Vessel did belong. To this
Oroonoko reply'd, He would engage his Honour to behave
himself in all friendly Order and Manner, and obey the
Command of the Captain, as he was Lord of the King's Vessel,
and General of those Men under his Command.

This was deliver'd to the still doubting Captain, who could
not resolve to trust a Heathen, he said, upon his Parole, a Man
that had no Sense or Notion of the God that he worshipp'd.
Oroonoko then reply'd, He was very sorry to hear that the
Captain pretended to the Knowledge and Worship of any
Gods, who had taught him no better Principles, than not to
credit as he would be credited. But they told him, the
Difference of their Faith occasion'd that Distrust: for the
Captain had protested to him upon the Word of a Christian,
and sworn in the Name of a great God; which if he should
violate, he must expect eternal Torments in the World to come.
"Is that all the Obligations he has to be just to his Oath? (reply'd
Oroonoko) Let him know, I swear by my Honour; which to
violate, would not only render me contemptible and despised
by all brave and honest Men, and so give my self perpetual
Pain, but it would be eternally offending and displeasing all
Mankind; harming, betraying, circumventing, and outraging all
Men. But Punishments hereafter are suffer'd by one's self; and
the World takes no Cognizance whether this God has reveng'd
'em or not, 'tis done so secretly, and deferr'd so long; while the
Man of no Honour suffers every Moment the Scorn and
Contempt of the honester World, and dies every Day
ignominiously in his Fame, which is more valuable than Life. I
speak not this to move Belief, but to shew you how you
mistake, when you imagine, that he who will violate his
Honour, will keep his Word with his *Gods*." So, turning from
him with a disdainful Smile, he refused to answer him, when

he urged him to know what Answer he should carry back to his Captain; so that he departed without saying any more.

The Captain pondering and consulting what to do, it was concluded, that nothing but *Oroonoko's* Liberty would encourage any of the rest to eat, except the *Frenchman*, whom the Captain could not pretend to keep Prisoner, but only told him, he was secur'd, because he might act something in Favour of the Prince; but that he should be freed as soon as they came to Land. So that they concluded it wholly necessary to free the Prince from his Irons, that he might shew himself to the rest; that they might have an Eye upon him, and that they could not fear a single Man.

This being resolved, to make the Obligation the greater, the Captain himself went to *Oroonoko*; where, after many Compliments, and Assurances of what he had already promis'd, he receiving from the Prince his Parole, and his Hand, for his good Behaviour, dismiss'd his Irons, and brought him to his own Cabin; where, after having treated and repos'd him a While, (for he had neither eat nor slept in four Days before) he besought him to visit those obstinate People in Chains, who refused all manner of Sustenance; and intreated him to oblige 'em to eat, and assure 'em of their Liberty the first Opportunity.

Oroonoko, who was too generous not to give Credit to his Words, shew'd himself to his People, who were transported with Excess of Joy at the Sight of their darling Prince; falling at his Feet, and kissing and embracing 'em; believing, as some divine Oracle, all he assur'd 'em. But he besought 'em to bear their Chains with that Bravery that became those whom he had seen act so nobly in Arms; and that they could not give him greater Proofs of their Love and Friendship, since 'twas all the Security the Captain (his Friend) could have against the Revenge, he said, they might possibly justly take for the Injuries sustained by him. And they all, with one Accord, assur'd him, that they could not suffer enough, when it was for his Repose and Safety.

After this, they no longer refus'd to eat, but took what was brought 'em, and were pleas'd with their Captivity, since by it they hoped to redeem the Prince, who, all the rest of the Voyage, was treated with all the Respect due to his Birth, tho' nothing could divert his Melancholy; and he would often sigh for *Imoinda*, and think this a Punishment due to his Misfortune, in having left that noble Maid behind him, that fatal Night, in the *Otan*, when he fled to the Camp.

Possess'd with a thousand Thoughts of past Joys with this fair young Person, and a thousand Griefs for her eternal Loss, he endur'd a tedious Voyage, and at last arriv'd at the Mouth of the River of *Surinam*, a Colony belonging to the King of *England*, and where they were to deliver some Part of their Slaves. There the Merchants and Gentlemen of the Country going on Board, to demand those Lots of Slaves they had already agreed on; and, amongst those, the Overseers of those Plantations where I then chanc'd to be: The Captain, who had given the Word, order'd his Men to bring up those noble Slaves in Fetters, whom I have spoken of; and having put 'em, some in one, and some in other Lots, with Women and Children, (which they call *Pickaninies*) they sold 'em off, as Slaves to several Merchants and Gentlemen; not putting any two in one Lot, because they would separate 'em far from each other; nor daring to trust 'em together, lest Rage and Courage should put 'em upon contriving some great Action, to the Ruin of the Colony.

Oroonoko was first seiz'd on, and sold to our Overseer, who had the first Lot, with seventeen more of all Sorts and Sizes, but not one of Quality with him. When he saw this, he found what they meant; for, as I said, he understood *English* pretty well; and being wholly unarm'd and defenceless, so as it was in vain to make any Resistance, he only beheld the Captain with a Look all fierce and disdainful, upbraiding him with Eyes that forc'd Blushes on his guilty Cheeks, he only cry'd in passing over the Side of the Ship; *Farewel, Sir, 'tis worth my Sufferings to gain so true a Knowledge, both of you, and of your Gods, by whom you swear.* And desiring those that held him to forbear their Pains, and telling 'em he would make no Resistance, he cry'd, *Come, my Fellow-Slaves, let us descend, and see if we can meet with more Honour and Honesty in the next World we shall touch upon.* So he nimbly leapt into the Boat, and shewing no more Concern, suffer'd himself to be row'd up the River, with his seventeen Companions.

The Gentleman that bought him, was a young *Cornish* Gentleman, whose Name was *Trefry*; a Man of great Wit, and fine Learning, and was carried into those Parts by the Lord—Governor, to manage all his Affairs. He reflecting on the last Words of *Oroonoko* to the Captain, and beholding the Richness of his Vest, no sooner came into the Boat, but he fix'd his Eyes on him; and finding something so extraordinary in his Face, his Shape and Mein, a Greatness of Look, and Haughtiness in his Air, and finding he spoke *English*, had a great Mind to be enquiring into his Quality and Fortune; which, though *Oroonoko* endeavour'd to hide, by only confessing he was above the Rank of common Slaves, *Trefry* soon found he was yet something greater than he confess'd; and from that Moment began to conceive so vast an Esteem for him, that he ever after lov'd him as his dearest Brother, and shew'd him all the Civilities due to so great a Man.

Trefry was a very good Mathematician, and a Linguist; could speak *French* and *Spanish;* and in the three Days they remain'd in the Boat, (for so long were they going from the Ship to the Plantation) he entertain'd *Oroonoko* so agreeably with his Art and Discourse, that he was no less pleas'd with *Trefry*, than he was with the Prince; and he thought himself, at least, fortunate in this, that since he was a Slave, as long as he would suffer himself to remain so, he had a Man of so excellent Wit and Parts for a Master. So that before they had finish'd their Voyage up the River, he made no Scruple of declaring to *Trefry* all his Fortunes, and most Part of what I have here related, and put himself wholly into the Hands of his new Friend, who he found resented all the Injuries were done him, and was charm'd with all the Greatnesses of his Actions; which were recited with that Modesty, and delicate Sense, as wholly vanquish'd him, and subdu'd him to his Interest. And he promis'd him, on his Word and Honour, he would find the Means to re-conduct him to his own Country again; assuring him, he had a perfect Abhorrence of so dishonourable an Action; and that he would sooner have dy'd, than have been the Author of such a Perfidy. He found the Prince was very much concerned to know what became of his Friends, and how they took their Slavery; and *Trefry* promised to take Care about the enquiring after their Condition, and that he should have an Account of 'em.

Tho', as *Oroonoko* afterwards said, he had little Reason to credit the Words of a *Backearary*; yet he knew not why, but he saw a kind of Sincerity, and aweful Truth in the Face of *Trefry*; he saw Honesty in his Eyes, and he found him wise and witty enough to understand Honour: for it was one of his Maxims, *A Man of Wit could not be a Knave or Villain.*

In their Passage up the River, they put in at several Houses for Refreshment; and ever when they landed, Numbers of People would flock to behold this Man: not but their Eyes were daily entertain'd with the Sight of Slaves; but the Fame of *Oroonoko* was gone before him, and all People were in Admiration of his Beauty. Besides, he had a rich Habit on, in which he was taken, so different from the rest, and which the Captain could not strip him of, because he was forc'd to surprize his Person in the Minute he sold him. When he found his Habit made him liable, as he thought, to be gazed at the more, he begged *Trefry* to give him something more befitting a Slave, which he did, and took off his Robes: Nevertheless, he shone thro' all, and his *Osenbrigs* (a sort of brown *Holland* Suit he had on) could not conceal the Graces of his Looks and Mein; and he had no less Admirers than when he had his dazling Habit on: The Royal Youth appear'd in spite of the Slave, and People could not help treating him after a different Manner, without designing it. As soon as they approached him, they venerated and esteemed him; his Eyes insensibly commanded Respect, and his Behaviour insinuated it into every Soul. So that there was nothing talked of but this young and gallant Slave, even by those who yet knew not that he was a Prince.

I ought to tell you, that the Christians never buy any Slaves but they give 'em some Name of their own, their native ones being likely very barbarous, and hard to pronounce; so that Mr. *Trefry* gave *Oroonoko* that of *Cæsar*; which name will live in that Country as long as that (scarce more) glorious one of the great *Roman*: for 'tis most evident he wanted no Part of the personal Courage of that *Cæsar*, and acted Things as memorable, had they been done in some Part of the World replenished with People and Historians, that might have given him his Due. But his Misfortune was, to fall in an obscure World, that afforded only a Female Pen to celebrate his Fame; tho' I doubt not but it had lived from others Endeavours, if the *Dutch*, who immediately after his Time took that Country, had not killed, banished and dispersed all those that were capable of giving the World this great Man's Life, much better than I have done. And Mr. *Trefry*, who design'd it, died before he began it, and bemoan'd himself for not having undertook it in Time.

For the future therefore I must call *Oroonoko Cæsar*; since by that Name only he was known in our Western World, and by that Name he was received on Shore at *Parham-House*, where he was destin'd a Slave. But if the King himself (God bless him) had come ashore, there could not have been greater Expectation by all the whole Plantation, and those neighbouring ones, than was on ours at that Time; and he was received more like a Governor than a Slave: Notwithstanding, as the Custom was, they assigned him his Portion of Land, his House and his Business up in the Plantation. But as it was more for Form, than any Design to put him to his Task, he endured no more of the Slave but the Name, and remain'd some Days in the House, receiving all Visits that were made him, without stirring towards that Part of the Plantation where the *Negroes* were.

At last, he would needs go view his Land, his House, and the Business assign'd him. But he no sooner came to the Houses of the Slaves, which are like a little Town by itself, the *Negroes* all having left Work, but they all came forth to behold him, and found he was that Prince who had, at several Times, sold most of 'em to these Parts; and from a Veneration they pay to great Men, especially if they know 'em, and from the Surprize and Awe they had at the Sight of him, they all cast themselves at his Feet, crying out, in their Language, *Live, O King! Long live, O King!* and kissing his Feet, paid him even Divine Homage.

Several *English* Gentlemen were with him, and what Mr. *Trefry* had told 'em was here confirm'd; of which he himself before had no other Witness than *Cæsar* himself: But he was infinitely glad to find his Grandeur confirmed by the Adoration of all the Slaves.

Cæsar, troubled with their Over-Joy, and Over-Ceremony, besought 'em to rise, and to receive him as their Fellow-Slave; assuring them he was no better. At which they set up with one Accord a most terrible and hideous Mourning and Condoling, which he and the *English* had much ado to appease: but at last they prevailed with 'em, and they prepared all their barbarous Musick, and every one kill'd and dress'd something of his own Stock (for every Family has their Land apart, on which, at their Leisure-times, they breed all eatable Things) and clubbing it together, made a most magnificent Supper, inviting their *Grandee Captain*, their *Prince*, to honour it with his Presence; which he did, and several *English* with him, where they all waited on him, some playing, others dancing before him all the Time, according to the Manners of their several Nations, and with unwearied Industry endeavouring to please and delight him.

While they sat at Meat, Mr. *Trefry* told *Cæsar*, that most of these young Slaves were undone in Love with a fine She-Slave, whom they had had about six Months on their Land; the Prince, who never heard the Name of *Love* without a Sigh, nor any Mention of it without the Curiosity of examining further into that Tale, which of all Discourses was most agreeable to him, asked, how they came to be so unhappy, as to be all undone for one fair Slave? *Trefry,* who was naturally amorous, and delighted to talk of Love as well as any Body, proceeded to tell him, they had the most charming Black that ever was beheld on their Plantation, about fifteen or sixteen Years old, as he guess'd; that for his Part he had done nothing but sigh for her ever since she came; and that all the White Beauties he had seen, never charm'd him so absolutely as this fine Creature had done; and that no Man, of any Nation, ever beheld her, that did not fall in love with her; and that she had all the Slaves perpetually at her Feet; and the whole Country resounded with the Fame of *Clemene,* for so (said he) we have christen'd her: but she denies us all with such a noble Disdain, that 'tis a Miracle to see, that she who can give such eternal Desires, should herself be all Ice and all Unconcern. She is adorn'd with the most graceful Modesty that ever beautify'd Youth; the softest Sigher—that, if she were capable of Love, one would swear she languished for some absent happy Man; and so retired, as if she fear'd a Rape even from the God of Day, or that the Breezes would steal Kisses from her delicate Mouth. Her Task of Work, some sighing Lover every Day makes it his Petition to perform for her; which she accepts blushing, and with Reluctancy, for Fear he will ask her a Look for a Recompence, which he dares not presume to hope; so great an Awe she strikes into the Hearts of her Admirers. "I do not wonder *(reply'd the Prince)* that *Clemene* should refuse Slaves, being, as you say, so beautiful; but wonder how she escapes those that can entertain her as you can do: or why, being your Slave, you do not oblige her to yield?" "I confess *(said* Trefry) when I have, against her Will, entertained her with Love so long, as to be transported with my Passion even above Decency, I have been ready to make Use of those Advantages of Strength and Force Nature has given me: But Oh! she disarms me with that Modesty and Weeping, so tender and so moving, that I retire, and thank my Stars she overcame me."

The Company laugh'd at his Civility to a Slave, and *Cæsar* only applauded the Nobleness of his Passion and Nature, since that Slave might be noble, or, what was better, have true Notions of Honour and Virtue in her. Thus passed they this Night, after having received from the Slaves all imaginable Respect and Obedience.

The next Day, *Trefry* ask'd *Cæsar* to walk when the Heat was allay'd, and designedly carried him by the Cottage of the fair Slave; and told him she whom he spoke of last Night lived there retir'd: *But* (says he) *I would not wish you to approach; for I am sure you will be in Love as soon as you behold her.* *Cæsar* assured him, he was Proof against all the Charms of that Sex; and that if he imagined his Heart could be so perfidious to love again after *Imoinda*, he believed he should tear it from his Bosom. They had no sooner spoke, but a little Shock-Dog, that *Clemene* had presented her, which she took great Delight in, ran out; and she, not knowing any Body was there, ran to get it in again, and bolted out on those who were just speaking of her: when seeing them, she would have run in again, but *Trefry* caught her by the Hand, and cry'd, Clemene, *however you fly a Lover, you ought to pay some Respect to this Stranger*, (pointing to *Cæsar*.) But she, as if she had resolved never to raise her Eyes to the Face of a Man again, bent 'em the more to the Earth, when he spoke, and gave the Prince the Leisure to look the more at her. There needed no long gazing, or Consideration, to examine who this fair Creature was; he soon saw *Imoinda* all over her; in a Minute he saw her Face, her Shape, her Air, her Modesty, and all that call'd forth his Soul with Joy at his Eyes, and left his Body destitute of almost Life: it stood without Motion, and for a Minute knew not that it had a Being; and, I believe, he had never come to himself, so oppress'd he was with Over-joy, if he had not met with this Allay, that he perceived *Imoinda* fall dead in the Hands of *Trefry*. This awaken'd him, and he ran to her Aid, and caught her in his Arms, where by Degrees she came to her self; and 'tis needless to tell with what Transports, what Extasies of Joy, they both a

While beheld each other, without speaking; then snatched each other to their Arms; then gaze again, as if they still doubted whether they possess'd the Blessing they grasped: but when they recover'd their Speech, 'tis not to be imagined what tender Things they express'd to each other; wondring what strange Fate had brought them again together. They soon inform'd each other of their Fortunes, and equally bewail'd their Fate; but at the same Time they mutually protested, that even Fetters and Slavery were soft and easy, and would be supported with Joy and Pleasure, while they could be so happy to possess each other, and to be able to make good their Vows. *Cæsar* swore he disdained the Empire of the World, while he could behold his *Imoinda*; and she despised Grandeur and Pomp, those Vanities of her Sex, when she could gaze on *Oroonoko*. He ador'd the very Cottage where she resided, and said, That little Inch of the World would give him more Happiness than all the Universe could do; and she vow'd it was a Palace, while adorned with the Presence of *Oroonoko*.

Trefry was infinitely pleased with this Novel, and found this *Clemene* was the fair Mistress of whom *Cæsar* had before spoke; and was not a little satisfy'd, that Heaven was so kind to the Prince as to sweeten his Misfortunes by so lucky an Accident; and leaving the Lovers to themselves, was impatient to come down to *Parham-House* (which was on the same Plantation) to give me an Account of what had happened. I was as impatient to make these Lovers a Visit, having already made a Friendship with *Cæsar*, and from his own Mouth learned what I have related; which was confirmed by his *Frenchman*, who was set on shore to seek his Fortune, and of whom they could not make a Slave, because a Christian; and he came daily to *Parham-Hill* to see and pay his Respects to his Pupil Prince. So that concerning and interesting myself in all that related to *Cæsar*, whom I had assured of Liberty as soon as the Governour arrived, I hasted presently to the Place where these Lovers were, and was infinitely glad to find this beautiful young Slave (who had already gain'd all our Esteems, for her

Modesty and extraordinary Prettiness) to be the same I had heard *Cæsar* speak so much of. One may imagine then we paid her a treble Respect; and tho' from her being carved in fine Flowers and Birds all over her Body, we took her to be of Quality before, yet when we knew *Clemene* was *Imoinda*, we could not enough admire her.

I had forgot to tell you, that those who are nobly born of that Country, are so delicately cut and raised all over the Fore-part of the Trunk of their Bodies, that it looks as if it were japan'd, the Works being raised like high Point round the Edges of the Flowers. Some are only carved with a little Flower, or Bird, at the Sides of the Temples, as was *Cæsar*; and those who are so carved over the Body, resemble our antient *Picts* that are figur'd in the Chronicles, but these Carvings are more delicate.

From that happy Day *Cæsar* took *Clemene* for his Wife, to the general Joy of all People; and there was as much Magnificence as the Country could afford at the Celebration of this Wedding: And in a very short Time after she conceived with Child, which made *Cæsar* even adore her, knowing he was the last of his great Race. This new Accident made him more impatient of Liberty, and he was every Day treating with *Trefrey* for his and *Clemene's* Liberty, and offer'd either Gold, or a vast Quantity of Slaves, which should be paid before they let him go, provided he could have any Security that he should go when his Ransom was paid. They fed him from Day to Day with Promises, and delay'd him till the Lord-Governor should come; so that he began to suspect them of Falshood, and that they would delay him till the Time of his Wife's Delivery, and make a Slave of the Child too; for all the Breed is theirs to whom the Parents belong. This Thought made him very uneasy, and his Sullenness gave them some Jealousies of him; so that I was obliged, by some Persons who fear'd a Mutiny (which is very fatal sometimes in those Colonies that abound so with Slaves, that they exceed the Whites in vast Numbers) to discourse with *Cæsar*, and to give him all the Satisfaction I possibly could: They knew he and *Clemene* were scarce an

Hour in a Day from my Lodgings; that they eat with me, and that I oblig'd them in all Things I was capable. I entertained them with the Lives of the *Romans*, and great Men, which charmed him to my Company; and her, with teaching her all the pretty Works that I was Mistress of, and telling her Stories of Nuns, and endeavouring to bring her to the Knowledge of the true God: But of all Discourses, *Cæsar* liked that the worst, and would never be reconciled to our Notions of the Trinity, of which he ever made a Jest; it was a Riddle he said would turn his Brain to conceive, and one could not make him understand what Faith was. However, these Conversations fail'd not altogether so well to divert him, that he liked the Company of us Women much above the Men, for he could not drink, and he is but an ill Companion in that Country that cannot. So that obliging him to love us very well, we had all the Liberty of Speech with him, especially my self, whom he call'd his *Great Mistress*; and indeed my Word would go a great Way with him. For these Reasons I had Opportunity to take Notice to him, that he was not well pleased of late, as he used to be; was more retired and thoughtful; and told him, I took it ill he should suspect we would break our Words with him, and not permit both him and *Clemene* to return to his own Kingdom, which was not so long a Way, but when he was once on his Voyage he would quickly arrive there. He made me some Answers that shew'd a Doubt in him, which made me ask, what Advantage it would be to doubt? It would but give us a Fear of him, and possibly compel us to treat him so as I should be very loth to behold; that is, it might occasion his Confinement. Perhaps this was not so luckily spoke of me, for I perceiv'd he resented that Word, which I strove to soften again in vain: However, he assur'd me, that whatsoever Resolutions he should take, he would act nothing upon the *White* People; and as for myself, and those upon that *Plantation* where he was, he would sooner forfeit his eternal Liberty, and Life itself, than lift his Hand against his greatest Enemy on that Place. He besought me to suffer no Fears upon his Account, for he could do nothing that Honour should not dictate; but he accused himself for having suffer'd Slavery so long; yet he charg'd that Weakness on Love alone, who was capable of making him neglect even Glory itself; and, for which, now he reproaches himself every Moment of the Day. Much more to this Effect he spoke, with an Air impatient enough to make me know he would not be long in Bondage; and tho' he suffer'd only the Name of a Slave, and had nothing of the Toil and Labour of one, yet that was sufficient to render him uneasy; and he had been too long idle, who us'd to be always in Action, and in Arms. He had a Spirit all rough and fierce, and that could not be tam'd to lazy Rest: And tho' all Endeavours were us'd to exercise himself in such Actions and Sports as this World afforded, as Running, Wrestling, Pitching the Bar, Hunting and Fishing, Chasing and Killing *Tygers* of a monstrous Size, which this Continent affords in abundance; and wonderful *Snakes*, such as *Alexander* is reported to have encounter'd at the River of *Amazons*, and which *Cæsar* took great Delight to overcome; yet these were not Actions great enough for his large Soul, which was still panting after more renown'd Actions.

Before I parted that Day with him, I got, with much ado, a Promise from him to rest yet a little longer with Patience, and wait the Coming of the Lord Governour, who was every Day expected on our Shore: He assur'd me he would, and this Promise he desired me to know was given perfectly in Complaisance to me, in whom he had an entire Confidence.

After this, I neither thought it convenient to trust him much out of our View, nor did the Country, who fear'd him; but with one Accord it was advis'd to treat him fairly, and oblige him to remain within such a Compass, and that he should be permitted, as seldom as could be, to go up to the Plantations of the *Negroes*; or, if he did, to be accompany'd by some that should be rather, in Appearance, Attendants than Spies. This Care was for some time taken, and *Cæsar* look'd upon it as a Mark of extraordinary Respect, and was glad his Discontent had oblig'd 'em to be more observant to him; he received new

Assurance from the Overseer, which was confirmed to him by the Opinion of all the Gentlemen of the Country, who made their Court to him. During this Time that we had his Company more frequently than hitherto we had had, it may not be unpleasant to relate to you the Diversions we entertain'd him with, or rather he us.

My Stay was to be short in that Country; because my Father dy'd at Sea, and never arriv'd to possess the Honour design'd him, (which was Lieutenant-General of six and thirty Islands, besides the Continent of *Surinam*) nor the Advantages he hop'd to reap by them: So that though we were oblig'd to continue on our Voyage, we did not intend to stay upon the Place. Though, in a Word, I must say thus much of it; That certainly had his late Majesty, of sacred Memory, but seen and known what a vast and charming World he had been Master of in that Continent, he would never have parted so easily with it to the *Dutch*. 'Tis a Continent, whose vast Extent was never yet known, and may contain more noble Earth than all the Universe beside; for, they say, it reaches from East to West one Way as far as *China*, and another to *Peru*: It affords all Things, both for Beauty and Use; 'tis there eternal Spring, always the very Months of *April, May*, and *June*; the Shades are perpetual, the Trees bearing at once all Degrees of Leaves, and Fruit, from blooming Buds to ripe Autumn: Groves of Oranges, Lemons, Citrons, Figs, Nutmegs, and noble Aromaticks, continually bearing their Fragrancies: The Trees appearing all like Nosegays, adorn'd with Flowers of different Kinds; some are all White, some Purple, some Scarlet, some Blue, some Yellow; bearing at the same Time ripe Fruit, and blooming young, or producing every Day new. The very Wood of all these Trees has an intrinsic Value, above common Timber; for they are, when cut, of different Colours, glorious to behold, and bear a Price considerable, to inlay withal. Besides this, they yield rich Balm, and Gums; so that we make our Candles of such an aromatic Substance, as does not only give a sufficient Light, but as they burn, they cast their Perfumes all about. Cedar is the

common Firing, and all the Houses are built with it. The very
Meat we eat, when set on the Table, if it be native, I mean of the
Country, perfumes the whole Room; especially a little Beast
call'd an *Armadillo*, a Thing which I can liken to nothing so
well as a *Rhinoceros*; 'tis all in white Armour, so jointed, that it
moves as well in it, as if it had nothing on: This Beast is about
the Bigness of Pig of six Weeks old. But it were endless to give
an Account of all the divers wonderful and strange Things that
Country affords, and which we took a great Delight to go in
Search of; tho' those Adventures are oftentimes fatal, and at
least dangerous: But while we had *Cæsar* in our Company on
these Designs, we fear'd no Harm, nor suffer'd any.

As soon as I came into the Country, the best House in it was
presented me, call'd *St. John's Hill*: It stood on a vast Rock of
white Marble, at the Foot of which, the River ran a vast Depth
down, and not to be descended on that Side; the little Waves
still dashing and washing the Foot of this Rock, made the
softest Murmurs and Purlings in the World; and the opposite
Bank was adorn'd with such vast Quantities of different
Flowers eternally blowing, and every Day and Hour new,
fenc'd behind 'em with lofty Trees of a thousand rare Forms
and Colours, that the Prospect was the most ravishing that
Sands can create. On the Edge of this white Rock, towards the
River, was a Walk, or Grove, of Orange and Lemon-Trees, about
half the Length of the *Mall* here, whose flowery and Fruit-
bearing Branches met at the Top, and hinder'd the Sun, whose
Rays are very fierce there, from entring a Beam into the Grove;
and the cool Air that came from the River, made it not only fit
to entertain People in, at all the hottest Hours of the Day, but
refresh the sweet Blossoms, and made it always sweet and
charming; and sure, the whole Globe of the World cannot
shew so delightful a Place as this Grove was: Not all the
Gardens of boasted *Italy* can produce a Shade to out-vie this,
which Nature had join'd with Art to render so exceeding fine;
and 'tis a Marvel to see how such vast Trees, as big as *English*
Oaks, could take Footing on so solid a Rock, and in so little

Earth as cover'd that Rock: But all Things by Nature there are rare, delightful, and wonderful. But to our Sports.

Sometimes we would go surprising, and in Search of young *Tygers* in their Dens, watching when the old ones went forth to forage for Prey; and oftentimes we have been in great Danger, and have fled apace for our Lives, when surpriz'd by the Dams. But once, above all other Times, we went on this Design, and *Cæsar* was with us; who had no sooner stoln a young *Tyger* from her Nest, but going off, we encounter'd the Dam, bearing a Buttock of a Cow, which she had torn off with her mighty Paw, and going with it towards her Den: We had only four Women, *Cæsar*, and an *English* Gentleman, Brother to *Harry Martin* the great *Oliverian*; we found there was no escaping this enraged and ravenous Beast. However, we Women fled as fast as we could from it; but our Heels had not saved our Lives, if *Cæsar* had not laid down her *Cub*, when he found the *Tyger* quit her Prey to make the more Speed towards him; and taking Mr. *Martin's* Sword, desired him to stand aside, or follow the Ladies. He obey'd him; and *Cæsar* met this monstrous Beast of mighty Size, and vast Limbs, who came with open Jaws upon him; and fixing his aweful stern Eyes full upon those of the Beast, and putting himself into a very steady and good aiming Posture of Defence, ran his Sword quite through his Breast, down to his very Heart, home to the Hilt of the Sword: The dying Beast stretch'd forth her Paw, and going to grasp his Thigh, surpriz'd with Death in that very Moment, did him no other Harm than fixing her long Nails in his Flesh very deep, feebly wounded him, but could not grasp the Flesh to tear off any. When he had done this, he hallow'd to us to return; which, after some Assurance of his Victory, we did, and found him lugging out the Sword from the Bosom of the *Tyger*, who was laid in her Blood on the Ground. He took up the *Cub*, and with an Unconcern that had nothing of the Joy or Gladness of Victory, he came and laid the Whelp at my Feet. We all extremely wonder'd at his daring, and at the Bigness of the Beast, which was about the Height of an Heifer, but of mighty great and strong Limbs.

Another time, being in the Woods, he kill'd a *Tyger*, that had long infested that Part, and borne away abundance of Sheep and Oxen, and other Things, that were for the Support of those to whom they belong'd. Abundance of People assail'd this Beast, some affirming they had shot her with several Bullets quite through the Body at several times; and some swearing they shot her through the very Heart; and they believed she was a Devil, rather than a mortal Thing. *Cæsar* had often said, he had a Mind to encounter this Monster, and spoke with several Gentlemen who had attempted her; one crying, I shot her with so many poison'd Arrows, another with his Gun in this Part of her, and another in that; so that he remarking all the Places where she was shot, fancy'd still he should overcome her, by giving her another Sort of a Wound than any had yet done; and one Day said (at the Table), "What Trophies and Garlands, Ladies, will you make me, if I bring you home the Heart of this ravenous Beast, that eats up all your Lambs and Pigs?" We all promis'd he should be rewarded at our Hands. So taking a Bow, which he chose out of a great many, he went up into the Wood, with two Gentlemen, where he imagin'd this Devourer to be. They had not pass'd very far into it, but they heard her Voice, growling and grumbling, as if she were pleas'd with something she was doing. When they came in View, they found her muzzling in the Belly of a new ravish'd Sheep, which she had torn open; and seeing herself approach'd, she took fast hold of her Prey with her fore Paws, and set a very fierce raging Look on *Cæsar*, without offering to approach him, for Fear at the same Time of loosing what she had in Possession: So that *Cæsar* remain'd a good while, only taking Aim, and getting an Opportunity to shoot her where he design'd. 'Twas some Time before he could accomplish it; and to wound her, and not kill her, would but have enrag'd her the more, and endanger'd him. He had a Quiver of Arrows at his Side, so that if one fail'd, he could be supply'd: At last, retiring a little, he gave her Opportunity to eat, for he found she was ravenous, and fell to as soon as she saw him retire, being more eager of her Prey, than of doing new Mischiefs; when he going softly to one Side of her, and hiding his Person behind certain Herbage, that grew high and thick, he took so good Aim, that, as he intended, he shot her just into the Eye, and the Arrow was sent with so good a Will, and so sure a Hand, that it stuck in her Brain, and made her caper, and become mad for a Moment or two; but being seconded by another Arrow, she fell dead upon the Prey. *Cæsar* cut her open with a Knife, to see where those Wounds were that had been reported to him, and why she did not die of 'em. But I shall now relate a Thing that, possibly, will find no Credit among Men; because 'tis a Notion commonly receiv'd with us, That nothing can receive a Wound in the Heart, and live: But when the Heart of this courageous Animal was taken out, there were seven Bullets of Lead in it, the Wound seam'd up with great Scars, and she liv'd with the Bullets a great While, for it was long since they were shot: This Heart the Conqueror brought up to us, and 'twas a very great Curiosity, which all the Country came to see; and which gave *Cæsar* Occasion of many fine Discourses of Accidents in War, and strange Escapes.

At other times he would go a Fishing; and discoursing on that Diversion, he found we had in that Country a very strange Fish, call'd a *Numb-Eel*, (an *Eel* of which I have eaten) that while it is alive, it has a Quality so cold, that those who are angling, tho' with a Line of ever so great a Length, with a Rod at the End of it, it shall in the same Minute the Bait is touch'd by this *Eel*, seize him or her that holds the Rod with a Numbness, that shall deprive 'em of Sense for a While; and some have fallen into the Water, and others drop'd, as dead, on the Banks of the Rivers where they stood, as soon as this Fish touches the Bait. *Cæsar* us'd to laugh at this, and believ'd it impossible a Man could lose his Force at the Touch of a Fish: and could not understand that Philosophy, that a cold Quality should be of that Nature; however, he had a great Curiosity to try whether it would have the same Effect on him it had on others, and often try'd, but in vain. At last, the sought-for Fish came to the Bait, as he stood angling on the Bank; and instead of throwing away the Rod, or giving it a sudden Twitch out of the Water, whereby he might have caught both the *Eel*, and have dismiss'd the Rod, before it could have too much Power over him; for Experiment-sake, he grasp'd it but the harder, and fainting, fell into the River; and being still possess'd of the Rod, the Tide carry'd him, senseless as he was, a great Way, till an *Indian* Boat took him up; and perceiv'd, when they touch'd him, a Numbness seize them, and by that knew the Rod was in his Hand; which with a Paddle, (that is a short Oar) they struck away, and snatch'd it into the Boat, *Eel* and all. If *Cæsar* was almost dead, with the Effect of this Fish, he was more so with that of the Water, where he had remain'd the Space of going a League, and they found they had much ado to bring him back to Life; but at last they did, and brought him home, where he was in a few Hours well recover'd and refresh'd, and not a little asham'd to find he should be overcome by an *Eel*, and that all the People, who heard his Defiance, would laugh at him. But we chear'd him up; and he being convinc'd, we had the *Eel* at Supper, which was a quarter of an Ell about, and most delicate Meat; and was of the more Value, since it cost so dear as almost the Life of so gallant a Man.

About this Time we were in many mortal Fears, about some Disputes the *English* had with the *Indians*; so that we could scarce trust our selves, without great Numbers, to go to any *Indian* Towns, or Place where they abode, for fear they should fall upon us, as they did immediately after my coming away; and the Place being in the Possession of the *Dutch*, they us'd them not so civilly as the *English*; so that they cut in Pieces all they could take, getting into Houses and hanging up the Mother, and all her Children about her; and cut a Footman, I left behind me, all in Joints, and nail'd him to Trees.

This Feud began while I was there; so that I lost half the Satisfaction I propos'd, in not seeing and visiting the *Indian* Towns. But one Day, bemoaning of our Misfortunes upon this

Account, *Cæsar* told us, we need not fear, for if we had a Mind to go, he would undertake to be our Guard. Some would, but most would not venture: About eighteen of us resolv'd, and took Barge; and after eight Days, arriv'd near an *Indian* Town: But approaching it, the Hearts of some of our Company fail'd, and they would not venture on Shore; so we poll'd, who would, and who would not. For my Part, I said, if *Cæsar* would, I would go. He resolv'd; so did my Brother, and my Woman, a Maid of good Courage. Now none of us speaking the Language of the People, and imagining we should have a half Diversion in gazing only; and not knowing what they said, we took a Fisherman that liv'd at the Mouth of the River, who had been a long Inhabitant there, and oblig'd him to go with us: But because he was known to the *Indians*, as trading among 'em, and being, by long living there, become a perfect *Indian* in Colour, we, who had a Mind to surprize 'em, by making them see something they never had seen, (that is, *White* People) resolv'd only my self, my Brother and Woman should go: So *Cæsar*, the Fisherman, and the rest, hiding behind some thick Reeds and Flowers that grew in the Banks, let us pass on towards the Town, which was on the Bank of the River all along. A little distant from the Houses, or Huts, we saw some dancing, others busy'd in fetching and carrying of Water from the River. They had no sooner spy'd us, but they set up a loud Cry, that frighted us at first; we thought it had been for those that should kill us, but it seems it was of Wonder and Amazement. They were all naked; and we were dress'd, so as is most commode for the hot Countries, very glittering and rich; so that we appear'd extremely fine; my own Hair was cut short, and I had a Taffety Cap, with black Feathers on my Head; my Brother was in a Stuff-Suit, with Silver Loops and Buttons, and abundance of green Ribbon. This was all infinitely surprising to them; and because we saw them stand still till we approach'd 'em, we took Heart and advanc'd, came up to 'em, and offer'd 'em our Hands; which they took, and look'd on us round about, calling still for more Company; who came

swarming out, all wondering, and crying out *Tepeeme*; taking
their Hair up in their Hands, and spreading it wide to those
they call'd out to; as if they would say (as indeed it signify'd)
Numberless Wonders, or not to be recounted, no more than to
number the Hair of their Heads. By Degrees they grew more
bold, and from gazing upon us round, they touch'd us, laying
their Hands upon all the Features of our Faces, feeling our
Breasts, and Arms, taking up one Petticoat, then wondering to
see another; admiring our Shoes and Stockings, but more our
Garters, which we gave 'em, and they ty'd about their Legs,
being lac'd with Silver Lace at the Ends; for they much esteem
any shining Things. In fine, we suffer'd 'em to survey us as they
pleas'd, and we thought they would never have done admiring
us. When *Cæsar*, and the rest, saw we were receiv'd with such
Wonder, they came up to us; and finding the *Indian* Trader
whom they knew, (for 'tis by these Fishermen, call'd *Indian*
Traders, we hold a Commerce with 'em; for they love not to go
far from home, and we never go to them) when they saw him
therefore, they set up a new Joy, and cry'd in their Language,
Oh, here's our Tiguamy, *and we shall know whether those
Things can speak.* So advancing to him, some of 'em gave him
their Hands, and cry'd, *Amora Tiguamy*; which is as much as,
How do you do? or, *Welcome Friend*; and all, with one din,
began to gabble to him, and ask'd, if we had Sense and Wit? If
we could talk of Affairs of Life and War, as they could do? If we
could hunt, swim, and do a thousand Things they use? He
answer'd 'em, We could. Then they invited us into their
Houses, and dress'd Venison and Buffalo for us; and going out,
gather'd a Leaf of a Tree, called a *Sarumbo* Leaf, of six Yards
long, and spread it on the Ground for a Table-Cloth; and
cutting another in Pieces, instead of Plates, set us on little low
Indian Stools, which they cut out of one entire Piece of Wood,
and paint in a sort of Japan-Work. They serve every one their
Mess on these Pieces of Leaves; and it was very good, but too
high-season'd with Pepper. When we had eat, my Brother and
I took out our Flutes, and play'd to 'em, which gave 'em new

Wonder; and I soon perceiv'd, by an Admiration that is natural to these People, and by the extreme Ignorance and Simplicity of 'em, it were not difficult to establish any unknown or extravagant Religion among them, and to impose any Notions or Fictions upon 'em. For seeing a Kinsman of mine set some Paper on Fire with a Burning-Glass, a Trick they had never before seen, they were like to have ador'd him for a God, and begg'd he would give 'em the Characters or Figures of his Name, that they might oppose it against Winds and Storms: which he did, and they held it up in those Seasons, and fancy'd, it had a Charm to conquer them, and kept it like a holy Relique. They are very superstitious, and call'd him the Great *Peeie*, that is, *Prophet*. They shewed us their *Indian Peeie*, a Youth of about sixteen Years old, as handsome as Nature could make a Man. They consecrate a beautiful Youth from his Infancy, and all Arts are used to compleat him in the finest Manner, both in Beauty and Shape: He is bred to all the little Arts and Cunning they are capable of; to all the legerdemain Tricks, and Slight of Hand, whereby he imposes on the Rabble; and is both a Doctor in Physick and Divinity: And by these Tricks makes the Sick believe he sometimes eases their Pains, by drawing from the afflicted Part little Serpents, or odd Flies, or Worms, or any strange Thing; and though they have besides undoubted good Remedies for almost all their Diseases, they cure the Patient more by Fancy than by Medicines, and make themselves feared, loved, and reverenced. This young *Peeie* had a very young Wife, who seeing my Brother kiss her, came running and kiss'd me. After this they kiss'd one another, and made it a very great Jest, it being so novel; and new Admiration and Laughing went round the Multitude, that they never will forget that Ceremony, never before us'd or known. *Cæsar* had a Mind to see and talk with their War-Captains, and we were conducted to one of their Houses, where we beheld several of the great Captains, who had been at Council: But so frightful a Vision it was to see 'em, no Fancy can create; no sad Dreams can represent so dreadful a Spectacle. For my Part, I took 'em

for Hobgoblins, or Fiends, rather than Men; But however their
Shapes appear'd, their Souls were very humane and noble; but
some wanted their Noses, some their Lips, some both Noses
and Lips, some their Ears, and others cut through each Cheek,
with long Slashes, through which their Teeth appear'd: They
had several other formidable Wounds and Scars, or rather
Dismembrings. They had *Comitias*, or little Aprons before
them; and Girdles of Cotton, with their Knives naked stuck in
it; a Bow at their Back, and a Quiver of Arrows on their Thighs;
and most had Feathers on their Heads of divers Colours. They
cry'd *Amora Tiguamy* to us, at our Entrance, and were pleas'd
we said as much to them: They seated us, and gave us Drink of
the best Sort, and wonder'd as much as the others had done
before to see us. *Cæsar* was marvelling as much at their Faces,
wondering how they should be all so wounded in War; he was
impatient to know how they all came by those frightful Marks
of Rage or Malice, rather than Wounds got in noble Battle:
They told us by our Interpreter, That when any War was
waging, two Men, chosen out by some old Captain whose
fighting was past, and who could only teach the Theory of War,
were to stand in Competition for the Generalship, or great War-
Captain; and being brought before the old Judges, now past
Labour, they are ask'd, What they dare do, to shew they are
worthy to lead an Army? When he who is first ask'd, making no
Reply, cuts off his Nose, and throws it contemptibly on the
Ground; and the other does something to himself that he
thinks surpasses him, and perhaps deprives himself of Lips
and an Eye: So they slash on 'till one gives out, and many have
dy'd in this Debate. And it's by a passive Valour they shew and
prove their Activity; a sort of Courage too brutal to be
applauded by our *Black* Hero; nevertheless, he express'd his
Esteem of 'em.

In this Voyage *Cæsar* begat so good an Understanding
between the *Indians* and the *English*, that there were no more
Fears or Heart-burnings during our Stay, but we had a perfect,
open, and free Trade with 'em. Many Things remarkable, and

worthy reciting, we met with in this short Voyage; because *Cæsar* made it his Business to search out and provide for our Entertainment, especially to please his dearly ador'd *Imoinda*, who was a Sharer in all our Adventures; we being resolv'd to make her Chains as easy as we could, and to compliment the Prince in that Manner that most oblig'd him.

As we were coming up again, we met with some *Indians* of strange Aspects; that is, of a larger Size, and other sort of Features, than those of our Country. Our *Indian Slaves*, that row'd us, ask'd 'em some Questions; but they could not understand us, but shew'd us a long Cotton String, with several Knots on it, and told us, they had been coming from the Mountains so many Moons as there were Knots: they were habited in Skins of a strange Beast, and brought along with 'em Bags of Gold-Dust; which, as well as they could give as to understand, came streaming in little small Channels down the high Mountains, when the Rains fell; and offer'd to be the Convoy to any Body, or Persons, that would go to the Mountains. We carry'd these Men up to *Parham*, where they were kept till the Lord-Governor came: And because all the Country was mad to be going on this Golden Adventure, the Governor, by his Letters, commanded (for they sent some of the Gold to him) that a Guard should be set at the Mouth of the River of *Amazons* (a River so call'd, almost as broad as the River of *Thames*) and prohibited all People from going up that River, it conducting to those Mountains or Gold. But we going off for *England* before the Project was further prosecuted, and the Governor being drown'd in a Hurricane, either the Design died, or the *Dutch* have the Advantage of it: And 'tis to be bemoan'd what his Majesty lost, by losing that Part of *America*.

Though this Digression is a little from my Story, however, since it contains some Proofs of the Curiosity and Daring of this great Man, I was content to omit nothing of his Character.

It was thus for some Time we diverted him; but now *Imoinda* began to shew she was with Child, and did nothing but sigh and weep for the Captivity of her Lord, herself, and the

Infant yet unborn; and believ'd, if it were so hard to gain the Liberty of two, 'twould be more difficult to get that for three. Her Griefs were so many Darts in the great Heart of *Cæsar*, and taking his Opportunity, one *Sunday*, when all the *Whites* were overtaken in Drink, as there were abundance of several Trades, and *Slaves* for four Years, that inhabited among the *Negro* Houses; and *Sunday* being their Day of Debauch, (otherwise they were a sort of Spies upon *Cæsar*) he went, pretending out of Goodness to 'em, to feast among 'em, and sent all his Musick, and order'd a great Treat for the whole Gang, about three hundred *Negroes*, and about an hundred and fifty were able to bear Arms, such as they had, which were sufficient to do Execution, with Spirits accordingly: For the *English* had none but rusty Swords, that no Strength could draw from a Scabbard; except the People of particular Quality, who took Care to oil 'em, and keep 'em in good Order: The Guns also, unless here and there one, or those newly carried from *England*, would do no Good or Harm; for 'tis the Nature of that Country to rust and eat up Iron, or any Metals but Gold and Silver. And they are very expert at the Bow, which the *Negroes* and *Indians* are perfect Masters of.

Cæsar, having singled out these Men from the Women and Children, made an Harangue to 'em, of the Miseries and Ignominies of Slavery; counting up all their Toils and Sufferings, under such Loads, Burdens and Drudgeries, as were fitter for Beasts than Men; senseless Brutes, than human Souls. He told 'em, it was not for Days, Months or Years, but for Eternity; there was no End to be of their Misfortunes: They suffer'd not like Men, who might find a Glory and Fortitude in Oppression; but like Dogs, that lov'd the Whip and Bell, and fawn'd the more they were beaten: That they had lost the divine Quality of Men, and were become insensible Asses, fit only to bear: Nay, worse; an Ass, or Dog, or Horse, having done his Duty, could lie down in Retreat, and rise to work again, and while he did his Duty, endur'd no Stripes; but Men, villanous, senseless Men, such as they, toil'd on all the tedious Week 'till

Black Friday; and then, whether they work'd or not, whether they were faulty or meriting, they, promiscuously, the Innocent with the Guilty, suffer'd the infamous Whip, the sordid Stripes, from their Fellow-Slaves, 'till their Blood trickled from all Parts of their Body; Blood, whose every Drop ought to be revenged with a Life of some of those Tyrants that impose it. "And why (*said he*) my dear Friends and Fellow-sufferers, should we be Slaves to an unknown People? Have they vanquished us nobly in Fight? Have they won us in Honourable Battle? And are we by the Chance of War become their Slaves? This would not anger a noble Heart; this would not animate a Soldier's Soul: No, but we are bought and sold like Apes or Monkeys, to be the Sport of Women, Fools and Cowards; and the Support of Rogues and Runagades, that have abandoned their own Countries for Rapine, Murders, Theft and Villanies. Do you not hear every Day how they upbraid each other with Infamy of Life, below the wildest Salvages? And shall we render Obedience to such a degenerate Race, who have no one human Virtue left, to distinguish them from the vilest Creatures? Will you, I say, suffer the Lash from such Hands?" *They all reply'd with one Accord*, "No, No, No; *Cæsar* has spoke like a great Captain, like a great King."

After this he would have proceeded, but was interrupted by a tall *Negro*, of some more Quality than the rest, his Name was *Tuscan*; who bowing at the Feet of *Cæsar*, cry'd, "My Lord, we have listen'd with Joy and Attention to what you have said; and, were we only Men, would follow so great a Leader through the World: But O! consider we are Husbands and Parents too, and have Things more dear to us than Life; our Wives and Children, unfit for Travel in those unpassable Woods, Mountains and Bogs. We have not only difficult Lands to overcome, but Rivers to wade, and Mountains to encounter; ravenous Beasts of Prey,"—*To this* Cæsar *reply'd*, "That Honour was the first Principle in Nature, that was to be obey'd; but as no Man would pretend to that, without all the Acts of Virtue, Compassion, Charity, Love, Justice and Reason, he found it not inconsistent with that, to take equal Care of their Wives and Children as they would of themselves; and that he did not design, when he led them to Freedom, and glorious Liberty, that they should leave that better Part of themselves to perish by the Hand of the Tyrant's Whip: But if there were a Woman among them so degenerate from Love and Virtue, to chuse Slavery before the Pursuit of her Husband, and with the Hazard of her Life, to share with him in his Fortunes; that such a one ought to be abandoned, and left as a Prey to the common Enemy."

To which they all agreed—and bowed. After this, he spoke of the impassable Woods and Rivers; and convinced them, the more Danger the more Glory. He told them, that he had heard of one *Hannibal*, a great Captain, had cut his Way through Mountains of solid Rocks; and should a few Shrubs oppose them, which they could fire before 'em? No, 'twas a trifling Excuse to Men resolved to die, or overcome. As for Bogs, they are with a little Labour filled and harden'd; and the Rivers could be no Obstacle, since they swam by Nature, at least by Custom, from the first Hour of their Birth: That when the Children were weary, they must carry them by Turns, and the Woods and their own Industry would afford them Food. To this they all assented with Joy.

Tuscan then demanded, what he would do: He said he would travel towards the Sea, plant a new Colony, and defend it by their Valour; and when they could find a Ship, either driven by Stress of Weather, or guided by Providence that Way, they would seize it, and make it a Prize, till it had transported them to their own Countries: at least they should be made free in his Kingdom, and be esteem'd as his Fellow-Sufferers, and Men that had the Courage and the Bravery to attempt, at least, for Liberty; and if they died in the Attempt, it would be more brave, than to live in perpetual Slavery.

They bow'd and kiss'd his Feet at this Resolution, and with one Accord vow'd to follow him to Death; and that Night was appointed to begin their March. They made it known to their Wives, and directed them to tie their Hamocks about their

Shoulders, and under their Arms, like a Scarf and to lead their Children that could go, and carry those that could not. The Wives, who pay an entire Obedience to their Husbands, obey'd, and stay'd for 'em where they were appointed: The Men stay'd but to furnish themselves with what defensive Arms they could get; and all met at the Rendezvouz, where *Cæsar* made a new encouraging Speech to 'em and led 'em out.

But as they could not march far that Night, on *Monday* early, when the Overseers went to call 'em all together, to go to work, they were extremely surprized, to find not one upon the Place, but all fled with what Baggage they had. You may imagine this News was not only suddenly spread all over the Plantation, but soon reached the neighbouring ones; and we had by Noon about 600 Men, they call the Militia of the Country, that came to assist us in the Pursuit of the Fugitives: But never did one see so comical an Army march forth to War. The Men of any Fashion would not concern themselves, tho' it were almost the Common Cause; for such Revoltings are very ill Examples, and have very fatal Consequences oftentimes, in many Colonies: But they had a Respect for *Cæsar*, and all Hands were against the *Parhamites* (as they called those of *Parham-Plantation*) because they did not in the first Place love the Lord-Governor; and secondly, they would have it that *Cæsar* was ill used, and baffled with: and 'tis not impossible but some of the best in the Country was of his Council in this Flight, and depriving us of all the Slaves; so that they of the better sort would not meddle in the Matter. The Deputy-Governor, of whom I have had no great Occasion to speak, and who was the most fawning fair-tongu'd Fellow in the World, and one that pretended the most Friendship to *Cæsar*, was now the only violent Man against him; and though he had nothing, and so need fear nothing, yet talked and looked bigger than any Man. He was a Fellow, whose Character is not fit to be mentioned with the worst of the Slaves: This Fellow would lead his Army forth to meet *Cæsar*, or rather to pursue him. Most of their Arms were of those Sort of cruel Whips they call *Cat with nine Tails*; some had rusty useless Guns for Shew; others old Basket Hilts, whose Blades had never seen the Light in this Age; and others had long Staffs and Clubs. Mr. *Trefry* went along, rather to be a Mediator than a Conqueror in such a Battle; for he foresaw and knew, if by fighting they put the *Negroes* into Despair, they were a sort of sullen Fellows, that would drown or kill themselves before they would yield; and he advis'd that fair Means was best: But *Byam* was one that abounded in his own Wit, and would take his own Measures.

It was not hard to find these Fugitives; for as they fled, they were forced to fire and cut the Woods before 'em: So that Night or Day they pursu'd 'em by the Light they made, and by the Path they had cleared. But as soon as *Cæsar* found that he was pursu'd, he put himself in a Posture of Defence, placing all the Woman and Children in the Rear; and himself, with *Tuscan* by his Side, or next to him, all promising to die or conquer. Encouraged thus, they never stood to parley, but fell on pell-mell upon the *English*, and killed some, and wounded a great many; they having Recourse to their Whips, as the best of their Weapons. And as they observed no Order, they perplexed the Enemy so sorely, with lashing 'em in the Eyes; and the Women and Children seeing their Husbands so treated, being of fearful and cowardly Dispositions, and hearing the *English* cry out, *Yield and Live! Yield, and be Pardon'd!* they all ran in amongst their Husbands and Fathers, and hung about them, crying out, *Yield! Yield, and leave* Cæsar *to their Revenge*; that by Degrees the Slaves abandon'd *Cæsar*, and left him only *Tuscan* and his Heroick *Imoinda*, who grown as big as she was, did nevertheless press near her Lord, having a Bow and a Quiver full of poisoned Arrows, which she managed with such Dexterity, that she wounded several, and shot the Governor into the Shoulder; of which Wound he had like to have died, but that an *Indian* Woman, his Mistress, sucked the Wound, and cleans'd it from the Venom: But however, he stir'd not from the Place till he had parly'd with *Cæsar*, who he found was resolved to die fighting, and would not be taken; no more

would *Tuscan* or *Imoinda*. But he, more thirsting after
Revenge of another Sort, than that of depriving him of Life,
now made use of all his Art of Talking and Dissembling, and
besought *Cæsar* to yield himself upon Terms which he himself
should propose, and should be sacredly assented to, and kept
by him. He told him, It was not that he any longer fear'd him,
or could believe the Force of two Men, and a young Heroine,
could overthrow all them, and with all the Slaves now on their
Side also; but it was the vast Esteem he had for his Person, the
Desire he had to serve so gallant a Man, and to hinder himself
from the Reproach hereafter, of having been the Occasion of
the Death of a Prince, whose Valour and Magnanimity
deserved the Empire of the World. He protested to him, he
looked upon his Action as gallant and brave, however tending
to the Prejudice of his Lord and Master, who would by it have
lost so considerable a Number of Slaves; that this Flight of his
should be look'd on as a Heat of Youth, and a Rashness of a too
forward Courage, and an unconsider'd Impatience of Liberty,
and no more; and that he labour'd in vain to accomplish that
which they would effectually perform as soon as any Ship
arrived that would touch on his Coast: "So that if you will be
pleased (*continued he*) to surrender yourself, all imaginable
Respect shall be paid you; and your Self, your Wife and Child,
if it be born here, shall depart free out of our Land." But *Cæsar*
would hear of no Composition; though *Byam* urged, if he
pursued and went on in his Design, he would inevitably
perish, either by great Snakes, wild Beasts or Hunger; and he
ought to have Regard to his Wife, whose Condition requir'd
Ease, and not the Fatigues of tedious Travel, where she could
not be secured from being devoured. But *Cæsar* told him,
there was no Faith in the White men, or the Gods they ador'd;
who instructed them in Principles so false, that honest Men
could not live amongst them; though no People profess'd so
much, none perform'd so little: That he knew what he had to
do when he dealt with Men of Honour; but with them a Man
ought to be eternally on his Guard, and never to eat and drink

with Christians, without his Weapon of Defence in his Hand; and, for his own Security, never to credit one Word they spoke. As for the Rashness and Inconsiderateness of his Action, he would confess the Governor is in the right; and that he was ashamed of what he had done in endeavouring to make those free, who were by Nature Slaves, poor wretched Rogues, fit to be used as Christian Tools; Dogs, treacherous and cowardly, fit for such Masters; and they wanted only but to be whipped into the Knowledge of the Christian Gods, to be the vilest of all creeping Things; to learn to worship such Deities as had not Power to make them just, brave, or honest: In fine, after a thousand Things of this Nature, not fit here to be recited, he told *Byam*, He had rather die, than live upon the same Earth with such Dogs. But *Trefry* and *Byam* pleaded and protested together so much, that *Trefry* believing the Governor to mean what he said, and speaking very cordially himself, generously put himself into *Cæsar's* Hands, and took him aside, and persuaded him, even with Tears, to live, by surrendring himself, and to name his Conditions. *Cæsar* was overcome by his Wit and Reasons, and in Consideration of *Imoinda*; and demanding what he desired, and that it should be ratify'd by their Hands in Writing, because he had perceived that was the common Way of Contract between Man and Man amongst the Whites; all this was performed, and *Tuscan's* Pardon was put in, and they surrender'd to the Governor, who walked peaceably down into the Plantation with them, after giving Order to bury their Dead. *Cæsar* was very much toil'd with the Bustle of the Day, for he had fought like a Fury; and what Mischief was done, he and *Tuscan* performed alone; and gave their Enemies a fatal Proof, that they durst do any Thing, and fear'd no mortal Force.

But they were no sooner arrived at the Place where all the Slaves receive their Punishments of Whipping, but they laid Hands on *Cæsar* and *Tuscan*, faint with Heat and Toil; and surprizing them, bound them to two several Stakes, and whipped them in a most deplorable and inhuman Manner, rending the very Flesh from their Bones, especially *Cæsar*, who was not perceived to make any Moan, or to alter his Face, only to roll his Eyes on the faithless Governor, and those he believed Guilty, with Fierceness and Indignation; and to complete his Rage, he saw every one of those Slaves who but a few Days before ador'd him as something more than Mortal, now had a Whip to give him some Lashes, while he strove not to break his Fetters; tho' if he had, it were impossible: but he pronounced a Woe and Revenge from his Eyes, that darted Fire, which was at once both aweful and terrible to behold.

When they thought they were sufficiently revenged on him, they unty'd him, almost fainting with Loss of Blood, from a thousand Wounds all over his Body; from which they had rent his Clothes, and led him bleeding and naked as he was, and loaded him all over with Irons; and then rubb'd his Wounds, to complete their Cruelty, with *Indian* Pepper, which had like to have made him raving mad; and, in this Condition made him so fast to the Ground, that he could not stir, if his Pains and Wounds would have given him Leave. They spared *Imoinda*, and did not let her see this Barbarity committed towards her Lord, but carried her down to *Parham*, and shut her up; which was not in Kindness to her, but for Fear she should die with the Sight, or miscarry, and then they should lose a young Slave, and perhaps the Mother.

You must know, that when the News was brought on *Monday* Morning, that *Cæsar* had betaken himself to the Woods, and carry'd with him all the *Negroes*, we were possess'd with extreme Fear, which no Persuasions could dissipate, that he would secure himself till Night, and then would come down and cut all our Throats. This Apprehension made all the Females of us fly down the River, to be secured; and while we were away, they acted this Cruelty; for I suppose I had Authority and Interest enough there, had I suspected any such Thing, to have prevented it: but we had not gone many Leagues, but the News overtook us, that *Cæsar* was taken and whipped liked a common Slave. We met on the River with Colonel *Martin*, a

Man of great Gallantry, Wit, and Goodness, and whom I have celebrated in a Character of my new Comedy, by his own Name, in Memory of so brave a Man: He was wise and eloquent, and, from the Fineness of his Parts, bore a great Sway over the Hearts of all the Colony: He was a Friend to *Cæsar*, and resented this false Dealing with him very much. We carried him back to *Parham*, thinking to have made an Accommodation; when he came, the first News we heard, was, That the Governor was dead of a Wound *Imoinda* had given him; but it was not so well. But it seems, he would have the Pleasure of beholding the Revenge he took on *Cæsar*; and before the cruel Ceremony was finished, he dropt down; and then they perceived the Wound he had on his Shoulder was by a venom'd Arrow, which, as I said, his *Indian* Mistress healed by sucking the Wound.

We were no sooner arrived, but we went up to the Plantation to see *Cæsar*; whom we found in a very miserable and unexpressible Condition; and I have a thousand Times admired how he lived in so much tormenting Pain. We said all Things to him, that Trouble, Pity and Good-Nature could suggest, protesting our Innocency of the Fact, and our Abhorrence of such Cruelties; making a thousand Professions and Services to him, and begging as many Pardons for the Offenders, till we said so much, that he believed we had no Hand in his ill Treatment; but told us, He could never pardon *Byam*; as for *Trefry*, he confess'd he saw his Grief and Sorrow for his Suffering, which he could not hinder, but was like to have been beaten down by the very Slaves, for speaking in his Defence: But for *Byam*, who was their Leader, their Head—and should, by his Justice and Honour, have been an Example to 'em—for him, he wished to live to take a dire Revenge of him; and said, *It had been well for him, if he had sacrificed me, instead of giving me the comtemptible Whip.* He refused to talk much; but begging us to give him our Hands, he took them, and protested never to lift up his to do us any Harm. He had a great Respect for Colonel *Martin*, and always took his Counsel like that of a Parent; and assured him, he would obey him in any Thing but his Revenge on *Byam*: "Therefore (*said he*) for his own Safety, let him speedly dispatch me; for if I could dispatch myself, I would not, till that Justice were done to my injured Person, and the Contempt of a Soldier: No, I would not kill myself, even after a Whipping, but will be content to live with that Infamy, and be pointed at by every grinning Slave, till I have completed my Revenge; and then you shall see, that *Oroonoko* scorns to live with the Indignity that was put on *Cæsar*." All we could do, could get no more Words from him; and we took Care to have him put immediately into a healing Bath, to rid him of his Pepper, and ordered a Chirurgeon to anoint him with healing Balm, which he suffer'd, and in some Time he began to be able to walk and eat. We failed not to visit him every Day, and to that End had him brought to an Apartment at *Parham*.

The Governor had no sooner recover'd, and had heard of the Menaces of *Cæsar*, but he called his Council, who (not to disgrace them, or burlesque the Government there) consisted of such notorious Villains as *Newgate* never transported; and, possibly, originally were such who understood neither the Laws of God or Man, and had no sort of Principles to make them worthy the Name of Men; but at the very Council-Table would contradict and fight with one another, and swear so bloodily, that 'twas terrible to hear and see 'em. (Some of 'em were afterwards hanged, when the *Dutch* took Possession of the Place, others sent off in Chains.) But calling these special Rulers of the Nation together, and requiring their Counsel in this weighty Affair, they all concluded, that (damn 'em) it might be their own Cases; and that *Cæsar* ought to be made an Example to all the *Negroes*, to fright 'em from daring to threaten their Betters, their Lords and Masters; and at this Rate no Man was safe from his own Slaves; and concluded, *nemine contradicente*, That *Cæsar* should be hanged.

Trefry then thought it Time to use his Authority, and told *Byam*, his Command did not extend to his Lord's Plantation; and that *Parham* was as much exempt from the Law as *White-*

Hall; and that they ought to more to touch the Servants of the Lord—(who there represented the King's Person) than they could those about the King himself; and that *Parham* was a Sanctuary; and tho' his Lord were absent in Person, his Power was still in being there, which he had entrusted with him, as far as the Dominions of his particular Plantations reached, and all that belonged to it; the rest of the Country, as *Byam* was Lieutenant to his Lord, he might exercise his Tyranny upon. *Trefry* had others as powerful, or more, that interested themselves in *Cæsar's* Life, and absolutely said, he should be defended. So turning the Governor, and his wise Council, out of Doors, (for they sat at *Parham-House*) we set a Guard upon our Lodging-Place, and would admit none but those we called Friends to us and *Cæsar*.

The Governor having remain'd wounded at *Parham*, till his Recovery was completed, *Cæsar* did not know but he was still there, and indeed for the most Part, his Time was spent there: for he was one that loved to live at other Peoples Expence, and if he were a Day absent, he was ten present there; and us'd to play, and walk, and hunt, and fish with *Cæsar*. So that *Cæsar* did not at all doubt, if he once recover'd Strength, but he should find an Opportunity of being revenged on him; though, after such a Revenge, he could not hope to live: for if he escaped the Fury of the *English* Mobile, who perhaps would have been glad of the Occasion to have killed him, he was resolved not to survive his Whipping; yet he had some tender Hours, a repenting Softness, which he called his Fits of Cowardice, wherein he struggled with Love for the Victory of his Heart, which took Part with his charming *Imoinda* there; but for the most Part, his Time was pass'd in melancholy Thoughts, and black Designs. He consider'd, if he should do this Deed, and die either in the Attempt, or after it, he left his lovely *Imoinda* a Prey, or at best a Slave to the enraged Multitude; his great Heart could not endure that Thought: *Perhaps* (said he) *she may be first ravish'd by every Brute; expos'd first to their nasty Lusts, and then a shameful Death*:

No, he could not live a Moment under that Apprehension, too insupportable to be borne. These were his Thoughts, and his silent Arguments with his Heart, as he told us afterwards: So that now resolving not only to kill *Byam*, but all those he thought had enraged him; pleasing his great Heart with the fancy'd Slaughter he should make over the whole Face of the Plantation; he first resolved on a Deed, (that however horrid it first appear'd to us all) when we had heard his Reasons, we thought it brave and just. Being able to walk, and, as he believed, fit for the Execution of his great Design, he begg'd *Trefry* to trust him into the Air, believing a Walk would do him good; which was granted him; and taking *Imoinda* with him, as he used to do in his more happy and calmer Days, he led her up into a Wood, where (after with a thousand Sighs, and long gazing silently on her Face, while Tears gush'd, in spite of him, from his Eyes) he told her his Design, first of killing her, and then his Enemies, and next himself, and the Impossibility of escaping, and therefore he told her the Necessity of dying. He found the heroick Wife faster pleading for Death, than he was to propose it, when she found his fix'd Resolution; and, on her Knees, besought him not to leave her a Prey to his Enemies. He (grieved to Death) yet pleased at her noble Resolution, took her up, and embracing of her with all the Passion and Languishment of a dying Lover, drew his Knife to kill this Treasure of his Soul, this Pleasure of his Eyes; while Tears trickled down his Cheeks, hers were smiling with Joy she should die by so noble a Hand, and be sent into her own Country (for that's their Notion of the next World) by him she so tenderly loved, and so truly ador'd in this: For Wives have a Respect for their Husbands equal to what any other People pay a Deity; and when a Man finds any Occasion to quit his Wife, if he love her, she dies by his Hand; if not, he sells her, or suffers some other to kill her. It being thus, you may believe the Deed was soon resolv'd on; and 'tis not to be doubted, but the parting, the eternal Leave-taking of two such Lovers, so greatly born, so sensible, so beautiful, so young, and so fond, must be very moving, as the Relation of it was to me afterwards.

All that Love could say in such Cases, being ended, and all the intermitting Irresolutions being adjusted, the lovely, young and ador'd Victim lays herself down before the Sacrificer; while he, with a Hand resolved, and a Heart-breaking within, gave the fatal Stroke, first cutting her Throat, and then severing her yet smiling Face from that delicate Body, pregnant as it was with the Fruits of tenderest Love. As soon as he had done, he laid the Body decently on Leaves and Flowers, of which he made a Bed, and conceal'd it under the same Cover-lid of Nature; only her Face he left yet bare to look on: But when he found she was dead, and past all Retrieve, never more to bless him with her Eyes, and soft Language, his Grief swell'd up to Rage; he tore, he rav'd, he roar'd like some Monster of the Wood, calling on the lov'd Name of *Imoinda*. A thousand Times he turned the fatal Knife that did the Deed towards his own Heart, with a Resolution to go immediately after her; but dire Revenge, which was now a thousand Times more fierce in his Soul than before, prevents him; and he would cry out, "No, since I have sacrific'd *Imoinda* to my Revenge, shall I lose that Glory which I have purchased so dear, as at the Price of the fairest, dearest, softest Creature that ever Nature made? No, no!" Then at her Name Grief would get the Ascendant of Rage, and he would lie down by her Side, and water her Face with Showers of Tears, which never were wont to fall from those Eyes; and however bent he was on his intended Slaughter, he had not Power to stir from the Sight of this dear Object, now more beloved, and more ador'd than ever.

He remained in this deplorable Condition for two Days, and never rose from the Ground where he had made her sad Sacrifice; at last rouzing from her Side, and accusing himself with living too long, now *Imoinda* was dead, and that the Deaths of those barbarous Enemies were deferred too long, he resolved now to finish the great Work: but offering to rise, he found his Strength so decay'd, that he reeled to and fro, like Boughs assailed by contrary Winds; so that he was forced to lie down again, and try to summon all his Courage to his Aid. He found his Brains turned round, and his Eyes were dizzy, and Objects appear'd not the same to him they were wont to do; his Breath was short, and all his Limbs surpriz'd with a Faintness he had never felt before. He had not eat in two Days, which was one Occasion of his Feebleness, but Excess of Grief was the greatest; yet still he hoped he should recover Vigour to act his Design, and lay expecting it yet six Days longer; still mourning over the dead Idol of his Heart, and striving every Day to rise, but could not.

In all this time you may believe we were in no little Affliction for *Cæsar* and his Wife; some were of Opinion he was escaped, never to return; others thought some Accident had happened to him: But however, we fail'd not to send out a hundred People several Ways, to search for him. A Party of about forty went that Way he took, among whom was *Tuscan*, who was perfectly reconciled to *Byam*: They had not gone very far into the Wood, but they smelt an unusual Smell, as of a dead Body; for Stinks must be very noisom, that can be distinguish'd among such a Quantity of natural Sweets, as every Inch of that Land produces: so that they concluded they should find him dead, or some body that was so; they pass'd on towards it, as loathsom as it was, and made such rustling among the Leaves that lie thick on the Ground, by continual falling, that *Cæsar* heard he was approach'd; and though he had, during the Space of these eight Days, endeavour'd to rise, but found he wanted Strength, yet looking up, and seeing his Pursuers, he rose, and reel'd to a neighbouring Tree, against which he fix'd his Back; and being within a dozen Yards of those that advanc'd and saw him, he call'd out to them, and bid them approach no nearer, if they would be safe. So that they stood still, and hardly believing their Eyes, that would persuade them that it was *Cæsar* that spoke to them, so much he was alter'd; they ask'd him, what he had done with his Wife, for they smelt a Stink that almost struck them dead? He pointing to the dead Body, sighing, cry'd, *Behold her there*. They put off the Flowers that cover'd her, with their Sticks, and found she was kill'd, and cry'd out, *Oh, Monster! that hast murder'd thy Wife*. Then asking him, why he did so cruel a Deed? He reply'd, He had no Leisure to answer impertinent Questions: "You may go back *(continued he)* and tell the faithless Governor, he may thank Fortune that I am breathing my last; and that my Arm is too feeble to obey my Heart, in what it had design'd him": But his Tongue faultering, and trembling, he could scarce end what he was saying. The *English* taking Advantage by his Weakness, cry'd, *Let us take him alive by all Means*. He heard 'em; and, as if he had reviv'd from a Fainting, or a Dream, he cried out, "No, Gentlemen, you are deceived; you will find no more *Cæsars* to be whipt; no more find a Faith in me; Feeble as you think me, I have Strength yet left to secure me from a second Indignity." They swore all anew; and he only shook his Head, and beheld them with Scorn. Then they cry'd out, *Who will venture on this single Man? Will nobody?* They stood all silent, while *Cæsar* replied, *Fatal will be the Attempt of the first Adventurer, let him assure himself*, (and, at that Word, held up his Knife in a menacing Posture:) *Look ye, ye faithless Crew*, said he, *'tis not Life I seek, nor am I afraid of dying*, (and at that Word, cut a Piece of Flesh from his own Throat, and threw it at 'em) *yet still I would live if I could, till I had perfected my Revenge: But, oh! it cannot be; I feel Life gliding from my Eyes and Heart; and if I make not haste, I shall fall a Victim to the shameful Whip*. At that, he rip'd up his own Belly, and took his Bowels and pull'd 'em out, with what Strength he could; while some, on their Knees imploring, besought him to hold his Hand. But when they saw him tottering, they cry'd out, *Will none venture on him?* A bold *Englishman* cry'd, *Yes, if he were the Devil*, (taking Courage when he saw him almost dead) and swearing a horrid Oath for his farewel to the World, he rush'd on him. *Cæsar* with his arm'd Hand, met him so fairly, as stuck him to the Heart, and he Fell dead at his feet. *Tuscan* seeing that, cry'd out, *I love thee, O Cæsar! and therefore will not let thee die, if possible*; and running to him, took him in his Arms; but, at the same time,

warding a Blow that *Cæsar* made at his Bosom, he receiv'd it
quite through his Arm; and *Cæsar* having not Strength to pluck
the Knife forth, tho' he attempted it, *Tuscan* neither pull'd it
out himself, nor suffer'd it to be pull'd out, but came down
with it sticking in his Arm; and the Reason he gave for it, was,
because the Air should not get into the Wound. They put their
Hands a-cross, and carry'd *Cæsar* between six of 'em, fainting
as he was, and they thought dead, or just dying; and they
brought him to *Parham*, and laid him on a Couch, and had the
Chirurgeon immediately to him, who dressed his Wounds, and
sow'd up his Belly, and us'd Means to bring him to Life, which
they effected. We ran all to see him; and, if before we thought
him so beautiful a Sight, he was now so alter'd, that his Face
was like a Death's-Head black'd over, nothing but Teeth and
Eye-holes: For some Days we suffer'd no Body to speak to him,
but caused Cordials to be poured down his Throat; which
sustained his Life, and in six or seven Days he recovered his
Senses: For, you must know, that Wounds are almost to a
Miracle cur'd in the *Indies*; unless Wounds in the Legs, which
they rarely ever cure.

When he was well enough to speak, we talk'd to him, and
ask'd him some Questions about his Wife, and the Reasons
why he kill'd her; and he then told us what I have related of that
Resolution, and of his Parting, and he besought us we would
let him die, and was extremely afflicted to think it was possible
he might live: He assur'd us, if we did not dispatch him, he
would prove very fatal to a great many. We said all we could to
make him live, and gave him new Assurances; but he begg'd we
would not think so poorly of him, or of his Love to *Imoinda*, to
imagine we could flatter him to Life again: But the Chirurgeon
assur'd him he could not live, and therefore he need not fear.
We were all (but *Cæsar*) afflicted at this News, and the Sight
was ghastly: His Discourse was sad; and the earthy Smell about
him so strong, that I was persuaded to leave the Place for some
time, (being my self but sickly, and very apt to fall into Fits of
dangerous Illness upon any extraordinary Melancholy.) The

Servants, and *Trefry*, and the Chirurgeons, promis'd all to take what possible Care they could of the Life of *Cæsar*; and I, taking Boat, went with other Company to Colonel *Martin's*, about three Days Journey down the River. But I was no sooner gone, than the Governor taking *Trefry*, about some pretended earnest Business, a Day's Journey up the River, having communicated his Design to one *Banister*, a wild *Irish* Man, one of the Council, a Fellow of absolute Barbarity, and fit to execute any Villany, but rich; he came up to *Parham*, and forcibly took *Cæsar*, and had him carried to the same Post where he was whipp'd; and causing him to be ty'd to it, and a great Fire made before him, he told him he should die like a Dog, as he was. *Cæsar* replied, This was the first piece of Bravery that ever *Banister* did, and he never spoke Sense till he pronounc'd that Word; and if he would keep it, he would declare, in the other World, that he was the only Man, of all the *Whites*, that ever he heard speak Truth. And turning to the Men that had bound him, he said, *My Friends, am I to die, or to be whipt?* And they cry'd, *Whipt! no, you shall not escape so well.* And then he reply'd, smiling, *A Blessing on thee*; and assur'd them they need not tie him, for he would stand fix'd like a Rock, and endure Death so as should encourage them to die: *But if you whip me* (said he) *be sure you tie me fast.*

He had learn'd to take Tobacco; and when he was assur'd he should die, he desir'd they would give him a Pipe in his Mouth, ready lighted; which they did: And the Executioner came, and first cut off his Members, and threw them into the Fire; after that, with an ill-favour'd Knife, they cut off his Ears and his Nose, and burn'd them; he still smoak'd on, as if nothing had touch'd him; then they hack'd off one of his Arms, and still he bore up and held his Pipe; but at the cutting off the other Arm, his Head sunk, and his Pipe dropt, and he gave up the Ghost, without a Groan, or a Reproach. My Mother and Sister were by him all the While, but not suffer'd to save him; so rude and wild were the Rabble, and so inhuman were the Justices who stood by to see the Execution, who after paid dear enough for their

Insolence. They cut *Cæsar* into Quarters, and sent them to several of the chief Plantations: One Quarter was sent to Colonel *Martin*; who refus'd it, and swore, he had rather see the Quarters of *Banister*, and the Governor himself, than those of *Cæsar*, on his Plantations; and that he could govern his *Negroes*, without terrifying and grieving them with frightful Spectacles of a mangled King.

Thus died this great Man, worthy of a better Fate, and a more sublime Wit than mine to write his Praise: Yet, I hope, the Reputation of my Pen is considerable enough to make his glorious Name to survive to all Ages, with that of the brave, the beautiful and the constant *Imoinda*.

THE FAIR JILT

OR
THE HISTORY OF PRINCE TARQUIN
AND MIRANDA

TO
HENRY PAIN, ESQ.

Sir,

Dedications are like Love, and no Man of Wit or Eminence escapes them; early or late, the Affliction of the Poet's Complement falls upon him; and Men are oblig'd to receive 'em as they do their Wives; *For better, for worse*; at lest with a feign'd Civility.

It was not Want of Respect, but Fear, that has hitherto made us keep clear of your Judgment, too piercing to be favourable to what is not nicely valuable. We durst not awaken your Criticism; and by begging your Protection in the Front of a Book, give you an Occasion to find nothing to deserve it. Nor can this little History lay a better Claim to that Honour, than those that have not pretended to it; which has but this Merit to recommend it, That it is Truth: Truth, which you so much admire. But 'tis a Truth that entertains you with so many Accidents diverting and moving, that they will need both a Patron, and an Assertor in this incredulous World. For however it may be imagin'd that Poetry (my Talent) has so greatly the Ascendant over me, that all I write must pass for Fiction, I now desire to have it understood that this is Reality, and Matter of Fact, and acted in this our latter Age: And that in the person of *Tarquin*, I bring a Prince to kiss your Hands, who own'd himself, and was receiv'd, as the last of the Race of the *Roman* Kings; whom I have often seen, and you have heard of; and whose Story is so well known to your self, and many Hundreds more: Part of which I had from the Mouth of this unhappy great Man, and was an Eye-Witness to the rest.

'Tis true, Sir, I present you with a Prince unfortunate, but still the more noble Object for your Goodness and Pity; who never valu'd a brave Man the less for being unhappy. And whither shou'd the Afflicted flee for Refuge but to the Generous? Amongst all the Race, he cannot find a better Man, or more certain Friend: Nor amongst all his Ancestors, match your greater Soul, and Magnificence of Mind. He will behold in one *English* Subject, a Spirit as illustrious, a Heart as fearless, a Wit and Eloquence as excellent, as *Rome* it self cou'd produce. Its Senate scarce boasted of a better States-man, nor Augustus of a more faithful Subject; as your Imprisonment and Sufferings, through all the Course of our late National Distractions, have sufficiently manifested: But nothing cou'd press or deject your great Heart; you were the same Man still, unmov'd in all Turns, easie and innocent; no Persecution being able to abate your constant good Humour, or wonted Gallantry.

If, Sir, you find here a Prince of less Fortitude and Vertue than your self, charge his Miscarriages on Love: a Weakness of that Nature you will easily excuse, (being so great a Friend to the Fair;) though possibly, he gave a Proof of it too Fatal to his Honour. Had I been to have form'd his Character, perhaps I had made him something more worthy of the Honour of your Protection: But I was oblig'd to pursue the Matter of Fact, and give a just Relation of that part of his Life which, possibly, was the only reproachful part of it. If he be so happy, as to entertain a Man of Wit and Business, I shall not fear his Welcome to the rest of the World: And 'tis only with your Passport he can hope to be so.

The particular Obligations I have to your Bounty and Goodness, O Noble Friend, and Patron of the *Muses*! I do not so much as pretend to acknowledge in this little Present; those being above the Poet's Pay, which is a sort of Coin, not currant in this Age: though perhaps may be esteem'd as Medals in the Cabinets of Men of Wit. If this be so happy to be of that Number, I desire no more lasting a Fame, that it may bear this Inscription, that I am,

SIR,

Your most Obliged, and

Most Humble Servant,

A. BEHN.

THE FAIR JILT

As Love is the most noble and divine Passion of the Soul, so it is that to which we may justly attribute all the real Satisfactions of Life; and without it Man is unfinish'd and unhappy.

There are a thousand things to be said of the Advantages this generous Passion brings to those, whose Hearts are capable of receiving its soft Impressions; for 'tis not every one that can be sensible of its tender Touches. How many Examples, from History and Observation, could I give of its wondrous Power; nay, even to a Degree of Transmigration! How many Idiots has it made wise! How many Fools eloquent! How many home-bred Squires accomplish'd! How many Cowards brave! And there is no sort of Species of Mankind on whom it cannot work some Change and Miracle, if it be a noble well-grounded Passion, except on the Fop in Fashion, the harden'd incorrigible Fop; so often wounded, but never reclaim'd: For still, by a dire Mistake, conducted by vast Opiniatrety, and a greater Portion of Self-love, than the rest of the Race of Man, he believes that Affectation in his Mein and Dress, that Mathematical Movement, that Formality in every Action, that a Face manag'd with Care, and soften'd into Ridicule, the languishing Turn, the Toss, and the Back-shake of the Periwig, is the direct Way to the Heart of the fine Person he adores; and instead of curing Love in his Soul, serves only to advance his Folly; and the more he is enamour'd, the more industriously he assumes (every Hour) the Coxcomb. These are Love's Play-things, a sort of Animals with whom he sports; and whom he never wounds, but when he is in good Humour, and always shoots laughing. 'Tis the Diversion of the little God, to see what a Fluttering and Bustle one of these Sparks, new-wounded, makes; to what fantastick Fooleries he has Recourse: The Glass is every Moment call'd to counsel, the Valet consulted and plagu'd for new Invention of Dress, the Footman and Scrutore perpetually employ'd; *Billet-doux* and *Madrigals* take up all his Mornings, till Play-time in dressing, till Night in gazing; still, like a Sun-flower, turn'd towards the Beams of the fair Eyes of his

Cœlia, adjusting himself in the most amorous Posture he can assume, his Hat under his Arm, while the other Hand is put carelesly into his Bosom, as if laid upon his panting Heart; his Head a little bent to one Side, supported with a World of Cravat-string, which he takes mighty Care not to put into Disorder; as one may guess by a never-failing and horrid Stiffness in his Neck; and if he had any Occasion to look aside, his whole Body turns at the same Time, for Fear the Motion of the Head alone should incommode the Cravat or Periwig: And sometimes the Glove is well manag'd, and the white Hand display'd. Thus, with a thousand other little Motions and Formalities, all in the common Place or Road of Foppery, he takes infinite Pains to shew himself to the Pit and Boxes, a most accomplish'd Ass. This is he, of all human Kind, on whom Love can do no Miracles, and who can no where, and upon no Occasion, quit one Grain of his refin'd Foppery, unless in a Duel, or a Battle, if ever his Stars should be so severe and ill-manner'd, to reduce him to the Necessity of either: Fear then would ruffle that fine Form he had so long preserv'd in nicest Order, with Grief considering, that an unlucky Chance-wound in his Face, if such a dire Misfortune should befal him, would spoil the Sale of it for ever.

Perhaps it will be urg'd, that since no Metamorphosis can be made in a Fop by Love, you must consider him one of those that only talks of Love, and thinks himself that happy Thing, a Lover; and wanting fine Sense enough for the real Passion, believes what he feels to be it. There are in the Quiver of the God a great many different Darts; some that wound for a Day, and others for a Year; they are all fine, painted, glittering Darts, and shew as well as those made of the noblest Metal; but the Wounds they make reach the Desire only, and are cur'd by possessing, while the short-liv'd Passion betrays the Cheat. But 'tis that refin'd and illustrious Passion of the Soul, whose Aim is Virtue, and whose end is Honour, that has the Power of changing Nature, and is capable of performing all those heroick Things, of which History is full.

How far distant Passions may be from one another, I shall be able to make appear in these following Rules. I'll prove to you the strong Effects of Love in some unguarded and ungovern'd Hearts; where it rages beyond the Inspirations of *a God all soft and gentle*, and reigns more like *a Fury from Hell*.

I do not pretend here to entertain you with a feign'd Story, or any Thing piec'd together with romantick Accidents; but every Circumstance, to a Tittle, is Truth. To a great Part of the Main I myself was an Eye-witness; and what I did not see, I was confirm'd of by Actors in the Intrigue, Holy Men, of the Order of St. *Francis*: But for the Sake of some of her Relations, I shall give my *Fair Jilt* a feign'd Name, that of *Miranda*; but my Hero must retain his own, it being too illustrious to be conceal'd.

You are to understand, that in all the Catholick Countries, where Holy Orders are establish'd, there are abundance of differing Kinds of Religious, both of Men and Women. Amongst the Women, there are those we call *Nuns*, that make solemn Vows of perpetual Chastity; There are others who make but a simple Vow, as for five or ten Years, or more or less; and that time expir'd, they may contract anew for longer time, or marry, or dispose of themselves as they shall see good; and these are ordinarily call'd *Galloping Nuns*: Of these there are several Orders; as *Canonesses, Begines, Quests, Swart-Sisters*, and *Jesuitesses*, with several others I have forgot. Of those of the *Begines* was our *Fair Votress*.

These Orders are taken up by the best Persons of the Town, young Maids of Fortune, who live together, not inclos'd, but in Palaces that will hold about fifteen hundred or two thousand of these *Filles Devotes*; where they have a regulated Government, under a sort of *Abbess*, or *Prioress*, or rather a *Governante*. They are oblig'd to a Method of Devotion, and are under a sort of Obedience. They wear a Habit much like our Widows of Quality in *England*, only without a *Bando*; and their Veil is of a thicker Crape than what we have here, thro' which one cannot see the Face; for when they go abroad, they cover themselves all over with it; but they put 'em up in the Churches, and lay 'em by in the Houses. Every one of these have a Confessor, who is to 'em a sort of Steward: For, you must know, they that go into these Places, have the Management of their own Fortunes, and what their Parents design 'em. Without the Advice of this Confessor, they act nothing, nor admit of a Lover that he shall not approve; at least, this Method ought to be taken, and is by almost all of 'em; tho' *Miranda* thought her Wit above it, as her Spirit was.

But as these Women are, as I said, of the best Quality, and live with the Reputation of being retir'd from the World a little more than ordinary, and because there is a sort of Difficulty to approach 'em, they are the People the most courted, and liable to the greatest Temptations; for as difficult as it seems to be, they receive Visits from all the Men of the best Quality, especially Strangers. All the Men of Wit and Conversation meet at the Apartments of these fair *Filles Devotes*, where all Manner of Gallantries are perform'd, while all the Study of these Maids is to accomplish themselves for these noble Conversations. They receive Presents, Balls, Serenades, and Billets; All the News, Wit, Verses, Songs, Novels, Musick, Gaming, and all fine Diversion, is in their Apartments, they themselves being of the best Quality and Fortune. So that to manage these Gallantries, there is no sort of Female Arts they are not practis'd in, no Intrigue they are ignorant of, and no Management of which they are not capable.

Of this happy Number was the fair *Miranda*, whose Parents being dead, and a vast Estate divided between her self and a young Sister, (who liv'd with an unmarry'd old Uncle, whose Estate afterwards was all divided between 'em) she put her self into this uninclos'd religious House; but her Beauty, which had all the Charms that ever Nature gave, became the Envy of the whole *Sisterhood*. She was tall, and admirably shaped; she had a bright Hair, and Hazle-Eyes, all full of Love and Sweetness: No Art could make a Face so fair as hers by Nature, which every Feature adorn'd with a Grace that Imagination cannot reach: Every Look, every Motion charm'd, and her black Dress shew'd the Lustre of her Face and Neck. She had an Air, though gay as so much Youth could inspire, yet so modest, so nobly reserv'd, without Formality, or Stiffness, that one who look'd on her would have imagin'd her Soul the Twin-Angel of her Body; and both together made her appear something divine. To this she had a great deal of Wit, read much, and retain'd all that serv'd her Purpose. She sung delicately, and danc'd well, and play'd on the Lute to a Miracle. She spoke several Languages naturally; for being Co-heiress to so great a Fortune, she was bred with the nicest Care, in all the finest Manners or Education; and was now arriv'd to her Eighteenth Year.

'Twere needless to tell you how great a Noise the Fame of this young Beauty, with so considerable a Fortune, made in the World: I may say, the World, rather than confine her Fame to the scanty Limits of a Town; it reach'd to many others: And there was not a Man of any Quality that came to *Antwerp*, or pass'd thro' the City, but made it his Business to see the lovely *Miranda*, who was universally ador'd: Her Youth and Beauty, her Shape, and Majesty of Mein, and Air of Greatness, charm'd all her Beholders; and thousands of People were dying by her Eyes, while she was vain enough to glory in her Conquests, and make it her Business to wound. She lov'd nothing so much as to behold sighing Slaves at her Feet, of the greatest Quality; and treated them all with an Affability that gave them Hope. Continual Musick, as soon as it was dark, and Songs of dying Lovers, were sung under her Windows; and she might well have made herself a great Fortune (if she had not been so already) by the rich Presents that were hourly made her; and every body daily expected when she would make some one happy, by suffering her self to be conquer'd by Love and Honour, by the Assiduities and Vows of some one of her Adorers. But *Miranda* accepted their Presents, heard their Vows with Pleasure, and willingly admitted all their soft Addresses; but would not yield her Heart, or give away that lovely Person to the Possession of one, who could please it self with so many. She was naturally amorous, but extremely inconstant: She lov'd one for his Wit, another for his Face, and a third for his Mein; but above all, she admir'd Quality: Quality alone had the Power to attach her entirely; yet not to one Man, but that Virtue was still admir'd by her in all: Where-ever she found that, she lov'd, or at least acted the Lover with such Art, that (deceiving well) she fail'd not to compleat her Conquest; and yet she never durst trust her fickle Humour with Marriage. She knew the Strength of her own Heart, and that it could not suffer itself to be confin'd to one Man, and wisely avoided those Inquietudes, and that Uneasiness of Life she was sure to find in that married State, which would, against her Nature, oblige her to the Embraces of one, whose Humour was, to love all the Young and the Gay. But Love, who had hitherto only play'd with her Heart, and given it nought but pleasing wanton Wounds, such as afforded only soft Joys, and not Plains, resolv'd, either out of Revenge to those Numbers she had abandon'd, and who had sigh'd so long in vain, or to try what Power he had upon so fickle a Heart, to send an Arrow dipp'd in the most tormenting Flames that rage in Hearts most sensible. He struck it home and deep, with all the Malice of an angry God.

There was a Church belonging to the *Cordeliers*, whither *Miranda* often repair'd to her Devotion; and being there one Day, accompany'd with a young Sister of the Order, after the Mass was ended, as 'tis the Custom, some one of the Fathers goes about the Church with a Box for Contribution, or Charity-Money: It happen'd that Day, that a young Father, newly initiated, carried the Box about, which, in his Turn, he brought to *Miranda*. She had no sooner cast her Eyes on this young Friar, but her Face was overspread with Blushes of Surprize: She beheld him stedfastly, and saw in his Face all the Charms of Youth, Wit, and Beauty; he wanted no one Grace that could form him for Love, he appear'd all that is adorable to the Fair Sex, nor could the mis-shapen Habit hide from her the lovely Shape it endeavour'd to cover, nor those delicate Hands that approach'd her too near with the Box. Besides the Beauty of his Face and Shape, he had an Air altogether great, in spite of his profess'd Poverty, it betray'd the Man of Quality; and that

Thought weigh'd greatly with *Miranda*. But Love, who did not design she should now feel any sort of those easy Flames, with which she had heretofore burnt, made her soon lay all those Considerations aside, which us'd to invite her to love, and now lov'd she knew not why.

She gaz'd upon him, while he bow'd before her, and waited for her Charity, till she perceiv'd the lovely Friar to blush, and cast his Eyes to the Ground. This awaken'd her Shame, and she put her Hand into her Pocket, and was a good while in searching for her Purse, as if she thought of nothing less than what she was about; at last she drew it out, and gave him a Pistole; but with so much Deliberation and Leisure, as easily betray'd the Satisfaction she took in looking on him; while the good Man, having receiv'd her Bounty, after a very low Obeysance, proceeded to the rest; and *Miranda* casting after him a Look all languishing, as long as he remain'd in the Church, departed with a Sign as soon as she saw him go out, and returned to her Apartment without speaking one Word all the Way to the young *Fille Devote*, who attended her; so absolutely was her Soul employ'd with this young Holy Man. *Cornelia* (so was this Maid call'd who was with her) perceiving she was so silent, who us'd to be all Wit and good Humour, and observing her little Disorder at the Sight of the young Father, tho' she was far from imagining it to be Love, took an Occasion, when she was come home, to speak of him. "Madam, *said she*, did you not observe that fine young *Cordelier*, who brought the Box?" At a Question that nam'd that Object of her Thoughts, *Miranda* blush'd; and she finding she did so, redoubled her Confusion, and she had scarce Courage enough to say,—*Yes, I did observe him*: And then, forcing herself to smile a little, continu'd, "And I wonder'd to see so jolly a young Friar of an Order so severe and mortify'd.— Madam, (*reply'd* Cornelia) when you know his *Story*, you will not wonder." *Miranda*, who was impatient to know all that concern'd her new Conqueror, oblig'd her to tell his Story; and *Cornelia* obey'd, and proceeded.

The Story of Prince Henrick

"You must know, Madam, that this young Holy Man is a Prince of *Germany*, of the House of ——, whose Fate it was, to fall most passionately in Love with a fair young Lady, who lov'd him with an Ardour equal to what he vow'd her. Sure of her Heart, and wanting only the Approbation of her Parents, and his own, which her Quality did not suffer him to despair of, he boasted of his Happiness to a young Prince, his elder Brother, a Youth amorous and fierce, impatient of Joys, and sensible of Beauty, taking Fire with all fair Eyes: He was his Father's Darling, and Delight of his fond Mother; and, by an Ascendant over both their Hearts, rul'd their Wills.

"This young Prince no sooner saw, but lov'd the fair Mistress of his Brother; and with an Authority of a Sovereign, rather than the Advice of a Friend, warn'd his Brother *Henrick* (this now young Friar) to approach no more this Lady, whom he had seen; and seeing, lov'd.

"In vain the poor surpriz'd Prince pleads his Right of Love, his Exchange of Vows, and Assurance of a Heart that could never be but for himself. In vain he urges his Nearness of Blood, his Friendship, his Passion, or his Life, which so entirely depended on the Possession of the charming Maid. All his Pleading serv'd but to blow his Brother's Flame; and the more he implores, the more the other burns; and while *Henrick* follows him, on his Knees, with humble Submissions, the other flies from him in Rages of transported Love; nor could his Tears, that pursu'd his Brother's Steps, move him to Pity: Hot-headed, vain-conceited of his Beauty, and greater Quality as elder Brother, he doubts not of Success, and resolv'd to sacrifice all to the Violence of his new-born Passion.

"In short, he speaks of his Design to his Mother, who promis'd him her Assistance; and accordingly proposing it first to the Prince her Husband, urging the Languishment of her Son, she soon wrought so on him, that a Match being concluded between the Parents of this young Beauty, and

Henrick's Brother, the Hour was appointed before she knew of the Sacrifice she was to be made. And while this was in Agitation, *Henrick* was sent on some great Affairs, up into *Germany*, far out of the Way; not but his boding Heart, with perpetual Sighs and Throbs, eternally foretold him his Fate.

"All the Letters he wrote were intercepted, as well as those she wrote to him. She finds herself every Day perplex'd with the Addresses of the Prince she hated; he was ever sighing at her Feet. In vain were all her reproaches, and all her Coldness, he was on the surer Side; for what he found Love would not do, Force of Parents would.

"She complains, in her Heart, of young *Henrick*, from whom she could never receive one Letter; and at last could not forbear bursting into Tears, in spite of all her Force, and feign'd Courage, when, on a Day, the Prince told her, that *Henrick* was withdrawn to give him Time to court her; to whom he said, he confess'd he had made some Vows, but did repent of 'em, knowing himself too young to make 'em good: That it was for that Reason he brought him first to see her; and for that Reason, that after that, he never saw her more, nor so much as took Leave of her; when, indeed, his Death lay upon the next Visit, his Brother having sworn to murder him; and to that End, put a Guard upon him, till he was sent into *Germany*.

"All this he utter'd with so many passionate Asseverations, Vows, and seeming Pity for her being so inhumanly abandon'd, that she almost gave Credit to all he had said, and had much ado to keep herself within the Bounds of Moderation, and silent Grief. Her Heart was breaking, her Eyes languish'd, and her Cheeks grew pale, and she had like to have fallen dead into the treacherous Arms of him that had reduc'd her to this Discovery; but she did what she could to assume her Courage, and to shew as little Resentment as possible for a Heart, like hers, oppress'd with Love, and now abandon'd by the dear Subject of its Joys and Pains.

"But, Madam, not to tire you with this Adventure, the Day arriv'd wherein our still weeping Fair Unfortunate was to be sacrific'd to the Capriciousness of Love; and she was carry'd to Court by her Parents, without knowing to what End, where she was even compell'd to marry the Prince.

"*Henrick*, who all this While knew no more of his Unhappiness, than what his Fears suggested, returns, and passes even to the Presence of his Father, before he knew any Thing of his Fortune; where he beheld his Mistress and his Brother, with his Father, in such a Familiarity, as he no longer doubted his Destiny. 'Tis hard to judge, whether the Lady, or himself, was most surpriz'd; she was all pale and unmoveable in her Chair, and *Henrick* fix'd like a Statue; at last Grief and Rage took Place of Amazement, and he could not forbear crying out, *Ah, Traytor! Is it thus you have treated a Friend and Brother? And you, O perjur'd Charmer! Is it thus you have rewarded all my Vows?* He could say no more; but reeling against the Door, had fallen in a Swoon upon the Floor, had not his Page caught him in his Arms, who was entring with him. The good old Prince, the Father, who knew not what all this meant, was soon inform'd by the young weeping Princess; who, in relating the Story of her Amour with *Henrick*, told her Tale in so moving a Manner, as brought Tears to the Old Man's Eyes, and Rage to those of her Husband; he immediately grew jealous to the last Degree: He finds himself in Possession ('tis true) of the Beauty he ador'd, but the Beauty adoring another; a Prince young and charming as the Light, soft, witty, and raging with an equal Passion. He finds this dreaded Rival in the same House with him, with an Authority equal to his own; and fancies, where two Hearts are so entirely agreed, and have so good an Understanding, it would not be impossible to find Opportunities to satisfy and ease that mutual Flame, that burnt so equally in both; he therefore resolved to send him out of the World, and to establish his own Repose by a Deed, wicked, cruel, and unnatural, to have him assassinated the first Opportunity he could find. This Resolution set him a little at Ease, and he strove to dissemble Kindness to *Henrick*, with all the Art he was capable of, suffering him to come often to the

Apartment of the Princess, and to entertain her oftentimes with Discourse, when he was not near enough to hear what he spoke; but still watching their Eyes, he found those of *Henrick* full of Tears, ready to flow, but restrain'd, looking all dying, and yet reproaching, while those of the Princess were ever bent to the Earth, and she as much as possible, shunning his Conversation. Yet this did not satisfy the jealous Husband; 'twas not her Complaisance that could appease him; he found her Heart was panting within, whenever *Henrick* approach'd her, and every Visit more and more confirmed his Death.

"The Father often found the Disorders of the Sons; the Softness and Address of the one gave him as much Fear, as the angry Blushings, the fierce Looks, and broken Replies of the other, whenever he beheld *Henrick* approach his Wife; so that the Father, fearing some ill Consequence of this, besought *Henrick* to withdraw to some other Country, or travel into *Italy*, he being now of an Age that required a View of the World. He told his Father, That he would obey his Commands, tho' he was certain, that Moment he was to be separated from the Sight of the fair Princess, his Sister, would be the last of his Life; and, in fine, made so pitiful a Story of his suffering Love, as almost moved the old Prince to compassionate him so far, as to permit him to stay; but he saw inevitable Danger in that, and therefore bid him prepare for his Journey.

"That which pass'd between the Father and *Henrick*, being a Secret, none talked of his departing from Court; so that the Design the Brother had went on; and making a Hunting-Match one Day, where most young People of Quality were, he order'd some whom he had hired to follow his Brother, so as if he chanced to go out of the Way, to dispatch him; and accordingly, Fortune gave 'em an Opportunity; for he lagg'd behind the Company, and turn'd aside into a pleasant Thicket of Hazles, where alighting, he walk'd on Foot in the most pleasant Part of it, full of Thought, how to divide his Soul between Love and Obedience. He was sensible that he ought not to stay; that he was but an Affliction to the young Princess, whose Honour could never permit her to ease any Part of his Flame; nor was he so vicious to entertain a Thought that should stain her Virtue. He beheld her now as his Brother's Wife, and that secured his Flame from all loose Desires, if her native Modesty had not been sufficient of itself to have done it, as well as that profound Respect he paid her; and he consider'd, in obeying his Father, he left her at Ease, and his Brother freed of a thousand Fears; he went to seek a Cure, which if he could not find, at last he could but die; and so he must, even at her Feet: However, that it was more noble to seek a Remedy for his Disease, than expect a certain Death by staying. After a thousand Reflections on his hard Fate, and bemoaning himself, and blaming his cruel Stars, that had doom'd him to die so young, after an Infinity of Sighs and Tears, Resolvings and Unresolvings, he, on the sudden, was interrupted by the trampling of some Horses he heard, and their rushing through the Boughs, and saw four Men make towards him: He had not time to mount, being walk'd some Paces from his Horse. One of the Men advanced, and cry'd, *Prince, you must die—I do believe thee,* (reply'd *Henrick*) *but not by a Hand so base as thine*: And at the same Time drawing his Sword, run him into the Groin. When the Fellow found himself so wounded, he wheel'd off and cry'd, *Thou art a Prophet, and hast rewarded my Treachery with Death.* The rest came up, and one shot at the Prince, and shot him in the Shoulder; the other two hastily laying hold (but too late) on the Hand of the Murderer, cry'd, *Hold, Traytor; we relent, and he shall not die.* He reply'd, *'Tis too late, he is shot; and see, he lies dead. Let us provide for ourselves, and tell the Prince, we have done the Work; for you are as guilty as I am.* At that they all fled, and left the Prince lying under a Tree, weltering in his Blood.

"About the Evening, the Forester going his Walks, saw the Horse, richly caparison'd, without a Rider, at the Entrance of the Wood; and going farther, to see if he could find its Owner, found there the Prince almost dead; he immediately mounts him on the Horse, and himself behind, bore him up, and carry'd him to the Lodge; where he had only one old Man, his Father, well skilled in Surgery, and a Boy. They put him to Bed; and the old Forester, with what Art he had, dress'd his Wounds, and in the Morning sent for an abler Surgeon, to whom the Prince enjoin'd Secrecy, because he knew him. The Man was faithful, and the Prince in Time was recover'd of his Wound; and as soon as he was well, he came to *Flanders*, in the Habit of a Pilgrim, and after some Time took the Order of St. *Francis*, none knowing what became of him, till he was profess'd; and then he wrote his own Story to the Prince his Father, to his Mistress, and his ungrateful Brother. The young Princess did not long survive his Loss, she languished from the Moment of his Departure; and he had this to confirm his devout Life, to know she dy'd for him.

"My Brother, Madam, was an Officer under the Prince his Father, and knew his Story perfectly well; from whose Mouth I had it."

What! (reply'd *Miranda* then) *is Father* Henrick *a Man of Quality? Yes, Madam,* (said *Cornelia*) *and has changed his Name to* Francisco. But *Miranda*, fearing to betray the Sentiments of her Heart, by asking any more Questions about him, turned the Discourse; and some Persons of Quality came in to visit her (for her Apartment was about six o'Clock, like the Presence-Chamber of a Queen, always filled with the greatest People): There meet all the *Beaux Esprits*, and all the Beauties. But it was visible *Miranda* was not so gay as she used to be; but pensive, and answering *mal a propos* to all that was said to her. She was a thousand times going to speak, against her Will, something of the charming Friar, who was never from her Thoughts; and she imagined, if he could inspire Love in a coarse, grey, ill-made Habit, a shorn Crown, a Hair-cord about his Waist, bare-legg'd, in Sandals instead of Shoes; what must he do, when looking back on Time, she beholds him in a Prospect of Glory, with all that Youth, and illustrious Beauty, set off by the Advantage of Dress and Equipage? She frames an

Idea of him all gay and splendid, and looks on his present Habit as some Disguise proper for the Stealths of Love; some feigned puton Shape, with the more Security to approach a Mistress, and make himself happy; and that the Robe laid by, she has the Lover in his proper Beauty, the same he would have been, if any other Habit (though ever so rich) were put off: In the Bed, the silent gloomy Night, and the soft Embraces of her Arms, he loses all the Friar, and assumes all the Prince; and that aweful Reverence, due alone to his Holy Habit, he exchanges for a thousand Dalliances, for which his Youth was made; for Love, for tender Embraces, and all the Happiness of Life. Some Moments she fancies him a Lover, and that the fair Object that takes up all his Heart, has left no Room for her there; but that was a Thought that did not long perplex her, and which, almost as soon as born, she turned to her Advantage. She beholds him a Lover, and therefore finds he has a Heart sensible and tender; he had Youth to be fir'd, as well as to inspire; he was far from the loved Object, and totally without Hope; and she reasonably consider'd, that Flame would of itself soon die, that had only Despair to feed on. She beheld her own Charms; and Experience, as well as her Glass, told her, they never failed of Conquest, especially where they designed it: And she believed *Henrick* would be glad, at least, to quench that Flame in himself, by an Amour with her, which was kindled by the young Princess of—his Sister.

These, and a thousand other Self-flatteries, all vain and indiscreet, took up her waking Nights, and now more retired Days; while Love, to make her truly wretched, suffered her to sooth herself with fond Imaginations; not so much as permitting her Reason to plead one Moment to save her from undoing: She would not suffer it to tell her, he had taken Holy Orders, made sacred and solemn Vows of everlasting Chastity, that it was impossible he could marry her, or lay before her any Argument that might prevent her Ruin; but Love, mad malicious Love, was always called to Counsel, and, like easy Monarchs, she had no Ears, but for Flatterers.

Well then, she is resolv'd to love, without considering to what End, and what must be the Consequence of such an Amour. She now miss'd no Day of being at that little Church, where she had the Happiness, or rather the Misfortune (so Love ordained) to see this Ravisher of her Heart and Soul; and every Day she took new Fire from his lovely Eyes. Unawares, unknown, and unwillingly, he gave her Wounds, and the Difficulty of her Cure made her rage the more: She burnt, she languish'd, and died for the young Innocent, who knew not he was the Author of so much Mischief.

Now she resolves a thousand Ways in her tortur'd Mind, to let him know her Anguish, and at last pitch'd upon that of writing to him soft Billets, which she had learn'd the Art of doing; or if she had not, she had now Fire enough to inspire her with all that could charm and move. These she deliver'd to a young Wench, who waited on her, and whom she had entirely subdu'd to her Interest, to give to a certain Lay-Brother of the Order, who was a very simple harmless Wretch, and who served in the Kitchen, in the Nature of a Cook, in the Monastery of *Cordeliers*. She gave him Gold to secure his Faith and Service; and not knowing from whence they came (with so good Credentials) he undertook to deliver the Letters to Father *Francisco*; which Letters were all afterwards, as you shall hear, produced in open Court. These Letters failed not to come every Day; and the Sense of the first was, to tell him, that a very beautiful young Lady, of a great Fortune, was in love with him, without naming her; but it came as from a third Person, to let him know the Secret, that she desir'd he would let her know whether she might hope any Return from him; assuring him, he needed but only see the fair Languisher, to confess himself her Slave.

This Letter being deliver'd him, he read by himself, and was surpriz'd to receive Words of this Nature, being so great a Stranger in that Place; and could not imagine or would not give himself the Trouble of guessing who this should be, because he never designed to make Returns.

The next Day, *Miranda*, finding no Advantage from her Messenger of Love, in the Evening sends another (impatient of Delay) confessing that she who suffer'd the Shame of writing and imploring, was the Person herself who ador'd him. 'Twas there her raging Love made her say all Things that discover'd the Nature of its Flame, and propose to flee with him to any Part of the World, if he would quit the Convent; that she had a Fortune considerable enough to make him happy; and that his Youth and Quality were not given him to so unprofitable and End as to lose themselves in a Convent, where Poverty and Ease was all the Business. In fine, she leaves nothing unurg'd that might debauch and invite him; not forgetting to send him her own Character of Beauty, and left him to judge of her Wit and Spirit by her Writing, and her Love by the Extremity of Passion she profess'd. To all which the lovely Friar made no Return, as believing a gentle Capitulation or Exhortation to her would but inflame her the more, and give new Occasions for her continuing to write. All her Reasonings, false and vicious, he despis'd, pity'd the Error of her Love, and was Proof against all she could plead. Yet notwithstanding his Silence, which left her in Doubt, and more tormented her, she ceas'd not to pursue him with her Letters, varying her Style; sometimes all wanton, loose and raving; sometimes feigning a Virgin-Modesty all over, accusing her self, blaming her Conduct, and sighing her Destiny, as one compell'd to the shameful Discovery by the Austerity of his Vow and Habit, asking his Pity and Forgiveness; urging him in Charity to use his Fatherly Care to persuade and reason with her wild Desires, and by his Counsel drive the God from her Heart, whose Tyranny was worse than that of a Fiend; and he did not know what his pious Advice might do. But still she writes in vain, in vain she varies her Style, by a Cunning, peculiar to a Maid possess'd with such a sort of Passion.

This cold Neglect was still Oil to the burning Lamp, and she tries yet more Arts, which for want of right Thinking were as fruitless. She has Recourse to Presents; her Letters came loaded with Rings of great Price, and Jewels, which Fops of Quality had given her. Many of this Sort he receiv'd, before he knew where to return 'em, or how; and on this Occasion alone he sent her a Letter, and restor'd her Trifles, as he call'd them: But his Habit having not made him forget his Quality and Education, he wrote to her with all the profound Respect imaginable; believing by her Presents, and the Liberality with which she parted with 'em, that she was of Quality. But the whole Letter, as he told me afterwards, was to persuade her from the Honour she did him, by loving him; urging a thousand Reasons, solid and pious, and assuring her, he had wholly devoted the rest of his Days to Heaven, and had no Need of those gay Trifles she had sent him, which were only fit to adorn Ladies so fair as herself, and who had Business with this glittering World, which he disdain'd, and had for ever abandon'd. He sent her a thousand Blessings, and told her, she should be ever in his Prayers, tho' not in his Heart, as she desir'd: And abundance of Goodness more he express'd, and Counsel he gave her, which had the same Effect with his Silence; it made her love but the more, and the more impatient she grew. She now had a new Occasion to write, she now is charm'd with his Wit; this was the new Subject. She rallies his Resolution, and endeavours to re-call him to the World, by all the Arguments that human Invention is capable of.

But when she had above four Months languish'd thus in vain, not missing one Day, wherein she went not to see him, without discovering herself to him; she resolv'd, as her last Effort, to shew her Person, and see what that, assisted by her Tears, and soft Words from her Mouth, could do, to prevail upon him.

It happen'd to be on the Eve of that Day when she was to receive the Sacrament, that she, covering herself with her Veil, came to *Vespers*, purposing to make Choice of the conquering Friar for her Confessor.

She approach'd him; and as she did so, she trembled with Love. At last she cry'd, *Father, my Confessor is gone for some Time from the Town, and I am oblig'd Tomorrow to receive, and beg you will be pleas'd to take my Confession.*

He could not refuse her; and let her into the *Sacristy*, where there is a Confession-Chair, in which he seated himself; and on one Side of him she kneel'd down, over-against a little Altar, where the Priests Robes lye, on which were plac'd some lighted Wax-Candles, that made the little Place very light and splendid, which shone full upon *Miranda*.

After the little Preparation usual in Confession, she turn'd up her Veil, and discover'd to his View the most wondrous Object of Beauty he had ever seen, dress'd in all the Glory of a young Bride; her Hair and Stomacher full of Diamonds, that gave a Lustre all dazling to her brighter Face and Eyes. He was surpriz'd at her amazing Beauty, and question'd whether he saw a Woman, or an Angel at his Feet. Her Hands, which were elevated, as if in Prayer, seem'd to be form'd of polish'd Alabaster; and he confess'd, he had never seen any Thing in Nature so perfect and so admirable.

He had some Pain to compose himself to hear her Confession, and was oblig'd to turn away his Eyes, that his Mind might not be perplex'd with an Object so diverting; when *Miranda*, opening the finest Mouth in the World, and discovering new Charms, began her Confession.

"Holy Father (*said she*) amongst the Number of my vile Offences, that which afflicts me to the greatest Degree, is, that I am in love: Not (*continued she*) that I believe simple and virtuous Love a Sin, when 'tis plac'd on an Object proper and suitable; but, my dear Father, (*said she, and wept*) I love with a Violence which cannot be contain'd within the Bounds of Reason, Moderation, or Virtue. I love a Man whom I cannot possess without a Crime, and a Man who cannot make me happy without being perjur'd. Is he marry'd? (*reply'd the Father.*) No; (*answer'd* Miranda.) Are you so? (*continued he.*) Neither, (*said she.*) Is he too near ally'd to you? (*said* Francisco:) a Brother, or Relation? Neither of these, (*said she.*) He is unenjoy'd, unpromis'd; and so am I: Nothing opposes our Happiness, or makes my Love a Vice, but you—'Tis you deny me Life: 'Tis you that forbid my Flame: 'Tis you will have me die, and seek my Remedy in my Grave, when I complain of Tortures, Wounds, and Flames. O cruel Charmer! 'tis for you I languish; and here, at your Feet, implore that Pity, which all my Addresses have fail'd of procuring me." —

With that, perceiving he was about to rise from his Seat, she held him by his Habit, and vow'd she would in that Posture follow him, where-ever he flew from her. She elevated her Voice so loud, he was afraid she might be heard, and therefore suffer'd her to force him into his Chair again; where being seated, he began, in the most passionate Terms imaginable, to dissuade her; but finding she the more persisted in Eagerness of Passion, he us'd all the tender Assurance that he could force from himself, that he would have for her all the Respect, Esteem and Friendship that he was capable of paying; that he had a real Compassion for her: and at last she prevail'd so far with him, by her Sighs and Tears, as to own he had a Tenderness for her, and that he could not behold so many Charms, without being sensibly touch'd by 'em, and finding all those Effects, that a Maid so fair and young causes in the Souls of Men of Youth and Sense: But that, as he was assured, he could never be so happy to marry her, and as certain he could not grant any Thing but honourable Passion, he humbly besought her not to expect more from him than such. And then began to tell her how short Life was, and transitory its Joys; how soon she would grow weary of Vice, and how often change to find real Repose in it, but never arrive to it. He made an End, by new Assurance of his eternal Friendship, but utterly forbad her to hope.

Behold her now deny'd, refus'd and defeated, with all her pleading Youth, Beauty, Tears, and Knees, imploring, as she lay, holding fast his *Scapular*, and embracing his Feet. What shall she do? She swells with Pride, Love, Indignation and Desire; her burning Heart is bursting with Despair, her Eyes grow fierce, and from Grief she rises to a Storm; and in her Agony of Passion, with Looks all disdainful, haughty, and full of Rage, she began to revile him, as the poorest of Animals; tells him his Soul was dwindled to the Meanness of his Habit, and his Vows of Poverty were suited to his degenerate Mind. "And (*said she*) since all my nobler Ways have fail'd me; and that, for a little Hypocritical Devotion, you resolve to lose the greatest Blessings of Life, and to sacrifice me to your Religious Pride and Vanity, I will either force you to abandon that dull Dissimulation, or you shall die, to prove your Sanctity real. Therefore answer me immediately, answer my Flame, my raging Fire, which your Eyes have kindled; or here, in this very Moment, I will ruin thee; and make no Scruple of revenging the Pains I suffer, by that which shall take away your Life and Honour."

The trembling young Man, who, all this While, with extreme Anguish of Mind, and Fear of the dire Result, had listen'd to her Ravings, full of Dread, demanded what she would have him do? When she reply'd—"Do that which thy Youth and Beauty were ordain'd to do:—this Place is private, a sacred Silence reigns here, and no one dares to pry into the Secrets of this Holy Place: We are as secure from Fears and Interruption, as in Desarts uninhabited, or Caves forsaken by wild Beasts. The Tapers too shall veil their Lights, and only that glimmering Lamp shall be Witness of our dear Stealths of Love—Come to my Arms, my trembling, longing Arms; and curse the Folly of thy Bigotry, that has made thee so long lose a Blessing, for which so many Princes sigh in vain."

At these Words she rose from his Feet, and snatching him in her Arms, he could not defend himself from receiving a thousand Kisses from the lovely Mouth of the charming Wanton; after which, she ran herself, and in an Instant put out the Candles. But he cry'd to her, "In vain, O too indiscreet Fair One, in vain you put out the Light; for Heaven still has Eyes, and will look down upon my broken Vows. I own your Power, I own I have all the Sense in the World of your charming Touches; I am frail Flesh and Blood, but—yet—yet I can resist; and I prefer my Vows to all your powerful Temptations.—I will be deaf and blind, and guard my Heart with Walls of Ice, and make you know, that when the Flames of true Devotion are kindled in a Heart, it puts out all other Fires; which are as ineffectual, as Candles lighted in the Face of the Sun.—Go, vain Wanton, and repent, and mortify that Blood which has so shamefully betray'd thee, and which will one Day ruin both thy Soul and Body." —

At these Words *Miranda*, more enrag'd, the nearer she imagin'd her self to Happiness, made no Reply; but throwing her self, in that Instant, into the Confessing-Chair, and violently pulling the young Friar into her Lap, she elevated her Voice to such a Degree, in crying out, *Help, Help! A Rape! Help, Help!* that she was heard all over the Church, which was full of People at the Evening's Devotion; who flock'd about the Door of the *Sacristy*, which was shut with a Spring-Lock on the Inside, but they durst not open the Door.

'Tis easily to be imagin'd, in what Condition our young Friar was, at this last devilish Stratagem of his wicked Mistress. He strove to break from those Arms that held him so fast; and his Bustling to get away, and her's to retain him, disorder'd her Hair and Habit to such a Degree, as gave the more Credit to her false Accusation.

The Fathers had a Door on the other Side, by which they usually enter'd, to dress in this little Room; and at the Report that was in an Instant made 'em, they hasted thither, and found *Miranda* and the good Father very indecently struggling; which they mis-interpreted, as *Miranda* desir'd; who, all in Tears, immediately threw her self at the Feet of the Provincial, who was one of those that enter'd; and cry'd, "O holy Father! revenge an innocent Maid, undone and lost to Fame and Honour, by that vile Monster, born of Goats, nurs'd by Tygers, and bred up on savage Mountains, where Humanity and Religion are Strangers. For, O holy Father, could it have enter'd into the Heart of Man, to have done so barbarous and horrid a Deed, as to attempt the Virgin-Honour of an unspotted Maid, and one of my Degree, even in the Moment of my Confession, in that holy Time, when I was prostrate before him and Heaven, confessing those Sins that press'd my tender Conscience; even then to load my Soul with the blackest of Infamies, to add to my Number a Weight that must sink me to Hell? Alas! under the Security of his innocent Looks, his holy Habit, and his aweful Function, I was led into this Room to make my Confession; where, he locking the Door, I had no sooner began, but he gazing on me, took fire at my fatal Beauty; and starting up, put out the Candles and caught me in his Arms; and raising me from the Pavement, set me in the Confession-Chair; and then—Oh, spare me the rest."

With that a Shower of Tears burst from her fair dissembling Eyes, and Sobs so naturally acted, and so well manag'd, as left no doubt upon the good Men, but all she had spoken was Truth.

"— At first, (*proceeded she*) I was unwilling to bring so great a Scandal on his Order, to cry out; but struggled as long as I had Breath; pleaded the Heinousness of the Crime, urging my Quality, and the Danger of the Attempt. But he, deaf as the Winds, and ruffling as a Storm, pursu'd his wild Design with so much Force and Insolence, as I at last, unable to resist, was wholly vanquish'd, robb'd of my native Purity. With what Life and Breath I had, I call'd for Assistance, both from Men and Heaven; but oh, alas! your Succours came too late:—You find me here a wretched, undone, and ravish'd Maid. Revenge me, Fathers; revenge me on the perfidious Hypocrite, or else give me a Death that may secure your Cruelty and Injustice from ever being proclaim'd over the World; or my Tongue will be eternally reproaching you, and cursing the wicked Author of my Infamy."

She ended as she began, with a thousand Sighs and Tears; and received from the Provincial all Assurances of Revenge.

The innocent betray'd Victim, all the while she was speaking, heard her with an Astonishment that may easily be imagined; yet shew'd no extravagant Signs of it, as those would do, who feign it, to be thought innocent; but being really so, he bore with an humble, modest, and blushing Countenance, all her

Accusations; which silent Shame they mistook for evident Signs of his Guilt.

When the Provincial demanded, with an unwonted Severity in his Eyes and Voice, what he could answer for himself? calling him Profaner of his Sacred Vows, and Infamy to the Holy Order; the injur'd, but innocently accus'd, only reply'd: "May Heaven forgive that bad Woman, and bring her to Repentance! For his Part, he was not so much in Love with Life, as to use many arguments to justify his Innocence; unless it were to free that Order from a Scandal, of which he had the Honour to be profess'd. But as for himself, Life or Death were Things indifferent to him, who heartily despis'd the World."

He said no more, and suffer'd himself to be led before the Magistrate; who committed him to Prison, upon the Accusation of this implacable Beauty; who, with so much feign'd Sorrow, prosecuted the Matter, even to his Tryal and Condemnation; where he refus'd to make any great Defence for himself. But being daily visited by all the Religious, both of his own and other Orders, they oblig'd him (some of 'em knowing the Austerity of his Life, others his Cause of Griefs that first brought him into Orders, and others pretending a nearer Knowledge, even of his Soul it self) to stand upon his Justification, and discover what he knew of that wicked Woman; whose Life had not been so exemplary for Virtue, not to have given the World a thousand Suspicions of her Lewdness and Prostitutions.

The daily Importunities of these Fathers made him produce her Letters: But as he had all the Gown-men on his Side, she had all the Hats and Feathers on her's; all the Men of Quality taking her Part, and all the Churchmen his. They heard his daily Protestations and Vows, but not a Word of what passed at Confession was yet discover'd: He held that as a Secret sacred on his Part; and what was said in Nature of a Confession, was not to be revealed, though his Life depended on the Discovery. But as to the Letters, they were forc'd from him, and expos'd; however, Matters were carry'd with so high a Hand against him, that they serv'd for no Proof at all of his Innocence, and he was at last condemn'd to be burn'd at the Market-Place.

After his Sentence was pass'd, the whole Body of Priests made their Addresses to the Marquis *Castel Roderigo*, the then Governor of *Flanders*, for a Reprieve; which, after much ado, was granted him for some Weeks, but with an absolute Denial of Pardon: So prevailing were the young Cavaliers of his Court, who were all Adorers of this Fair Jilt.

About this time, while the poor innocent young *Henrick* was thus languishing in Prison, in a dark and dismal Dungeon, and *Miranda*, cured of her Love, was triumphing in her Revenge, expecting and daily giving new Conquests; and who, by this time, had re-assum'd all her wonted Gaiety; there was a great Noise about the Town, that a Prince of mighty Name, and fam'd for all the Excellencies of his Sex, was arriv'd; a Prince young, and gloriously attended, call'd Prince *Tarquin*.

We had often heard of this great Man, and that he was making his Travels in *France* and *Germany*: And we had also heard, that some Years before, he being about Eighteen Years of Age, in the Time when our King *Charles*, of blessed Memory, was in *Brussels*, in the last Year of his Banishment, that all on a sudden, this young Man rose up upon 'em like the Sun, all glorious and dazling, demanding Place of all the Princes in that Court. And when his Pretence was demanded, he own'd himself Prince *Tarquin*, of the Race of the last Kings of *Rome*, made good his Title, and took his Place accordingly. After that he travell'd for about six Years up and down the World, and then arriv'd at *Antwerp*, about the Time of my being sent thither by King *Charles*.

Perhaps there could be nothing seen so magnificent as this Prince: He was, as I said, extremely handsome, from Head to Foot exactly form'd, and he wanted nothing that might adorn that native Beauty to the best Advantage. His Parts were suitable to the rest: He had an Accomplishment fit for a Prince, an Air haughty, but a Carriage affable, easy in Conversation, and very entertaining, liberal and good-natur'd, brave and inoffensive. I have seen him pass the Streets with twelve Footmen, and four Pages; the Pages all in green Velvet Coats lac'd with Gold, and white Velvet Tunicks; the Men in Cloth, richly lac'd with Gold; his Coaches, and all other Officers, suitable to a great Man.

He was all the Discourse of the Town; some laughing at his Title, others reverencing it: Some cry'd, that he was an Imposter; others, that he had made his Title as plain, as if *Tarquin* had reign'd but a Year ago. Some made Friendships with him, others would have nothing to say to him: But all wonder'd where his Revenue was, that supported this Grandeur; and believ'd, tho' he could make his Descent from the *Roman* Kings very well out, that he could not lay so good a Claim to the *Roman* Land. Thus every body meddled with what they had nothing to do; and, as in other Places, thought themselves on the surer Side, if, in these doubtful Cases, they imagin'd the worst.

But the Men might be of what Opinion they pleas'd concerning him; the Ladies were all agreed that he was a Prince, and a young handsome Prince, and a Prince not to be resisted: He had all their Wishes, all their Eyes, and all their Hearts. They now dress'd only for him; and what Church he grac'd, was sure, that Day, to have the Beauties, and all that thought themselves so.

You may believe, our amorous *Miranda* was not the least Conquest he made. She no sooner heard of him, which was as soon as he arriv'd, but she fell in love with his very Name. *Jesu!*—A young King of *Rome*! Oh, it was so novel, that she doated on the Title; and had not car'd whether the rest had been Man or Monkey almost: She was resolved to be the *Lucretia* that this young *Tarquin* should ravish.

To this End, she was no sooner up the next Day, but she sent him a *Billet Doux*, assuring him how much she admired his Fame; and that being a Stranger in the Town, she begged the Honour of introducing him to all the *Belle* Conversations, &c. which he took for the Invitation of some Coquet, who had

Interest in fair Ladies; and civilly return'd her an Answer, that he would wait on her. She had him that Day watched to Church; and impatient to see what she heard so many People flock to see, she went also to the same Church; those sanctified Abodes being too often profaned by such Devotees, whose Business is to ogle and ensnare.

But what a Noise and Humming was heard all over the Church, when *Tarquin* enter'd! His Grace, his Mein, his Fashion, his Beauty, his Dress, and his Equipage surprized all that were present: And by the good Management and Care of *Miranda*, she got to kneel at the Side of the Altar, just over against the Prince, so that, if he would, he could not avoid looking full upon her. She had turned up her Veil, and all her Face and Shape appear'd such, and so inchanting, as I have described; and her Beauty heighten'd with Blushes, and her Eyes full of Spirit and Fire, with Joy, to find the young *Roman* Monarch so charming, she appear'd like something more than mortal, and compelled his Eyes to a fixed gazing on her Face: She never glanc'd that Way, but she met them; and then would feign so modest a Shame, and cast her Eyes downwards with such inviting Art, that he was wholly ravished and charmed, and she over-joy'd to find he was so.

The Ceremony being ended, he sent a Page to follow that Lady Home, himself pursuing her to the Door of the Church, where he took some holy Water, and threw upon her, and made her a profound Reverence. She forc'd an innocent Look, and a modest Gratitude in her Face, and bow'd, and passed forward, half assur'd of her Conquest; leaving her, to go home to his Lodging, and impatiently wait the Return of his Page. And all the Ladies who saw this first Beginning between the Prince and *Miranda*, began to curse and envy her Charms, who had deprived them of half their Hopes.

After this, I need not tell you, he made *Miranda* a Visit; and from that Day never left her Apartment, but when he went home at Nights, or unless he had Business; so entirely was he conquer'd by this Fair One. But the Bishop, and several Men of Quality, in Orders, that profess'd Friendship to him, advised him from her Company; and spoke several Things to him, that might (if Love had not made him blind) have reclaimed him from the Pursuit of his Ruin. But whatever they trusted him with, she had the Art to wind herself about his Heart, and make him unravel all his Secrets; and then knew as well, by feign'd Sighs and Tears, to make him disbelieve all; so that he had no Faith but for her; and was wholly inchanted and bewitch'd by her. At last, in spite of all that would have opposed it, he marry'd this famous Woman, possess'd by so many great Men and Strangers before, while all the World was pitying his Shame and Misfortunes.

Being marry'd, they took a great House; and as she was indeed a great Fortune, and now a great Princess, there was nothing wanting that was agreeable to their Quality; all was splendid and magnificent. But all this would not acquire them the World's Esteem; they had an Abhorrence for her former Life, and despised her; and for his espousing a Woman so infamous, they despised him. So that though they admir'd, and gazed upon their Equipage, and glorious Dress, they foresaw the Ruin that attended it, and paid her Quality little Respect.

She was no sooner married, but her Uncle died; and dividing his Fortune between *Miranda* and her Sister, leaves the young Heiress, and all her Fortune, entirely in the Hands of the Princess.

We will call this Sister *Alcidiana*; she was about fourteen Years of Age, and now had chosen her Brother, the Prince, for her Guardian. If *Alcidiana* were not altogether so great a Beauty as her Sister, she had Charms sufficient to procure her a great many Lovers, though her Fortune had not been so considerable as it was; but with that Addition, you may believe, she wanted no Courtships from those of the best Quality; tho' every body deplor'd her being under the Tutorage of a Lady so expert in all the Vices of her Sex, and so cunning a Manager of Sin, as was the Princess; who, on her Part, failed not, by all the Caresses, and obliging Endearments, to engage the Mind of this young Maid, and to subdue her wholly to her Government.

All her Senses were eternally regaled with the most bewitching Pleasures they were capable of: She saw nothing but Glory and Magnificence, heard nothing but Musick of the sweetest Sounds; the richest Perfumes employ'd her Smelling; and all she eat and touch'd was delicate and inviting; and being too young to consider how this State and Grandeur was to be continu'd, little imagined her vast Fortune was every Day diminishing, towards its needless Support.

When the Princess went to Church, she had her Gentleman bare before her, carrying a great Velvet Cushion, with great Golden Tassels, for her to kneel on, and her Train borne up a most prodigious Length, led by a Gentleman Usher, bare; follow'd by innumerable Footmen, Pages, and Women. And in this State she would walk in the Streets, as in those Countries it is the Fashion for the great Ladies to do, who are well; and in her Train two or three Coaches, and perhaps a rich Velvet Chair embroider'd, would follow in State.

It was thus for some time they liv'd, and the Princess was daily press'd by young sighing Lovers, for her Consent to marry *Alcidiana*; but she had still one Art or other to put them off, and so continually broke all the great Matches that were proposed to her, notwithstanding their Kindred and other Friends had industriously endeavour'd to make several great Matches for her; but the Princess was still positive in her Denial, and one Way or other broke all. At last it happened, there was one proposed, yet more advantageous, a young Count, with whom the young Maid grew passionately in Love, and besought her Sister to consent that she might have him, and got the Prince to speak in her Behalf; but he had no sooner heard the secret Reasons *Miranda* gave him, but (entirely her Slave) he chang'd his Mind, and suited it to hers, and she, as before, broke off that Amour: Which so extremely incensed *Alcidiana*, the she, taking an Opportunity, got from her Guard, and ran away, putting her self into the Hands of a wealty Merchant, her Kinsman, and one who bore the greatest Authority in the City; him she chuses for her Guardian, resolving to be no longer a Slave to the Tyranny of her Sister. And so well she ordered Matters, that she writ this young Cavalier, her last Lover, and retrieved him; who came back to *Antwerp* again, to renew his Courtship.

Both Parties being agreed, it was no hard Matter to persuade all but the Princess. But though she opposed it, it was resolved on, and the Day appointed for Marriage, and the Portion demanded; demanded only, but never to be paid, the best Part of it being spent. However, she put them off from Day to Day, by a thousand frivolous Delays; and when she saw they would have Recourse to Force, and all that her Magnificence would be at an End, if the Law should prevail against her; and that without this Sister's Fortune, she could not long support her Grandeur; she bethought herself of a Means to make it all her own, by getting her Sister made away; but she being out of her Tuition, she was not able to accomplish so great a Deed of Darkness. But since it was resolved it must be done, she contrives a thousand Stratagems; and at last pitches upon an effectual one.

She had a Page call'd *Van Brune*, a Youth of great Address and Wit, and one she had long managed for her Purpose. This Youth was about seventeen Years of Age, and extremely beautiful; and in the Time when *Alcidiana* lived with the Princess, she was a little in Love with this handsome Boy; but it was checked in its Infancy, and never grew up to a Flame: Nevertheless, *Alcidiana* retained still a sort of Tenderness for him, while he burn'd in good Earnest with Love for the Princess.

The Princess one Day ordering this Page to wait on her in her Closet, she shut the Door; and after a thousand Questions of what he would undertake to serve her, the amorous Boy finding himself alone, and caress'd by the fair Person he ador'd, with joyful Blushes that beautify'd his Face, told her "There was nothing upon Earth, he would not do, to obey her least Commands." She grew more familiar with him, to oblige him; and seeing Love dance in his Eyes, of which she was so good a Judge, she treated him more like a Lover, than a Servant; till at last the ravished Youth, wholly transported out of himself, fell at her Feet, and impatiently implor'd to receive her Commands quickly, that he might fly to execute them; for he was not able to bear her charming Words, Looks, and Touches, and retain his Duty. At this she smil'd, and told him, the Work was of such a Nature, as would mortify all Flames about him; and he would have more Need of Rage, Envy, and Malice, than the Aids of a Passion so soft as what she now found him capable of. He assur'd her, he would stick at nothing, tho' even against his Nature, to recompense for the Boldness he now, through his Indiscretion, had discover'd. She smiling, told him, he had committed no Fault; and that possibly, the Pay he should receive for the Service she required at his Hands, should be—what he most wish'd for in the World. At this he bow'd to the Earth; and kissing her Feet, bad her command: And then she boldly told him, *'Twas to kill her Sister* Alcidiana. The Youth, without so much as starting or pausing upon the Matter, told her, *It should be done*; and bowing low, immediately went out of the Closet. She call'd him back, and would have given him some Instruction; but he refused it, and said, "The Action and the Contrivance should be all his own." And offering to go again, she—again recalled him; putting into his Hand a Purse of a hundred Pistoles, which he took, and with a low Bow departed.

He no sooner left her Presence, but he goes directly, and buys a Dose of Poison, and went immediately to the House where *Alcidiana* lived; where desiring to be brought to her Presence, he fell a weeping; and told her, his Lady had fallen out with him, and dismissed him her Service, and since from a Child he had been brought up in the Family, he humbly besought *Alcidiana* to receive him into hers, she being in a few Days to be marry'd. There needed not much Intreaty to a Thing that pleased her so well, and she immediately received him to Pension: And he waited some Days on her, before he could get an Opportunity to administer his devilish Potion. But one

Night, when she drank Wine with roasted Apples, which was usual with her; instead of Sugar, or with the Sugar, the baneful Drug was mixed, and she drank it down.

About this Time, there was a great Talk of this Page's coming from one Sister, to go to the other. And Prince *Tarquin*, who was ignorant of the Design from the Beginning to the End, hearing some Men of Quality at his Table speaking of *Van Brune's* Change of Place (the Princess then keeping her Chamber upon some trifling Indisposition) he answer'd, "That surely they were mistaken, that he was not dismissed from the Princess's Service:" And calling some of his Servants, he asked for *Van Brune*; and whether any Thing had happen'd between her Highness and him, that had occasion'd his being turned off. They all seem'd ignorant of this Matter; and those who had spoken of it, began to fancy there was some Juggle in the Case, which Time would bring to Light.

The ensuing Day 'twas all about the Town, that *Alcidiana* was poison'd; and though not dead, yet very near it; and that the Doctors said, she had taken Mercury. So that there was never so formidable a Sight as this fair young Creature; her Head and Body swoln, her Eyes starting out, her Face black, and all deformed: So that diligent Search was made, who it should be that did this; who gave her Drink and Meat. The Cook and Butler were examined, the Footman called to an Account; but all concluded, she received nothing but from the Hand of her new Page, since he came into her Service. He was examined, and shew'd a thousand guilty Looks: And the Apothecary, then attending among the Doctors, proved he had bought Mercury of him three or four Days before; which he could not deny; and making many Excuses for his buying it, betray'd him the more; so ill he chanced to dissemble. He was immediately sent to be examined by the Margrave or Justice, who made his *Mittimus*, and sent him to Prison.

'Tis easy to imagine, in what Fears and Confusion the Princess was at this News: She took her Chamber upon it, more to hide her guilty Face, than for any Indisposition. And the Doctors apply'd such Remedies to *Alcidiana*, such Antidotes against the Poison, that in a short Time she recover'd; but lost the finest Hair in the World, and the Complexion of her Face ever after.

It was not long before the Trials for Criminals came on; and the Day being arrived, *Van Brune* was try'd the first of all; every Body having already read his Destiny, according as they wished it; and none would believe, but just indeed as it was: So that for the Revenge they hoped to see fall upon the Princess, every one wished he might find no Mercy, that she might share of his Shame and Misery.

The Sessions-House was filled that Day with all the Ladies, and chief of the Town, to hear the Result of his Trial; and the sad Youth was brought, loaded with Chains, and pale as Death; where every Circumstance being sufficiently proved against him, and he making but a weak Defence for himself, he was convicted, and sent back to Prison, to receive his Sentence of Death on the Morrow; where he owned all, and who set him on to do it. He own'd 'twas not Reward of Gain he did it for, but Hope he should command at his Pleasure the Possession of his Mistress, the Princess, who should deny him nothing, after having entrusted him with so great a Secret; and that besides, she had elevated him with the Promise of that glorious Reward, and had dazzled his young Heart with so charming a Prospect, that blind and mad with Joy, he rushed forward to gain the desired Prize, and thought on nothing but his coming Happiness: That he saw too late the Follies of his presumptuous Flame, and cursed the deluding Flatteries of the fair Hypocrite, who had soothed him to his Undoing: That he was a miserable Victim to her Wickedness; and hoped he should warn all young Men, by his Fall, to avoid the Dissimulation of the deceiving Fair: That he hoped they would have Pity on his Youth, and attribute his Crime to the subtle Persuasions alone of his Mistress the Princess: And that since *Alcidiana* was not dead, they would grant him Mercy, and permit him to live to repent of his grievous Crime, in some Part of the World, whither they might banish him.

He ended with Tears, that fell in abundance from his Eyes; and immediately the Princess was apprehended, and brought to Prison, to the same Prison where yet the poor young Father *Francisco* was languishing, he having been from Week to Week repriev'd, by the Intercession of the Fathers; and possibly she there had Time to make some Reflections.

You may imagine *Tarquin* left no Means unessay'd, to prevent the Imprisonment of the Princess, and the publick Shame and Infamy she was likely to undergo in this Affair: But the whole City being over-joy'd that she should be punished, as an Author of all this Mischief, were generally bent against her, both Priests, Magistrates and People; the whole Force of the Stream running that Way, she found no more Favour than the meanest Criminal. The Prince therefore, when he saw 'twas impossible to rescue her from the Hands of Justice, suffer'd with Grief unspeakable, what he could not prevent, and led her himself to the Prison, follow'd by all his People, in as much State as if he had been going to his Marriage; where, when she came, she was as well attended and served as before, he never stirring one Moment from her.

The next Day, she was tried in open and common Court; here she appeared in Glory, led by *Tarquin*, and attended according to her Quality: And she could not deny all the Page had alledged against her, who was brought thither also in Chains; and after a great many Circumstances, she was found Guilty, and both received Sentence; the Page to be hanged till he was dead, on a Gibbet in the Market-Place; and the Princess to stand under the Gibbet, with a Rope about her Neck, the other End of which was to be fastned to the Gibbet where the Page was hanging; and to have an Inscription, in large Characters, upon her Back and Breast, of the Cause why; where she was to stand from ten in the Morning to twelve.

This Sentence, the People with one Accord, believed too favourable for so ill a Woman, whose Crimes deserved Death; equal to that of *Van Brune*. Nevertheless, there were some who said, it was infinitely more severe than Death it self.

The following *Friday* was the Day of Execution, and one need not tell of the Abundance of People, who were flocked together in the Market-Place: And all the Windows were taken down, and filled with Spectators, and the Tops of Houses; when at the Hour appointed, the fatal Beauty appear'd. She was dress'd in a black Velvet Gown, with a rich Row of Diamonds all down the fore Part of her Breast, and a great Knot of Diamonds at the Peak behind; and a Petticoat of flower'd Gold, very rich, and laced; with all Things else suitable. A Gentleman carry'd her great Velvet Cushion before her, on which her Prayer-Book, embroider'd, was laid; her Train was borne up by a Page, and the Prince led her, bare; followed by his Footmen, Pages, and other Officers of his House.

When they arrived at the Place of Execution, the Cushion was laid on the Ground, upon a *Portugal* Mat, spread there for that Purpose; and the Princess stood on the Cushion, with her Prayer-Book in her Hand, and a Priest by her Side; and was accordingly tied up to the Gibbet.

She had not stood there ten Minutes, but she had the Mortification (at least one would think it so to her) to see her sad Page, *Van Brune*, approach, fair as an Angel, but languishing and pale. That Sight moved all the Beholders with as much Pity, as that of the Princess did with Disdain and Pleasure.

He was dressed all in Mourning, and very fine Linen, bare-headed, with his own Hair, the fairest that could be seen, hanging all in Curls on his Back and Shoulders, very long. He had a Prayer-Book of black Velvet in his Hand, and behaved himself with much Penitence and Devotion.

When he came under the Gibbet, he seeing his Mistress in that Condition, shew'd an infinite Concern, and his fair Face was cover'd over with Blushes; and falling at her Feet, he humbly ask'd her Pardon for having been the Occasion of so great an Infamy to her, by a weak Confession, which the Fears of Youth, and Hopes of Life, had obliged him to make, so greatly to her Dishonour; for indeed he wanted that manly

Strength, to bear the Efforts of dying, as he ought, in Silence, rather than of commiting so great a Crime against his Duty, and Honour itself; and that he could not die in Peace, unless she would forgive him. The Princess only nodded her Head, and cried, *I do* —

And after having spoken a little to his Father-Confessor, who was with him, he chearfully mounted the Ladder, and in Sight of the Princess he was turned off, while a loud Cry was heard thro' all the Market-Place, especially from the Fair Sex; he hanged there till the Time the Princess was to depart; and then she was put into a rich embroider'd Chair, and carry'd away, *Tarquin* going into his, for he had all that Time stood supporting the Princess under the Gallows, and was very weary. She was sent back, till her Releasement came, which was that Night about seven o'Clock; and then she was conducted to her own House in great State, with a Dozen White Wax Flambeaux about her Chair.

If the Guardian of *Alcidiana*, and her Friends, before were impatient of having the Portion out of the Hands of these Extravagants, it is not to be imagined, but they were now much more so; and the next Day they sent an Officer, according to Law, to demand it, or to summon the Prince to give Reasons why he would not pay it. The Officer received for Answer, That the Money should be call'd in, and paid in such a Time, setting a certain Time, which I have not been so curious as to retain, or put in my Journal-Observations; but I am sure it was not long, as may be easily imagin'd, for they every Moment suspected the Prince would pack up, and be gone, some time or other, on the sudden; and for that Reason they would not trust him without Bail, or two Officers to remain in his House, to watch that nothing should be remov'd or touch'd. As for Bail, or Security, he could give none; every one slunk their Heads out of the Collar, when it came to that: So that he was oblig'd, at his own Expence, to maintain Officers in his House.

The Princess finding her self reduced to the last Extremity, and that she must either produce the Value of a hundred thousand Crowns, or see the Prince her Husband lodged for ever in a Prison, and all their Glory vanish; and that it was impossible to fly, since guarded; she had Recourse to an Extremity, worse than the Affair of *Van Brune*. And in order to this, she first puts on a world of Sorrow and Concern, for what she feared might arrive to the Prince: And indeed, if ever she shed Tears which she did not dissemble, it was upon this Occasion. But here she almost over-acted: She stirred not from her Bed, and refused to eat, or sleep, or see the Light; so that the Day being shut out of her Chamber, she lived by Wax-lights, and refus'd all Comfort and Consolation.

The Prince, all raving with Love, tender Compassion and Grief, never stirred from her Bed-side, nor ceas'd to implore, that she would suffer herself to live. But she, who was not now so passionately in Love with *Tarquin*, as she was with the Prince; nor so fond of the Man as his Titles, and of Glory; foresaw the total Ruin of the last, if not prevented by avoiding the Payment of this great Sum; which could not otherwise be, than by the Death of *Alcidiana*: And therefore, without ceasing, she wept, and cry'd out, "She could not live, unless *Alcidiana* died. This *Alcidiana (continued she)* who has been the Author of my Shame; who has expos'd me under a Gibbet, in the Publick Market-Place—Oh!—I am deaf to all Reason, blind to natural Affection. I renounce her, I hate her as my mortal Foe, my Stop to Glory, and the Finisher of my Days, e'er half my Race of Life be run."

Then throwing her false, but snowy, charming Arms about the Neck her Heart-breaking Lord, and Lover, who lay sighing, and listening by her Side, he was charmed and bewitch'd into saying all Things that appeased her; and lastly, told her, "*Alcidiana* should be no longer any Obstacle to her Repose; but that, if she would look up, and cast her Eyes of Sweetness and Love upon him, as heretofore; forget her Sorrow, and redeem her lost Health; he would take what Measures she should propose to dispatch this fatal Stop to her Happiness, out of the Way."

These Words failed not to make her caress him in the most endearing Manner that Love and Flattery could invent; and she kiss'd him to an Oath, a solemn Oath, to perform what he had promised; and he vow'd liberally. And she assumed in an Instant her Good-Humour, and suffer'd a Supper to be prepared, and did eat; which in many Days before she had not done: So obstinate and powerful was she in dissembling well.

The next Thing to be consider'd was, which Way this Deed was to be done; for they doubted not, but when it was done, all the World would lay it upon the Princess, as done by her Command: But she urged, Suspicion was no Proof; and that they never put to Death any one, but when they had great and certain Evidence who were the Offenders. She was sure of her own Constancy, that Racks and Tortures should never get the Secret from her Breast; and if he were as confident on his Part, there was no Danger. Yet this Preparation she made towards laying the Fact on others, that she caused several Letters to be wrote from *Germany*, as from the Relations of *Van Brune*, who threaten'd *Alcidiana* with Death, for depriving their Kinsman (who was a Gentleman) of his Life, though he had not taken away hers. And it was the Report of the Town, how this young Maid was threaten'd. And indeed, the Death of the Page had so afflicted a great many, that *Alcidiana* had procured her self abundance of Enemies upon that Account, because she might have saved him if she had pleased; but, on the contrary, she was a Spectator, and in full Health and Vigour, at his Execution: And People were not so much concerned for her at this Report, as they would have been.

The Prince, who now had, by reasoning the Matter soberly with *Miranda*, found it absolutely necessary to dispatch *Alcidiana*, resolved himself, and with his own Hand, to execute it; not daring to trust to any of his most favourite Servants, though he had many, who possibly would have obey'd him; for they loved him as he deserved, and so would all the World, had he not been so purely deluded by this fair Enchantress. He therefore, as I said, resolved to keep this great Secret to himself; and taking a Pistol, charged well with two Bullets, he watch'd an Opportunity to shoot her as she should go out or into her House, or Coach, some Evening.

To this End he waited several Nights near her Lodgings, but still, either she went not out, or when she return'd, she was so guarded with Friends, her Lover, and Flambeaux, that he could not aim at her without endangering the Life of some other. But one Night above the rest, upon a *Sunday*, when he knew she would be at the Theatre, for she never missed that Day seeing the Play, he waited at the Corner of the Stadt-House, near the Theatre, with his Cloak cast over his Face, and a black Periwig, all alone, with his Pistol ready cock'd; and remain'd not very long but he saw her Kinsman's Coach come along; 'twas almost dark, Day was just shutting up her Beauties, and left such a Light to govern the World, as serv'd only just to distinguish one Object from another, and a convenient Help to Mischief. He saw alight out of the Coach only one young Lady, the Lover, and then the destin'd Victim; which he (drawing near) knew rather by her Tongue than Shape. The Lady ran into the Play-House, and left *Alcidiana* to be conducted by her Lover into it: Who led her to the Door, and went to give some Order to the Coachman; so that the Lover was about twenty Yards from *Alcidiana*; when she stood the fairest Mark in the World, on the Threshold of the Entrance of the Theatre, there being many Coaches about the Door, so that hers could not come so near. *Tarquin* was resolved not to lose so fair an Opportunity, and advanc'd, but went behind the Coaches; and when he came over-against the Door, through a great booted Velvet Coach, that stood between him and her, he shot; and she having the Train of her Gown and Petticoat on her Arm, in great Quantity, he missed her Body, and shot through her Clothes, between her Arm and her Body. She, frighten'd to find something hit her, and to see the Smoke, and hear the Report of the Pistol; running in, cried, *I am shot, I am dead.*

This Noise quickly alarm'd her Lover; and all the Coachmen

and Footmen immediately ran, some one Way, and some another. One of 'em seeing a Man haste away in a Cloak; he being a lusty, bold *German*, stopped him; and drawing upon him, bad him stand, and deliver his Pistol, or he would run him through.

Tarquin being surprised at the Boldness of this Fellow to demand his Pistol, as if he positively knew him to be the Murderer (for so he thought himself, since he believed *Alcidiana* dead) had so much Presence of Mind as to consider, if he suffered himself to be taken, he should poorly die a publick Death; and therefore resolv'd upon one Mischief more, to secure himself from the first: And in the Moment that the *German* bad him deliver his Pistol, he cried, *Though I have no Pistol to deliver, I have a Sword to chastise thy Insolence.* And throwing off his Cloak, and flinging his Pistol from him, he drew, and wounded, and disarmed the Fellow.

This Noise of Swords brought every body to the Place; and immediately the Bruit ran, *The Murderer was taken, the Murderer was taken*; Tho' none knew which was he, nor as yet so much as the Cause of the Quarrel between the two fighting Men; for it was now darker than before. But at the Noise of the Murderer being taken, the Lover of *Alcidiana*, who by this Time found his Lady unhurt, all but the Trains of her Gown and Petticoat, came running to the Place, just as *Tarquin* had disarm'd the *German*, and was ready to kill him; when laying hold of his Arm, they arrested the Stroke, and redeemed the Footman.

They then demanded who this Stranger was, at whose Mercy the Fellow lay; but the Prince, who now found himself venturing for his last Stake, made no Reply; but with two Swords in his Hands went to fight his Way through the Rabble; And tho' there were above a hundred Persons, some with Swords, others with long Whips, (as Coachmen) so invincible was the Courage of this poor unfortunate Gentleman at that Time, that all these were not able to seize him; but he made his Way through the Ring that encompassed him, and ran away;

but was, however, so closely pursued, the Company still gathering as they ran, that toiled with fighting, oppressed with Guilt, and Fear of being taken, he grew fainter and fainter, and suffered himself, at last, to yield to his Pursuers, who soon found him to be Prince *Tarquin* in Disguise: And they carry'd him directly to Prison, being *Sunday*, to wait the coming Day, to go before a Magistrate.

In an Hour's Time the whole fatal Adventure was carried all over the City, and every one knew that *Tarquin* was the intended Murderer of *Alcidiana*; and not one but had a real Sorrow and Compassion for him. They heard how bravely he had defended himself, how many he had wounded before he could be taken, and what numbers he had fought through: And even those that saw his Valour and Bravery, and who had assisted at his being seiz'd, now repented from the Bottom of their Hearts their having any Hand in the Ruin of so gallant a Man; especially since they knew the Lady was not hurt. A thousand Addresses were made to her, not to prosecute him; but her Lover, a hot-headed Fellow, more fierce than brave, would by no Means be pacified, but vowed to pursue him to the Scaffold.

The *Monday* came, and the Prince being examined, confessed the Matter of Fact, since there was no Harm done; believing a generous Confession the best of his Game: But he was sent back to closer Imprisonment, loaded with Irons, to expect the next Sessions. All his Household-Goods were seiz'd, and all they could find, for the Use of *Alcidiana*. And the Princess, all in Rage, tearing her Hair, was carried to the same Prison, to behold the cruel Effects of her hellish Designs.

One need not tell here how sad and horrid this Meeting appear'd between her Lord and her: Let it suffice, it was the most melancholy and mortifying Object that ever Eyes beheld. On *Miranda's* Part, 'twas sometimes all Rage and Fire, and sometimes all Tears and Groans; but still 'twas sad Love, and mournful Tenderness on his. Nor could all his Sufferings, and the Prospect of Death itself, drive from his Soul one Spark of that Fire the obstinate God had fatally kindled there: And in the midst of all his Sighs, he would re-call himself, and cry,—*I have* Miranda *still*.

He was eternally visited by his Friends and Acquaintance; and this last Action of Bravery had got him more than all his former Conduct had lost. The Fathers were perpetually with him; and all join'd with one common Voice in this, That he ought to abandon a Woman so wicked as the Princess; and that however Fate dealt with him, he could not shew himself a true Penitent, while he laid the Author of so much Evil in his Bosom: That Heaven would never bless him, till he had renounced her: And on such Conditions he would find those that would employ their utmost Interest to save his Life, who else would not stir in this Affair. But he was so deaf to all, that he could not so much as dissemble a Repentance for having married her.

He lay a long Time in Prison, and all that Time the poor Father *Francisco* remained there also: And the good Fathers who daily visited these two amorous Prisoners, the Prince and Princess; and who found, by the Management of Matters, it would go very hard with *Tarquin*, entertained 'em often with holy Matters relating to the Life to to come; from which, before his Trial, he gathered what his Stars had appointed, and that he was destin'd to die.

This gave an unspeakable Torment to the now repenting Beauty, who had reduced him to it; and she began to appear with a more solid Grief: Which being perceived by the good Fathers, they resolved to attack her on the yielding Side; and after some Discourse upon the Judgment for Sin, they came to reflect on the Business of Father *Francisco*; and told her, she had never thriven since her accusing of that Father, and laid it very home to her Conscience; assuring her that they would do their utmost in her Service, if she would confess that secret Sin to all the World, so that she might atone for the Crime, by the saving that good Man. At first she seemed inclined to yield; but Shame of being her own Detector, in so vile a Matter, recalled her Goodness, and she faintly persisted in it.

At the End of six Months, Prince *Tarquin* was called to his Tryal; where I will pass over the Circumstances, which are only what is usual in such criminal Cases, and tell you, that he being found guilty of the Intent of killing *Alcidiana*, was condemned to lose his Head in the Market-Place, and the Princess to be banished her Country.

After Sentence pronounced, to the real Grief of all the Spectators, he was carry'd back to Prison, and now the Fathers attack her anew; and she, whose Griefs daily encreased, with a Languishment that brought her very near her Grave, at last confess'd all her Life, all the Lewdness of her Practices with several Princes and great Men, besides her Lusts with People that served her, and others in mean Capacity: And lastly, the whole Truth of the young Friar; and how she had drawn the Page, and the Prince her Husband, to this design'd Murder of her Sister. This she signed with her Hand, in the Presence of the Prince, her Husband, and several Holy Men who were present. Which being signify'd to the Magistrates, the Friar was immediately deliver'd from his Irons (where he had languished more than two whole Years) in great Triumph, with much Honour, and lives a most exemplary pious Life, as he did before; for he is now living in *Antwerp*.

After the Condemnation of these two unfortunate Persons, who begot such different Sentiments in the Minds of the People (the Prince, all the Compassion and Pity imaginable; and the Princess, all the Contempt and Despite;) they languished almost six Months longer in Prison; so great an Interest there was made, in order to the saving his Life, by all the Men of the Robe. On the other side, the Princes, and great Men of all Nations, who were at the Court of *Brussels*, who bore a secret Revenge in their Hearts against a Man who had, as they pretended, set up a false Title, only to take Place of them; who indeed was but a Merchant's Son of *Holland*, as they said; so incens'd them against him, that they were too hard at Court for the Church-men. However, this Dispute gave the Prince his Life some Months longer than was expected;

which gave him also some Hope, that a Reprieve for ninety Years would have been granted, as was desired. Nay, Father *Francisco* so interested himself in this Concern, that he writ to his Father, and several Princes of *Germany*, with whom the Marquis *Castel Roderigo* was well acquainted, to intercede with him for the saving of *Tarquin*; since 'twas more by his Persuasions, than those of all who attacked her, that made *Miranda* confess the Truth of her Affair with him. But at the End of six Months, when all Applications were found fruitless and vain, the Prince receiv'd News, that in two Days he was to die, as his Sentence had been before pronounced, and for which he prepared himself with all Chearfulness.

On the following *Friday*, as soon as it was light, all People of any Condition came to take their Leaves of him; and none departed with dry Eyes, or Hearts unconcern'd to the last Degree: For *Tarquin*, when he found his Fate inevitable bore it with a Fortitude that shewed no Signs of Regret; but address'd himself to all about him with the same chearful, modest, and great Air, he was wont to do in his most flourishing Fortune. His Valet was dressing him all the Morning, so many Interruptions they had by Visitors; and he was all in Mourning, and so were all his Followers; for even to the last he kept up his Grandeur, to the Amazement of all People. And indeed, he was so passionately belov'd by them, that those he had dismiss'd, serv'd him voluntarily, and would not be persuaded to abandon him while he liv'd.

The Princess was also dress'd in Mourning, and her two Women; and notwithstanding the unheard-of Lewdness and Villanies she had confess'd of her self, the Prince still ador'd her; for she had still those Charms that made him first do so; nor, to his last Moment, could he be brought to wish, that he had never seen her; but on the contrary, as a Man yet vainly proud of his Fetters, he said, "All the Satisfaction this short Moment of Life could afford him, was, that he died in endeavouring to serve *Miranda*, his adorable Princess."

After he had taken Leave of all, who thought it necessary to leave him to himself for some Time, he retir'd with his Confessor; where they were about an Hour in Prayer, all the Ceremonies of Devotion that were fit to be done, being already past. At last the Bell toll'd, and he was to take Leave of the Princess, as his last Work of Life, and the most hard he had to accomplish. He threw himself at her Feet, and gazing on her as she sat more dead than alive, overwhelm'd with silent Grief, they both remain'd some Moments speechless; and then, as if one rising Tide of Tears had supply'd both their Eyes, it burst out in Streams at the same Instant: and when his Sighs gave Way, he utter'd a thousand Farewels, so soft, so passionate, and moving, that all who were by were extremely touch'd with it, and said, *That nothing could be seen more deplorable and melancholy.* A thousand Times they bad Farewel, and still some tender Look, or Word, would prevent his going; then embrace, and bid Farewel again. A thousand Times she ask'd his Pardon for being the Occasion of that fatal Separation; a thousand Times assuring him, she would follow him, for she could not live without him. And Heaven knows when their soft and sad Caresses would have ended, had not the Officers assur'd him 'twas Time to mount the Scaffold. At which Words the Princess fell fainting in the Arms of her Woman, and they led *Tarquin* out of Prison.

When he came to the Market-Place, whither he walked on Foot, follow'd by his own Domesticks, and some bearing a black Velvet Coffin with Silver Hinges; the Head's-man before him with his fatal Scimiter drawn, his Confessor by his Side, and many Gentlemen and Churchmen, with Father *Francisco* attending him, the People showring Millions of Blessings on him, and beholding him with weeping Eyes, he mounted the Scaffold; which was strewed with some Saw-dust, about the Place where he was to kneel, to receive the Blood: For they behead People kneeling, and with the Back-Stroak of a Scimiter; and not lying on a Block, and with an Axe, as we in *England.* The Scaffold had a low Rail about it, that every body might more conveniently see. This was hung with black, and all that State that such a Death could have, was here in most decent Order.

He did not say much upon the Scaffold: The Sum of what he said to his Friends was, to be kind, and take Care of the poor Penitent his Wife: To others, recommending his honest and generous Servants, whose Fidelity was so well known and commended, that they were soon promised Preferment. He was some time in Prayer, and a very short time in speaking to his Confessor; then he turned to the Head's-man, and desired him to do his Office well, and gave him twenty *Louis d'Ors*; and undressing himself with the Help of his Valet and Page, he pull'd off his Coat, and had underneath a white Sattin Waistcoat: He took off his Periwig, and put on a white Sattin Cap, with a Holland one done with Point under it, which he pulled over his Eyes; then took a chearful Leave of all, and kneel'd down, and said, "When he lifted up his Hands the third Time, the Head's-man should do his Office." Which accordingly was done, and the Head's-man gave him his last Stroke, and the Prince fell on the Scaffold. The People with one common Voice, as if it had been but one entire one, pray'd for his Soul; and Murmurs of Sighs were heard from the whole Multitude, who scrambled for some of the bloody Saw-dust, to keep for his Memory.

The Head's-man going to take up the Head, as the Manner is, to shew it to the People, he found he had not struck it off, and that the Body stirr'd; with that he stepped to an Engine, which they always carry with 'em, to force those who may be refractory; thinking, as he said, to have twisted the Head from the Shoulders, conceiving it to hang but by a small Matter of Flesh. Tho' 'twas an odd Shift of the Fellow's, yet 'twas done, and the best Shift he could suddenly propose. The Margrave, and another Officer, old Men, were on the Scaffold, with some of the Prince's Friends, and Servants; who seeing the Head's-man put the Engine about the Neck of the Prince, began to call out, and the People made a great Noise. The Prince, who found himself yet alive; or rather, who was past thinking but had some Sense of Feeling left, when the Head's-man took him up, and set his Back against the Rail, and clapp'd the Engine about his Neck, got his two Thumbs between the Rope and his Neck, feeling himself press'd there; and struggling between Life and Death, and bending himself over the Rail backward, while the Head's-man pulled forward, he threw himself quite over the Rail, by Chance, and not Design, and fell upon the Heads and Shoulders of the People, who were crying out with amazing Shouts of Joy. The Head's-man leap'd after him, but the Rabble had lik'd to have pull'd him to Pieces: All the City was in an Uproar, but none knew what the Matter was, but those who bore the Body of the Prince, whom they found yet living; but how, or by what strange Miracle preserv'd, they knew not, nor did examine; but with one Accord, as if the whole Crowd had been one Body, and had had but one Motion, they bore the Prince on their Heads about a hundred Yards from the Scaffold, where there is a Monastery of Jesuits; and there they secur'd him. All this was done, his beheading, his falling, and his being secur'd, almost in a Moment's Time; the People rejoiceing, as at some extraordinary Victory won. One of the Officers being, as I said, an old timorous Man, was so frighten'd at the Accident, the Bustle, the Noise, and the Confusion, of which he was wholly ignorant, that he dy'd with Amazement and Fear; and the other was fain to be let blood.

The Officers of Justice went to demand the Prisoner, but they demanded in vain; the Jesuits had now a Right to protect him, and would do so. All his overjoy's Friends went to see in what Condition he was, and all of Quality found Admittance: They saw him in Bed, going to be dress'd by the most skilful Surgeons, who yet could not assure him of Life. They desired no body should speak to him, or ask him any Questions. They found that the Head's-man had struck him too low, and had cut him into the Shoulder-bone. A very great Wound, you may be sure; for the Sword, in such Executions, carries an extreme Force: However, so great Care was taken on all Sides, and so greatly the Fathers were concern'd for him, that they found an

Amendment, and Hopes of a good Effect of their incomparable Charity and Goodness.

At last, when he was permitted to speak, the first News he ask'd was after the Princess. And his Friends were very much afflicted to find, that all his Loss of Blood had not quenched that Flame, not let out that which made him still love that bad Woman. He was sollicited daily to think no more of her: And all her Crimes are laid so open to him, and so shamefully represented; and on the other Side, his Virtues so admir'd; and which, they said, would have been eternally celebrated, but for his Folly with this infamous Creature; that at last, by assuring him of all their Assistance if he abandon'd her; and to renounce him, and deliver him up, if he did not; they wrought so far upon him, as to promise, he would suffer her to go alone into Banishment, and would not follow her, or live with her any more. But alas! this was but his Gratitude that compell'd this Complaisance, for in his Heart he resolv'd never to abandon her; nor was he able to live, and think of doing it: However, his Reason assur'd him, he could not do a Deed more justifiable, and one that would regain his Fame sooner.

His Friends ask'd him some Questions concerning his Escape; and since he was not beheaded, but only wounded, why he did not immediately rise up? But he replied, he was so absolutely prepossessed, that at the third lifting up his Hands he should receive the Stroke of Death, that at the same Instant the Sword touch'd him, he had no Sense; nay, not even of Pain, so absolutely dead he was with Imagination; and knew not that he stirr'd, as the Head's-man found he did; nor did he remember any Thing, from the lifting up of his Hands, to his fall; and then awaken'd, as out of a Dream, or rather a Moment's Sleep without Dream, he found he liv'd, and wonder'd what was arriv'd to him, or how he came to live; having not, as yet, any Sense of his Wound, tho' so terrible an one.

After this, *Alcidiana*, who was extremely afflicted for having been the Prosecutor of this great Man; who, baking this last Design against her, which she knew was at the Instigation of her Sister, had oblig'd her with all the Civility imaginable; now sought all Means possible of getting his Pardon, and that of her Sister; tho' of an hundred thousand Crowns, which she should have paid her, she could get but ten thousand; which was from the Sale of her rich Beds, and some other Furniture. So that the young Count, who before should have marry'd her, now went off for want of Fortune; and a young Merchant (perhaps the best of the two) was the Man to whom she was destin'd.

At last, by great Intercession, both their Pardons were obtain'd; and the Prince, who would be no more seen in a Place that had prov'd every way so fatal to him, left *Flanders*, promising never to live with the Fair Hypocrite more; but e'er he departed, he wrote her a Letter, wherein he order'd her, in a little Time, to follow him into *Holland*; and left a Bill of Exchange with one of his trusty Servants, whom he had left to wait upon her, for Money for her Accommodation; so that she was now reduced to one Woman, one Page, and this Gentleman. The Prince, in this Time of his Imprisonment, had several Bills of great Sums from his Father, who was exceeding rich, and this all the Children he had in the World, and whom he tenderly loved.

As soon as *Miranda* was come into *Holland*, she was welcom'd with all imaginable Respect and Endearment by the old Father; who was impos'd upon so, as that he knew not she was the fatal Occasion of all these Disasters to his Son; but rather look'd on her as a Woman, who had brought him an hundred and fifty thousand Crowns, which his Misfortunes had consum'd. But, above all, she was receiv'd by *Tarquin* with a Joy unspeakable; who, after some Time, to redeem his Credit, and gain himself a new Fame, put himself into the *French* Army, where he did Wonders; and after three Campaigns, his Father dying, he return'd home, and retir'd to a Country-House; where, with his Princess, he liv'd as a private Gentleman, in all the Tranquillity of a Man of good Fortune. They say *Miranda* has been very penitent for her Life past, and gives Heaven the Glory for having given her these Afflictions that have reclaim'd her, and brought her to as perfect a State of Happiness, as this troublesome World, can afford.

Since I began this Relation, I heard that Prince *Tarquin*, dy'd about three Quarters of a Year ago.

THE HISTORY OF THE NUN
OR
THE FAIR VOW-BREAKER

To the Most Illustrious Princess, The Dutchess of Mazarine

Madam,

There are none of an Illustrious Quality, who have not been made, by some Poet or other, the Patronesses of his Distress'd Hero, or Unfortunate Damsel; and such Addresses are Tributes, due only to the most Elevated, where they have always been very well receiv'd, since they are the greatest Testimonies we can give, of our Esteem and Veneration.

Madam, when I survey'd the whole Toor of Ladies at Court, which was adorn'd by you, who appear'd there with a Grace and Majesty, peculiar to Your Great Self only, mix'd with an irresistible Air of Sweetness, Generosity, and Wit, I was impatient for an Opportunity, to tell Your Grace, how infinitely one of Your own Sex ador'd You, and that, among all the numerous Conquest, Your Grace has made over the Hearts of Men, Your Grace had not subdu'd a more entire Slave; I assure you, Madam, there is neither Compliment nor Poetry, in this humble Declaration, but a Truth, which has cost me a great deal of Inquietude, for that Fortune has not set me in such a Station, as might justifie my Pretence to the honour and satisfaction of being ever near Your Grace, to view eternally that lovely Person, and hear that surprizing Wit; what can be more grateful to a Heart, than so great, and so agreeable, an Entertainment? And how few Objects are there, that can render it so entire a Pleasure, as at once to hear you speak, and to look upon your Beauty? A Beauty that is heighten'd, if possible, with an air of Negligence, in Dress, wholly Charming, as if your Beauty disdain'd those little Arts of your Sex, whose Nicety alone is their greatest Charm, while yours, Madam, even without the Assistance of your exalted Birth, begets an Awe and Reverence in all that do approach you, and every one is proud, and pleas'd, in paying you Homage their several ways, according to their Capacities and Talents; mine, Madam, can only be exprest by my Pen, which would be infinitely honour'd, in being permitted to celebrate your great Name for ever, and perpetually to serve, where it has so great an inclination.

In the mean time, Madam, I presume to lay this little Trifle at your Feet; the Story is true, as it is on the Records of the Town, where it was transacted; and if my fair unfortunate VOW-BREAKER do not deserve the honour of your Graces Protection, at least, she will be found worthy of your Pity; which will be a sufficient Glory, both for her, and,

Madam,

Your Graces most humble,

and most obedient Servant,

A. BEHN.

THE HISTORY OF THE NUN

Of all the sins, incident to Human Nature, there is none, of which Heaven has took so particular, visible, and frequent Notice, and Revenge, as on that of *Violated Vows*, which never go unpunished; and the *Cupids* may boast what they will, for the encouragement of their Trade of Love, that Heaven never takes cognisance of Lovers broken Vows and Oaths, and that 'tis the only Perjury that escapes the Anger of the *Gods*; But I verily believe, if it were search'd into, we should find these frequent Perjuries, that pass in the World for so many Gallantries only, to be the occasion of so many unhappy Marriages, and the cause of all those Misfortunes, which are so frequent to the Nuptiall'd Pair. For not one of a Thousand, but, either on his side, or on hers, has been perjur'd, and broke Vows made to some fond believing Wretch, whom they have abandon'd and undone. What Man that does not boast of the Numbers he has thus ruin'd, and, who does not glory in the shameful Triumph? Nay, what Woman, almost, has not a pleasure in Deceiving, taught, perhaps, at first, by some dear false one, who had fatally instructed her Youth in an Art she ever after practis'd, in Revenge on all those she could be too hard for, and conquer at their own Weapons? For, without all dispute, Women are by Nature more Constant and Just, than Men, and did not their first Lovers teach them the trick of Change, they would be *Doves*, that would never quit their Mate, and, like *Indian* Wives, would leap alive into the Graves of their deceased Lovers, and be buried quick with 'em. But Customs of Countries change even Nature her self, and long Habit takes her place: The Women are taught, by the Lives of the Men, to live up to all their Vices, and are become almost as inconstant; and 'tis but Modesty that makes the difference, and, hardly, inclination; so deprav'd the nicest Appetites grow in time, by bad Examples.

But, as there are degrees of Vows, so there are degrees of Punishments for Vows, there are solemn Matrimonial Vows, such as contract and are the most effectual Marriage, and have the most reason to be so; there are a thousand Vows and Friendships, that pass between Man and Man, on a thousand Occasions; but there is another Vow, call'd a *Sacred Vow*, made to God only; and, by which, we oblige our selves eternally to serve him with all Chastity and Devotion: This Vow is only taken, and Made, by those that enter into Holy Orders, and, of all broken Vows, these are those, that receive the most severe and notorious Revenges of God; and I am almost certain, there is not one Example to be produc'd in the World, where Perjuries of this nature have past unpunish'd, nay, that have not been persu'd with the greatest and most rigorous of Punishments. I could my self, of my own knowledge, give an hundred Examples of the fatal Consequences of the Violation of Sacred Vows; and who ever make it their business, and are curious in the search of such Misfortunes, shall find, as I say, that they never go unregarded.

The young Beauty therefore, who dedicates her self to Heaven, and weds her self for ever to the service of God, ought, first, very well to consider the Self-denial she is going to put upon her youth, her fickle faithless deceiving Youth, of one Opinion to day, and of another to morrow; like Flowers, which never remain in one state or fashion, but bud to day, and blow by insensible degrees, and decay as imperceptibly. The Resolution, we promise, and believe we shall maintain, is not in our power, and nothing is so deceitful as human Hearts.

I once was design'd an humble Votary in the House of Devotion, but fancying my self not endu'd with an obstinacy of Mind, great enough to secure me from the Efforts and Vanities of the World, I rather chose to deny my self that Content I could not certainly promise my self, than to languish (as I have seen some do) in a certain Affliction; tho' possibly, since, I have sufficiently bewailed that mistaken and inconsiderate Approbation and Preference of the false ungrateful World, (full of nothing but Nonsense, Noise, false Notions, and Contradiction) before the Innocence and Quiet of a Cloyster;

nevertheless, I could wish, for the prevention of abundance of Mischiefs and Miseries, that Nunneries and Marriages were not to be enter'd into, 'till the Maid, so destin'd, were of a mature Age to make her own Choice; and that Parents would not make use of their justly assum'd Authority to compel their Children, neither to the one or the other; but since I cannot alter Custom, nor shall ever be allow'd to make new Laws, or rectify the old ones, I must leave the Young Nuns inclos'd to their best Endeavours, of making a Virtue of Necessity; and the young Wives, to make the best of a bad Market.

In *Iper*, a Town, not long since in the Dominions of the King of *Spain*, and now in possession of the King of *France*, there liv'd a Man of Quality, of a considerable Fortune, call'd, Count *Henrick de Vallary*, who had a very beautiful Lady, by whom, he had one Daughter, call'd *Isabella*, whose Mother dying when she was about two years old to the unspeakable Grief of the Count, her Husband, he resolv'd never to partake of any Pleasure more, that this transitory World could court him with, but determin'd, with himself, to dedicate his Youth, and future Days, to Heaven, and to take upon him Holy Orders; and, without considering, that, possibly, the young *Isabella*, when she grew to Woman, might have Sentiments contrary to those that now possest him, he design'd she should also become a Nun; However, he was not so positive in that Resolution, as to put the matter wholly out of her Choice, but divided his Estate; one half he carried with him to the Monastery of *Jesuits*, of which number, he became one; and the other half, he gave with *Isabella*, to the Monastery, of which, his only Sister was Lady *Abbess*, of the Order of St. *Augustine*; but so he ordered the matter, that if, at the Age of Thirteen, *Isabella* had not a mind to take Orders, or that the Lady *Abbess* found her Inclination averse to a Monastick Life, she should have such a proportion of the Revenue, as should be fit to marry her to a Noble Man, and left it to the discretion of the Lady *Abbess*, who was a Lady of known Piety, and admirable strictness of Life, and so nearly related to *Isabella*, that there was no doubt made of her Integrity and Justice.

The little *Isabella* was carried immediately (in her Mourning for her dead Mother) into the Nunnery, and was receiv'd as a very diverting Companion by all the young Ladies, and, above all, by her Reverend Aunt, for she was come just to the Age of delighting her Parents; she was the prettiest forward Pratler in the World, and had a thousand little Charms to please, besides the young Beauties that were just budding in her little Angel Face: So that she soon became the dear lov'd Favourite of the whole House; and as she was an Entertainment to them all, so they made it their study to find all the Diversions they could for the pretty *Isabella*; and as she grew in Wit and Beauty every day, so they fail'd not to cultivate her Mind; and delicate Apprehension, in all that was advantageous to her Sex, and whatever Excellency any one abounded in, she was sure to communicate it to the young *Isabella*, if one could Dance, another Sing, another play on this Instrument, and another on that; if this spoke one Language, and that another; if she had Wit, and she Discretion, and a third, the finest Fashion and Manners; all joyn'd to compleat the Mind and Body of this beautiful young Girl; Who, being undiverted with the less noble, and less solid, Vanities of the World, took to these Virtues, and excell'd in all; and her Youth and Wit being apt for all Impressions, she soon became a greater Mistress of their Arts, than those who taught her; so that at the Age of eight or nine Years, she was thought fit to receive and entertain all the great Men and Ladies, and the Strangers of any Nation, at the *Grate*; and that with so admirable a Grace, so quick and piercing a Wit, and so delightful and sweet a Conversation, that she became the whole Discourse of the Town, and Strangers spread her Fame, as prodigious, throughout the Christian World; for Strangers came daily to hear her talk, and sing, and play, and to admire her Beauty; and Ladies brought their Children, to shame 'em into good Fashion and Manners, with looking on the lovely young *Isabella*.

The Lady *Abbess*, her Aunt, you may believe, was not a little proud of the Exellencies and Virtues of her fair *Niece*, and omitted nothing that might adorn her Mind; because, not only of the vastness of her Parts and Fame, and the Credit she would do her House, by residing there for ever; but also, being very loth to part with her considerable Fortune, which she must resign, if she returned into the World, she us'd all her Arts and Stratagems to make her become a *Nun*, to which all the fair Sisterhood contributed their Cunning, but it was altogether needless; her Inclination, the strictness of her Devotion, her early Prayers, and those continual, and innate Stedfastness, and Calm, she was Mistress of; her Ignorance of the World's Vanities, and those that uninclos'd young Ladies count Pleasures and Diversions, being all unknown to her, she thought there was no Joy out of a *Nunnery*, and no Satisfactions on the other side of a *Grate*.

The Lady *Abbess*, seeing, that of her self she yielded faster than she could expect; to discharge her Conscience to her Brother, who came frequently to visit his Darling *Isabella*, would very often discourse to her of the Pleasures of the World, telling her, how much happier she would think her self, to be the Wife of some gallant young Cavalier, and to have Coaches and Equipages; to see the World, to behold a thousand Rarities she had never seen, to live in Splendor, to eat high, and wear magnificent Clothes, to be bow'd to as she pass'd, and have a thousand Adorers, to see in time a pretty Offspring, the products of Love, that should talk, and look, and delight, as she did, the Heart of their Parents; but to all, her Father and the Lady *Abbess* could say of the World, and its Pleasures, *Isabella* brought a thousand Reasons and Arguments, so Pious, so Devout, that the *Abbess* was very well pleased, to find her (purposely weak) Propositions so well overthrown; and gives an account of her daily Discourses to her Brother, which were no less pleasing to him; and tho' *Isabella* went already dress'd as richly as her Quality deserv'd, yet her Father, to try the utmost that the World's Vanity could do, upon her young Heart, orders the most Glorious Clothes should be bought her, and that the Lady *Abbess* should suffer her to go abroad with those Ladies of Quality, that were her Relations, and her Mother's Acquaintance; that she should visit and go on the Toore, (that is, the Hide Park there) that she should see all that was diverting, to try, whether it were not for want of Temptation to Vanity, that made her leave the World, and love an inclos'd Life.

As the Count had commanded, all things were performed; and *Isabella* arriving at her Thirteenth Year of Age, and being pretty tall of Stature, with the finest Shape that Fancy can create, with all the Adornment of a perfect brown-hair'd Beauty, Eyes black and lovely, Complexion fair; to a Miracle, all her Features of the rarest proportion, the Mouth red, the Teeth white, and a thousand Graces in her Meen and Air; she came no sooner abroad, but she had a thousand Persons fighting for love of her; the Reputation her Wit had acquir'd, got her Adorers without seeing her, but when they saw her, they found themselves conquer'd and undone; all were glad she was come into the World, of whom they had heard so much, and all the Youth of the Town dress'd only for *Isabella de Valerie*, the rose like a new Star that Eclips'd all the rest, and which set the World a-gazing. Some hop'd, and some despair'd, but all lov'd while *Isabella* regarded not their Eyes, their distant darling Looks of Love, and their signs of Adoration; she was civil and affable to all, but so reserv'd, that none durst tell her his Passion, or name that strange and abhorr'd thing, *Love*, to her; the Relations with whom she went abroad every day, were fein to force her out, and when she went, 'twas the motive of Civility, and not Satisfaction, that made her go; whatever she saw, she beheld with no admiration, and nothing created wonder in her, tho' never so strange and Novel. She survey'd all things with an indifference, that tho' it was not sullen, was far from Transport, so that her evenness of Mind was infinitely admir'd and prais'd. And now it was, that, young as she was, her Conduct and Discretion appear'd equal to her Wit and Beauty, and she encreas'd daily in Reputation, insomuch, that the Parents of abundance of young Noble Men, made it their business to endeavour to marry their Sons to so admirable and noble a Maid, and one, whose Virtues were the Discourse of all the World; the *Father*, the Lady *Abbess*, and those who had her abroad, were solicited to make an Alliance; for the Father, he would give no answer, but left it to the discretion of *Isabella*, who could not be persuaded to hear any thing of that nature; so that for a long time she refus'd her company to all those, who propos'd any thing of Marriage to her; she said, she had seen nothing in the World that was worth her Care, or the venturing the losing of Heaven for, and therefore was resolv'd to dedicate her self to that; that the more she saw of the World, the worse she lik'd it, and pity'd the Wretches that were condemn'd to it; that she had consider'd it, and found no one Inclination that forbad her immediate Entrance into a Religious Life; to which, her Father, after using all the Arguments he could, to make her take good heed of what she went about, to consider it well; and had urg'd all the Inconveniencies of Severe Life, Watchings, Midnight Risings in all Weathers and Seasons to Prayers, hard Lodging, course Diet, and homely Habit, with a thousand other things of Labour and Work us'd among the *Nuns*; and finding her still resolv'd and inflexible to all contrary persuasions, he consented, kiss'd her, and told her, She had argu'd according to the wish of his Soul, and that he never believ'd himself truly happy, till this moment that he was assur'd, she would become a Religious.

This News, to the Heart-breaking of a thousand Lovers, was spread all over the Town, and there was nothing but Songs of Complaint, and of her retiring, after she had shewn her self to the World, and vanquish'd so many Hearts; all Wits were at work on this Cruel Subject, and one begat another, as is usual in such Affairs. Amongst the number of these Lovers, there was a young Gentleman, Nobly born, his name was *Villenoys*, who was admirably made, and very handsom, had travell'd and accomplish'd himself, as much as was possible for one so young to do; he was about Eighteen, and was going to the

Siege of *Candia*, in a very good Equipage, but, overtaken by his Fate, surpris'd in his way to Glory, he stopt at *Ipers*, so fell most passionately in love with this Maid of Immortal Fame; but being defeated in his hopes by this News, was the Man that made the softest Complaints to this fair Beauty, and whose violence of Passion oppress'd him to that degree, that he was the only Lover, who durst himself tell her, he was in love with her; he writ Billets so soft and tender, that she had, of all her Lovers, most compassion for *Villenoys*, and dain'd several times, in pity of him, to send him answers to his Letters, but they were such, as absolutely forbad him to love her; such as incited him to follow Glory, the Mistress that could noblest reward him; and that, for her part, her Prayers should always be, that he might be victorious, and the Darling of that Fortune he was going to court; and that she, for her part, had fix'd her Mind on Heaven, and no Earthly Thought should bring it down; but she should ever retain for him all Sisterly Respect, and begg'd, in her Solitudes, to hear, whether her Prayers had prov'd effectual or not, and if Fortune were so kind to him, as she should perpetually wish.

When *Villenoys* found she was resolv'd, he design'd to persue his Journy, but could not leave the Town, till he had seen the fatal Ceremony of *Isabella's* being made a *Nun*, which was every day expected; and while he stay'd, he could not forbear writing daily to her, but receiv'd no more Answers from her, she already accusing her self of having done too much, for a Maid in her Circumstances; but she confess'd, of all she had seen, she lik'd *Villenoys* the best; and if she ever could have lov'd, she believ'd it would have been *Villenoys*, for he had all the good Qualities, and grace, that could render him agreeable to the Fair; besides, that he was only Son to a very rich and noble Parent, and one that might very well presume to lay claim to a Maid of *Isabella's* Beauty and Fortune.

As the time approach'd, when he must eternally lose all hope, by *Isabella's* taking Orders, he found himself less able to bear the Efforts of that Despair it possess'd him with, he languish'd with the thought, so that it was visible to all his Friends, the decays it wrought on his Beauty and Gaiety: So that he fell at last into a Feaver; and 'twas the whole Discourse of the Town, That *Villenoys* was dying for the Fair *Isabella*; his Relations, being all of Quality, were extreamly afflicted at his Misfortune, and joyn'd their Interests yet, to dissuade this fair young Victoress from an act so cruel, as to inclose herself in a *Nunnery*, while the finest of all the youths of Quality was dying for her, and ask'd her, If it would not be more acceptable to Heaven to save a Life, and perhaps a Soul, than to go and expose her own to a thousand Tortures? They assur'd her, *Villenoys* was dying, and dying Adoring her; that nothing could save his Life, but her kind Eyes turn'd upon the fainting Lover; a Lover, that could breath nothing, but her Name in Sighs; and find satisfaction in nothing, but weeping and crying out, "I dye for Isabella!" This Discourse fetch'd abundance of Tears from the fair Eyes of this tender Maid; but, at the same time, she besought them to believe, these Tears ought not to give them hope, she should ever yield to save his Life, by quitting her Resolution, of becoming a *Nun*; but, on the contrary, they were Tears, that only bewail'd her own Misfortune, in having been the occasion of the death of any Man, especially, a Man, who had so many Excellencies, as might have render'd him entirely Happy and Glorious for a long race of Years, had it not been his ill fortune to have seen her unlucky Face. She believ'd, it was for her Sins of Curiosity, and going beyond the Walls of the Monastery, to wander after the Vanities of the foolish World, that had occasion'd this Misfortune to the young Count of *Villenoys*, and she would put a severe Penance on her Body, for the Mischiefs her Eyes had done him; she fears she might, by something in her looks, have intic'd his Heart, for she own'd she saw him, with wonder at his Beauty, and much more she admir'd him, when she found the Beauties of his Mind; she confess'd, she had given him hope, by answering his Letters; and that when she found her Heart grow a little more than usually tender, when she thought on him, she believ'd it a

Crime, that ought to be check'd by a Virtue, such as she pretended to profess, and hop'd she should ever carry to her Grave; and she desired his Relations to implore him, in her Name, to rest contented, in knowing he was the first, and should be the last, that should ever make an impression on her Heart; that what she had conceiv'd there, for him, should remain with her to her dying day, and that she besought him to live, that she might see, he both deserv'd this Esteem she had for him, and to repay it her, otherwise he would dye in her debt, and make her Life ever after reposeless.

This being all they could get from her, they return'd with Looks that told their Message; however, they render'd those soft things *Isabella* had said, in so moving a manner, as fail'd not to please, and while he remain'd in this condition, the Ceremonies were compleated, of making *Isabella* a *Nun*; which was a Secret to none but *Villenoys*, and from him it was carefully conceal'd, so that in a little time he recover'd his lost health, at least, so well, as to support the fatal News, and upon the first hearing it, he made ready his Equipage, and departed immediately for *Candia*; where he behav'd himself very gallantly, under the Command of the Duke De *Beaufort*, and, with him, return'd to *France*, after the loss of that noble City to the *Turks*.

In all the time of his absence, that he might the sooner establish his Repose, he forbore sending to the fair Cruel *Nun*, and she heard no more of *Villenoys* in above two years; so that giving her self wholly up to Devotion, there was never seen any one, who led so Austere and Pious a Life, as this young *Votress*; she was a Saint in the Chapel, and an Angel at the *Grate*: She there laid by all her severe Looks, and mortify'd Discourse, and being at perfect peace and tranquility within, she was outwardly all gay, sprightly, and entertaining, being satisfy'd, no Sights, no Freedoms, could give any temptations to worldly desires; she gave a loose to all that was modest, and that Virtue and Honour would permit, and was the most charming Conversation that ever was admir'd; and the whole World that pass'd through *Iper*, of Strangers, came directed and recommended to the lovely *Isabella*; I mean, those of Quality: But however Diverting she was at the *Grate*, she was most exemplary Devout in the Cloister, doing more Penance, and imposing a more rigid Severity and Task on her self, than was requir'd, giving such rare Examples to all the *Nuns* that were less Devout, that her Life was a Proverb, and a President, and when they would express a very Holy Woman indeed, they would say, "She was a very *ISABELLA*."

There was in this *Nunnery*, a young *Nun*, call'd, Sister *Katteriena*, Daughter to the Grave *Vanhenault*, that is to say, an Earl, who liv'd about six Miles from the Town, in a noble *Villa*; this Sister *Katteriena* was not only a very beautiful Maid, but very witty, and had all the good qualities to make her be belov'd, and had most wonderfully gain'd upon the Heart of the fair *Isabella*, she was her Chamber-Fellow and Companion in all her Devotions and Diversions, so that where one was, there was the other, and they never went but together to the *Grate*, to the Garden, or to any place, whither their *Affairs* call'd either. This young *Katteriena* had a Brother, who lov'd her intirely, and came every day to see her, he was about twenty Years of Age, rather tall than middle Statur'd, his Hair and Eyes brown, but his Face exceeding beautiful, adorn'd with a thousand Graces, and the most nobly and exactly made, that 'twas possible for Nature to form; to the Fineness and Charms of his Person, he had an Air in his Meen and Dressing, so very agreeable, besides rich, that 'twas impossible to look on him, without wishing him happy, because he did so absolutely merit being so. His Wit and his Manner was so perfectly Obliging, a Goodness and Generosity so Sincere and Gallant, that it would even have aton'd for Ugliness. As he was eldest Son to so great a Father, he was kept at home, while the rest of his Brothers were employ'd in Wars abroad; this made him of a melancholy Temper, and fit for soft Impressions; he was very Bookish, and had the best Tutors that could be got, for Learning and Languages, and all that could compleat a Man; but was unus'd to Action, and of a temper Lazy, and given to

Repose, so that his Father could hardly ever get him to use any Exercise, or so much as ride abroad, which he would call, Losing Time from his Studies: He car'd not for the Conversation of Men, because he lov'd not Debauch, as they usually did; so that for Exercise, more than any Design, he came on Horseback every day to *Iper* to the *Monastery*, and would sit at the *Grate*, entertaining his Sister the most part of the Afternoon, and, in the Evening, retire; he had often seen and convers'd with the lovely *Isabella*, and found from the first sight of her, he had more Esteem for her, than any other of her Sex: But as Love very rarely takes Birth without Hope; so he never believ'd that the Pleasure he took in beholding her, and in discoursing with her, was Love, because he regarded her, as a Thing consecrate to Heaven, and never so much as thought to wish, she were a Mortal fit for his Addresses; yet he found himself more and more fill'd with Reflections on her which was not usual with him; he found she grew upon his Memory, and oftner came there, than he us'd to do, that he lov'd his Studies less, and going to *Iper* more; and, that every time he went, he found a new Joy at his Heart that pleas'd him; he found, he could not get himself from the *Grate*, without Pain; nor part from the sight of that all-charming Object, without Sighs; and if, while he was there, any persons came to visit her, whose Quality she could not refuse the honour of her sight to, he would blush, and pant with uneasiness, especially, if they were handsom, and fit to make Impressions: And he would check this Uneasiness in himself, and ask his Heart, what it meant, by rising and beating in those Moments, and strive to assume an Indifferency in vain, and depart dissatisfy'd, and out of humour.

On the other side, *Isabella* was not so Gay as she us'd to be, but, on the sudden, retir'd her self more from the *Grate* than she us'd to do, refus'd to receive Visits every day, and her Complexion grew a little pale and languid; she was observ'd not to sleep, or eat, as she us'd to do, nor exercise in those little Plays they made, and diverted themselves with, now and then;

she was heard to sigh often, and it became the Discourse of the whole House, that she was much alter'd: The Lady *Abbess*, who lov'd her with a most tender Passion, was infinitely concern'd at this Change, and endeavour'd to find out the Cause, and 'twas generally believ'd, she was too Devout, for now she redoubled her Austerity; and in cold Winter Nights, of Frost and Snow, would be up at all Hours, and lying upon the cold Stones, before the Altar, prostrate at Prayers: So that she receiv'd Orders from the Lady *Abbess*, not to harass her self so very much, but to have a care of her Health, as well as her Soul; but she regarded not these Admonitions, tho' even persuaded daily by her *Katteriena*, whom she lov'd every day more and more.

But, one Night, when they were retir'd to their Chamber, amongst a thousand things that they spoke of, to pass away a tedious Evening, they talk'd of Pictures and Likenesses, and *Katteriena* told *Isabella*, that before she was a *Nun*, in her more happy days, she was so like her Brother *Bernardo Henault*, (who was the same that visited them every day) that she would, in Men's Clothes, undertake, she should not have known one from t'other, and fetching out his *Picture*, she had in a Dressing-Box, she threw it to *Isabella*, who, at the first sight of it, turns as pale as Ashes, and, being ready to swound, she bid her take it away, and could not, for her Soul, hide the sudden surprise the *Picture* brought: *Katteriena* had too much Wit, not to make a just Interpretation of this Change, and (as a Woman) was naturally curious to pry farther, tho' Discretion should have made her been silent, for Talking, in such cases, does but make the Wound rage the more; "Why, my dear Sister, (said *Katteriena*) is the likeness of my Brother so offensive to you?" *Isabella* found by this, she had discover'd too much, and that Thought put her by all power of excusing it; she was confounded with Shame, and the more she strove to hide it, the more it disorder'd her; so that she (blushing extremely) hung down her Head, sigh'd, and confess'd all by her Looks. At last, after a considering Pause, she cry'd, "My dearest Sister, I do confess, I was surpriz'd at the sight of Monsieur *Henault,* and much more than ever you have observ'd me to be at the sight of his Person, because there is scarce a day wherein I do not see that, and know beforehand I shall see him; I am prepar'd for the Encounter, and have lessen'd my Concern, or rather Confusion, by that time I come to the *Grate,* so much Mistress I am of my Passions, when they give me warning of their approach, and sure I can withstand the greatest assaults of Fate, if I can but foresee it; but if it surprize me, I find I am as feeble a Woman, as the most unresolv'd; you did not tell me, you had this Picture, nor say, you would shew me such a Picture; but when I least expect to see that Face, you shew it me, even in my Chamber."

"Ah, my dear Sister! (reply'd *Katteriena*) I believe, that Paleness, and those Blushes, proceed from some other cause, than the Nicety of seeing the Picture of a Man in your Chamber."

"You have too much Wit, (reply'd *Isabella*) to be impos'd on by such an Excuse, if I were so silly to make it; but oh! my dear Sister! it was in my Thoughts to deceive you; could I have concealed my Pain and Sufferings, you should never have known them; but since I find it impossible, and that I am too sincere to make use of Fraud in any thing, 'tis fit I tell you, from what cause my change of Colour proceeds, and to own to you, I fear, 'tis Love, if ever therefore, oh gentle pitying Maid! thou wert a Lover? If ever thy tender Heart were touch'd with that Passion? Inform me, oh! inform me, of the nature of that cruel Disease, and how thou found'st a Cure?"

While she was speaking these words, she threw her Arms about the Neck of the fair *Katteriena,* and bath'd her Bosom (where she hid her Face) with a shower of Tears; *Katteriena,* embracing her with all the fondness of a dear Lover, told her, with a Sigh, that she could deny her nothing, and therefore confess'd to her, she had been a Lover, and that was the occasion of her being made a *Nun,* her Father finding out the Intrigue, which fatally happen'd to be with his own Page, a

Youth of extraordinary Beauty. "I was but Young, (said she) about Thirteen, and knew not what to call the new-known Pleasure that I felt; when e're I look'd upon the young *Arnaldo*, my Heart would heave, when e're he came in view, and my disorder'd Breath came doubly from my Bosom; a Shivering seiz'd me, and my Face grew wan; my Thought was at a stand, and Sense it self, for that short moment, lost its Faculties; But when he touch'd me, oh! no hunted Deer, tir'd with his flight, and just secur'd in Shades, pants with a nimbler motion than my Heart; at first, I thought the Youth had had some Magick Art, to make one faint and tremble at his touches; but he himself, when I accus'd his Cruelty, told me, he had no Art, but awful Passion, and vow'd that when I touch'd him, he was so; so trembling, so surprized, so charm'd, so pleas'd. When he was present, nothing could displease me, but when he parted from me; then 'twas rather a soft silent Grief, that eas'd itself by sighing, and by hoping, that some kind moment would restore my joy. When he was absent, nothing could divert me, howe're I strove, howe're I toyl'd for Mirth; no Smile, no Joy, dwelt in my Heart or Eyes; I could not feign, so very well I lov'd, impatient in his absence, I would count the tedious parting Hours, and pass them off like useless Visitants, whom we wish were gon; these are the Hours, where Life no business has, at least, a Lover's Life. But, oh! what Minutes seem'd the happy Hours, when on his Eyes I gaz'd, and he on mine, and half our Conversation lost in Sighs, Sighs, the soft moving Language of a Lover!"

"No more, no more, (reply'd *Isabella*, throwing her Arms again about the Neck of the transported *Katteriena*) thou blow'st my Flame by thy soft Words, and mak'st me know my Weakness, and my Shame: I love! I love! and feel those differing Passions!"—Then pausing a moment, she proceeded,—"Yet so didst thou, but hast surmounted it. Now thou hast found the Nature of my Pain, oh! tell me thy saving Remedy?" "Alas! (reply'd *Katteriena*) tho' there's but one Disease, there's many Remedies: They say, possession's one, but that to me seems a

Riddle; Absence, they say, another, and that was mine; for *Arnaldo* having by chance lost one of my Billets, discover'd the Amour, and was sent to travel, and my self forc'd into this Monastery, where at last, Time convinc'd me, I had lov'd below my Quality, and that sham'd me into Holy Orders." "And is it a Disease, (reply'd *Isabella*) that People often recover?" "Most frequently, (said *Katteriena*) and yet some dye of the Disease, but very rarely." "Nay then, (said *Isabella*) I fear, you will find me one of these Martyrs; for I have already oppos'd it with the most severe Devotion in the World: But all my Prayers are vain, your lovely Brother persues me into the greatest Solitude; he meets me at my very Midnight Devotions, and interrupts my Prayers; he gives me a thousand Thoughts, that ought not to enter into a Soul dedicated to Heaven; he ruins all the Glory I have achiev'd, even above my Sex, for Piety of Life, and the Observation of all Virtues. Oh *Katteriena*! he has a Power in his Eyes, that transcends all the World besides: And, to shew the weakness of Human Nature, and how vain all our Boastings are, he has done that in one fatal Hour, that the persuasions of all my Relations and Friends, Glory, Honour, Pleasure, and all that can tempt, could not perform in Years; I resisted all but *Henault's* Eyes, and they were Ordain'd to make me truly wretched; But yet with thy Assistance, and a Resolution to see him no more, and my perpetual Trust in Heaven, I may, perhaps, overcome this Tyrant of my Soul, who, I thought, had never enter'd into holy Houses, or mix'd his Devotions and Worship with the true Religion; but, oh! no Cells, no Cloysters, no Hermitages, are secur'd from his Efforts."

This Discourse she ended with abundance of Tears, and it was resolv'd, since she was devoted for ever to a Holy Life, That it was best for her to make it as easy to her as was possible; in order to it, and the banishing this fond and useless Passion from her Heart, it was very necessary, she should see *Henault* no more: At first, *Isabella* was afraid, that, in refusing to see him, he might mistrust her Passion; but *Katteriena* who was both Pious and Discreet, and endeavour'd truly to cure her of so violent a Disease, which must, she knew, either end in her death or destruction, told her, She would take care of that matter, that it should not blemish her Honour; and so leaving her a while; after they had resolved on this, she left her in a thousand Confusions, she was now another Woman than what she had hitherto been; she was quite alter'd in every Sentiment, thought and Notion; she now repented, she had promis'd not to see *Henault*; she trembled and even fainted, for fear she should see him no more; she was not able to bear that thought, it made her rage within, like one possest, and all her Virtue could not calm her; yet since her word was past, and, as she was, she could not, without great Scandal, break it in that point, she resolv'd to dye a thousand Deaths, rather than not perform her Promise made to *Katteriena*; but 'tis not to be express'd what she endur'd; what Fits, Pains, and Convulsions, she sustain'd; and how much ado she had to dissemble to Dame *Katteriena*, who soon return'd to the afflicted Maid; the next day, about the time that *Henault* was to come, as he usually did, about two or three a Clock after Noon, 'tis impossible to express the uneasiness of *Isabella*; she ask'd, a thousand times, "What, is not your Brother come?" When Dame *Katteriena* would reply, "Why do you ask?" She would say, "Because I would be sure not to see him." "You need not fear, Madam, (reply'd *Katteriena*) for you shall keep your Chamber." She need not have urg'd that, for *Isabella* was very ill without knowing it, and in a Feaver.

At last, one of the *Nuns* came up, and told Dame *Katteriena*, that her Brother was at the *Grate*, and she desired, he should be bid come about to the Private *Grate* above stairs, which he did, and she went to him, leaving *Isabella* even dead on the Bed, at the very name of *Henault*: But the more she conceal'd her Flame, the more violently it rag'd, which she strove in vain by Prayers, and those Recourses of Solitude to lessen; all this did but augment the Pain, and was Oyl to the Fire, so that she now could hope, that nothing but Death would put an end to her Griefs, and her Infamy. She was eternally thinking on him, how handsome his Face, how delicate every Feature, how charming his Air, how graceful his Meen, how soft and good his Disposition, and how witty and entertaining his Conversation. She now fancy'd, she was at the *Grate*, talking to him as she us'd to be, and blest those happy Hours she past then, and bewail'd her Misfortune, that she is no more destin'd to be so Happy, then gives a loose to Grief; Griefs, at which, no Mortals, but Despairing Lovers, can guess, or how tormenting they are; where the most easie Moments are, those, wherein one resolves to kill ones self, and the happiest Thought is Damnation; but from these Imaginations, she endeavours to fly, all frighted with horror; but, alas! whither would she fly, but to a Life more full of horror? She considers well, she cannot bear Despairing Love, and finds it impossible to cure her Despair; she cannot fly from the Thoughts of the Charming *Henault*, and 'tis impossible to quit 'em; and, at this rate, she found, Life could not long support it self, but would either reduce her to Madness, and so render her an hated Object of Scorn to the Censuring World, or force her Hand to commit a Murder upon her self. This she had found, this she had well consider'd, nor could her fervent and continual Prayers, her nightly Watchings, her Mortifications on the cold Marble in long Winter Season, and all her Acts of Devotion abate one spark of this shameful Feaver of Love, that was destroying her within. When she had rag'd and struggled with this unruly Passion, 'till she was quite tir'd and breathless, finding all her force in vain, she fill'd her fancy with a thousand charming *Ideas* of the lovely *Henault*, and, in that soft fit, had a mind to satisfy her panting Heart, and give it one Joy more, by beholding the Lord of its Desires, and the Author of its Pains: Pleas'd, yet trembling, at this Resolve, she rose from the Bed where she was laid, and softly advanc'd to the Stair-Case, from whence there open'd that Room where Dame *Katteriena* was, and where there was a private *Grate*, at which, she was entertaining her *Brother*; they were earnest in Discourse, and so loud, that *Isabella* could easily hear all they said, and the first words were from *Katteriena*, who, in a sort of Anger, cry'd, "Urge me no more! My Virtue is too nice, to become an Advocate for a Passion, that can tend to nothing but your Ruin; for, suppose I should tell the fair *Isabella*, you dye for her, what can it avail you? What hope can any Man have, to move the Heart of a Virgin, so averse to Love? A Virgin, whose Modesty and Virtue is so very curious, it would fly the very word, Love, as some monstrous Witchcraft, or the foulest of Sins, who would loath me for bringing so lewd a Message, and banish you her Sight, as the Object of her Hate and Scorn; is it unknown to you, how many of the noblest Youths of *Flanders* have address'd themselves to her in vain, when yet she was in the World? Have you been ignorant, how the young Count de *Villenoys* languished, in vain, almost to Death for her? And, that no Persuasions, no Attractions in him, no wordly Advantages, or all his Pleadings, who had a Wit and Spirit capable of prevailing on any Heart, less severe and harsh, than hers? Do you not know, that all was lost on this insensible fair one, even when she was a proper Object for the Adoration of the Young and Amorous? And can you hope, now she has so entirely wedded her future days to Devotion, and given all to Heaven; nay, lives a Life here more like a Saint, than a Woman; rather an Angel, than a mortal Creature? Do you imagin, with any Rhetorick you can deliver, now to turn the Heart, and whole Nature, of this Divine Maid, to consider your Earthly Passion? No, 'tis fondness, and an injury to her Virtue, to harbour such a Thought; quit it, quit it, my dear Brother! before it ruin your Repose." "Ah, Sister! (replied the dejected *Henault*) your Counsel comes too late, and your Reasons are of too feeble force, to rebate those Arrows, the Charming *Isabella's* Eyes have fix'd in my Heart and Soul; and I am undone, unless she know my Pain, which I shall dye, before I shall ever dare mention to her; but you, young Maids, have a thousand Familiarities together, can jest, and play, and say a thousand things between Railery and Earnest, that may first hint what you would deliver, and insinuate into each others Hearts a kind of Curiosity to know more; for naturally, (my dear Sister) Maids, are curious and vain; and however Divine the Mind of the fair *Isabella* may be, it bears the Tincture still of Mortal Woman."

"Suppose this true, how could this Mortal part about her Advantage you, (said *Katteriena*) all that you can expect from this Discovery, (if she should be content to hear it, and to return you pity) would be, to make her wretched, like your self? What farther can you hope?" "Oh! talk not, (replied *Henault*) of so much Happiness! I do not expect to be so blest, that she should pity me, or love to a degree of Inquietude; 'tis sufficient, for the ease of my Heart, that she know its Pains, and what it suffers for her; that she would give my Eyes leave to gaze upon her, and my Heart to vent a Sigh now and then; and, when I dare, to give me leave to speak, and tell her of my Passion; This, this, is all, my Sister." And, at that word, the Tears glided down his Cheeks, and he declin'd his Eyes, and set a Look so charming, and so sad, that *Isabella*, whose Eyes were fix'd upon him, was a thousand times ready to throw her self into the Room, and to have made a Confession, how sensible she was of all she had heard and seen: But, with much ado, she contain'd and satisfy'd her self, with knowing, that she was ador'd by him whom she ador'd, and, with Prudence that is natural to her, she withdrew, and waited with patience the event of their Discourse. She impatiently long'd to know, how *Katteriena* would manage this Secret her Brother had given her, and was pleas'd, that the Friendship and Prudence of that Maid had conceal'd her Passion from her Brother; and now contented and joyful beyond imagination, to find her self belov'd, she knew she could dissemble her own Passion and make him the first Aggressor; the first that lov'd, or at least, that should seem to do so. This Thought restores her so great a part of her Peace of Mind, that she resolv'd to see him, and to dissemble with *Katteriena* so far, as to make her believe, she had subdu'd that Passion, she was really asham'd to own; she now, with her Woman's Skill, begins to practise an Art she never before understood, and has recourse to Cunning, and resolves to seem to reassume her former Repose: But hearing *Katteriena* approach, she laid her self again on her Bed, where she had left her, but compos'd her Face to more chearfulness, and put on a Resolution that indeed deceiv'd the Sister, who was extreamly pleased, she said, to see her look so well: When *Isabella* reply'd, "Yes, I am another Woman now; I hope Heaven has heard, and granted, my long and humble Supplications, and driven from my Heart this tormenting God, that has so long disturb'd my purer Thoughts." "And are you sure, (said Dame *Katteriena*) that this wanton Deity is repell'd by the noble force of your Resolutions? Is he never to return?" "No, (replied *Isabella*) never to my Heart." "Yes, (said *Katteriena*) if you should see the lovely Murderer of your Repose, your Wound would bleed anew." At this, *Isabella* smiling with a little Disdain, reply'd, "Because you once to love, and *Henault's* Charms defencelsss found me, ah! do you think I have no Fortitude? But so in Fondness lost, remiss in Virtue, that when I have resolv'd, (and see it necessary for my after-Quiet) to want the power of keeping that Resolution? No, scorn me, and despise me then, as lost to all the Glories of my Sex, and all that Nicety I've hitherto preserv'd." There needed no more from a Maid of *Isabella's* Integrity and Reputation, to convince any one of the Sincerity of what she said, since, in the whole course of her Life, she never could be charg'd with an Untruth, or an Equivocation; and *Katteriena* assur'd her, she believ'd her, and was infinitely glad she had vanquish'd a Passion, that would have prov'd destructive to her Repose: *Isabella* reply'd, She had not altogether vanquish'd her Passion, she did not boast of so absolute a power over her soft Nature, but had resolv'd things great, and Time would work the Cure; that she hop'd, *Katteriena* would make such Excuses to her Brother, for her not appearing at the *Grate* so gay and entertaining as she us'd, and, by a little absence, she should retrieve the Liberty she had lost: But she desir'd, such Excuses might be made for her, that young *Henault* might not perceive the Reason. At the naming him, she had much ado not to shew some Concern extraordinary, and *Katteriena* assur'd her, She had now a very good Excuse to keep from the *Grate*, when he was at it; "For, (said she) now you have resolv'd, I may tell you, he is dying for you, raving in Love, and has this day made me promise to him, to give you some account of his Passion, and to make you sensible of his Languishment: I had not told you this, (reply'd *Katteriena*) but that I believe you fortify'd with brave Resolution and Virtue, and that this knowledge will rather put you more upon your Guard, than you were before." While she spoke, she fixed her Eyes on *Isabella*, to see what alteration it would make in her Heart and Looks; but the Master-piece of this young Maid's Art was shewn in this minute, for she commanded her self so well, that her very Looks dissembled and shew'd no concern at a Relation, that made her Soul dance with Joy; but it was, what she was prepar'd for, or else I question her Fortitude. But, with a Calmness, which absolutely subdu'd *Katteriena*, she reply'd, "I am almost glad he has confess'd a Passion for me, and you shall confess to him, you told me of it, and that I absent my self from the *Grate*, on purpose to avoid the sight of a Man, who durst love me, and confess it; and I assure you, my dear Sister! (continued she, dissembling) You could not have advanc'd my Cure by a more effectual way, than telling me of his Presumption." At that word, *Katteriena* joyfully related to her all that had pass'd between young *Henault* and her self, and how he implor'd her Aid in this Amour; at the end of which Relation, *Isabella* smil'd, and carelesly reply'd, "I pity him." And so going to their Devotion, they had no more Discourse of the Lover.

In the mean time, young *Henault* was a little satisfy'd, to know, his Sister would discover his Passion to the lovely *Isabella*; and though he dreaded the return, he was pleas'd that she should know, she had a Lover that ador'd her, though even without hope; for though the thought of possessing *Isabella*, was the most ravishing that could be; yet he had a dread upon him, when he thought of it, for he could not hope to accomplish that, without Sacrilege; and he was a young Man, very Devout, and even bigotted in Religion; and would often question and debate within himself, that, if it were possible, he should come to be belov'd by this Fair Creature, and that it were possible for her, to grant all that Youth in Love could require, whether he should receive the Blessing offer'd? And though he ador'd the Maid, whether he should not abhor the *Nun* in his Embraces? 'Twas an undetermin'd Thought, that chill'd his Fire as often as it approach'd; but he had too many that rekindled it again with the greater Flame and Ardor.

His impatience to know, what Success *Katteriena* had, with the Relation she was to make to *Isabella* in his behalf, brought him early to *Iper* the next day. He came again to the private *Grate*, where his Sister receiving him, and finding him, with a sad and dejected Look, expect what she had to say; she told him, That Look well became the News she had for him, it being such, as ought to make him, both Griev'd, and Penitent; for, to obey him, she had so absolutely displeas'd *Isabella*, that she was resolv'd never to believe her her Friend more, "Or to see you, (said she) therefore, as you have made me commit a Crime against my Conscience, against my Order, against my Friendship, and against my Honour, you ought to do some brave thing; take some noble Resolution, whorthy of your Courage, to redeem all; for your Repose, I promis'd, I would let Isabella know you lov'd, and, for the mitigation of my Crime, you ought to let me tell her, you have surmounted your Passion, as the last Remedy of Life and Fame."

At these her last words, the Tears gush'd from his Eyes, and he was able only, a good while, to sigh; at last, cry'd, "What! see her no more! see the Charming *Isabella* no more!" And then vented the Grief of his Soul in so passionate a manner, as his Sister had all the Compassion imaginable for him, but thought it great Sin and Indiscretion to cherish his Flame: So that, after a while, having heard her Counsel, he reply'd, "And is this all, my Sister, you will do to save a Brother?" "All! (reply'd she) I would not be the occasion of making a *NUN* violate her Vow, to save a Brother's Life, no, nor my own; assure your self of this, and take it as my last Resolution: Therefore, if you will be content with the Friendship of this young Lady, and so behave your self, that we may find no longer the Lover in the Friend, we shall reassume our former Conversation, and live with you, as we ought; otherwise, your Presence will continually banish her from the *Grate*, and, in time, make both her you love, and your self, a Town Discourse."

Much more to this purpose she said, to dissuade him, and bid him retire, and keep himself from thence, till he could resolve to visit them without a Crime; and she protested, if he did not do this, and master his foolish Passion, she would let her Father understand his Conduct, who was a Man of temper so very precise, that should he believe, his Son should have a thought of Love to a Virgin vow'd to Heaven, he would abandon him to Shame, and eternal Poverty, by disinheriting him of all he could: Therefore, she said, he ought to lay all this to his Heart, and weigh it with his unheedy Passion. While the Sister talk'd thus wisely, *Henault* was not without his Thoughts, but consider'd as she spoke, but did not consider in the right place; he was not considering, how to please a Father, and save an Estate, but how to manage the matter so, to establish himself, as he was before with *Isabella*; for he imagin'd, since already she knew his Passion, and that if after that she would be prevail'd with to see him, he might, some lucky Minute or other, have the pleasure of speaking for himself, at least, he should again see and talk to her, which was a joyful Thought in the midst of so many dreadful ones: And, as if he had known what pass'd in *Isabella's* Heart, he, by a strange sympathy, took the same measures to deceive *Katteriena*, a well-meaning young Lady, and easily impos'd on from her own Innocence, he resolv'd to dissemble Patience, since he must have that Virtue, and own'd, his Sister's Reasons were just, and ought to be persu'd; that she had argu'd him into half his Peace, and that he would endeavour to recover the rest; that Youth ought to be pardon'd a thousand Failings, and Years would reduce him to a condition of laughing at his Follies of Youth, but that grave Direction was not yet arriv'd: And so desiring, she would pray for his Conversion, and that she would recommend him to the Devotions of the Fair *Isabella*, he took his leave, and came no more to the *Nunnery* in ten Days; in all which time, none but Impatient Lovers can guess, what Pain and Languishments *Isabella* suffer'd, not knowing the Cause of his Absence, nor daring to enquire; but she bore it out so admirably, that Dame *Katteriena* never so much as suspected she had any Thoughts of that nature that perplex'd her, and now believ'd indeed she had conquer'd all her Uneasiness: And one day, when *Isabella* and she were alone together, she ask'd that fair Dissembler, if she did not admire at the Conduct and Resolution of her Brother? "Why!" (reply'd *Isabella* unconcernedly, while her Heart was fainting within, for fear of ill News:) With that, *Katteriena* told her the last Discourse she had with her Brother, and how at last she had persuaded him (for her sake) to quit his Passion; and that he had promis'd, he would endeavour to surmount it; and that, that was the reason he was absent now, and they were to see him no more, till he had made a Conquest over himself. You may assure your self, this News was not so welcom to *Isabella*, as *Katteriena* imagin'd; yet still she dissembled, with a force, beyond what the most cunning Practitioner could have shewn, and carry'd her self before People, as if no Pressures had lain upon her Heart; but when alone retir'd, in order to her Devotion, she would vent her Griefs in the most deplorable manner, that a distress'd distracted Maid could do, and which, in spite of all her severe Penances, she found no abatement of.

At last *Henault* came again to the *Monastery*, and, with a Look as gay as he could possibly assume, he saw his Sister, and told her, He had gain'd an absolute Victory over his Heart; and desir'd, he might see *Isabella*, only to convince, both her, and *Katteriena*, that he was no longer a Lover of that fair Creature, that had so lately charm'd him; that he had set Five thousand

Pounds a Year, against a fruitless Passion, and found the solid Gold much the heavier in the Scale: And he smil'd, and talk'd the whole Day of indifferent things, with his Sister, and ask'd no more for *Isabella*; nor did *Isabella* look, or ask, after him, but in her Heart. Two Months pass'd in this Indifference, till it was taken notice of, that Sister *Isabella* came not to the *Grate*, when *Henault* was there, as she us'd to do; this being spoken to Dame *Katteriena*, she told it to *Isabella*, and said, "The *NUNS* would believe, there was some Cause for her Absence, if she did not appear again": That if she could trust her Heart, she was sure she could trust her Brother, for he thought no more of her, she was confident; this, in lieu of pleasing, was a Dagger to the Heart of *Isabella*, who thought it time to retrieve the flying Lover, and therefore told *Katteriena*, She would the next Day entertain at the Low *Grate*, as she was wont to do, and accordingly, as soon as any People of Quality came, she appear'd there, where she had not been two Minutes, but she saw the lovely *Henault*, and it was well for both, that People were in the Room, they had else both sufficiently discover'd their Inclinations, or rather their not to be conceal'd Passions; after the General Conversation was over, by the going away of the Gentlemen that were at the *Grate, Katteriena* being employ'd elsewhere, *Isabella* was at last left alone with *Henault*; but who can guess the Confusion of these two Lovers, who wish'd, yet fear'd, to know each others Thoughts? She trembling with a dismal Apprehension, that he lov'd no more; and he almost dying with fear, she should Reproach or Upbraid him with his Presumption; so that both being possess'd with equal Sentiments of Love, Fear, and Shame, they both stood fix'd with dejected Looks and Hearts, that heav'd with stifled Sighs. At last, *Isabella*, the softer and tender-hearted of the two, tho' not the most a Lover perhaps, not being able to contain her Love any longer within the bounds of Dissimulation or Discretion, being by Nature innocent, burst out into Tears, and all fainting with pressing Thoughts within, she fell languishly into a Chair that stood there, while the distracted *Henault*, who could not come to her Assistance, and finding Marks of Love, rather than Anger or Disdain, in that Confusion of *Isabella's*, throwing himself on his Knees at the *Grate*, implor'd her to behold him, to hear him, and to pardon him, who dy'd every moment for her, and who ador'd her with a violent Ardor; but yet, with such an one, as should (tho' he perish'd with it) be conformable to her Commands; and as he spoke, the Tears stream'd down his dying Eyes, that beheld her with all the tender Regard that ever Lover was capable of; she recover'd a little, and turn'd her too beautiful Face to him, and pierc'd him with a Look, that darted a thousand Joys and Flames into his Heart, with Eyes, that told him her Heart was burning and dying for him; for which Assurances, he made Ten thousand Asseverations of his never-dying Passion, and expressing as many Raptures and Exesses of Joy, to find her Eyes and Looks confess, he was not odious to her, and that the knowledge he was her Lover, did not make her hate him: In fine, he spoke so many things all soft and moving, and so well convinc'd her of his Passion, that she at last was compell'd by a mighty force, absolutely irresistible, to speak.

"Sir, (said she) perhaps you will wonder, where I, a Maid, brought up in the simplicity of Virtue, should learn the Confidence, not only to hear of Love from you, but to confess I am sensible of the most violent of its Pain my self; and I wonder, and am amazed at my own Daring, that I should have the Courage, rather to speak, than dye, and bury it in silence; but such is my Fate. Hurried by an unknown Force, which I have endeavoured always, in vain, to resist, I am compell'd to tell you, I love you, and have done so from the first moment I saw you; and you are the only Man born to give me Life or Death, to make me Happy or Blest; perhaps, had I not been confin'd, and, as it were, utterly forbid by my Vow, as well as my Modesty, to tell you this, I should not have been so miserable to have fallen thus low, as to have confess'd my Shame; but our Opportunities of Speaking are so few, and Letters so impossible to be sent without discovery, that perhaps this is the only time I shall ever have to speak with you alone." And, at that word the Tears flow'd abundantly from her Eyes, and gave *Henault* leave to speak. "Ah Madam! (said he) do not, as soon as you have rais'd me to the greatest Happiness in the World, throw me with one word beneath your Scorn, much easier 'tis to dye, and know I am lov'd, than never, never, hope to hear that blessed sound again from that beautiful Mouth: Ah, Madam! rather let me make use of this one opportunity our happy Luck has given us, and contrive how we may for ever see, and speak, to each other; let us assure one another, there are a thousand ways to escape a place so rigid, as denies us that Happiness; and denies the fairest Maid in the World, the privilege of her Creation, and the end to which she was form'd to Angelical." And seeing *Isabella* was going to speak, lest she should say something, that might dissuade from an Attempt so dangerous and wicked, he persu'd to tell her, it might be indeed the last moment Heaven would give 'em, and besought her to answer him what he implor'd, whether she would fly with him from the *Monastery*? At this Word, she grew pale, and started, as at some dreadful Sound, and cry'd, "Hah! what is't you say? Is it possible, you should propose a thing so wicked? And can it enter into your Imagination, because I have so far forget my Virtue, and my Vow, to become a Lover, I should therefore fall to so wretched a degree of Infamy and Reprobation? No, name it to me no more, if you would see me; and if it be as you say, a Pleasure to be belov'd by me; for I will sooner dye, than yield to what . . . Alas! I but too well approve!" These last words, she spoke with a fainting Tone, and the Tears fell anew from her fair soft Eyes. "If it be so," said he, (with a Voice so languishing, it could scarce be heard) "If it be so, and that you are resolv'd to try, if my Love be eternal without Hope, without expectation of any other Joy, than seeing and adoring you through the *Grate*; I am, and must, and will be contented, and you shall see, I can prefer the Sighing to these cold Irons, that separate us, before all the Possessions of the rest of the World; that I chuse rather to lead my Life here, at this cruel

Distance from you, for ever, than before the Embrace of all the
Fair; and you shall see, how pleas'd I will be, to languish here;
but as you see me decay, (for surely so I shall) do not triumph
o're my languid Looks, and laugh at my Pale and meager Face;
but, Pitying, say, How easily I might have preserv'd that Face,
those Eyes, and all that Youth and Vigour, now no more, from
this total Ruine I now behold it in, and love your Slave that
dyes, and will be daily and visibly dying, as long as my Eyes can
gaze on that fair Object, and my Soul be fed and kept alive with
her Charming Wit and Conversation; if Love can live on such
Airy Food, (tho' rich in it self, yet unfit, alone, to sustain Life) it
shall be for ever dedicated to the lovely *ISABELLA*: But, oh! that
time cannot be long! Fate will not lend her Slave many days,
who loves too violently, to be satisfy'd to enjoy the fair Object
of his Desires, no otherwise than at a *Grate*."

He ceas'd speaking, for Sighs and Tears stopt his Voice, and
he begg'd the liberty to sit down; and his Looks being quite
alter'd, *ISABELLA* found her self touch'd to the very Soul, with a
concern the most tender, that ever yielding Maid was oppress'd
with: She had no power to suffer him to Languish, while she by
one soft word could restore him, and being about to say a
thousand things that would have been agreeable to him, she
saw herself approach'd by some of the *Nuns*, and only had time
to say, "If you love me, live and hope." The rest of the *Nuns*
began to ask *Henault* of News, for he always brought them all
that was Novel in the Town, and they were glad still of his Visits,
above all other, for they heard, how all Amours and Intrigues
pass'd in the World, by this young Cavalier. These last words of
Isabella's were a Cordial to his Soul, and he, from that, and to
conceal the present Affair, endeavour'd to assume all the Gaity
he could, and told 'em all he could either remember, or invent,
to please 'em, tho' he wish'd them a great way off at that time.

Thus they pass'd the day, till it was a decent hour for him to
quit the *Grate*, and for them to draw the Curtain; all that Night
did *Isabella* dedicate to Love, she went to Bed, with a
Resolution, to think over all she had to do, and to consider,

how she should manage this great Affair of her Life: I have already said, she had try'd all that was possible in Human Strength to perform, in the design of quitting a Passion so injurious to her Honour and Virtue, and found no means possible to accomplish it: She had try'd Fasting long, Praying fervently, rigid Penances and Pains, severe Disciplines, all the Mortification, almost to the destruction of Life it self, to conquer the unruly Flame; but still it burnt and rag'd but the more; so, at last, she was forc'd to permit that to conquer her, she could not conquer, and submitted to her Fate, as a thing destin'd her by Heaven it self; and after all this opposition, she fancy'd it was resisting even Divine Providence, to struggle any longer with her Heart; and this being her real Belief, she the more patiently gave way to all the Thoughts that pleas'd her.

As soon as she was laid, without discoursing (as she us'd to do) to *Katteriena*, after they were in Bed, she pretended to be sleepy, and turning from her, setled her self to profound Thinking, and was resolv'd to conclude the Matter, between her Heart, and her Vow of Devotion, that Night, and she, having no more to determine, might end the Affair accordingly, the first opportunity she should have to speak to *Henault*, which was, to fly, and marry him; or, to remain for ever fix'd to her Vow of Chastity. This was the Debate; she brings Reason on both sides: Against the first, she sets the Shame of a Violated Vow, and considers, where she shall shew her Face after such an Action; to the Vow, she argues, that she was born in Sin, and could not live without it; that she was Human, and no Angel, and that, possibly, that Sin might be as soon forgiven, as another; that since all her devout Endeavours could not defend her from the Cause, Heaven ought to execute the Effect; that as to shewing her Face, so she saw that of *Henault* always turned (Charming as it was) towards her with love; what had she to do with the World, or car'd to behold any other?

Some times, she thought, it would be more Brave and Pious to dye, than to break her Vow; but she soon answer'd that, as false Arguing, for Self-Muroder was the worst of Sins, and in the

Deadly Number. She could, after such an Action, live to repent, and, of two Evils, she ought to chuse the least; she dreads to think, since she had so great a Reputation for Virtue and Piety, both in the *Monastery*, and in the World, what they both would say, when she should commit an Action so contrary to both these, she posest; but, after a whole Night's Debate, Love was strongest, and gain'd the Victory. She never went about to think, how she should escape, because she knew it would be easy, the keeping of the Key of the *Monastery*, was often intrusted in her keeping, and was, by turns, in the hands of many more, whose Virtue and Discretion was Infallible, and out of Doubt; besides, her Aunt being the Lady *Abbess*, she had greater privilege than the rest; so that she had no more to do, she thought, than to acquaint *Henault* with her Design, as soon as she should get an opportunity. Which was not quickly; but, in the mean time, *Isabella's* Father dy'd, which put some little stop to our Lover's Happiness, and gave her a short time of Grief; but Love, who, while he is new and young, can do us Miracles, soon wip'd her Eyes, and chas'd away all Sorrows from her Heart, and grew every day more and more impatient, to put her new Design in Execution, being every day more resolv'd. Her Father's Death had remov'd one Obstacle, and secur'd her from his Reproaches; and now she only wants Opportunity, first, to acquaint *Henault*, and then to fly.

She waited not long, all things concurring to her desire; for *Katteriena* falling sick, she had the good luck, as she call'd it then, to entertain *Henault* at the *Grate* oftentimes alone; the first moment she did so, she entertain'd him with the good News, and told him, She had at last vanquish'd her Heart in favour of him, and loving him above all things, Honour, her Vow or Reputation, had resolv'd to abandon her self wholly to him, to give her self up to love and serve him, and that she had no other Consideration in the World; but *Henault*, instead of returning her an Answer, all Joy and Satisfaction, held down his Eyes, and Sighing, with a dejected Look, he cry'd, "Ah, Madam! Pity a Man so wretched and undone, as not to be sensible of this Blessing as I ought." She grew pale at this Reply, and trembling, expected he would proceed: "'Tis not (continued he) that I want Love, tenderest Passion, and all the desire Youth and Love can inspire; But, Oh, Madam! when I consider, (for raving mad in Love as I am for your sake, I do consider) that if I should take you from this Repose, Nobly Born and Educated, as you are; and, for that Act, should find a rigid Father deprive me of all that ought to support you, and afford your Birth, Beauty, and Merits, their due, what would you say? How would you Reproach me?" He sighing, expected her Answer, when Blushes overspreading her Face, she reply'd, in a Tone all haughty and angry, "Ah, *Henault*! Am I then refus'd, after having abandon'd all things for you? Is it thus, you reward my Sacrific'd Honour, Vows, and Virtue? Cannot you hazard the loss of Fortune to possess *Isabella*, who loses all for you!" Then bursting into Tears, at her misfortune of Loving, she suffer'd him to say, "Oh, Charming fair one! how industrious is your Cruelty, to find out new Torments for an Heart, already press'd down with the Severities of Love? Is it possible, you can make so unhappy a Construction of the tenderest part of my Passion? And can you imagin it want of Love in me, to consider, how I shall preserve and merit the vast Blessing Heaven has given me? Is my Care a Crime? And would not the most deserving Beauty of the World hate me, if I should, to preserve my Life, and satisfy the Passion of my fond Heart, reduce her to the Extremities of Want and Misery? And is there any thing, in what I have said, but what you ought to take for the greatest Respect and tenderness!" "Alas! (reply'd *Isabella* sighing) young as I am, all unskilful in Love I find, but what I feel, that Discretion is no part of it; and Consideration, inconsistent with the Nobler Passion, who will subsist of its own Nature, and Love unmixed with any other Sentiment? And 'tis not pure, if it be otherwise: I know, had I mix'd Discretion with mine, my Love must have been less, I never thought of living, but my Love; and, if I consider'd at all, it was, that Grandure and Magnificence were useless Trifles to Lovers, wholly needless and troublesom. I thought of living in some loanly Cottage, far from the noise of crowded busie Cities, to walk with thee in Groves, and silent Shades, where I might hear no Voice but thine; and when we had been tir'd, to sit us done by some cool murmuring Rivulet, and be to each a World, my Monarch thou, and I thy Sovereign Queen, while Wreaths of Flowers shall crown our happy Heads, some fragrant Bank our Throne, and Heaven our Canopy: Thus we might laugh at Fortune, and the Proud, despise the duller World, who place their Joys in mighty Shew and Equipage. Alas! my Nature could not bear it, I am unus'd to Wordly Vanities, and would boast of nothing but my *Henault*; no Riches, but his Love; no Grandure, but his Presence." She ended speaking, with Tears, and he reply'd, "Now, now, I find, my *Isabella* loves indeed, when she's content to abandon the World for my sake; Oh! thou hast named the only happy Life that suits my quiet Nature, to be retir'd, has always been my Joy! But to be so with thee! Oh! thou hast charm'd me with a Thought so dear, as has for ever banish'd all my Care, but how to receive thy Goodness! Please think no more what my angry Parent may do, when he shall hear, how I have dispos'd of my self against his Will and Pleasure, but trust to Love and Providence; no more! be gone all Thoughts, but those of *Isabella!*"

As soon as he had made an end of expressing his Joy, he fell to consulting how, and when, she should escape; and since it was uncertain, when she should be offer'd the Key, for she would not ask for it, she resolv'd to give him notice, either by word of Mouth, or a bit of Paper she would write in, and give him through the *Grate* the first opportunity; and, parting for that time, they both resolv'd to get up what was possible for their Support, till Time should reconcile Affairs and Friends, and to wait the happy hour.

Isabella's dead Mother had left Jewels, of the value of £2000 to her Daughter, at her Decease, which Jewels were in the possession, now, of the Lady *Abbess*, and were upon Sale, to be added to the Revenue of the *Monastery*; and as *Isabella* was the most Prudent of her Sex, at least, had hitherto been so esteem'd, she was intrusted with all that was in possession of the Lady *Abbess*, and 'twas not difficult to make her self Mistress of all her own Jewels; as also, some 3 or £400 in Gold, that was hoarded up in her Ladyship's Cabinet, against any Accidents that might arrive to the *Monastery*; these *Isabella* also made her own, and put up with the Jewels; and having acquainted *Henault*, with the Day and Hour of her Escape, he got together what he could, and waiting for her, with his Coach, one Night, when no body was awake but her self, when rising softly, as she us'd to do, in the Night, to her Devotion, she stole so dexterously out of the *Monastery*, as no body knew any thing of it; she carry'd away the Keys with her, after having lock'd all the Doors, for she was intrusted often with all. She found *Henault* waiting in his Coach, and trusted none but an honest Coachman that lov'd him; he receiv'd her with all the Transports of a truly ravish'd Lover, and she was infinitely charm'd with the new Pleasure of his Embraces and Kisses.

They drove out of Town immediately, and because she durst not be seen in that Habit, (for it had been immediate Death for both) they drove into a Thicket some three Miles from the Town, where *Henault* having brought her some of his younger Sister's Clothes, he made her put off her Habit, and put on those; and, rending the other, they hid them in a Sand-pit, covered over with Broom, and went that Night forty Miles from *Iper*, to a little Town upon the River *Rhine*, where, changing their Names, they were forthwith married, and took a House in a Country Village, a Farm, where they resolv'd to live retir'd, by the name of *Beroone*, and drove a Farming Trade; however, not forgetting to set Friends and Engines at work, to get their Pardon, as Criminals, first, that had trangress'd the Law; and, next, as disobedient Persons, who had done contrary to the Will and Desire of their Parents: *Isabella* writ to her Aunt the most moving Letters in the World, so did *Henault* to his Father; but she was a long time, before she could gain so much as an answer from her Aunt, and *Henault* was so unhappy, as never to gain one from his Father; who no sooner heard the News that was spread over all the Town and Country, that young *Henault* was fled with the so fam'd *Isabella*, a *Nun*, and singular for Devotion and Piety of Life, but he immediately setled his Estate on his younger Son, cutting *Henault* off with all his Birthright, which was £5000 a Year. This News, you may believe, was not very pleasing to the young Man, who tho' in possession of the loveliest Virgin, and now Wife, that ever Man was bless'd with; yet when he reflected, he should have children by her, and these and she should come to want, (he having been magnificently Educated, and impatient of scanty Fortune) he laid it to Heart, and it gave him a thousand Uneasinesses in the midst of unspeakable Joys; and the more he strove to hide his Sentiments from *Isabella*, the more tormenting it was within; he durst not name it to her, so insuperable a Grief it would cause in her, to hear him complain; and tho' she could live hardly, as being bred to a devout and severe Life, he could not, but must let the Man of Quality shew it self; even in the disguise of an humbler Farmer: Besides all this, hs found nothing of his Industry thrive, his Cattel still dy'd in the midst of those that were in full Vigour and Health of other Peoples; his Crops of Wheat and Barly, and other Grain, tho' manag'd by able and knowing Husbandmen, were all, either Mildew'd, or Blasted, or some Misfortune still arriv'd to him; his Coach-Horses would fight and kill one another, his Barns sometimes be fir'd; so that it became a Proverb all over the Country, if any ill Luck had arriv'd to any body, they would say, "They had Monsieur *BEROONE'S* Luck." All these Reflections did but add to his Melancholy, and he grew at last to be in some want, insomuch, that *Isabella*, who had by her frequent Letters, and submissive Supplications, to her Aunt, (who lov'd her tenderly) obtain'd her Pardon, and her Blessing; she now press'd her for some Money, and besought her to consider, how great a Fortune she had brought to the *Monastery*, and implor'd, she would allow her some Sallary out of it, for she had been marry'd two Years, and most of what she had was exhausted. The Aunt, who found, that what was done, could not be undone, did, from time to time, supply her so, as one might have liv'd very decently on that very Revenue; but that would not satisfy the great Heart of *Henault*. He was now about three and twenty Years old, and *Isabella* about eighteen, too young, and too lovely a Pair, to begin their Misfortunes so soon; they were both the most Just and Pious in the World; they were Examples of Goodness, and Eminent for Holy Living, and for perfect Loving, and yet nothing thriv'd they undertook; they had no Children, and all their Joy was in each other; at last, one good Fortune arriv'd to them, by the Solicitations of the Lady *Abbess*, and the *Bishop*, who was her near Kinsman, they got a Pardon for *Isabella's* quitting the *Monastery*, and marrying, so that she might now return to her own Country again. *Henault* having also his Pardon, they immediately quit the place, where they had remain'd for two Years, and came again into *Flanders*, hoping, the change of place might afford 'em better Luck.

Henault then began again to solicit his Cruel Father, but nothing would do, he refus'd to see him, or to receive any Letters from him; but, at last, he prevail'd so far with him, as that he sent a Kinsman to him, to assure him, if he would leave his Wife, and go into the *French* Campagn, he would Equip him as well as his Quality requir'd, and that, according as he behav'd himself, he should gain his Favour; but if he liv'd Idly at home, giving up his Youth and Glory to lazy Love, he would have no more to say to him, but race him out of his Heart, and out of his Memory.

He had setled himself in a very pretty House, furnished with what was fitting for the Reception of any Body of Quality that would live a private Life, and they found all the Respect that their Merits deserv'd from all the World, every body entirely loving and endeavouring to serve them; and *Isabella* so perfectly had the Ascendent over her Aunt's Heart, that she procur'd from her all that she could desire, and much more than she could expect. She was perpetually progging and saving all that she could, to enrich and advance her, and, at last, pardoning and forgiving *Henault*, lov'd him as her own Child; so that all things look'd with a better Face than before, and never was so dear and fond a Couple seen, as *Henault* and *Isabella*; but, at last, she prov'd with Child, and the Aunt, who might reasonably believe, so young a Couple would have a great many Children, and foreseeing there was a no Provision likely to be made them, unless he pleas'd his Father, for if the Aunt should chance to dye, all their Hope was gone; she therefore daily solicited him to obey his Father, and go to the Camp; and that having atchiev'd Fame and Renown, he would return a Favourite to his Father, and Comfort to his Wife: After she had solicited in vain, for he was not able to endure the thought of leaving *Isabella*, melancholy as he was with his ill Fortune; the *Bishop*, kinsman to *Isabella*, took him to task, and urg'd his Youth and Birth, and that he ought not to wast both without Action, when all the World was employ'd; and, that since his Father had so great a desire he should go into a Campagn, either to serve the *Venetian* against the *Turks*, or into the *French* Service, which he lik'd best; he besought him to think of it; and since he had satisfy'd his Love, he should and ought to satisfy his Duty, it being absolutely necessary for the wiping off the Stain of his Sacrilege, and to gain him the favour of Heaven, which, he found, had hitherto been averse to all he had undertaken: In fine, all his Friends, and all who lov'd him, joyn'd in this Design, and all thought it convenient, nor was he insensible of the Advantage it might bring him; but Love, which every day grew fonder and fonder in his Heart, oppos'd all their Reasonings, tho' he saw all the Brave Youth of the Age preparing to go, either to one Army, or the other.

At last, he lets *Isabella* know, what Propositions he had made him, both by his Father, and his Relations; at the very first Motion, she almost fainted in his Arms, while he was speaking, and it possess'd her with so intire a Grief, that she miscarry'd, to the insupportable Torment of her tender Husband and Lover, so that, to re-establish her Repose, he was forc'd to promise not

177

to go; however, she consider'd all their Circumstances, and weigh'd the Advantages that might redound both to his Honour and Fortune, by it; and, in a matter of a Month's time, with the Persuasions and Reasons of her Friends, she suffer'd him to resolve upon going, her self determining to retire to the *Monastery*, till the time of his Return; but when she nam'd the *Monastery*, he grew pale and disorder'd, and obliged her to promise him, not to enter into it any more, for fear they should never suffer her to come forth again; so that he resolv'd not to depart, till she had made a Vow to him, never to go again within the Walls of a Religious House, which had already been so fatal to them. She promis'd, and he believ'd.

Henault, at last, overcame his Heart, which pleaded so for his Stay, and sent his Father word, he was ready to obey him, and to carry the first Efforts of his Arms against the common Foes of Christendom, the *Turks*; his Father was very well pleas'd at this, and sent him Two thousand Crowns, his Horses and Furniture sutable to his Quality, and a Man to wait on him; so that it was not long e're he got himself in order to be gone, after a dismal parting.

He made what hast he could to the *French* Army, then under the Command of the Monsignior, the Duke of *Beaufort*, then at *Candia*, and put himself a Voluntier under his Conduct; in which Station was *Villenoys*, who, you have already heard, was so passionate a Lover of *Isabella*, who no sooner heard of *Henault's* being arriv'd, and that he was Husband to *Isabella*, but he was impatient to learn, by what strange Adventure he came to gain her, even from her Vow'd Retreat, when he, with all his Courtship, could not be so happy, tho' she was then free in the World, and Unvow'd to Heaven.

As soon as he sent his Name to *Henault*, he was sent for up, for *Henault* had heard of *Villenoys*, and that he had been a Lover of *Isabella*; they receiv'd one another with all the endearing Civility imaginable for the aforesaid Reason, and for that he was his Country-man, tho' unknown to him, *Villenoys* being gone to the Army, just as *Henault* came from the *Jesuits*

College. A great deal of Endearment pass'd between them, and they became, from that moment, like two sworn Brothers, and he receiv'd the whole Relation from *Henault*, of his Amour.

It was not long before the Siege began anew, for he arriv'd at the beginning of the Spring, and, as soon as he came, almost, they fell to Action; and it happen'd upon a day, that a Party of some Four hundred Men resolv'd to sally out upon the Enemy, as, when ever they could, they did; but as it is not my business to relate the History of the War, being wholly unacquainted with the Terms of Battels, I shall only say, That these Men were led by *Villenoys*, and that *Henault* would accompany him in this Sally, and that they acted very Noble, and great Things, worthy of a Memory in the History of that Siege; but this day, particularly, they had an occasion to shew their Valour, which they did very much to their Glory; but, venturing too far, they were ambush'd, in the persuit of the Party of the Enemies, and being surrounded, *Villenoys* had the unhappiness to see his gallant Friend fall, fighting and dealing of Wounds around him, even as he descended to the Earth, for he fell from his Horse at the same moment that he kill'd a *Turk*; and *Villenoys* could neither assist him, nor had he the satisfaction to be able to rescue his dead Body from under the Horses, but, with much ado, escaping with his own Life, got away, in spite of all that follow'd him, and recover'd the Town, before they could overtake him: He passionately bewail'd the Loss of this brave young Man, and offer'd any Recompence to those, that would have ventur'd to have search'd for his dead Body among the Slain; but it was not fit to hazard the Living, for unnecessary Services to the Dead; and tho' he had a great mind to have Interr'd him, he rested content with what he wish'd to pay his Friends Memory, tho' he could not: So that all the Service now he could do him, was, to write to *Isabella*, to whom he had not writ, tho' commanded by her so to do, in three Years before, which was never since she took Orders. He gave her an Account of the Death of her Husband, and how Gloriously he fell fighting for the Holy Cross, and how much Honour he had won, if it had been his Fate to have outliv'd that great, but unfortunate, Day, where, with 400 Men, they had kill'd 1500 of the Enemy. The General *Beaufort* himself had so great a Respect and Esteem for this young Man, and knowing him to be of Quality, that he did him the honour to bemoan him, and to send a Condoling Letter to *Isabella*, how much worth her Esteem he dy'd, and that he had Eterniz'd his Memory with the last Gasp of his Life.

When this News arriv'd, it may be easily imagin'd, what Impressions, or rather Ruins, it made in the Heart of this fair Mourner; the Letters came by his Man, who saw him fall in Battel, and came off with those few that escap'd with *Villenoys*; he brought back what Money he had, a few Jewels, with *Isabella's* Picture that he carry'd with him and had left in his Chamber in the Fort at *Candia*, for fear of breaking it in Action. And now *Isabella's* Sorrow grew to the Extremity, she thought, she could not suffer more than she did by his Absence, but she now found a Grief more killing; she hung her Chamber with Black, and liv'd without the Light of Day: Only Wax Lights, that let her behold the Picture of this Charming Man, before which she sacrific'd Floods of Tears. He had now been absent about ten Months, and she had learnt just to live without him, but Hope preserv'd her then; but now she had nothing, for which to wish to live. She, for about two Months after the News arriv'd, liv'd without seeing any Creature but a young Maid, that was her Woman; but extream Importunity oblig'd her to give way to the Visits of her Friends, who endeavour'd to restore her Melancholy Soul to its wonted Easiness; for, however it was oppress'd within, by *Henault's* Absence, she bore it off with a modest Chearfulness; but now she found, that Fortitude and Virtue fail'd her, when she was assur'd, he was no more: She continu'd thus Mourning, and thus inclos'd, thespace of a whole Year, never suffering the Visit of any Man, but of a near Relation; so that she acquir'd a Reputation, such as never any young Beauty had, for she was now but Nineteen, and her Face and Shape more excellent than ever; she daily increas'd in Beauty, which, joyn'd to her Exemplary Piety, Charity, and all other excellent Qualities, gain'd her a wonderous Fame, and begat an Awe and Reverence in all that heard of her, and there was no Man of any Quality, that did not Adore her. After her Year was up, she went to the Churches, but would never be seen any where else abroad, but that was enough to procure her a thousand Lovers; and some, who had the boldness to send her Letters, which, if she receiv'd, she gave no Answer to, and many she sent back unread and unseal'd: So that she would encourage none, tho' their Quality was far beyond what she could hope; but she was resolv'd to marry no more, however her Fortune might require it.

It happen'd, that, about this time, *Candia* being unfortunately taken by the *Turks*, all the brave Men that escap'd the Sword, return'd, among them, *Villenoys*, who no sooner arriv'd, but he sent to let *Isabella* know of it, and to beg the Honour of waiting on her; desirous to learn what Fate befel her dear Lord, she suffer'd him to visit her, where he found her, in her Mourning, a thousand times more Fair, (at least, he fancy'd so) than ever she appear'd to be; so that if he lov'd her before, he now ador'd her; if he burnt then, he rages now; but the awful Sadness, and soft Languishment of her Eyes, hinder'd him from the presumption of speaking of his Passion to her, tho' it would have been no new thing; and his first Visit was spent in the Relation of every Circumstance of *Henault's* Death; and, at his going away, he begg'd leave to visit her sometimes, and she gave him permission: He lost no time, but made use of the Liberty she had given him; and when his Sister, who was a great Companion of *Isabella's*, went to see her, he would still wait on her; so that, either with his own Visits, and those of his Sister's, he saw *Isabella* every day, and had the good luck to see, he diverted her, by giving her Relations of Transactions of the Siege, and the Customs and Manners of the *Turks*: All he said, was with so good a Grace, that he render'd every thing agreeable; he was, besides, very Beautiful, well made, of Quality and Fortune, and fit to inspire Love.

He made his Visits so often, and so long, that, at last, he took the Courage to speak of his Passion, which, at first, *Isabella* would by no means hear of, but, by degrees, she yielded more and more to listen to his tender Discourse; and he liv'd thus with her two Years, before he could gain any more upon her Heart, than to suffer him to speak of Love to her; but that, which subdu'd her quite was, That her Aunt, the Lady *Abbess*, dy'd, and with her, all the Hopes and Fortune of *Isabella*, so that she was left with only a Charming Face and Meen, a Virtue, and a Discretion above her Sex, to make her Fortune within the World; into a Religious House, she was resolv'd not to go, because her Heart deceiv'd her once, and she durst not trust it again, whatever it promis'd.

The death of this Lady made her look more favourably on *Villenoys*; but yet, she was resolv'd to try his Love to the utmost, and keep him off, as long as 'twas possible she could subsist, and 'twas for Interest she married again, tho' she lik'd the Person very well; and since she was forc'd to submit her self to be a second time a Wife, she thought, she could live better with *Villenoys*, than any other, since for him she ever had a great Esteem; and fancy'd the Hand of Heaven had pointed out her Destiny, which she could not avoid, without a Crime.

So that when she was again importun'd by her impatient Lover, she told him, She had made a Vow to remain three Years, at least, before she would marry again, after the Death of the best of Men and Husbands, and him who had the Fruits of her early Heart; and, notwithstanding all the Solicitations of *Villenoys*, she would not consent to marry him, till her Vow of Widowhood was expir'd.

He took her promise, which he urg'd her to give him, and to shew the height of his Passion in his obedience; he condescends to stay her appointed time, tho' he saw her every day, and all his Friends and Relations made her Visits upon this new account, and there was nothing talk'd on, but this design'd Wedding, which, when the time was expir'd, was perform'd accordingly with great Pomp and Magnificence, for

Villenoys had no Parents to hinder his Design; or if he had, the Reputation and Virtue of this Lady would have subdu'd them.

The Marriage was celebrated in this House, where she liv'd ever since her Return from *Germany*, from the time she got her Pardon; and when *Villenoys* was preparing all things in a more magnificent Order at his Villa, some ten Miles from the City, she was very melancholy, and would often say, She had been us'd to such profound Retreat, and to live without the fatigue of Noise and Equipage, that, she fear'd, she should never endure that Grandeur, which was proper for his Quality; and tho' the House, in the Country, was the most beautifully Situated in all *Flanders*, she was afraid of a numerous Train, and kept him, for the most part, in this pretty City Mansion, which he Adorn'd and Enlarg'd, as much as she would give him leave; so that there wanted nothing, to make this House fit to receive the People of the greatest Quality, little as it was: But all the Servants and Footmen, all but one *Valet*, and the Maid, were lodg'd abroad, for *Isabella*, not much us'd to the sight of Men about her, suffer'd them as seldom as possible, to come in her Presence, so that she liv'd more like a *Nun* still, than a Lady of the World; and very rarely any Maids came about her, but *Maria*, who had always permission to come, when ever she pleas'd, unless forbidden.

As *Villenoys* had the most tender and violent Passion for his Wife, in the World, he suffer'd her to be pleas'd at any rate, and to live in what Method she best lik'd, and was infinitely satisfy'd with the Austerity and manner of her Conduct, since in his Arms, and alone, with him, she wanted nothing that could Charm; so that she was esteemed the fairest and best of Wives, and he the most happy of all Mankind. When she would go abroad, she had her Coaches Rich and Gay, and her Livery ready to attend her in all the Splendour imaginable; and he was always buying one rich Jewel, or Necklace, or some great Rarity or other, that might please her; so that there was nothing her Soul could desire, which it had not, except the Assurance of Eternal Happiness, which she labour'd incessantly to gain. She had no Discontent, but because she was not bless'd with a

Child; but she submits to the pleasure of Heaven, and endeavour'd, by her good Works, and her Charity, to make the Poor her Children, and was ever doing Acts of Virtue, to make the Proverb good, *That more are the Children of the Barren, than the Fruitful Woman.* She liv'd in this Tranquility, belov'd by all, for the space of five Years, and Time (and perpetual Obligations from *Villenoys*, who was the most indulgent and indearing Man in the World) had almost worn out of her Heart the Thought of *Henault*, or if she remember'd him, it was in her Prayers, or sometimes with a short sigh, and no more, tho' it was a great while, before she could subdue her Heart to that Calmness; but she was prudent, and wisely bent all her Endeavours to please, oblige, and caress, the deserving Living, and to strive all she could, to forget the unhappy Dead, since it could not but redound to the disturbance of her Repose, to think of him; so that she had now transferr'd all that Tenderness she had for him, to *Villenoys*.

Villenoys, of all Diversions, lov'd Hunting, and kept, at his Country House, a very famous Pack of Dogs, which he us'd to lend, sometimes, to a young Lord, who was his dear Friend, and his Neighbour in the Country, who would often take them, and be out two or three days together, where he heard of Game, and oftentimes *Villenoys* and he would be a whole Week at a time exercising in this Sport, for there was no Game near at hand. This young Lord had sent him a Letter, to invite him fifteen Miles farther than his own *Villa*, to hunt, and appointed to meet him at his Country House, in order to go in search of this promis'd Game; So that *Villenoys* got about a Week's Provision, of what Necessaries he thought he should want in that time; and taking only his *Valet*, who lov'd the Sport, he left *Isabella* for a Week to her Devotion, and her other innocent Diversions of fine Work, at which she was Excellent, and left the Town to go meet this young Challenger.

When *Villenoys* was at any time out, it was the custom of *Isabella* to retire to her Chamber, and to receive no Visits, not even the Ladies, so absolutely she devoted her self to her

Husband: All the first day she pass'd over in this manner, and Evening being come, she order'd her Supper to be brought to her Chamber, and, because it was Washing-day the next day, she order'd all her Maids to go very early to Bed, that they might be up betimes, and to leave only *Maria* to attend her; which was accordingly done. This *Maria* was a young Maid, that was very discreet, and, of all things in the World, lov'd her Lady, whom she had liv'd with, ever since she came from the *Monastery*.

When all were in Bed, and the little light Supper just carry'd up to the Lady, and only, as I said, *Maria* attending, some body knock'd at the Gate, it being about Nine of the Clock at Night; so *Maria* snatching up a Candle, went to the Gate, to see who it might be; when she open'd the Door, she found a Man in a very odd Habit, and a worse Countenance, and asking, Who he would speak with? He told her, Her Lady: My Lady (reply'd *Maria*) does not use to receive Visits at this hour; Pray, what is your Business? He reply'd, That which I will deliver only to your Lady, and that she may give me Admittance, pray, deliver her this Ring: And pulling off a small Ring, with *Isabella's* Name and Hair in it, he gave it *Maria*, who, shutting the Gate upon him, went in with the Ring; as soon as *Isabella* saw it, she was ready to swound on the Chair where she sate, and cry'd, Where had you this? *Maria* reply'd, An old rusty Fellow at the Gate gave it me, and desired, it might be his Pasport to you; I ask'd his Name, but he said, You knew him not, but he had great News to tell you. *Isabella* reply'd, (almost swounding again) Oh, *Maria*! I am ruin'd. The Maid, all this while, knew not what she meant, nor, that that was a Ring given to *Henault* by her Mistress, but endeavouring to recover her, only ask'd her, What she should say to the old Messenger? *Isabella* bid her bring him up to her, (she had scarce Life to utter these last words) and before she was well recover'd, *Maria* enter'd with the Man; and *Isabella* making a Sign to her, to depart the Room, she was left alone with him.

Henault (for it was he) stood trembling and speechless before her, giving her leisure to take a strict Survey of him; at first finding no Feature nor Part of *Henault* about him, her Fears began to lessen, and she hop'd, it was not he, as her first Apprehensions had suggested; when he (with the Tears of Joy standing in his Eyes, and not daring suddenly to approach her, for fear of encreasing that Disorder he saw in her pale Face) began to speak to her, and cry'd, Fair Creature! is there no Remains of your *Henault* left in this Face of mine, all o'ergrown with Hair? Nothing in these Eyes, sunk with eight Years Absence from you, and Sorrows? Nothing in this Shape, bow'd with Labour and Griefs, that can inform you? I was once that happy Man you lov'd! At these words, Tears stop'd his Speech, and *Isabella* kept them Company, for yet she wanted Words. Shame and Confusion fill'd her Soul, and she was not able to lift her Eyes up, to consider the Face of him, whose Voice she knew so perfectly well. In one moment, she run over a thousand Thoughts. She finds, by his Return, she is not only expos'd to all the Shame imaginable; to all the Upbraiding, on his part, when he shall know she is marry'd to another; but all the Fury and Rage of *Villenoys*, and the Scorn of the Town, who will look on her as an Adulteress: She sees *Henault* poor, and knew, she must fall from all the Glory and Tranquility she had for five happy Years triumph'd in; in which time, she had known no Sorrow, or Care, tho' she had endur'd a thousand with *Henault*. She dyes, to think, however, that he should know, she had been so lightly in Love with him, to marry again; and she dyes, to think, that *Villenoys* must see her again in the Arms of *Henault*; besides, she could not recal her Love, for Love, like Reputation, once fled, never returns more. 'Tis impossible to love, and cease to love, (and love another) and yet return again to the first Passion, tho' the Person have all the Charms, or a thousand times more than it had, when it first conquer'd. This Mistery in Love, it may be, is not generally known, but nothing is more certain. One may a while suffer the Flame to languish, but here may be a reviving Spark in the Ashes, rak'd up, that may burn anew; but when 'tis quite extinguish'd, it never returns or rekindles.

'Twas so with the Heart of *Isabella*; had she believ'd, *Henault* had been living, she had lov'd to the last moment of their Lives; but, alas! the Dead are soon forgotten, and she now lov'd only *Villenoys*.

After they had both thus silently wept, with very different sentiments, she thought 'twas time to speak; and dissembling as well as she could, she caress'd him in her Arms, and told him, She could not express her Surprize and Joy for his Arrival. If she did not Embrace him heartily, or speak so Passionately as she us'd to do, he fancy'd it her Confusion, and his being in a condition not so fit to receive Embraces from her; and evaded them as much as 'twas possible for him to do, in respect to her, till he had dress'd his Face, and put himself in order; but the Supper being just brought up, when he knock'd, she order'd him to sit down and Eat, and he desir'd her not to let *Maria* know who he was, to see how long it would be, before she knew him or would call him to mind. But *Isabella* commanded *Maria*, to make up a Bed in such a Chamber, without disturbing her Fellows, and dismiss'd her from waiting at Table. The Maid admir'd, what strange, good, and joyful News, this Man had brought her Mistress, that he was so Treated, and alone with her, which never any Man had yet been; but she never imagin'd the Truth, and knew her Lady's Prudence too well, to question her Conduct. While they were at Supper, *Isabella* oblig'd him to tell her, How he came to be reported Dead; of which, she receiv'd Letters, both from Monsieur *Villenoys*, and the Duke of *Beaufort*, and by his Man the News, who saw him Dead? He told her, That, after the Fight, of which, first, he gave her an account, he being left among the Dead, when the Enemy came to Plunder and strip 'em, they found, he had Life in him, and appearing as an Eminent Person, they thought it better Booty to save me, (continu'd he) and get my Ransom, than to strip me, and bury me among the Dead; so they bore me off to a Tent, and recover'd me to Life; and, after that, I was recover'd of my Wounds, and sold, by the Soldier that had taken me, to a Spahee, who kept me a Slave, setting a great Ransom on me, such as I was not able to pay. I writ several times, to give you, and my Father, an account of my Misery, but receiv'd no Answer, and endur'd seven Years of Dreadful Slavery: When I found, at last, an opportunity to make my Escape, and from that time, resolv'd, never to cut the Hair of this Beard, till I should either see my dearest *Isabella* again, or hear some News of her. All that I fear'd, was, That she was Dead; and, at that word, he fetch'd a deep Sigh; and viewing all things so infinitely more Magnificent than he had left 'em, or, believ'd, she could afford; and, that she was far more Beautiful in Person, and Rich in Dress, than when he left her: He had a thousand Torments of Jealousie that seiz'd him, of which, he durst not make any mention, but rather chose to wait a little, and see, whether she had lost her Virtue: He desir'd, he might send for a Barber, to put his Face in some handsomer Order, and more fit for the Happiness 'twas that Night to receive; but she told him, No Dress, no Disguise, could render him more Dear and Acceptable to her, and that to morrow was time enough, and that his Travels had render'd him more fit for Repose, than Dressing. So that after a little while, they had talk'd over all they had a mind to say, all that was very indearing on his side, and as much Concern as she could force, on hers; she conducted him to his Chamber, which was very rich, and which gave him a very great addition of Jealousie: However, he suffer'd her to help him to Bed, which she seem'd to do, with all the tenderness in the World; and when she had seen him laid, she said, She would go to her Prayers, and come to him as soon as she had done, which being before her usual Custom, it was not a wonder to him she stay'd long, and he, being extreamly tir'd with his Journy, fell asleep. 'Tis true, *Isabella* essay'd to Pray, but alas! it was in vain, she was distracted with a thousand Thoughts what to do, which the more she thought, the more it distracted her; she was a thousand times about to end her Life, and, at one stroke, rid her self of the Infamy, that, she saw, must inevitably fall upon her; but Nature was frail, and the Tempter strong: And after a thousand Convulsions, even

worse than Death it self, she resolv'd upon the Murder of
Henault, as the only means of removing all Obstacles to her
future Happiness; she resolv'd on this, but after she had done
so, she was seiz'd with so great Horror, that she imagin'd, if she
perform'd it, she should run Mad; and yet, if she did not, she
should be also Frantick, with the Shames and Miseries that
would befal her; and believing the Murder the least Evil, since
she could never live with him, she fix'd her Heart on that; and
causing her self to be put immediately to Bed, in her own Bed,
she made *Maria* go to hers, and when all was still, she softly
rose, and taking a Candle with her, only in her Night-Gown and
Slippers, she goes to the Bed of the Unfortunate *Henault*, with
a Penknife in her hand; but considering, she knew not how to
conceal the Blood, should she cut his Throat, she resolves to
Strangle him, or Smother him with a Pillow; that last thought
was no sooner borne, but put in Execution; and, as he soundly
slept, she smother'd him without any Noise, or so much as his
Strugling; But when she had done this dreadful Deed, and saw
the dead Corps of her once-lov'd Lord, lye Smiling (as it were)
upon her, she fell into a Swound with the Horror of the Deed,
and it had been well for her she had there dy'd; but she reviv'd
again, and awaken'd to more and new Horrors, she flyes all
frighted from the Chamber, and fancies, the Phantom of her
dead Lord persues her; she runs from Room to Room, and
starts and stares, as if she saw him continually before her. Now
all that was ever Soft and Dear to her, with him, comes into her
Heart, and, she finds, he conquers anew, being Dead, who
could not gain her Pity, while Living.

While she was thus flying from her Guilt, in vain, she hears
one knock with Authority at the Door: She is now more
affrighted, if possible, and knows not whither to fly for Refuge;
she fancies, they are already the Officers of Justice, and that
Ten thousand Tortures and Wrecks are fastening on her, to
make her confess the horrid Murder; the knocking increases,
and so loud, that the Laundry Maids believing it to be the
Woman that us'd to call them up, and help them to Wash, rose,

and, opening the Door, let in *Villenoys*; who having been at his Country *Villa*, and finding there a Footman, instead of his Friend, who waited to tell him, His Master was fallen sick of the Small Pox, and could not wait on him, he took Horse, and came back to his lovely *Isabella*; but running up, as he us'd to do, to her Chamber, he found her not, and seeing a Light in another Room, he went in, but found *Isabella* flying from him, out at another Door, with all the speed she could, he admires at this Action, and the more, because his Maid told him Her Lady had been a Bed a good while; he grows a little Jealous, and persues her, but still she flies; at last he caught her in his Arms, where she fell into a swound, but quickly recovering, he set her down in a Chair, and, kneeling before her, implor'd to know what she ayl'd, and why she fled from him, who ador'd her? She only fix'd a ghastly Look upon him, and said, She was not well: "Oh! (said he) put not me off with such poor Excuses, *Isabella* never fled from me, when Ill, but came to my Arms, and to my Bosom, to find a Cure; therefore, tell me, what's the matter?" At that, she fell a weeping in a most violent manner, and cry'd, She was for ever undone: He, being mov'd with Love and Compassion, conjur'd her to tell what she ayl'd: "Ah! (said she) thou and I, and all of us, are undone!" At this, he lost all Patience, and rav'd, and cry'd, Tell me, and tell me immediately, what's the matter? When she saw his Face pale, and his Eyes fierce, she fell on her knees, and cry'd, "Oh! you can never Pardon me, if I should tell you, and yet, alas! I am innocent of Ill, by all that's good, I am." But her Conscience accusing her at that word, she was silent. If thou art Innocent, said *Villenoys*, taking her up in his Arms, and kissing her wet Face, "By all that's Good, I Pardon thee, what ever thou hast done.' 'Alas! (said she) Oh! but I dare not name it, 'till you swear." "By all that's Sacred, (reply'd he) and by whatever Oath you can oblige me to; by my inviolable Love to thee, and by thy own dear Self, I swear, whate'er it be, I do forgive thee; I know, thou art too good to commit a Sin I may not with Honour, pardon."

With this, and hearten'd by his Caresses, she told him, That

Henault was return'd; and repeating to him his Escape, she said, She had put him to Bed, and when he expected her to come, she fell on her Knees at the Bedside, and confess'd, She was married to *Villenoys*; at that word (said she) he fetch'd a deep Sigh or two, and presently after, with a very little struggling, dy'd; and, yonder, he lyes still in the Bed. After this, she wept so abundantly, that all *Villenoys* could do, could hardly calm her Spirits; but after, consulting what they should do in this Affair, *Villenoys* ask'd her, Who of the House saw him? She said, Only *Maria*, who knew not who he was; so that, resolving to save *Isabella's* Honour, which was the only Misfortune to come, *Villenoys* himself propos'd the carrying him out to the Bridge, and throwing him into the River, where the Stream would carry him down to the Sea, and lose him; or, if he were found, none could know him. So *Villenoys* took a Candle, and went and look'd on him, and found him altogether chang'd, that no Body would know who he was; he therefore put on his Clothes, which was not hard for him to do, for he was scarce yet cold, and comforting again *Isabella*, as well as he could, he went himself into the Stable, and fetched a Sack, such as they us'd for Oats, a new Sack, whereon stuck a great Needle, with a Pack-thread in it; this Sack he brings into the House, and shews to *Isabella*, telling her, He would put the Body in there, for the better convenience of carrying it on his Back. *Isabella* all this while said but little, but, fill'd with Thoughts all Black and Hellish, she ponder'd within, while the Fond and Passionate *Villenoys* was endeavouring to hide her Shame, and to make this an absolute Secret: She imagin'd, that could she live after a Deed so black, *Villenoys* would be eternal reproaching her, if not with his Tongue, at least with his Heart, and embolden'd by one Wickedness, she was the readier for another, and another of such a Nature, as has, in my Opinion, far less Excuse, than the first; but when Fate begins to afflict, she goes through stitch with her Black Work.

When *Villenoys*, who would, for the Safety of *Isabella's* Honour, be the sole Actor in the disposing of this Body; and since he was Young, Vigorous, and Strong, and able to bear it, would trust no one with the Secret, he having put up the Body, and ty'd it fast, set it on a Chair, turning his Back towards it, with the more conveniency to take it upon his Back, bidding *Isabella* give him the two Corners of the Sack in his Hands; telling her, They must do this last office for the Dead, more, in order to the securing their Honour and Tranquility hereafter, than for any other Reason, and bid her be of good Courage, till he came back, for it was not far to the Bridge, and it being the dead of the Night, he should pass well enough. When he had the Sack on his Back, and ready to go with it, she cry'd, Stay, my Dear, some of his Clothes hang out, which I will put in; and, with that, taking the Pack-needle with the Thread, sew'd the Sack, with several strong Stitches, to the Collar of *Villenoy's* Coat, without his perceiving it, and bid him go now; and when you come to the Bridge, (said she) and that you are throwing him over the Rail, (which is not above Breast high) be sure you give him a good swing, least the Sack should hang on any thing at the side of the Bridge, and not fall into the Stream; I'le warrant you, (said *Villenoys*) I know how to secure his falling. And going his way with it, Love lent him Strength, and he soon arriv'd at the Bridge; where, turning his Back to the Rail, and heaving the Body over, he threw himself with all his force backward, the better to swing the Body into the River, whose weight (it being made fast to his Collar) pull'd *Villenoys* after it, and both the live and the dead Man falling into the River, which, being rapid at the Bridge, soon drown'd him, especially when so great a weight hung to his Neck; so that he dy'd, without considering what was the occasion of his Fate.

Isabella remain'd the most part of the Night sitting in her Chamber, without going to Bed, to see what would become of her Damnable Design; but when it was towards Morning, and she heard no News, she put herself into Bed, but not to find Repose or Rest there, for that she thought impossible, after so great a Barbarity as she had committed; No, (said she) it is but just I should for ever wake, who have, in one fatal Night, destroy'd two such Innocents. Oh! what Fate, what Destiny, is mine? Under what cursed Planet was I born, that Heaven it self could not divert my Ruine? It was not many Hours since I thought my self the most happy and blest of Women, and now am fallen to the Misery of one of the worst Fiends of Hell.

Such were her Thoughts, and such her Cryes, till the Light brought on new Matter for Grief; for, about Ten of the Clock, News was brought, that Two Men were found dead in the River, and that they were carry'd to the Town-Hall, to lye there, till they were own'd: Within an hour after, News was brought in, that one of these Unhappy Men was *Villenoys*; his *Valet*, who, all this while, imagin'd him in Bed with his Lady, ran to the Hall, to undeceive the People, for he knew, if his Lord were gone out, he should have been call'd to Dress him; but finding it, as 'twas reported, he fell a weeping, and wringing his Hands, in a most miserable manner, he ran home with the News; where, knocking at his Lady's Chamber Door, and finding it fast lock'd, he almost hop'd again, he was deceiv'd; but *Isabella* rising, and opening the Door, *Maria* first enter'd weeping, with the News, and then brought the *Valet*, to testify the fatal Truth of it. *Isabella*, tho' it were nothing but what she expected to hear, almost swounded in her Chair; nor did she feign it, but felt really all the Pangs of Killing Grief; and was so alter'd with her Night's Watching and Grieving, that this new Sorrow look'd very Natural in her. When she was recover'd, she asked a thousand Questions about him, and question'd the Possibility of it; for (said she) he went out this Morning early from me, and had no signs, in his Face, of any Grief or Discontent. Alas! (said the *Valet*) Madam, he is not his own Murderer, some one has done it in Revenge; and then told her, how he was found fasten'd to a Sack, with a dead strange Man ty'd up within it; and every body concludes, that they were both first murder'd, and then drawn to the River, and thrown both in. At the Relation of this Strange Man, she seem'd more amaz'd than before, and commanding the *Valet* to go to the Hall, and to take Order about the Coroner's sitting on the Body of *Villenoys*, and then to have it

193

brought home: She called *Maria* to her, and, after bidding her shut the Door, she cry'd, Ah, *Maria*! I will tell thee what my Heart imagins; but first, (said she) run to the Chamber of the Stranger, and see, if he be still in Bed, which I fear he is not; she did so, and brought word, he was gone; then (said she) my Forebodings are true. When I was in Bed last night, with *Villenoys* (and at that word, she sigh'd as if her Heart-Strings had broken) I told him, I had lodg'd a Stranger in my House, who was by, when my first Lord and Husband fell in Battel; and that, after the Fight, finding him yet alive, he spoke to him, and gave him that Ring you brought me last Night; and conjur'd him, if ever his Fortune should bring him to *Flanders*, to see me, and give me that Ring, and tell me—(with that, she wept, and could scarce speak) a thousand tender and endearing things, and then dy'd in his Arms. For my dear *Henault's* sake (said she) I us'd him nobly, and dismiss'd you that Night, because I was asham'd to have any Witness of the Griefs I paid his Memory: All this I told to *Villenoys*, whom I found disorder'd; and, after a sleepless Night, I fancy he got up, and took this poor Man, and has occasion'd his Death: At that, she wept anew, and *Maria*, to whom, all that her Mistress said, was Gospel, verily believ'd it so, without examining Reason; and *Isabella* conjuring her, since none of the House knew of the old Man's being there, (for Old he appear'd to be) that she would let it for ever be a Secret, and, to this she bound her by an Oath; so that none knowing *Henault*, altho' his Body was expos'd there for three Days to Publick View: When the Coroner had Set on the Bodies, he found, they had been first Murder'd some way or other, and then afterwards tack'd together, and thrown into the River, they brought the Body of *Villenoys* home to his House, where, it being laid on a Table, all the House infinitely bewail'd it; and *Isabella* did nothing but swound away, almost as fast as she recover'd Life; however, she would, to compleat her Misery, be led to see this dreadful Victim of her Cruelty, and, coming near the Table, the Body, whose Eyes were before close shut, now open'd themselves wide, and fix'd them on *Isabella*, who, giving a great Schreek, fell down in a swound, and the Eyes clos'd again; they had much ado to bring her to Life, but, at last, they did so, and led her back to her Bed, where she remain'd a good while. Different Opinions and Discourses were made, concerning the opening of the Eyes of the Dead Man, and viewing *Isabella*; but she was a Woman of so admirable a Life and Conversation, of so undoubted a Piety and Sanctity of Living, that not the least Conjecture could be made, of her having a hand in it, besides the improbability of it; yet the whole thing was a Mystery, which, they thought, they ought to look into: But a few Days after, the Body of *Villenoys* being interr'd in a most magnificent manner, and, by Will all he had, was long since setled on *Isabella*, the World, instead of Suspecting her, Ador'd her the more, and every Body of Quality was already hoping to be next, tho' the fair Mourner still kept her Bed, and Languish'd daily.

It happen'd, not long after this, there came to the Town a *French* Gentleman, who was taken at the Siege of *Candia*, and was Fellow-Slave with *Henault*, for seven Years, in *Turky*, and who had escap'd with *Henault*, and came as far as *Liege* with him, where, having some Business and Acquaintance with a Merchant, he stay'd some time; but when he parted with *Henault*, he ask'd him, Where he should find him in *Flanders?* *Henault* gave him a Note, with his Name, and Place of Abode, if his Wife were alive; if not, to enquire at his Sister's, or his Father's. This *French* Man came at last, to the very House of *Isabella*, enquiring for this Man, and receiv'd a strange Answer, and was laugh'd at; He found, that was the House, and that the Lady; and enquiring about the Town, and speaking of *Henault's* Return, describing the Man, it was quickly discover'd, to be the same that was in the Sack: He had his Friend taken up (for he was buried) and found him the same, and, causing a *Barber* to Trim him, when his bushy Beard was off, a great many People remember'd him; and the *French* Man affirming, he went to his own Home, all *Isabella's* Family, and her self, were cited before the Magistrate of Justice, where, as soon as she was accus'd, she confess'd the whole Matter of Fact, and, without any Disorder, deliver'd her self in the Hands of Justice, as the Murderess of two Husbands (both belov'd) in one Night: The whole World stood amaz'd at this; who knew her Life a Holy and Charitable Life, and how dearly and well she had liv'd with her Husbands, and every one bewail'd her Misfortune, and she alone was the only Person, that was not afflicted for her self; she was Try'd, and Condemn'd to lose her Head; which Sentence, she joyfully receiv'd, and said, Heaven, and her Judges, were too Merciful to her, and that her Sins had deserv'd much more.

While she was in Prison, she was always at Prayers, and very Chearful and Easie, distributing all she had amongst, and for the Use of, the Poor of the Town, especially to the Poor Widows; exhorting daily, the Young, and the Fair, that came perpetually to visit her, never to break a Vow; for that was first the Ruine of her, and she never since prosper'd, do whatever other good Deeds she could. When the day of Execution came, she appear'd on the Scaffold all in Mourning, but with a Meen so very Majestick and Charming, and a Face so surprizing Fair, where no Languishment or Fear appear'd, but all Chearful as a Bride, that she set all Hearts a flaming, even in that mortifying Minute of Preparation for Death: She made a Speech of half an Hour long, so Eloquent, so admirable a warning to the *Vow-Breakers*, that it was as amazing to hear her, as it was to behold her.

After she had done with the help of *Maria*, she put off her Mourning Vail, and, without any thing over her Face, she kneel'd down, and the Executioner, at one Blow, sever'd her Beautiful Head from her Delicate Body, being then in her Seven and Twentieth Year. She was generally Lamented, and Honourably Bury'd.

THE ADVENTURE OF THE
BLACK LADY

THE ADVENTURE OF THE BLACK LADY

About the Beginning of last *June* (as near as I can remember) *Bellamora* came to Town from *Hampshire*, and was obliged to lodge the first Night at the same Inn where the Stage-Coach set up. The next Day she took Coach for *Covent-Garden*, where she thought to find Madam *Brightly*, a Relation of hers, with whom she design'd to continue for about half a Year undiscover'd, if possible, by her Friends in the Country: and order'd therefore her Trunk, with her Clothes, and most of her Money and Jewels, to be brought after her to Madame *Brightly's* by a strange Porter, whom she spoke to in the Street as she was taking Coach; being utterly unacquainted with the neat Practices of this fine City. When she came to *Bridges-Street*, where indeed her Cousin had lodged near three or four Years since, she was strangely surprized that she could not learn anything of her; no, nor so much as meet with anyone that had ever heard of her Cousin's Name: Till, at last, describing Madam *Brightly* to one of the House-keepers in that Place, he told her, that there was such a kind of Lady, whom he had sometimes seen there about a Year and a half ago; but that he believed she was married and remov'd towards *Sobo*. In this Perplexity she quite forgot her Trunk and Money, *&c*, and wander'd in her Hackney-Coach all over St. *Anne's* Parish; inquiring for Madam *Brightly*, still describing her Person, but in vain; for no Soul could give her any Tale or Tidings of such a Lady. After she had thus fruitlessly rambled, till she, the Coachman, and the very Horses were even tired, by good Fortune for her, she happen'd on a private House, where lived a good, discreet, ancient Gentlewoman, who was fallen to Decay, and forc'd to let Lodgings for the best Part of her Livelihood: From whom she understood, that there was such a kind of Lady, who had lain there somewhat more than a Twelvemonth, being near three Months after she was married; but that she was now gone abroad with the Gentleman her Husband, either to the Play, or to take the fresh Air; and she believ'd would not return till Night. This Discourse of the Good Gentlewoman's so elevated *Bellamora's* drooping Spirits, that after she had beg'd the liberty of staying there till they came home, she discharg'd the Coachman in all haste, still forgetting her Trunk, and the more valuable Furniture of it.

When they were alone, *Bellamora* desired she might be permitted the Freedom to send for a Pint of Sack; which, with some little Difficulty, was at last allow'd her. They began then to chat for a matter of half an Hour of things indifferent: and at length the ancient Gentlewoman ask'd the fair Innocent (I must not say foolish) one, of what Country, and what her Name was: to both which she answer'd directly and truly, tho' it might have prov'd not discreetly. She then enquir'd of *Bellamora* if her Parents were living, and the Occasion of her coming to Town. The fair unthinking Creature reply'd, that her Father and Mother were both dead; and that she had escap'd from her Uncle, under the pretence of making a Visit to a young Lady, her Cousin, who was lately married, and liv'd above twenty Miles from her Uncle's, in the Road to *London*, and that the Cause of her quitting the Country, was to avoid the hated Importunities of a Gentleman, whose pretended Love to her she fear'd had been her eternal Ruin. At which she wept and sigh'd most extravagantly. The discreet Gentlewoman endeavour'd to comfort her by all the softest and most powerful Arguments in her Capacity; promising her all the friendly Assistance that she could expect from her, during *Bellamora's* stay in Town: which she did with so much Earnestness, and visible Integrity, that the pretty innocent Creature was going to make her a full and real Discovery of her imaginary insupportable Misfortunes; and (doubtless) had done it, had she not been prevented by the Return of the Lady, whom she hop'd to have found her Cousin *Brightly*. The Gentleman, her Husband just saw her within Doors, and orderd the Coach to drive to some of his Bottle-Companions; which gave the Women the better Opportunity of entertaining one another, which happen'd to be with some Surprize on all

Sides. As the Lady was going up into her Apartment, the Gentlewoman of the House told her there was a young Lady in the Parlour, who came out of the Country that very Day on purpose to visit her: The Lady stept immediately to see who it was, and *Bellamora* approaching to receive her hop'd-for Cousin, stop'd on the sudden just as she came to her; and sigh'd out aloud, Ah, Madam! I am lost—It is not your Ladyship I seek. No, Madam (return'd the other) I am apt to think you did not intend me this Honour. But you are as welcome to me, as you could be to the dearest of your Acquaintance: Have you forgot me, Madame *Bellamora*? (continued she.) That Name startled the other: However, it was with a kind of Joy. Alas! Madam, (replied the young one) I now remember that I have been so happy to have seen you; but where and when, my Memory can't tell me. 'Tis indeed some Years since, (return'd the Lady) But of that another time.—Mean while, if you are unprovided of a Lodging, I dare undertake, you shall be welcome to this Gentlewoman. The Unfortunate returned her Thanks; and whilst a Chamber was preparing for her, the Lady entertain'd her in her own. About Ten o'Clock they parted, *Bellamora* being conducted to her Lodging by the Mistress of the House, who then left her to take what Rest she could amidst her so many Misfortunes; returning to the other Lady, who desir'd her to search into the Cause of *Bellamora's* Retreat to Town.

The next Morning the good Gentlewoman of the House coming up to her, found *Bellamora* almost drown'd in Tears, which by many kind and sweet Words she at last stopp'd; and asking whence so great Signs of Sorrow should proceed, vow'd a most profound Secrecy if she would discover to her their Occasion; which, after some little Reluctancy, she did, in this manner.

I was courted (said she) above three Years ago, when my Mother was yet living, by one Mr. *Fondlove*, a Gentleman of good Estate, and true Worth; and one who, I dare believe, did then really love me: He continu'd his Passion for me, with all the earnest and honest Sollicitations imaginable, till some Months before my Mother's Death; who, at that time, was most desirous to see me disposed of in Marriage to another Gentleman, of much better Estate than Mr. *Fondlove*; but one whose Person and Humour did by no means hit with my Inclinations: And this gave *Fondlove* the unhappy Advantage over me. For, finding me one Day all alone in my Chamber, and lying on my Bed, in as mournful and wretched a Condition to my then foolish Apprehension, as now I am, he urged his Passion with such Violence, and accursed Success for me, with reiterated Promises of Marriage, whensoever I pleas'd to challenge 'em, which he bound with the most sacred Oaths, and most dreadful Execrations: that partly with my Aversion to the other, and partly with my Inclinations to pity him, I ruin'd my self.—Here she relaps'd into a greater Extravagance of Grief than before; which was so extreme that it did not continue long. When therefore she was pretty well come to herself, the antient Gentlewoman ask'd her, why she imagin'd herself ruin'd: To which she answer'd, I am great with Child by him, Madam, and wonder you did not perceive it last Night. Alas! I have not a Month to go: I am asham'd, ruin'd, and damn'd, I fear, for ever lost. Oh! fie, Madam, think not so, (said the other) for the Gentleman may yet prove true, and marry you. Ay, Madam (replied *Bellamora*) I doubt not that he would marry me; for soon after my Mother's Death, when I came to be at my own Disposal, which happen'd about two Months after, he offer'd, nay most earnestly sollicited me to it, which still he perseveres to do. This is strange! (return'd the other) and it appears to me to be your own Fault, that you are yet miserable. Why did you not, or why will you not consent to your own Happiness? Alas! (cry'd *Bellamora*) 'tis the only Thing I dread in this World: For, I am certain, he can never love me after. Besides, ever since I have abhorr'd the Sight of him: and this is the only Cause that obliges me to forsake my Uncle, and all my Friends and Relations in the Country, hoping in this populous and publick Place to be most private, especially, Madam, in your House, and in your Fidelity and Discretion. Of the last you may assure yourself, Madam, (said the other:) but what Provision have you made for the Reception of the young Stranger that you carry about you? Ah, Madam! (cryd *Bellamora*) you have brought to my Mind another Misfortune: Then she acquainted her with the suppos'd loss of her Money and Jewels, telling her withall, that she had but three Guineas and some Silver left, and the Rings she wore, in her present possession. The good Gentlewoman of the House told her, she would send to enquire at the Inn where she lay the first Night she came to Town; for, haply, they might give some Account of the Porter to whom she had entrusted her Trunk; and withal repeated her Promise of all the Help in her Power, and for that time left her much more compos'd than she found her. The good Gentlewoman went directly to the other Lady, her Lodger, to whom she recounted *Bellamora's* mournful Confession; at which the Lady appear'd mightily concern'd: and at last she told her Landlady, that she would take Care that *Bellamora* should lie in according to her Quality: For, added she, the Child, it seems, is my own Brother's.

As soon as she had din'd, she went to the *Exchange*, and bought Child-bed Linen; but desired that *Bellamora* might not have the least Notice of it: And at her return dispatch'd a Letter to her Brother *Fondlove* in *Hampshire*, with an Account of every Particular; which soon brought him up to Town, without satisfying any of his or her Friends with the Reason of his sudden Departure. Mean while, the good Gentlewoman of the House had sent to the *Star Inn* on *Fish-street-Hill*, to demand the Trunk, which she rightly suppos'd to have been carried back thither: For by good Luck, it was a Fellow that ply'd thereabouts, who brought it to *Bellamora's* Lodgings that very Night, but unknown to her. *Fondlove* no sooner got to *London*, but he posts to his Sister's Lodgings, where he was advis'd not to be seen of *Bellamora* till they had work'd farther upon her, which the Landlady began in this manner; she told her that her Things were miscarried, and she fear'd, lost; that she had but a little Money her self, and if the Overseers of the Poor (justly so call'd from their over-looking 'em) should have the least Suspicion of a strange and unmarried Person, who was entertain'd in her House big with Child, and so near her Time as *Bellamora* was, she should be troubled, if they could not give Security to the Parish to twenty or thirty Pounds, that they should not suffer by her, which she could not; or otherwise she must be sent to the House of Correction, and her Child to a Parish-Nurse. This Discourse, one may imagine, was very dreadful to a Person of her Youth, Beauty, Education, Family and Estate: However, she resolutely protested, that she had rather undergo all this, than be expos'd to the Scorn of her Friends and Relations in the Country. The other told her then, that she must write down to her Uncle a Farewell-Letter, as if she were just going aboard the Pacquet-Boat for *Holland*, that he might not send to enquire for her in Town, when he should understand she was not at her new-married Cousin's in the Country; which accordingly she did, keeping her self close Prisoner to her Chamber; where she was daily visited by *Fondlove's* Sister and the Landlady, but by no Soul else, the first dissembling the Knowledge she had of her Misfortunes. Thus she continued for above three Weeks, not a Servant being suffer'd to enter her Chamber, so much as to make her Bed, lest they should take Notice of her great Belly: but for all this Caution, the Secret had taken Wind, by the means of an Attendant of the other Lady below, who had over-heard her speaking of it to her Husband. This soon got out of Doors, and spread abroad, till it reach'd the long Ears of the Wolves of the Parish, who next Day design'd to pay her a Visit: But *Fondlove*, by good Providence, prevented it; who, the Night before, was usher'd into *Bellamora's* Chamber by his Sister, his Brother-in-Law, and the Landlady. At the Sight of him she had like to have swoon'd away: but he taking her in his Arms, began again, as he was wont to do, with Tears in his Eyes, to beg that she would marry him ere she was deliver'd; if not for his, nor her own, yet for the Child's Sake, which she hourly expected; that it might not be born out of Wedlock, and so be made uncapable of inheriting either of their Estates; with a great many more pressing Arguments on all Sides: To which at last she consented; and an honest officious Gentleman, whom they had before provided, was call'd up, who made an End of the Dispute: So to Bed they went together that Night; next Day to the *Exchange*, for several pretty Businesses that Ladies in her Condition want. Whilst they were abroad, came the Vermin of the Parish, (I mean, the Overseers of the Poor, who eat the Bread from 'em) to search for a young Blackhair'd Lady (for so was *Bellamora*) who was either brought to Bed, or just ready to lie down. The Landlady shew'd 'em all the Rooms in her House, but no such Lady could be found. At last she bethought her self, and led 'em into her Parlour, where she open'd a little Closet-door, and shew'd 'em a black Cat that had just kitten'd: assuring 'em, that she should never trouble the Parish as long as she had Rats or Mice in the House; and so dismiss'd 'em like Loggerheads as they came.

THE COURT OF THE KING
OF BANTAM

THE COURT OF THE KING OF BANTAM

This Money certainly is a most devilish Thing! I'm sure the Want of it had like to have ruin'd my dear *Philibella*, in her Love to *Valentine Goodland*; who was really a pretty deserving Gentleman, Heir to about fifteen hundred Pounds a Year; which, however, did not so much recommend him, as the Sweetness of his Temper, the Comeliness of his Person, and the Excellency of his Parts: In all which Circumstances my obliging Acquaintance equal'd him, unless in the Advantage of their Fortune. Old Sir *George Goodland* knew of his Son's Passion for *Philibella*; and tho' he was generous, and of a Humour sufficiently complying, yet he could by no means think it convenient, that his only Son should marry with a young Lady of so slender a Fortune as my Friend, who had not above five hundred Pound, and that the Gift of her Uncle Sir *Philip Friendly*: tho' her Virtue and Beauty might have deserv'd, and have adorn'd the Throne of an *Alexander* or a *Cæsar*.

Sir *Philip* himself, indeed, was but a younger Brother, tho' of a good Family, and of a generous Education; which, with his Person, Bravery, and Wit, recommended him to his Lady *Philadelphia*, Widow of Sir *Bartholomew Banquier*, who left her possess'd of two thousand Pounds *per Annum*, besides twenty thousand Pounds in Money and Jewels; which oblig'd him to get himself dubb'd, that she might not descend to an inferior Quality. When he was in Town, he liv'd—let me see! in the *Strand*; or, as near as I can remember, somewhere about *Charing-Cross*; where first of all Mr. *Would-be King*, a Gentleman of a large Estate in Houses, Land and Money, of a haughty, extravagant and profuse Humour, very fond of every new Face, had the Misfortune to fall passionately in love with *Philibella*, who then liv'd with her Uncle.

This Mr. *Would-be* it seems had often been told, when he was yet a Stripling, either by one of his Nurses, or his own Grandmother, or by some other Gypsy, that he should infallibly be what his Sirname imply'd, a King, by Providence or Chance, ere he dy'd, or never. This glorious Prophecy had so great an Influence on all his Thoughts and Actions, that he distributed and dispers'd his Wealth sometimes so largely, that one would have thought he had undoubtedly been King of some Part of the *Indies*; to see a Present made today of a Diamond Ring, worth two or three hundred Pounds, to Madam *Flippant*; tomorrow, a large Chest of the finest *China* to my Lady *Fleecewell*; and next Day, perhaps, a rich Necklace of large Oriental Pearl, with a Locket to it of Saphires, Emeralds, Rubies, *&c.*, to pretty Miss *Ogle-me*, for an amorous Glance, for a Smile, and (it may be, tho' but rarely) for the mighty Blessing of one single Kiss. But such were his Largesses, not to reckon his Treats, his Balls, and Serenades besides, tho' at the same time he had marry'd a virtuous Lady, and of good Quality: But her Relation to him (it may be fear'd) made her very disagreeable: For a Man of his Humour and Estate can no more be satisfy'd with one Woman, than with one Dish of Meat; and to say Truth, 'tis something unmodish. However, he might have dy'd a pure Celibate, and altogether unexpert of Women, had his good or bad Hopes only terminated in Sir *Philip's* Niece. But the brave and haughty Mr. *Would-be* was not to be baulk'd by Appearances of Virtue, which he thought all Womankind only did affect; besides, he promis'd himself the Victory over any Lady whom he attempted, by the Force of his damn'd Money, tho' her Virtue were ever so real and strict.

With *Philibella* he found another pretty young Creature, very like her, who had been a *quondam* Mistress to Sir *Philip*: He, with young *Goodland*, was then diverting his Mistress and Niece at a Game at Cards, when *Would-be* came to visit him; he found 'em very merry, with a Flask or two of Claret before 'em, and Oranges roasting by a large Fire, for it was *Christmas-time*. The Lady *Friendly* understanding that this extraordinary Man was with Sir *Philip* in the Parlour, came in to 'em, to make the number of both Sexes equal, as well as in Hopes to make up a Purse of Guineas toward the Purchase of some new fine

Business that she had in her Head, from his accustom'd Design of losing at Play to her. Indeed, she had Part of her Wish, for she got twenty Guineas of him; *Philibella* ten; and *Lucy*, Sir *Philip's* quondam, five: Not but that *Would-be* intended better Fortune to the young ones, than he did to Sir *Philip's* Lady; but her Ladyship was utterly unwilling to give him over to their Management, tho' at the last, when they were all tir'd with the Cards, after *Would-be* had said as many obliging things as his present Genius would give him leave, to *Philibella* and *Lucy*, especially to the first, not forgetting his Baisemains to the Lady *Friendly*, he bid the Knight and *Goodland* adieu; but with a Promise of repeating his Visit at six a-clock in the Evening on *Twelfth-Day*, to renew the famous and antient Solemnity of chusing King and Queen; to which Sir *Philip* before invited him, with a Design yet unknown to you, I hope.

As soon as he was gone, every one made their Remarks on him, but with very little or no Difference in all their Figures of him. In short, all Mankind, had they ever known him, would have universally agreed in this his Character, That he was an Original; since nothing in Humanity was ever so vain, so haughty, so profuse, so fond, and so ridiculously ambitious, as Mr. *Would-be King*. They laugh'd and talk'd about an Hour longer, and then young *Goodland* was oblig'd to see *Lucy* home in his Coach; tho' he had rather have sat up all Night in the same House with *Philibella*, I fancy, of whom he took but an unwilling Leave; which was visible enough to every one there, since they were all acquainted with his Passion for my fair Friend.

About twelve a-clock on the Day prefix'd, young *Goodland* came to dine with Sir *Philip*, whom he found just return'd from Court, in a very good Humour. On the Sight of *Valentine*, the Knight ran to him, and embracing him, told him, That he had prevented his Wishes, in coming thither before he sent for him, as he had just then design'd. The other return'd, that he therefore hoped he might be of some Service to him, by so happy a Prevention of his intended Kindness. No doubt (reply'd Sir *Philip*) the Kindness, I hope, will be to us both; I am assur'd it will, if you will act according to my Measures. I desire no better Prescriptions for my Happiness (return'd *Valentine*) than what you shall please to set down to me: But is it necessary or convenient that I should know 'em first? It is, (answer'd Sir *Philip*) let us sit, and you shall understand 'em.— I am very sensible (continu'd he) of your sincere and honourable Affection and Pretension to my Niece, who, perhaps, is as dear to me as my own Child could be, had I one; nor am I ignorant how averse Sir *George* your Father is to your Marriage with her, insomuch that I am confident he would disinherit you immediately upon it, merely for want of a Fortune somewhat proportionable to your Estate: but I have now contrived the Means to add two or three thousand Pounds to the five hundred I have design'd to give with her; I mean, if you marry her, *Val*, not otherwise; for I will not labour so for any other Man. What inviolable Obligations you put upon me! (cry'd *Goodland*.) No Return, by way of Compliments, good *Val*, (said the Knight:) Had I not engag'd to my Wife, before Marriage, that I would not dispose of any part of what she brought me, without her Consent, I would certainly make *Philibella's*. Fortune answerable to your Estate: And besides, my Wife is not yet full eight and twenty, and we may therefore expect Children of our own, which hinders me from proposing any thing more for the Advantage of my Niece.—But now to my Instructions;—*King* will be here this Evening without fail, and, at some Time or other tonight, will shew the Haughtiness of his Temper to you, I doubt not, since you are in a manner a Stranger to him: Be sure therefore you seem to quarrel with him before you part, but suffer as much as you can first from his Tongue; for I know he will give you Occasions enough to exercise your passive Valour. I must appear his Friend, and you must retire Home, if you please, for this Night, but let me see you as early as your Convenience will permit tomorrow: my late Friend *Lucy* must be my Niece too. Observe this, and leave the rest to me. I shall most punctually, and will in all things be directed by you, (said *Valentine*,) I had forgot to tell you (said *Friendly*) that I have so order'd matters, that he must be King tonight, and *Lucy* Queen, by the Lots in the Cake. By all means (return'd *Goodland*;) it must be Majesty.

Exactly at six a'clock came *Wou'd-be* in his Coach and six, and found Sir *Philip*, and his Lady, *Goodland*, *Philibella*, and *Lucy* ready to receive him; *Lucy* as fine as a Dutchess, and almost as beautiful as she was before her Fall. All things were in ample Order for his Entertainment. They play'd till Supper was serv'd in, which was between eight and nine. The Treat was very seasonable and splendid. Just as the second Course was set on the Table, they were all on a sudden surpriz'd, except *Would-be*, with a Flourish of Violins, and other Instruments, which proceeded to entertain 'em with the best and newest Airs in the last new Plays, being then in the Year 1683. The Ladies were curious to know to whom they ow'd the chearful part of their Entertainment: On which he call'd out, Hey! *Tom Farmer! Aleworth! Eccles! Hall!* and the rest of you! Here's a Health to these Ladies, and all this honourable Company. They bow'd; he drank, and commanded another Glass to be fill'd, into which he put something yet better than the Wine, I mean, ten Guineas: Here, *Farmer*, (said he then) this for you and your Friends. We humbly thank the honourable Mr. *Would-be King*. They all return'd, and struck up with more Spriteliness than before. For Gold and Wine, doubtless, are the best Rosin for Musicians.

After Supper they took a hearty Glass or two to the King, Queen, Duke, &c. And then the mighty Cake, teeming with the Fate of this extraordinary Personage, was brought in, the Musicians playing an Overture at the Entrance of the *Alimental Oracle*; which was then cut and consulted, and the royal Bean and Pea fell to those to whom Sir *Philip* had design'd 'em. 'Twas then the Knight began a merry Bumper, with three Huzza's, and, *Long live King* Would-be! to *Goodland*, who echo'd and pledg'd him, putting the Glass about to the harmonious Attendants; while the Ladies drank their own

213

Quantities among themselves, *To his aforesaid Majesty*. Then of course you may believe Queen *Lucy's* Health went merrily round, with the same Ceremony: After which he saluted his Royal Consort, and condescended to do the same Honour to the two other Ladies.

Then they fell a dancing, like Lightning; I mean, they mov'd as swift, and made almost as little Noise; But his Majesty was soon weary of that; for he long'd to be making love both to *Philibella* and *Lucy*, who (believe me) that Night might well enough have passed for a Queen.

They fell then to Questions and Commands; to cross Purposes: *I think a Thought, what is it like?* &c. In all which, his *Would-be* Majesty took the Opportunity of shewing the Excellency of his Parts, as, How fit he was to govern! How dextrous at mining and countermining! and, How he could reconcile the most contrary and distant Thoughts! The Musick, at last, good as it was, grew troublesome and too loud; which made him dismiss them: And then he began to this effect, addressing himself to *Philibella*: Madam, had Fortune been just, and were it possible that the World should be govern'd and influenc'd by two Suns, undoubtedly we had all been Subjects to you, from this Night's Chance, as well as to that Lady, who indeed alone can equal you in the Empire of Beauty, which yet you share with her Majesty here present, who only could dispute it with you, and is only superior to you in Title. My Wife is infinitely oblig'd to your Majesty, (interrupted Sir *Philip*) who in my Opinion, has greater Charms, and more than both of them together. You ought to think so, Sir *Philip* (returned the new dubb'd King) however you should not liberally have express'd your self, in Opposition and Derogation to Majesty:—Let me tell you 'tis a saucy Boldness that thus has loos'd your Tongue!—What think you, young Kinsman and Counsellor? (said he to *Goodland*.) With all Respect due to your sacred Title, (return'd *Valentene*, rising and bowing) Sir *Philip* spoke as became a truly affectionate Husband; and it had been Presumption in him, unpardonable, to have seem'd to prefer her Majesty, or that other sweet Lady, in his Thoughts, since your Majesty has been pleas'd to say so much and so particularly of their Merits: 'T would appear as if he durst lift up his Eyes, with Thoughts too near the Heaven you only would enjoy. And only can deserve, you should have added, (said *King*, no longer *Would-be*.) How! may it please your Majesty (cry'd *Friendly*) both my Nieces! tho' you deserve ten thousand more, and better, would your Majesty enjoy them both? Are they then both your Nieces? (asked *Chance's King*). Yes, both, Sir (return'd the Knight,) her Majesty's the eldest, and in that Fortune has shewn some Justice. So she has (reply'd the titular Monarch: My Lot is fair (pursu'd he) tho' I can be bless'd but with one.

Let Majesty with Majesty be join'd,
To get and leave a Race of Kings behind.

Come, Madam (continued he, kissing *Lucy*, this, as an Earnest of our future Endeavours. I fear (return'd the pretty Queen) your Majesty will forget the unhappy *Statira*, when you return to the Embraces of your dear and beautiful *Roxana*. There is none beautiful but you (reply'd the titular King) unless this Lady, to whom I yet could pay my Vows most zealously, were't not that Fortune has thus pre-engaged me. But, Madam (continued he) to shew that still you hold our Royal Favour, and that, next to our Royal Consort, we esteem you, we greet you thus (kissing *Philibella*;) and as a Signal of our continued Love, wear this rich Diamond: (here he put a Diamond Ring on her Finger, worth three hundred Pounds.) Your Majesty (pursu'd he to *Lucy*) may please to wear this Necklace, with this Locket of Emeralds. Your Majesty is bounteous as a God! (said *Valentine*.) Art thou in Want, young Spark? (ask'd the King of *Bantam*) I'll give thee an Estate shall make thee merit the Mistress of thy Vows, be she who she will. That is my other Niece, Sir, (cry'd *Friendly*.) How! how! presumptious Youth! How are thy Eyes and Thoughts exalted? ha! To Bliss your

Majesty must never hope for, (reply'd *Goodland*.) How now! thou Creature of the basest Mold! Not hope for what thou dost aspire to! *Mock-King*; thou canst not, dar'st not, shalt not hope it: (return'd *Valentine* in a heat.) Hold, *Val*, (cry'd Sir *Philip*) you grow warm, forget your Duty to their Majesties, and abuse your Friends, by making us suspected. Good-night, dear *Philibella*, and my Queen! Madam, I am your Ladyship's Servant (said Goodland:) Farewel, Sir *Philip*: Adieu, thou Pageant! thou Property-King! I shall see thy Brother on the Stage ere long; but first I'll visit thee: and in the meantime, by way of Return to thy proffer'd Estate, I shall add a real Territory to the rest of thy empty Titles; for from thy Education, barbarous manner of Conversation, and Complexion, I think I may justly proclaim thee, *King of* Bantam—So, *Hail, King that Would-be! Hail thou King of* Christmas! *All-hail, Wou'd-be King of* Bantam—and so he left 'em.—They all seem'd amazed, and gaz'd on one another, without speaking a Syllable; 'till Sir *Philip* broke the Charm, and sigh'd out, Oh, the monstrous Effects of Passion! Say rather, Oh, the foolish Effects of a mean Education! (interrupted his Majesty of *Bantam*.) For Passions were given us for Use, Reason to govern and direct us in the Use, and Education to cultivate and refine that Reason. But (pursu'd he) for all his Impudence to me, which I shall take a time to correct, I am oblig'd to him, that at last he has found me out a Kingdom to my Title; and if I were Monarch of that Place (believe me, Ladies) I would make you all Princesses and Duchesses; and thou, my old Companion, *Friendly*, should rule the Roast with me. But these Ladies should be with us there, where we could erect Temples and Altars to 'em; build Golden Palaces of Love, and Castles—in the Air (interrupted her Majesty, *Lucy* I. smiling.) 'Gad take me (cry'd King *Wou'd-be*) thou dear Partner of my Greatness, and shalt be, of all my Pleasures! thy pretty satirical Observation has oblig'd me beyond Imitation. I think your Majesty is got into a Vein of Rhiming tonight, (said *Philadelphia*.) Ay! Pox of that young insipid Fop, we could else have been as great as an Emperor of *China*, and as witty as

Horace in his Wine; but let him go, like a pragmatical, captious, giddy Fool as he is! I shall take a Time to see him. Nay, Sir, (said *Philibella*) he has promis'd your Majesty a Visit in our Hearing. Come, Sir, I beg your Majesty to pledge me this Glass to your long and happy Reign; laying aside all Thoughts of ungovern'd Youth: Besides, this Discourse must needs be ungrateful to her Majesty, to whom, I fear, he will be marry'd within this Month! How! (cry'd *King and no King*) married to my Queen! I must not, cannot suffer it! Pray restrain your self a little, Sir (said Sir *Philip*) and when once these Ladies have left us, I will discourse your Majesty further about this Business. Well, pray, Sir *Philip*, (said his Lady) let not your Worship be pleas'd to sit up too long for his Majesty: About five o'Clock I shall expect you; 'tis your old Hour. And yours, Madam, to wake to receive me coming to Bed—Your Ladyship understands me, (return'd *Friendly*.) You're merry, my Love, you're merry, (cry'd *Philadelphia*:) Come, Niece, to Bed! to Bed! Ay, (said the Knight) Go, both of you and sleep together, if you can, without the Thoughts of a Lover, or a Husband. His Majesty was pleas'd to wish them a good Repose; and so, with a Kiss, they parted for that time.

Now we're alone (said Sir *Philip*) let me assure you, Sir, I resent this Affront done to you by Mr. *Goodland*, almost as highly as you can: and tho' I can't wish that you should take such Satisfaction, as perhaps some other hotter Sparks would; yet let me say, his Miscarriage ought not to go unpunish'd in him. Fear not (reply'd t'other) I shall give him a sharp Lesson. No, Sir (return'd *Friendly*) I would not have you think of a bloody Revenge; for 'tis that which possibly he designs on you: I know him brave as any Man. However, were it convenient that the Sword should determine betwixt you, you should not want mine: The Affront is partly to me, since done in my House; but I've already laid down safer Measures for us, tho' of more fatal Consequence to him: that is, I've form'd them in my Thoughts. Dismiss your Coach and Equipage, all but one Servant, and I will discourse it to you at large. 'Tis now past Twelve; and if you please, I would invite you to take up as easy a Lodging here, as my House will afford. (Accordingly they were dismiss'd, and he proceeded:)—As I hinted to you before, he is in love with my youngest Niece, *Philibella*; but her Fortune not exceeding five hundred Pound, his Father will assuredly disinherit him, if he marries her: tho' he has given his Consent that he should marry her eldest Sister, whose Father dying ere he knew his Wife was with child of the youngest, left *Lucy* three thousand Pounds, being as much as he thought convenient to match her handsomly; and accordingly the Nuptials of young *Goodland* and *Lucy* are to be celebrated next *Easter*. They shall not, if I can hinder them (interrupted his offended Majesty.) Never endeavour the Obstruction (said the Knight) for I'll shew you the Way to a dearer Vengeance: Women are Women, your Majesty knows; she may be won to your Embraces before that time, and then you antedate him your Creature. A Cuckold, you mean (cry'd King in Fancy:) O exquisite Revenge! but can you consent that I should attempt it? What is't to me? We live not in *Spain*, where all the Relations of the Family are oblig'd to vindicate a Whore: No, I would wound him in his most tender Part. But how shall we compass it? (ask'd t'other.) Why thus, throw away three thousand Pounds on the youngest Sister, as a Portion, to make her as happy as she can be in her new Lover, Sir *Frederick Flygold*, an extravagant young Fop, and wholly given over to Gaming; so, ten to one, but you may retrieve your Money of him, and have the two Sisters at your Devotion. Oh, thou my better Genius than that which was given to me by Heaven at my Birth! What Thanks, what Praises shall I return and sing to thee for this! (cry'd King *Conundrum*.) No Thanks, no Praises, I beseech your Majesty, since in this I gratify my self—You think I am your Friend? and, you will agree to this? (said *Friendly*, by way of Question.) Most readily, (returned the Fop King:) Would it were broad Day, that I might send for the Money to my Banker's; for in all my Life, in all my Frolicks, Encounters and Extravagances, I never had one so grateful, and so pleasant as this will be, if you are in earnest, to gratify both my Love and Revenge! That I am in earnest, you will not doubt, when you see with what Application I shall pursue my Design: In the mean Time, *My Duty to your Majesty; To our good Success in this Affair.* While he drank, t'other return'd, *With all my Heart;* and pledg'd him. Then *Friendly* began afresh: Leave the whole Management of this to me; only one thing more I think necessary, that you make a Present of five hundred Guineas to her Majesty, the Bride that must be. By all means (return'd the wealthy King of *Bantam*;) I had so design'd before. Well, Sir (said Sir *Philip*) what think you of a set Party or two at *Piquet*, to pass away a few Hours, till we can sleep? A seasonable and welcome Proposition (returned the King;) but I won't play above twenty Guineas the Game, and forty the Lurch. Agreed (said *Friendly*;) first call in your Servant; mine is here already. The Slave came in, and they began, with unequal Fortune at first; for the Knight had lost a hundred Guineas to Majesty, which he paid in Specie; and then propos'd fifty Guineas the Game, and a hundred the Lurch. To which t'other consented; and without winning more than three Games, and those not together, made shift to get three thousand two hundred Guineas in debt to Sir *Philip*; for which Majesty was pleas'd to give him Bond, whether *Friendly* would or no,

Seal'd and deliver'd in the Presence of,
The Mark of *(W.) Will. Watchful.*
And, *(S) Sim. Slyboots.*

A couple of delicate Beagles, their mighty Attendants.

It was then about the Hour that Sir *Philip's* (and, it may be, other Ladies) began to yawn and stretch; when the Spirits refresh'd, troul'd about, and tickled the Blood with Desires of Action; which made Majesty and Worship think of a Retreat to Bed: where in less than half an Hour, or before ever he cou'd say his Prayers, I'm sure the first fell fast asleep; but the last, perhaps, paid his accustom'd Devotion, ere he begun his Progress to the Shadow of Death. However, he waked earlier than his Cully Majesty, and got up to receive young *Goodland*, who came according to his Word, with the first Opportunity. Sir *Philip* receiv'd him with more than usual Joy, tho' not with greater Kindness, and let him know every Syllable and Accident that had pass'd between them till they went to Bed: which you may believe was not a little pleasantly surprizing to *Valentine*, who began then to have some Assurance of his Happiness with *Philibella*. His Friend told him, that he must now be reconcil'd to his *Mock-Majesty*, tho' with some Difficulty; and so taking one hearty Glass a-piece, he left *Valentine* in the Parlour to carry the ungrateful News of his Visit to him that Morning. King — was in an odd sort of taking, when he heard that *Valentine* was below; and had been, as Sir *Philip* inform'd *Majesty*, at *Majesty's* Palace, to enquire for him there: But when he told him, that he had already school'd him on his own Behalf, for the Affront done in his House, and that he believ'd he could bring his Majesty off without any loss of present Honour, his Countenance visibly discover'd his past Fear, and present Satisfaction; which was much encreas'd too, when *Friendly* shewing him his Bond for the Money he won of him at play, let him know, that if he paid three thousand Guineas to *Philibella*, he would immediately deliver him up his Bond, and not expect the two hundred Guineas overplus. His Majesty of *Bantam* was then in so good a Humour, that he could have made Love to Sir *Philip*; nay, I believe he could have kiss'd *Valentine*, instead of seeming angry. Down they came, and saluted like Gentlemen: But after the Greeting was over, *Goodland* began to talk something of Affront, Satisfaction, Honour, &c. when immediately *Friendly* interpos'd, and after a little seeming Uneasiness and Reluctancy, reconcil'd the hot and cholerick Youth to the cold phlegmatick King.

Peace was no sooner proclaim'd, than the King of *Bantam* took his Rival and late Antagonist with him in his own Coach, not excluding Sir *Philip* by any means, to *Locket's*, where they din'd: Thence he would have 'em to Court with him, where he met the Lady *Flippant*, the Lady *Harpy*, the Lady *Crocodile*,

Madam *Tattlemore*, Miss *Medler*, Mrs. *Gingerly*, a rich Grocer's Wife, and some others, besides Knights and Gentlemen of as good Humours as the Ladies; all whom he invited to a Ball at his own House, the Night following; his own Lady being then in the Country. Madam *Tattlemore*, I think was the first he spoke to in Court, and whom first he surpriz'd with the happy News of his Advancement to the Title of King of *Bantam*. How wondrous hasty was she to be gone, as soon as she heard it! 'Twas not in her Power, because not in her Nature, to stay long enough to take a civil Leave of the Company; but away she flew, big with the empty Title of a fantastick King, proclaiming it to every one of her Acquaintance, as she passed through every Room, till she came to the *Presence-Chamber*, where she only whisper'd it; but her Whispers made above half the honourable Company quit the Presence of the King of *Great-Britain*, to go make their Court to his Majesty of *Bantam*: some cry'd, *God bless your Majesty!* Some *Long live the King of* Bantam! Others, *All Hail to your Sacred Majesty*; In short, he was congratulated on all Sides. Indeed I don't hear that his Majesty King *Charles* II. ever sent an Ambassador to compliment him; tho' possibly, he saluted him by his Title the first time he saw him afterwards: For, you know, he is a wonderful good-natur'd and well-bred Gentleman.

After he thought the Court of *England* was universally acquainted with his mighty Honour, he was pleas'd to think fit to retire to his own more private Palace, with Sir *Philip* and *Goodland*, whom he entertain'd that Night very handsomly, till about seven o'Clock; when they went together to the Play, which was that Night, *A King and no King*. His Attendant-Friends could not forbear smiling, to think how aptly the Title of the Play suited his Circumstances. Nor could he choose but take Notice of it behind the Scenes, between Jest and Earnest; telling the Players how kind Fortune had been the Night past, in disposing the Bean to him; and justifying what one of her Prophetesses had foretold some Years since. I shall now no more regard (said he) that old doating Fellow *Pythagoras's*

Saying *Abstineto a Fabis*, That is, (added he, by way of Construction) *Abstain from Beans*: for I find the Excellency of 'em in Cakes and Dishes; from the first, they inspire the Soul with mighty Thoughts; and from the last our Bodies receive a strong and wholesom Nourishment. That is, (said a Wag among those sharp Youths, I think 'twas my Friend the Count) these puff you up in Mind, Sir, those in Body. They had some further Discourse among the Nymphs of the Stage, ere they went into the Pit; where Sir *Philip* spread the News of his Friend's Accession to the Title, tho' not yet to the Throne of *Bantam*; upon which he was there again complimented on that Occasion. Several of the Ladies and Gentlemen who saluted him, he invited to the next Night's Ball at his Palace.

The Play done, they took each of them a Bottle at the *Rose*, and parted till Seven the Night following; which came not sooner than desired: for he had taken such Care, that all things were in readiness before Eight, only he was not to expect the Musick till the End of the Play. About Nine, Sir *Philip*, his Lady, *Goodland, Philibella*, and *Lucy* came. Sir *Philip* return'd him *Rabelais*, which he had borrow'd of him, wherein the Knight had written, in an old odd sort of a Character, this Prophecy of his own making; with which he surpriz'd the Majesty of *Bantam*, who vow'd he had never taken Notice of it before; but he said, he perceiv'd it had been long written by the Character; and here it follows, as near as I can remember:

> *When* M. D. C. *come* L. *before,*
> *Three* XXX's, *two* II's *and one* I. *more*;
> *Then* K I N G, *tho' now but Name to thee,*
> *Shall both thy Name and Title be.*

They had hardly made an End of reading it, ere the whole Company, and more than he had invited, came in, and were receiv'd with a great deal of Formality and Magnificence. *Lucy* was there attended as his Queen; and *Philibella*, as the Princess her Sister. They danc'd then till they were weary; and

afterwards retired to another large Room, where they found
the Tables spread and furnished with all the most seasonable
cold Meat; which was succeeded by the choicest Fruits, and the
richest Desert of Sweetmeats that Luxury could think on, or at
least that this Town could afford. The Wines were all most
excellent in their Kind; and their Spirits flew about thro' every
Corner of the House: There was scarce a Spark sober in the
whole Company, with drinking repeated Glasses to the Health
of the King of *Bantam,* and his Royal Consort, with the
Princess *Philibella's* who sat together under a Royal Canopy of
State, his Majesty between the two beautiful Sisters: only
Friendly and *Goodland* wisely manag'd that part of the
Engagement where they were concern'd, and preserv'd
themselves from the Heat of the Debauch.

Between Three and Four most of them began to draw off,
laden with Fruit and Sweetmeats, and rich Favours compos'd of
Yellow, Green, Red and White, the Colours of his new Majesty of
Bantam. Before Five they were left to themselves; when the
Lady *Friendly* was discompos'd, for want of Sleep, and her usual
Cordial, which obliged Sir *Philip* to wait on her Home, with his
two Nieces: But his Majesty would by no means part with
Goodland; whom, before Nine that Morning, he made as drunk
as a Lord, and by Consequence, one of his Peers; for Majesty was
then, indeed, as great as an Emperor: He fancy'd himself
Alexander, and young *Valentine* his *Hephestion;* and did so be-
buss him, that the young Gentleman fear'd he was fallen into the
Hands of an *Italian.* However, by the kind Persuasions of his
condescending and dissembling Majesty, he ventur'd to go into
Bed with him; where King *Would-be* fell asleep, hand-over-head:
and not long after, *Goodland,* his new-made Peer, follow'd him
to the cool Retreats of *Morpheus.*

About Three the next Afternoon they both wak'd, as by
consent, and called to dress. And after that Business was over,
I think they swallow'd each of 'em a Pint of *Old-Hock,* with a
little Sugar, by the way of healing. Their Coaches were got
ready in the mean time; but the Peer was forced to accept of

the Honour of being carried in his Majesty's to Sir *Philip's*, whom they found just risen from Dinner, with *Philadelphia* and his two Nieces. They sat down, and ask'd for something to relish a Glass of Wine, and Sir *Philip* order'd a cold Chine to be set before 'em, of which they eat about an Ounce a-piece; but they drank more by half, I dare say.

After their little Repast, *Friendly* call'd the *Would-be-Monarch* aside, and told him, that he would have him go to the Play that Night, which was *The London-Cuckolds*; promising to meet him there in less than half an Hour after his Departure: telling him withal, that he would surprize him with a much better Entertainment than the Stage afforded. *Majesty* took the Hint, imagining, and that rightly, that the Knight had some Intrigue in his Head, for the Promotion of the Commonwealth of Cuckoldom: In order therefore to his Advice, he took his leave about a quarter of an Hour after.

When he was gone, Sir *Philip* thus bespoke his pretended Niece: Madam, I hope your Majesty will not refuse me the Honour of waiting on you to a Place where you will meet with better Entertainment than your Majesty can expect from the best Comedy in Christendom. *Val*, (continued he) you must go with us, to secure me against the Jealousy of my Wife. That, indeed (return'd his Lady) is very material; and you are mightily concern'd not to give me Occasion, I must own. You see I am now, (replied he:) But—come! on with Hoods and Scarf! (pursued he, to *Lucy*.) Then addressing himself again to his Lady; Madam, (said he) we'll wait on you. In less Time than I could have drank a Bottle to my Share, the Coach was got ready, and on they drove to the Play-House. By the way, said *Friendly* to *Val*.—Your Honour, noble Peer, must be set down at *Long's*; for only *Lucy* and I must be seen to his Majesty of *Bantam*: And now, I doubt not, you understand what you must trust to.—To be robb'd of her Majesty's Company, I warrant (return'd the other) for these long three Hours. Why (cry'd *Lucy*) you don't mean, I hope, to leave me with his Majesty of *Bantam*? 'Tis for thy Good, Child! 'Tis for thy Good (return'd

Friendly.) To the *Rose* they got then; where *Goodland* alighted, and expected Sir *Philip*; who led *Lucy* into the King's Box, to his new Majesty; where, after the first Scene, he left them together. The over-joy'd fantastick Monarch would fain have said some fine obliging Things to the Knight, as he was going out; but *Friendly's* Haste prevented 'em, who went directly to *Valentine*, took one Glass, call'd a Reckoning, mounted his Chariot, and away Home they came: where I believe he was welcome to his Lady; for I never heard any thing to the contrary.

In the mean Time, his Majesty had not the Patience to stay out half the Play, at which he was saluted by above twenty Gentlemen and Ladies by his new and mighty Title: but out he led Miss Majesty ere the third Act was half done; pretending, that it was so damn'd a bawdy Play, that he knew her Modesty had been already but too much offended at it; so into his Coach he got her. When they were seated, she told him she would go to no Place with him, but to the Lodgings her Mother had taken for her, when she first came to Town, and which still she kept. Your Mother, Madam, (cry'd he) why, is Sir *Philip's* Sister living then? His Brother's Widow is, Sir, (she reply'd.) Is she there? (he ask'd.) No, Sir, (she return'd;) she is in the Country. Oh, then we will go thither to chuse. The Coach-man was then order'd to drive to *Jermain-Street*; where, when he came in to the Lodgings, he found 'em very rich and modishly furnish'd. He presently call'd one of his Slaves, and whisper'd him to get three or four pretty Dishes for Supper; and then getting a Pen, Ink and Paper, writ a Note to *C—d* the Goldsmith with *Temple-Bar*, for five hundred guineas; which *Watchful* brought him, in less than an Hour's time, when they were just in the Height of Supper; *Lucy* having invited her Landlady, for the better Colour of the Matter. His *Bantamite* Majesty took the Gold from his Slave, and threw it by him in the Window, that *Lucy* might take Notice of it; (which you may assure yourself she did, and after Supper wink'd on the goodly Matron of the House to retire, which she immediately obey'd.) Then his Majesty began his Court very earnestly and hotly, throwing the naked Guineas into her Lap: which she seemed to refuse with much Disdain; but upon his repeated Promises, confirm'd by unheard of Oaths and Imprecations, that he would give her Sister three thousand Guineas to her Portion, she began by Degrees to mollify, and let the Gold lie quietly in her Lap: And the next Night, after he had drawn Notes on two or three of his Bankers, for the Payment of three thousand Guineas to Sir *Philip*, or Order, and received his own Bond, made for what he had lost at Play, from *Friendly*, she made no great Difficulty to admit his Majesty to her Bed. Where I think fit to leave 'em for the present; for (perhaps) they had some private Business.

The next Morning before the Titular King was (I won't say up, or stirring, but) out of Bed, young *Goodland* and *Philibella* were privately marry'd; the Bills being all accepted and paid in two Days Time. As soon as ever the fantastick Monarch could find in his Heart to divorce himself from the dear and charming Embraces of his beautiful Bedfellow, he came flying to Sir *Philip*, with all the Haste that Imagination big with Pleasure could inspire him with, to discharge it self to a suppos'd Friend. The Knight told him, that he was really much troubled to find that his Niece had yielded so soon and easily to him; however, he wish'd him Joy: To which the other return'd, that he could never want it, whilst he had the Command of so much Beauty, and that without the ungrateful Obligations of Matrimony, which certainly are the most nauseous, hateful, pernicious and destructive of Love imaginable. Think you so, Sir? (ask'd the Knight;) we shall hear what a Friend of mine will say on such an Occasion, tomorrow about this Time: but I beseech your Majesty to conceal your Sentiments of it to him, lest you make him as uneasy as you seem to be in that Circumstance. Be assur'd I will, (return'd the other:) But when shall I see the sweet, the dear, the blooming, the charming *Philibella*? She will be with us at Dinner. Where's her Majesty? (ask'd Sir *Philip*) Had you enquir'd before, she had been here; for, look, she comes! *Friendly* seems to regard her with a Kind of Displeasure, and whisper'd Majesty, that he should express no particular Symptoms of Familiarity with *Lucy* in his House, at any Time, especially when *Goodland* was there, as then he was above with his Lady and *Philibella*, who came down presently after to Dinner.

About Four o'Clock, as his Majesty had intrigu'd with her, *Lucy* took a Hackney-Coach, and went to her Lodgings; whither about an Hour after, he follow'd her, Next Morning, at nine, he came to *Friendly's*, who carry'd him up to see his new-married Friends—But (O Damnation to Thoughts!) what Torments did he feel, when he saw young *Goodland* and *Philibella* in bed together; the last of which return'd him humble and hearty Thanks for her Portion and Husband, as the first did for his Wife. He shook his Head at Sir *Philip*, and without speaking one Word, left 'em, and hurry'd to *Lucy*, to lament the ill Treatment he had met with from *Friendly*. They coo'd and bill'd as long as he was able; she (sweet Hypocrite) seeming to bemoan his Misfortunes; which he took so kindly, that when he left her, which was about three in the Afternoon, he caus'd a Scrivener to draw up an Instrument, wherein he settled a hundred Pounds a Year on *Lucy* for her Life, and gave her a hundred Guineas more against her Lying-in: (For she told him, and indeed 'twas true, that she was with child, and knew her self to be so from a very good Reason—) And indeed she was so—by the *Friendly* Knight. When he return'd to her, he threw the obliging Instrument into her Lap; (it seems he had a particular Kindness for that Place—) then call'd for Wine, and something to eat; for he had not drank a Pint to his Share all the Day, (tho' he had ply'd it at the Chocolate-House.—) The Landlady, who was invited to sup with 'em, bid 'em good-night, about eleven; when they went to bed, and partly slept till about six; when they were entertain'd by some Gentleman of their Acquaintance, who play'd and sung very finely, by way of *Epithalamium*, these Words and more:

Joy to great Bantam!
Live long, love and wanton!
And thy Royal Consort!
For both are of one Sort, &c.

The rest I have forgot. He took some Offence at the Words; but more at the Visit that Sir *Philip*, and *Goodland*, made him, about an Hour after, who found him in Bed with his Royal Consort; and after having wish'd 'em Joy, and thrown their Majesties own Shoes and Stockings at their Head, retir'd. This gave Monarch in Fancy so great a Caution that he took his Royal Consort into the Country, (but above forty Miles off the Place where his own Lady was) where, in less than eight Months, she was deliver'd of a Princely Babe, who was Christen'd by the Heathenish Name of *Hayoumorecake Bantam*, while her Majesty lay in like a pretty Queen.

THE NUN
OR
THE PERJUR'D BEAUTY
A TRUE NOVEL

THE NUN
OR THE PERJUR'D BEAUTY

Don *Henrique* was a Person of great Birth, of a great Estate, of a Bravery equal to either, of a most generous Education, but of more Passion than Reason: He was besides of an opener and freer Temper than generally his Countrymen are (I mean, the *Spaniards*) and always engag'd in some Love-Intrigue or other.

One Night as he was retreating from one of those Engagements, Don *Sebastian*, whose Sister he had abus'd with a Promise of Marriage, set upon him at the Corner of a Street, in *Madrid*, and by the Help of three of his Friends, design'd to have dispatch'd him on a doubtful Embassy to the Almighty Monarch: But he receiv'd their first Instructions with better Address than they expected, and dismiss'd his Envoy first, killing one of Don *Sebastian's* Friends. Which so enrag'd the injur'd Brother, that his Strength and Resolution seem'd to be redoubled, and so animated his two surviving Companions, that (doubtless) they had gain'd a dishonourable Victory, had not Don *Antonio* accidentally come in to the Rescue; who after a short Dispute, kill'd one of the two who attack'd him only; whilst Don *Henrique*, with the greatest Difficulty, defended his Life, for some Moments, against *Sebastian*, whose Rage depriv'd him of Strength, and gave his Adversary the unwish'd Advantage of his seeming Death, tho' not without bequeathing some bloody Legacies to Don *Henrique*. *Antonio* had receiv'd but one slight Wound in the left Arm, and his surviving Antagonist none; who however thought it not adviseable to begin a fresh Dispute against two, of whose Courage he had but too fatal a Proof, tho' one of 'em was sufficiently disabled. The Conquerors, on the other Side, politickly retreated, and quitting the Field to the Conquer'd, left the Living to bury the Dead, if he could, or thought convenient.

As they were marching off, Don *Antonio*, who all this while knew not whose Life he had so happily preserv'd, told his Companion in Arms, that he thought it indispensibly necessary that he should quarter with him that Night, for his further Preservation. To which he prudently consented, and went, with no little Uneasiness, to his Lodgings; where he surpriz'd *Antonio* with the Sight of his dearest Friend. For they had certainly the nearest Sympathy in all their Thoughts, that ever made two brave Men unhappy: And, undoubtedly, nothing but Death, or more fatal Love, could have divided them. However, at present, they were united and secure.

In the mean time, Don *Sebastian's* Friend was just going to call Help to carry off the Bodies, as the —— came by; who seeing three Men lie dead, seiz'd the fourth; who as he was about to justify himself, by discovering one of the Authors of so much Blood-shed, was interrupted by a Groan from his supposed dead Friend Don *Sebastian*; whom, after a brief Account of some Part of the Matter, and the Knowledge of his Quality, they took up, and carried to his House; where, within a few Days, he was recovered past the Fear of Death. All this While *Henrique* and *Antonio* durst not appear, so much as by Night; nor could be found, tho' diligent and daily Search was made after the first; but upon Don *Sebastian's* Recovery, the Search ceasing, they took the Advantage of the Night, and, in Disguise, retreated to *Seville*. 'Twas there they thought themselves most secure, where indeed they were in the greatest Danger; for tho' (haply) they might there have escap'd the murderous Attempt of Don *Sebastian*, and his Friends, yet they could not there avoid the malicious Influence of their Stars.

This City gave Birth to *Antonio*, and to the Cause of his greatest Misfortunes, as well as of his Death. Dona *Ardelia* was born there, a Miracle of Beauty and Falshood. 'Twas more than a Year since Don *Antonio* had first seen and loved her. For 'twas impossible any Man should do one without the other. He had had the unkind Opportunity of speaking and conveying a Billet to her at Church; and to his greater Misfortune, the next Time he found her there, he met with too Kind a Return both from her Eyes and from her Hand, which privately slipt a Paper into his; in which he found abundantly more than he expected, directing him in that, how he should proceed, in order to carry her off from her Father with the least Danger he could look for in such an Attempt; since it would have been vain and fruitless to have asked her of her Father, because their Families had been at Enmity for several Years; tho' *Antonio* was as well descended as she, and had as ample a Fortune; nor was his Person, according to his Sex, any way inferior to her's; and certainly, the Beauties of his Mind were more excellent, especially if it be an Excellence to be constant.

He had made several Attempts to take Possession of her; but all prov'd ineffectual; however, he had the good Fortune not to be known, tho' once or twice he narrowly escap'd with Life, bearing off his Wounds with Difficulty.—(Alas, that the Wounds of Love should cause those of Hate!) Upon which she was strictly confin'd to one Room, whose only Window was towards the Garden, and that too was grated with Iron; and, once a Month, when she went to Church, she was constantly and carefully attended by her Father, and a Mother-in -Law, worse than a *Duegna*. Under this miserable Confinement *Antonio* understood she still continued, at his Return to *Seville*, with Don *Henrique*, whom he acquainted with his invincible Passion for her; lamenting the Severity of her present Circumstances, that admitted of no Prospect of Relief; which caus'd a generous Concern in Don *Henrique*, both for the Sufferings of his Friend, and of the Lady. He proposed several Ways to Don *Antonio*, for the Release of the fair Prisoner; but none of them was thought practicable, or at least likely to succeed. But *Antonio*, who (you may believe) was then more nearly engag'd, bethought himself of an Expedient that would undoubtedly reward their Endeavours. 'Twas, that Don *Henrique*, who was very well acquainted with *Ardelia's* Father, should make him a Visit, with Pretence of begging his Consent and Admission to make his Addresses to his Daughter; which, in all Probability, he could not refuse to Don *Henrique's* Quality and Estate; and then this Freedom of Access to her would give him the Opportunity of delivering the Lady to his

Friend. This was thought so reasonable, that the very next Day it was put in Practice; and with so good Success, that Don *Henrique* was received by the Father of *Ardelia* with the greatest and most respectful Ceremony imaginable: And when he made the Proposal to him of marrying his Daughter, it was embraced with a visible Satisfaction and Joy in the Air of his Face. This their first Conversation ended with all imaginable Content on both Sides; Don *Henrique* being invited by the Father to Dinner the next Day, when Dona *Ardelia* was to be present; who, at that Time, was said to be indispos'd, (as 'tis very probable she was, with so close an Imprisonment.) *Henrique* returned to *Antonio*, and made him happy with the Account of his Reception; which could not but have terminated in the perfect Felicity of *Antonio*, had his Fate been just to the Merits of his Love. The Day and Hour came which brought *Henrique*, with a private Commission from his Friend, to *Ardelia*. He saw her;—(ah! would he had only seen her veil'd!) and, with the first Opportunity, gave her the Letter, which held so much Love, and so much Truth, as ought to have preserved him in the Empire of her Heart. It contained, besides, a Discovery of his whole Design upon her Father, for the compleating of their Happiness; which nothing then could obstruct but her self. But *Henrique* had seen her; he had gaz'd, and swallowed all her Beauties at his Eyes. How greedily his Soul drank the strong Poison in! But yet his Honour and his Friendship were strong as ever, and bravely fought against the Usurper Love, and got a noble Victory; at least he thought and wish'd so. With this, and a short Answer to his Letter, *Henrique* return'd to the longing *Antonio*; who, receiving the Paper with the greatest Devotion, and kissing it with the greatest Zeal, open'd and read these Words to himself:

Don Antonio,
  YOU have, at last, made Use of the best and only Expedient for my Enlargement; for which I thank you, since I know it is purely the Effect of your Love. Your Agent has a mighty

Influence on my Father: And you may assure yourself, that as you have advis'd and desir'd me, he shall have no less on me, who am

Your's entirely,

And only your's,

ARDELIA.

Having respectfully and tenderly kiss'd the Name, he could not chuse but shew the *Billet* to his Friend; who reading that Part of it which concern'd himself, started and blush'd: Which *Antonio* observing, was curious to know the Cause of it. *Henrique* told him, That he was surpriz'd to find her express so little Love, after so long an Absence. To which his Friend reply'd for her, That, doubtless, she has not Time enough to attempt so great a Matter as a perfect Account of her Love; and added, that it was Confirmation enough to him of its Continuance, since she subscrib'd her self his entirely, and only his.—How blind is Love! Don *Henrique* knew how to make it bear another Meaning; which, however, he had the Discretion to conceal. *Antonio*, who was as real in his Friendship, as constant in his Love, ask'd him what he thought of her Beauty? To which the other answer'd, that he thought it irresistable to any, but to a Soul preposses'd, and nobly fortify'd with a perfect Friendship:—Such as is thine, my *Henrique*, (added *Antonio*;) yet as sincere and perfect as that is, I know you must, nay, I know you do love her. As I ought to do, (reply'd *Henrique*.) Yes, yes, (return'd his Friend) it must be so; otherwise the Sympathy which unites our Souls would be wanting, and consequently our Friendship were in a State of Imperfection. How industriously you would argue me into a Crime, that would tear and destroy the Foundation of the strongest Ties of Truth and Honour! (said *Henrique*.) But (he continu'd) I hope within a few Days, to put it out of my Power to be guilty of so great a Sacrilege. I can't determine (said *Antonio*) if I knew that you lov'd one another, whether I could easier part with my Friend, or my Mistress. Tho' what you say, is highly generous, (reply'd

Henrique) yet give me Leave to urge, that it looks like a Trial of Friendship, and argues you inclinable to Jealousy: But, pardon me, I know it to be sincerely meant by you; and must therefore own, that 'tis the best, because 'tis the noblest Way of securing both your Friend and Mistress. I need not make use of any Arts to secure me of either, (reply'd *Antonio*) but expect to enjoy 'em both in a little Time.

Henrique, who was a little uneasy with a Discourse of this Nature, diverted it, by reflecting on what had pass'd at *Madrid*, between them two and Don *Sebastian* and his Friends; which caus'd *Antonio* to bethink himself of the Danger to which he expos'd his Friend, by appearing daily, tho' in Disguise: For, doubtless, Don *Sebastian* would pursue his Revenge to the utmost Extremity. These Thoughts put him upon desiring his Friend, for his own Sake, to hasten the Performance of his Attempt; and accordingly, each Day Don *Henrique* brought *Antonio* nearer the Hopes of Happiness, while he himself was hourly sinking into the lowest State of Misery. The last Night before the Day in which *Antonio* expected to be bless'd in her Love, Don *Henrique* had a long and fatal Conference with her about her Liberty. Being then with her alone in an Arbour of the Garden, which Privilege he had had for some Days; after a long Silence, and observing Don *Henrique* in much Disorder, by the Motion of his Eyes, which were sometimes stedfastly fix'd on the Ground, then lifted up to her or Heaven, (for he could see nothing more beautiful on Earth) she made use of the Privilege of her Sex, and began the Discourse first, to this Effect:—Has any Thing happened, Sir, since our Retreat hither, to occasion that Disorder which is but too visible in your Face, and too dreadful in your continued Silence? Speak, I beseech you, Sir, and let me know if I have any Way unhappily contributed to it! No, Madam, (replyed he) my Friendship is now likely to be the only Cause of my greatest Misery; for Tomorrow I must be guilty of an unpardonable Crime, in betraying the generous Confidence which your noble Father has plac'd in me: Tomorrow (added he, with a piteous Sigh) I must deliver you into the Hands of one whom your Father hates even to Death, instead of doing myself the Honour of becoming his Sonin-law within a few Days more.—But—I will consider and remind myself, that I give you into the Hands of my Friend; of my Friend, that loves you better than his Life, which he has often expos'd for your Sake; and what is more than all, to my Friend, whom you love more than any Consideration on Earth.—And must this be done? (she ask'd.) Is it inevitable as Fate?—Fix'd as the Laws of Nature, Madam, (reply'd he) don't you find the Necessity of it, *Ardelia*? (continued he, by Way of Question:) Does not your Love require it? Think, you are going to your dear *Antonio*, who alone can merit you, and whom only you can love. Were your last Words true (returned she) I should yet be unhappy in the Displeasure of a dear and tender Father, and infinitely more, in being the Cause of your Infidelity to him: No, Don *Henrique* (continued she) I could with greater Satisfaction return to my miserable Confinement, than by any Means disturb the Peace of your Mind, or occasion one Moment's Interruption of your Quiet.—Would to Heaven you did not, (sigh'd he to himself.) Then addressing his Words more distinctly to her, cry'd he, Ah, cruel! ah, unjust *Ardelia*! these Words belong to none but *Antonio*; why then would you endeavour to persuade me, that I do, or even can merit the Tenderness of such an Expression?— Have a Care! (pursued he) have a Care, *Ardelia*! your outward Beauties are too powerful to be resisted; even your Frowns have such a Sweetness that they attract the very Soul that is not strongly prepossessed with the noblest Friendship, and the highest Principles of Honour: Why then, alas! did you add such sweet and Charming Accents? Why—ah, Don *Henrique*! (she interrupted) why did you appear to me so charming in your Person, so great in your Friendship, and so illustrious in your Reputation? Why did my Father, ever since your first Visit, continually fill my Ears and Thoughts with noble Characters and glorious Ideas, which yet but imperfectly and faintly represent the inimitable Original!—But—(what is most severe and cruel) why, Don *Henrique*, why will you defeat my Father in his Ambition of your Alliance, and me of those glorious Hopes with which you had bless'd my Soul, by casting me away from you to *Antonio*!—Ha! (cry'd he, starting) what said you, Madam? What did *Ardelia* say? That I had bless'd your Soul with Hopes! That I would cast you away to *Antonio*!—Can they who safely arrive in their wish'd-for Port, be said to be shipwreck'd? Or, can an adject indigent Wretch make a King?—These are more than Riddles, Madam; and I must not think to expound 'em. No, (said she) let it alone, Don *Henrique*; I'll ease you of that Trouble, and tell you plainly that I love you. Ah! (cry'd he) now all my Fears are come upon me!—How! (ask'd she) were you afraid I should love you? Is my Love so dreadful then? Yes, when misplac'd (reply'd he;) but 'twas your Falshood that I fear'd: Your Love was what I would have sought with the utmost Hazard of my Life, nay, even of my future Happiness, I fear, had you not been engag'd: strongly oblig'd to love elsewhere, both by your own Choice and Vows, as well as by his dangerous Services, and matchless Constancy. For which (said she) I do not hate him, tho' his Father kill'd my Uncle: Nay, perhaps (continu'd she) I have a Friendship for him, but no more. No more, said you, Madam? (cry'd he;)—but tell me, did you never love him? Indeed, I did, (reply'd she;) but the Sight of you has better instructed me, both in my Duty to my Father, and in causing my Passion for you, without whom I shall be eternally miserable. Ah, then pursue your honourable Proposal, and made my Father happy in my Marriage! It must not be (return'd Don *Henrique*) my Honour, my Friendship forbids it. No (she return'd) your Honour requires it; and if your Friendship opposes your Honour, it can have no sure and solid Foundation. Female Sophistry! (cry'd *Henrique*;) but you need no Art nor Artifice, *Ardelia*, to make me love you: Love you! (pursu'd he:) By that bright Sun, the Light and Heat of all the World, you are my only Light and Heat—Oh, Friendship! Sacred Friendship, now assist me!—(Here for a Time he paus'd, and then afresh proceeded thus,)—You told me, or my Ears deceiv'd me, that you lov'd me, *Ardelia*. I did, she reply'd; and that I do love you, is as true as that I told you so. 'Tis well;—But would it were not so! Did ever Man receive a Blessing thus?—Why, I could wish I did not love you, *Ardelia*! But that were impossible—At least unjust, (interrupted she.) Well then (he went on) to shew you that I do sincerely consult your particular Happiness, without any regard to my own, Tomorrow I will give you to Don *Antonio*; and as a Proof of your Love to me, I expect your ready Consent to it. To let you see, Don *Henrique*, how perfectly and tenderly I love you, I will be sacrificed Tomorrow to Don *Antonio*, and to your Quiet. Oh, strongest, dearest Obligation!—cry'd *Henrique*: Tomorrow then, as I have told your Father, I am to bring you to see the dearest Friend I have on Earth, who dares not appear within this City for some unhappy Reasons, and therefore cannot be present at our Nuptials; for which Cause, I could not but think it my Duty to one so nearly related to my Soul, to make him happy in the Sight of my beautiful Choice, e'er yet she be my Bride. I hope (said she) my loving Obedience may merit your Compassion; and that at last, e'er the Fire is lighted that must consume the Offering, I mean the Marriage-Tapers (alluding to the old *Roman* Ceremony) that you or some other pitying Angel, will snatch me from the Altar. Ah, no more, *Ardelia*! say no more (cry'd he) we must be cruel, to be just to our selves. (Here their Discourse ended, and they walked into the House, where they found the good old Gentleman and his Lady, with whom he stay'd till about an Hour after Supper, when he returned to his Friend with joyful News, but a sorrowful Heart.)

Antonio was all Rapture with the Thoughts of the approaching Day; which tho' it brought Don *Henrique* and his dear *Ardelia* to him, about five o'Clock in the Evening, yet at the same Time brought his last and greatest Misfortune. He saw her then at a She Relation's of his, above three Miles from *Seville*, which was the Place assigned for their fatal Interview. He saw her, I say; but ah! how strange! how altered from the dear, kind *Ardelia* she was when last he left her! 'Tis true, he flew to her with Arms expanded, and with so swift and eager a Motion, that she could not avoid, nor get loose from his Embrace, till he had kissed, and sighed, and dropt some Tears, which all the Strength of his Mind could not restrain; whether they were the Effects of Joy, or whether (which rather may be feared) they were the Heat-drops which preceded and threaten'd the Thunder and Tempest that should fall on his Head, I cannot positively say; yet all this she was then forced to endure, e'er she had Liberty to speak, or indeed to breathe. But as soon as she had freed herself from the loving Circle that should have been the dear and lov'd Confinement or Centre of a Faithful Heart, she began to dart whole Showers of Tortures on him from her Eyes; which that Mouth that he had just before so tenderly and sacredly kiss'd, seconded with whole Volleys of Deaths crammed in every Sentence, pointed with the keenest Affliction that ever pierc'd a Soul. *Antonio*, (she began) you have treated me now as if you were never like to see me more: and would to Heaven you were not!—Ha! (cry'd he, starting and staring wildly on her;) What said you, Madam? What said you, my *Ardelia*? If you like the Repetition, take it? (reply'd she, unmoved) *Would to Heaven you were never like to see me more!* Good! very Good! (cry'd he, with a Sigh that threw him trembling into a Chair behind him, and gave her the Opportunity of proceeding thus:)—Yet, *Antonio*, I must not have my Wish; I must continue with you, not out of Choice, but by Command, by the strictest and severest Obligation that ever bound Humanity; Don *Henrique*, your Friend, commands it; Don *Henrique*, the dearest Object of my Soul, enjoins it; Don *Henrique*, whose only Aversion I am, will have it so. Oh, do not wrong me, Madam! (cry'd Don *Henrique*.) Lead me, lead me a little more by the Light of your Discourse, I beseech you (said Don *Antonio*) that I may see your Meaning! for hitherto 'tis Darkness all to me. Attend therefore with your best Faculties (pursu'd *Ardelia*) and know, That I do most sincerely and most passionately love Don *Henrique*; and as a Proof of my Love to him, I have this Day consented to be delivered up to you by him; not for your Sake in the least, *Antonio*, but purely to sacrifice all the Quiet of my

Life to his Satisfaction. And now, Sir (continued she, addressing her self to Don *Henrique*) now, Sir, if you can be so cruel, execute your own most dreadful Decree, and join our Hands, though our Hearts never can meet. All this to try me! It's too much, *Ardelia*—(said *Antonio:*) And then turning to Don *Henrique*, he went on, Speak thou! if yet thou art not Apostate to our Friendship! Yet speak, however! Speak, though the Devil has been tampering with thee too! Thou art a Man, a Man of Honour once. And when I forfeit my just Title to that (interrupted Don *Henrique*) may I be made most miserable!— May I lose the Blessings of thy Friendship!—May I lose thee!— Say on then, *Henrique*! (cry'd *Antonio:*) And I charge thee, by all the sacred Ties of Friendship, say, Is this a Trial of me? Is't Illusion, Sport, or shameful murderous Truth?—Oh, my Soul burns within me, and I can bear no longer!—Tell! Speak! Say on!—(Here, with folded Arms, and Eyes fixed stedfastly on *Henrique*, he stood like a Statue, without Motion; unless sometimes, when his swelling Heart raised his overcharged Breast.) After a little Pause, and a hearty Sigh or two, *Henrique* began;—Oh, *Antonio*! Oh my Friend! prepare thy self to hear yet more dreadful Accents!—I am (pursu'd he) unhappily the greatest and most innocent Criminal that e'er till now offended:—I love her, *Antonio*,—I love *Ardelia* with a Passion strong and violent as thine!—Oh! summon all that us'd to be more than Man about thee, to suffer to the End of my Discourse, which nothing but a Resolution like thine can bear! I know it by myself.—Tho' there be Wounds, Horror, and Death in each Syllable (interrupted *Antonio*) yet prithee now go on, but with all Haste. I will, (returned Don *Henrique*) tho' I feel my own Words have the same cruel Effects on me. I say, again, my Soul loves *Ardelia*: And how can it be otherwise? Have we not both the self-same Appetites, the same Disgusts? How then could I avoid my Destiny, that has decreed that I should love and hate just as you do? Oh, hard Necessity! that obliged you to use me in the Recovery of this Lady! Alas, can you think that any Man of Sense or Passion could have seen, and not have lov'd her! Then how should I, whose Thoughts are Unisons to yours, evade those Charms that had prevail'd on you?—And now, to let you know, 'tis no Illusion, no Sport, but serious and amazing woeful Truth, *Ardelia* best can tell you whom she loves. What I have already said, is true, by Heaven (cry'd she) 'tis you, Don *Henrique*, whom I only love, and who alone can give me Happiness: Ah, would you would!—With you, *Antonio*, I must remain unhappy, wretched, cursed: Thou art my Hell; Don *Henrique* is my Heaven. And thou art mine, (returned he) which here I part with to my dearest Friend. Then taking her Hand, Pardon me, *Antonio*, (pursued he) that I thus take my last Farewel of all the Tastes of Bliss from your *Ardelia*, at this Moment. (At which Words he kiss'd her Hand, and gave it to Don *Antonio*; who received it, and gently pressed it close to his Heart, as if he would have her feel the Disorders she had caus'd there.) Be happy, *Antonio*, (cry'd *Henrique*:) Be very tender of her; Tomorrow early I shall hope to see thee.—*Ardelia* (pursued he) All Happiness and Joy surround thee! May'st thou ne'er want those Blessings thou can'st give *Antonio*!—Farewel to both! (added he, going out.) Ah (cry'd she) Farewel to all Joys, Blessings, Happiness, if you forsake me.—Yet do not go!—Ah, cruel! (continu'd she, seeing him quit the Room) but you shall take my Soul with you. Here she swooned away in Don *Antonio's* Arms; who, though he was happy that he had her fast there, yet was obliged to call in his Cousin, and *Ardelia's* Attendants, e'er she could be perfectly recovered. In the mean while Don *Henrique* had not the Power to go out of Sight of the House, but wandred to and fro about it, distracted in his Soul; and not being able longer to refrain her Sight, her last Words still resounding in his Ears, he came again into the Room where he left her with Don *Antonio*, just as she revived, and called him, exclaiming on his Cruelty, in leaving her so soon. But when, turning her Eyes towards the Door, she saw him; Oh! with what eager Haste she flew to him! then clasped him round the Waist, obliging him, with all the tender Expressions that the Soul of a Lover, and a Woman's too, is capable of uttering, not to leave her in the Possession of Don *Antonio*. This so amaz'd her slighted Lover, that he knew not, at first, how to proceed in this tormenting Scene; but at last, summoning all his wonted Resolution, and Strength of Mind, he told her, He would put her out of his Power, if she would consent to retreat for some few Hours to a Nunnery that was not above half a Mile distant from thence, till he had discoursed his Friend, Don *Henrique* something more particularly than hitherto, about this Matter: To which she readily agreed, upon the Promise that Don *Henrique* made her, of seeing her with the first Opportunity. They waited on her then to the Convent, where she was kindly and respectfully received by the Lady Abbess; but it was not long before her Grief renewing with greater Violence, and more afflicting Circumstances, had obliged them to stay with her till it was almost dark, when they once more begged the Liberty of an Hour's Absence; and the better to palliate their Design, *Henrique* told her, that he would make use of her Father Don *Richardo's* Coach, in which they came to Don *Antonio's*, for so small a Time: which they did, leaving only *Eleonora* her Attendant with her, with out whom she had been at a Loss, among so many fair Strangers; Strangers, I mean, to her unhappy Circumstances: Whilst they were carry'd near a Mile farther, where, just as 'twas dark, they lighted from the Coach, Don *Henrique*, ordering the Servants not to stir thence till their Return from their private Walk, which was about a Furlong, in a Field that belong'd to the Convent. Here Don *Antonio* told Don *Henrique*, That he had not acted honourably; That he had betray'd him, and robb'd him at once both of a Friend and Mistress. To which t'other returned, That he understood his Meaning, when he proposed a particular Discourse about this Affair, which he now perceived must end in Blood: But you may remind your self (continued he) that I have kept my Promise in delivering her to you. Yes, (cry'd *Antonio*) after you had practis'd foully and basely on her. Not at all! (returned *Henrique*) It was her Fate that brought this Mischief on her; for I urged the Shame and Scandal of Inconstancy, but all in vain, to

her. But don't you love her, *Henrique?* (the other ask'd.) Too
well, and cannot live without her, though I fear I may feel the
cursed Effects of the same Inconstancy: However, I had quitted
her all to you, but you see how she resents it. And you shall see,
Sir, (cry'd *Antonio*, drawing his Sword in a Rage) how I resent it.
Here, without more Words, they fell to Action; to bloody Action.
(Ah! how wretched are our Sex, in being the unhappy Occasion
of so many fatal Mischiefs, even between the dearest Friends!)
They fought on each Side with the greatest Animosity of Rivals,
forgetting all the sacred Bonds of their former Friendship; till
Don *Antonio* fell, and said, dying, "Forgive me, *Henrique!* I was
to blame; I could not live without her:—I fear she will betray thy
Life, which haste and preserve, for my sake—Let me not die all at
once!—Heaven pardon both of us!—Farewel! Oh, haste! Farewel!
(*returned Don* Henrique) Farewel, thou bravest, truest Friend!
Farewel thou noblest Part of me!—And Farewel all the Quiet of
my Soul." Then stooping, he kissed his Cheek; but, rising, he
found he must retire in time, or else must perish through Loss
of Blood, for he had received two or three dangerous Wounds,
besides others of less Consequence: Wherefore he made all the
convenient Haste he could to the Coach, into which, by the
Help of the Footmen, he got, and order'd 'em to drive him
directly to Don *Richardo's* with all imaginable Speed; where he
arriv'd in little more than half an Hour's Time, and was received
by *Ardelia's* Father with the greatest Confusion and Amazement that is expressible, seeing him return'd without his
Daughter, and so desperately wounded. Before he thought it
convenient to ask him any Question more than to enquire of his
Daughter's Safety, to which he receiv'd a short but satisfactory
Answer, Don *Richardo* sent for an eminent and able Surgeon,
who probed and dress'd Don *Henrique's* Wounds, who was
immediately put to Bed; not without some Despondency of his
Recovery; but (thanks to his kind Stars, and kinder
Constitution!) he rested pretty well for some Hours that Night,
and early in the Morning, *Ardelia's* Father, who had scarce
taken any Rest all that Night, came to visit him, as soon as he

understood from the Servants who watched with him, that he was in a Condition to suffer a short Discourse; which, you may be sure, was to learn the Circumstances of the past Night's Adventure; of which Don *Henrique* gave him a perfect and pleasant Account, since he heard that Don *Antonio*, his mortal Enemy, was killed; the Assurance of whose Death was the more delightful to him, since, by this Relation, he found that *Antonio* was the Man, whom his Care of his Daughter had so often frustrated. Don *Henrique* had hardly made an End of his Narration, e'er a Servant came hastily to give *Richardo* Notice, that the Officers were come to search for his Son-in-Law that should have been; whom the Old Gentleman's wise Precaution had secured in a Room so unsuspected, that they might as reasonably have imagined the entire Walls of his House had a Door made of Stones, as that there should have been one to that close Apartment: He went therefore boldly to the Officers, and gave them all the Keys of his House, with free Liberty to examine every Room and Chamber; which they did, but to no Purpose; and Don *Henrique* lay there undiscover'd, till his Cure was perfected.

In the mean time *Ardelia*, who that fatal Night but too rightly guess'd that the Death of one or both her Lovers was the Cause that they did not return to their Promise, the next Day fell into a high Fever, in which her Father found her soon after he had clear'd himself of those who come to search for a Lover. The Assurance which her Father gave her of *Henrique's* Life, seemed a little to revive her; but the Severity of *Antonio's* Fate was no Way obliging to her, since she could not but retain the Memory of his Love and Constancy; which added to her Afflictions, and heightened her Distemper, insomuch that *Richardo* was constrain'd to leave her under the Care of the good Lady Abbess, and to the diligent Attendance of *Eleonora*, not daring to hazard her Life in a Removal to his own House. All their Care and Diligence was however ineffectual; for she languished even to the least Hope of Recovery, till immediately after the first Visit of Don *Henrique*, which was the first he made in a Month's Time, and that by Night *incognito*, with her Father, her Distemper visibly retreated each Day: Yet when at last she enjoy'd a perfect Health of Body, her Mind grew sick, and she plunged into a deep Melancholy; which made her entertain a positive Resolution of taking the Veil at the End of her Novitiate; which accordingly she did, notwithstanding all the Intreaties, Prayers, and Tears both of her Father and Lover. But she soon repented her Vow, and often wish'd that she might by any Means see and speak to Don *Henrique*, by whose Help she promised to her self a Deliverance out of her voluntary Imprisonment: Nor were his Wishes wanting to the same Effect, tho' he was forced to fly into *Italy*, to avoid the Prosecution of *Antonio's* Friends. Thither she pursu'd him; nor could he any way shun her, unless he could have left his Heart at a Distance from his Body: Which made him take a fatal Resolution of returning to *Seville* in Disguise, where he wander'd about the Convent every Night like a Ghost (for indeed his Soul was within, while his inanimate Trunk was without) till at last he found Means to convey a Letter to her, which both surprized and delighted her. The Messenger that brought it her was one of her Mother-in-Law's Maids, whom he had known before, and met accidentally one Night as he was going his Rounds, and she coming out from *Ardelia*; with her he prevail'd, and with Gold obliged her to Secrecy and Assistance: Which proved so successful, that he understood from *Ardelia* her strong Desire of Liberty, and the Continuance of her Passion for him, together with the Means and Time most convenient and likely to succeed for her Enlargement. The Time was the fourteenth Night following, at twelve o'Clock, which just compleated a Month since his Return thither; at which Time they both promised themselves the greatest Happiness on Earth. But you may observe the Justice of Heaven, in their Disappointment.

Don *Sebastian*, who still pursu'd him with a most implacable Hatred, had traced him even to *Italy*, and there narrowly missing him, posted after him to *Toledo*; so sure and secret was his Intelligence! As soon as he arriv'd, he went directly to the Convent where his Sister *Elvira* had been one of the Profess'd, ever since Don *Henrique* had forsaken her, and where *Ardelia* had taken her repented Vow. *Elvira* had all along conceal'd the Occasion of her coming thither from *Ardelia*; and tho' she was her only Confident, and knew the whole Story of her Misfortunes, and heard the Name of Don *Henrique* repeated a hundred Times a Day, whom still she lov'd most perfectly, yet never gave her beautiful Rival any Cause of Suspicion that she lov'd him, either by Words or Looks: Nay more, when she understood that Don *Henrique* came to the Convent with *Ardelia* and *Antonio*, and at other Times with her Father; yet she had so great a Command of her self, as to refrain seeing him, or to be seen by him; nor ever intended to have spoken or writ to him, had not her Brother Don *Sebastian* put her upon the cruel Necessity of doing the last; who coming to visit his Sister (as I have said before) found her with Dona *Ardelia*, whom he never remembred to have seen, nor who ever had seen him but twice, and that was about six Years before, when she was but ten Years of Age, when she fell passionately in Love with him, and continu'd her Passion till about the fourteenth Year of her Empire, when unfortunate *Antonio* first began his Court to her. Don *Sebastian* was really a very desirable Person, being at that time very beautiful, his Age not exceeding six and twenty, of a sweet Conversation, very brave, but revengeful and irreconcilable (like most of his Countrymen) and of an honourable Family. At the Sight of him *Ardelia* felt her former Passion renew; which proceeded and continued with such Violence, that it utterly defac'd the Ideas of *Antonio* and *Henrique*. (No Wonder that she who could resolve to forsake her God for Man, should quit one Lover for another.) In short, she then only wished that he might love her equally, and then she doubted not of contriving the Means of their Happiness betwixt 'em. She had her Wish, and more, if possible; for he lov'd her beyond the Thought of any other present or future Blessing, and fail'd not to let her know it, at the second Interview; when he receiv'd the greatest Pleasure he could have wish'd, next to the Joys of a Bridal Bed: For she confessed her Love to him, and presently put him upon thinking on the Means of her Escape; but not finding his Designs so likely to succeed, as those Measures she had sent to Don *Henrique*, she communicates the very same to Don *Sebastian*, and agreed with him to make use of them on that very Night, wherein she had obliged Don *Henrique* to attempt her Deliverance: The Hour indeed was different, being determined to be at eleven. *Elvira*, who was present at the Conference, took the Hint; and not being willing to disoblige a Brother who had so hazarded his Life in Vindication of her, either does not, or would not seem to oppose his Inclinations at that Time: However, when he retired with her to talk more particularly of his intended Revenge on Don *Henrique*, who he told her lay somewhere absconded in *Toledo*, and whom he had resolved, as he assured her, to sacrifice to her injur'd Honour, and his Resentments; she oppos'd that his vindictive Resolution with all the forcible Arguments in a virtuous and pious Lady's Capacity, but in vain: so that immediately upon his Retreat from the Convent, she took the Opportunity of writing to Don *Henrique* as follows, the fatal Hour not being then seven Nights distant.

Don *Henrique*,
My Brother is now in Town, in Pursuit of your Life; nay more, of your Mistress, who has consented to make her Escape from the Convent, at the same Place of it, and by the same Means on which she had agreed to give her self entirely to you, but the Hour is eleven. I know, Henrique, *your* Ardelia *is dearer to you than your Life: But your Life, your dear Life, is more desired than any Thing in this World, by*

Your injur'd and forsaken
ELVIRA.

This she delivered to *Richardo's* Servant, whom *Henrique*

had gained that Night, as soon as she came to visit *Ardelia*, at her usual Hour, just as she went out of the Cloister.

Don *Henrique* was not a little surprized with this *Billet*; however, he could hardly resolve to forbear his accustom'd Visits to *Ardelia*, at first: But upon more mature Consideration, he only chose to converse with her by Letters, which still press'd her to be mindful of her Promise, and of the Hour, not taking notice of any Caution that he had received of her Treachery. To which she still return'd in Words that might assure him of her Constancy.

The dreadful Hour wanted not a Quarter of being perfect, when Don *Henrique* came; and having fixed his Rope-Ladder to that Part of the Garden-Wall, where he was expected, *Ardelia*, who had not stir'd from that very Place for a Quarter of an Hour before, prepar'd to ascend by it; which she did, as soon as his Servant had returned and fixed it on the inner-side of the Wall: On the Top of which, at a little Distance, she found another fasten'd, for her to descend on the out-side, whilst Don *Henrique* eagerly waited to receive her. She came at last, and flew into his Arms; which made *Henrique* cry out in a Rapture, *Am I at last once more happy in having my* Ardelia *in my Possession*! She, who knew his Voice, and now found she was betray'd, but knew not by whom, shriek'd out, *I am ruin'd! help! help!—Loose me, I charge you*, Henrique! *Loose me*! At that very Moment, and at those very Words, came *Sebastian*, attended by only one Servant; and hearing *Henrique* reply, *Not all the Powers of Hell shall snatch you from me*, drawing his Sword, without one Word, made a furious Pass at him: but his Rage and Haste misguided his Arm, for his Sword went quite through *Ardelia's* Body, who only said, *Ah, wretched Maid!* and drop'd from *Henrique's* Arms, who then was obliged to quit her, to preserve his own Life, if possible: however he had not had so much Time as to draw, had not *Sebastian* been amazed at this dreadful Mistake of his Sword; but presently recollecting himself, he flew with redoubled Rage to attack *Henrique*; and his Servant had seconded him, had not *Henrique's*, who was now descended, otherwise diverted him. They fought with the greatest Animosity on both Sides, and with equal Advantage; for they both fell together: *Ah, my* Ardelia, *I come to thee now!* (*Sebastian* groan'd out,)—*'Twas this unlucky Arm, which now embraces thee, that killed thee. Just Heaven!* (she sigh'd out,)—*Oh, yet have Mercy!* (Here they both dy'd.) *Amen*, (cry'd *Henrique*, dying) *I want it most—Oh*, Antonio! *Oh*, Elvira! *Ah, there's the Weight that sinks me down.—And yet I wish Forgiveness.—Once more, sweet Heaven, have Mercy!* He could not out-live that last Word; which was echo'd by *Elvira*, who all this while stood weeping, and calling out for Help, as she stood close to the Wall in the Garden.

This alarmed the Rest of the Sisters, who rising, caus'd the Bell to be rung out, as upon dangerous Occasions it used to be; which rais'd the Neighbourhood, who came time enough to remove the dead Bodies of the two Rivals, and of the late fallen Angel *Ardelia*. The injur'd and neglected *Elvira*, whose Piety designed quite contrary Effects, was immediately seiz'd with a violent Fever; which, as it was violent, did not last long: for she dy'd within four and twenty Hours, with all the happy Symptoms of a departing Saint.

THE UNFORTUNATE BRIDE

OR
THE BLIND LADY A BEAUTY

THE UNFORTUNATE BRIDE
OR THE BLIND LADY A BEAUTY

Frankwit and *Wildvill*, were two young Gentlemen of very considerable Fortunes, both born in *Staffordshire*, and, during their Minority, both educated together, by which Opportunity they contracted a very inviolable Friendship, a Friendship which grew up with them; and though it was remarkably known to every Body else, they knew it not themselves; they never made Profession of it in Words, but Actions; so true a Warmth their Fires could boast, as needed not the Effusion of their Breath to make it live. *Wildvill* was of the richest Family, but *Frankwit* of the noblest; *Wildvill* was admired for outward Qualifications, as Strength, and manly Proportions, *Frankwit* for a much softer Beauty, for his inward Endowments, Pleasing in his Conversation, of a free, and moving Air, humble in his Behaviour, and if he had any Pride, it was but just enough to shew that he did not affect Humility; his Mind bowed with a Motion as unconstrained as his Body, nor did he force this Vertue in the least, but he allowed it only. So aimable he was, that every Virgin that had Eyes, knew too she had a Heart, and knew as surely she should lose it. His *Cupid* could not be reputed blind, he never shot for him, but he was sure to wound. As every other Nymph admired him, so he was dear to all the Tuneful Sisters; the Muses were fired with him as much as their own radiant God *Apollo*; their loved Springs and Fountains were not so grateful to their Eyes as he, him they esteemed their *Helicon* and *Parnassus* too; in short, when ever he pleased, he could enjoy them all. Thus he enamour'd the whole Female Sex, but amongst all the sighing Captives of his Eyes, *Belvira* only boasted Charms to move him; her Parents lived near his, and even from their Childhood they felt mutual Love, as if their Eyes, at their first meeting, had struck out such Glances, as had kindled into amorous Flame. And now *Belvira* in her fourteenth Year, (when the fresh Spring of young Virginity began to cast more lively Bloomings in her Cheeks, and softer Longings in her Eyes) by her indulgent Father's Care was sent to *London* to a Friend, her Mother being lately dead: When, as if Fortune ordered it so, *Frankwit's* Father took a Journey to the other World, to let his Son the better enjoy the Pleasures and Delights of this: The young Lover now with all imaginable haste interred his Father, nor did he shed so many Tears for his Loss, as might in the least quench the Fire which he received from his *Belvira's* Eyes, but (Master of seventeen Hundred Pounds a Year, which his Father left him) with all the Wings of Love flies to *London*, and sollicits *Belvira* with such Fervency, that it might be thought he meant Death's Torch should kindle *Hymen's*; and now as soon as he arrives at his Journey's end, he goes to pay a Visit to the fair Mistress of his Soul, and assures her, That tho' he was absent from her, yet she was still with him; and that all the Road he travell'd, her beauteous Image danced before him, and like the ravished Prophet, he saw his Diety in every Bush; in short, he paid her constant Visits, the Sun ne'er rose or set, but still he saw it in her Company, and every Minute of the Day he counted by his Sighs. So incessantly he importuned her that she could no longer hold out, and was pleased in the surrender of her Heart, since it was he was Conqueror; and therefore felt a Triumph in her yielding. Their Flames now joyned, grew more and more, glowed in their Cheeks, and lightened in their Glances: Eager they looked, as if there were Pulses beating in their Eyes; and all endearing, at last she vowed, that *Frankwit* living she would ne'er be any other Man's. Thus they past on some time, while every Day rowl'd over fair; Heaven showed an Aspect all serene, and the Sun seemed to smile at what was done. He still caressed his Charmer, with an Innocence becoming his Sincerity; he lived upon her tender Breath, and basked in the bright Lustre of her Eyes, with Pride, and secret Joy.

He saw his Rivals languish for that Bliss, those Charms, those Raptures and extatick Transports, which he engrossed alone. But now some eighteen Months (some Ages in a Lover's Kalendar) winged with Delights, and fair *Belvira* now grown fit for riper Joys, knows hardly how she can deny her pressing Lover, and herself, to crown their Vows, and joyn their Hands as well as Hearts. All this while the young Gallant wash'd himself clean of that shining Dirt, his Gold; he fancied little of Heaven dwelt in his yellow Angels, but let them fly away, as it were on their own golden Wings; he only valued the smiling Babies in *Belvira's* Eyes. His Generosity was boundless, as his Love, for no Man ever truly loved, that was not generous. He thought his Estate, like his Passion, was a sort of a *Pontick* Ocean, it could never know an Ebb; But now he found it could be fathom'd, and that the Tide was turning, therefore he sollicits with more impatience the consummation of their Joys, that both might go like Martyrs from their Flames immediately to Heaven; and now at last it was agreed between them, that they should both be one, but not without some Reluctancy on the Female side; for 'tis the Humour of our Sex, to deny most eagerly those Grants to Lovers, for which most tenderly we sigh, so contradictory are we to our selves, as if the Deity had made us with a seeming Reluctancy to his own Designs; placing as much Discords in our Minds, as there is Harmony in our Faces. We are a sort of aiery Clouds, whose Lightning flash out one way, and the Thunder another. Our Words and Thoughts can ne'er agree. So this young charming Lady thought her Desires could live in their own longings, like Misers wealth-devouring Eyes; and e'er she consented to her Lover, prepared him first with speaking Looks, and then with a fore-running Sigh, applyed to the dear Charmer thus: "*Frankwit*, I am afraid to venture the Matrimonial Bondage, it may make you think your self too much confined, in being only free to one." "Ah! my dear *Belvira*," he replied, "That one, like *Manna*, has the Taste of all, why should I be displeased to be confined to Paradice, when it was the Curse of our Forefathers to be set at large, tho' they had the whole World to roam in: You have, my love, ubiquitary Charms, and you are all in all, in every Part." "Ay, but," reply'd *Belvira*, "we are all like Perfumes, and too continual Smelling makes us seem to have lost our Sweets, I'll be judged by my Cousin *Celesia* here, if it be not better to live still in mutual Love, without the last Enjoyment." (I had forgot to tell my Reader that *Celesia* was an Heiress, the only Child of a rich *Turkey* Merchant, who, when he dyed, left her Fifty thousand Pound in Money, and some Estate in Land; but, poor Creature, she was Blind to all these Riches, having been born without the use of Sight, though in all other Respects charming to a wonder.) "Indeed," says *Celesia*, (for she saw clearly in her Mind) "I admire you should ask my Judgment in such a Case, where I have never had the least Experience; but I believe it is but a sickly Soul which cannot nourish its Offspring of Desires without preying upon the Body." "Believe me," reply'd *Frankwit*, "I bewail your want of Sight, and I could almost wish you my own Eyes for a Moment, to view your charming Cousin, where you would see such Beauties as are too dazling to be long beheld; and if too daringly you gazed, you would feel the Misfortune of the loss of Sight, much greater than the want of it: And you would acknowledge, that in too presumptuously seeing, you would be blinder then, than now unhappily you are."

"Ah! I must confess," reply'd *Belvira*, "my poor, dear Cousin is Blind, for I fancy she bears too great an Esteem for *Frankwit*, and only longs for Sight to look on him." "Indeed," reply'd *Celesia*, "I would be glad to see *Frankwit*, for I fancy he's as dazling, as he but now describ'd his Mistress, and if I fancy I see him, sure I do see him, for Sight is Fancy, is it not? or do you feel my Cousin with your Eyes?" "This is indeed, a charming Blindness," reply'd *Frankwit*, "and the fancy of your Sight excels the certainty of ours. Strange! that there should be such Glances even in blindness? You, fair Maid, require not Eyes to conquer, if your Night has such Stars, what Sunshine would you Day of Sight have, if ever you should see?" "I fear those Stars you talk of," said *Belvira*, "have some Influence on you, and by the Compass you sail by now, I guess you are steering to my Cousin. She is indeed charming enough to have been another Offspring of bright *Venus*, Blind like her Brother

Cupid." "That *Cupid*," reply'd *Celesia*, "I am afraid has shot me, for methinks I would not have you marry *Frankwit*, but rather live as you do without the last Enjoyment, for methinks if he were marry'd, he would be more out of Sight than he already is.' 'Ah, Madam," return'd *Frankwit*, "Love is no Camelion, it cannot feed on Air alone." "No but," rejoyn'd *Celesia*, "you Lovers that are not Blind like Love it self, have am'rous Looks to feed on." "Ah! believe it,' said *Belvira*, "'tis better, *Frankwit*, not to lose Paradice by too much Knowledge; Marriage Enjoyments does but wake you from your sweet golden Dreams: Pleasure is but a Dream, dear *Frankwit*, but a Dream, and to be waken'd." "Ah! Dearest, but unkind *Belvira*," answer'd *Frankwit*, "sure there's no waking from Delight, in being lull'd on those soft Breasts of thine." "Alas! (reply'd the Bride to be) it is that very lulling wakes you; Women enjoy'd, are like Romances read, or Raree-shows once seen, meer Tricks of the slight of Hand, which, when found out, you only wonder at your selves for wondering so before at them. 'Tis Expectation endears the Blessing; Heaven would not be Heaven, could we tell what 'tis. When the Plot's out you have done with the Play, and when the last Act's done, you see the Curtain drawn with great indifferency." "O my *Belvira*," answered *Frankwit*, "that Expectation were indeed a Monster which Enjoyment could not satisfy: I should take no pleasure," he rejoin'd, 'running from Hill to Hill, like Children chasing that Sun, which I could never catch." "O thou shalt have it then, that Sun of Love," reply'd *Belvira*, fir'd by this Complaint, and gently rush'd into Arms, (rejoyn'd) so *Phœbus* rushes radiant and unsullied, into a gilded Cloud. "Well then, my dear *Belvira*," answered *Frankwit*, "be assured I shall be ever yours, as you are mine; fear not you shall never draw Bills of Love upon me so fast, as I shall wait in readiness to pay them; but now I talk of Bills, I must retire into *Cambridgeshire*, where I have a small Concern as yet unmortgaged, I will return thence with a Brace of thousand Pounds within a Week at furthest, with which our Nuptials, by their Celebration, shall be worthy of our Love. And

then, my Life, my Soul, we shall be join'd, never to part again."
This tender Expression mov'd *Belvira* to shed some few Tears,
and poor *Celesia* thought herself most unhappy that she had
not Eyes to weep with too; but if she had, such was the
greatness of her Grief, that sure she would have soon grown
Blind with weeping. In short, after a great many soft Vows, and
Promises of an inviolable Faith, they parted with a pompous
sort of pleasing Woe; their Concern was of such a mixture of
Joy and Sadness, as the Weather seems, when it both rains and
shines. And now the last, the very last Adieu's was over, for the
Farewels of Lovers hardly ever end, and *Frankwit* (the Time
being Summer) reach'd *Cambridge* that Night, about Nine a
Clock; (Strange! that he should have made such Haste to fly
from what so much he lov'd!) and now, tir'd with the fatigue of
his Journey, he thought fit to refresh himself by writing some
few Lines to his belov'd *Belvira*; for a little Verse after the dull
Prose Company of his Servant, was as great an Ease to him,
(from whom it flow'd as naturally and unartificially, as his Love
or his Breath) as a Pace or Hand-gallop, after a hard, uncouth,
and rugged Trot. He therefore, finding his *Pegasus* was no way
tir'd with his Land-travel, takes a short Journey thro' the Air,
and writes as follows:

My dearest dear Belvira,

YOU knew my Soul, you knew it yours before,
I told it all, and now can tell no more;
Your Presents never wants fresh Charms to move,
But now more strange, and unknown Pow'r you prove, ⎫
For now your very Absence 'tis I love. ⎭
Something there is which strikes my wandring View,
And still before my Eyes I fancy you.
Charming you seem, all charming, heavenly fair, ⎫
Bright as a Goddess, does my Love appear, ⎬
You seem, *Belvira*, what indeed you are. ⎭
Like the Angelick Off-spring of the Skies,

With beatifick Glories in your Eyes:
Sparkling with radiant Lustre all Divine,
Angels, and Gods! oh Heavens! how bright they shine!
Are you *Belvira*? can I think you mine!
Beyond ev'n Thought, I do thy Beauties see,
Can such a Heaven of Heavens be kept for me!
Oh be assur'd, I shall be ever true,
I must —
For if I would, I can't be false to you.
Oh! how I wish I might no longer stay,
Tho' I resolve I will no Time delay,
One Tedious Week, and then I'll fleet away.
Tho' Love be blind, he shall conduct my Road,
Wing'd with almighty Love, to your Abode,
I'll fly, and grow Immortal as a God.
Short is my stay, yet my impatience strong,
Short tho' it is, alas! I think it long.
I'll come, my Life, new Blessings to pursue,
Love then shall fly a Flight he never flew,
I'll stretch his balmy Wings; I'm yours,—*Adieu.*

Frankwit.

This Letter *Belvira* receiv'd with unspeakable Joy, and laid it up safely in her Bosom; laid it, where the dear Author of it lay before, and wonderfully pleas'd with his Humour of writing Verse, resolv'd not to be at all behind-hand with him, and so writ as follows:

My dear Charmer,

YOU knew before what Power your Love could boast,
But now your constant Faith confirms me most.
Absent Sincerity the best assures,
Love may do much, but Faith much more allures,
For now your Constancy has bound me yours.
I find, methinks, in Verse some Pleasure too,

I cannot want a Muse, who write to you.
Ah! soon return, return, my charming Dear,
Heav'n knows how much we Mourn your Absence here:
My poor *Celesia* now would Charm your Soul,
Her Eyes, once Blind, do now Divinely rowl.
An aged Matron has by Charms unknown,
Given her clear Sight as perfect as thy own.
And yet, beyond her Eyes, she values thee,
'Tis for thy Sake alone she's glad to see.
She begg'd me, pray remember her to you,
That is a Task which now I gladly do.
Gladly, since so I only recommend
A dear Relation, and a dearer Friend,
Ne're shall my Love—but here my Note must end.

> *Your ever true* Belvira.

When this Letter was written, it was strait shown to *Celesia*, who look'd upon any Thing that belong'd to *Frankwit*, with rejoycing Glances; so eagerly she perus'd it, that her tender Eyes beginning to Water, she cry'd out, (fancying she saw the Words dance before her View) "Ah! Cousin, Cousin, your Letter is running away, sure it can't go itself to *Frankwit*." A great Deal of other pleasing innocent Things she said, but still her Eyes flow'd more bright with lustrous Beams, as if they were to shine out; now all that glancing Radiancy which had been so long kept secret, and, as if, as soon as the Cloud of Blindness once was broke, nothing but Lightnings were to flash for ever after. Thus in mutual Discourse they spent their Hours, while *Frankwit* was now ravished with the Receipt of this charming Answer of *Belvira's*, and blest his own Eyes which discovered to him the much welcome News of fair *Celesia's*. Often he read the Letters o'er and o'er, but there his Fate lay hid, for twas that very Fondness proved his Ruin. He lodg'd at a Cousin's House of his, and there, (it being a private Family) lodged likewise a Blackamoor Lady, then a Widower; a whimsical Knight had taken a Fancy to enjoy her: *Enjoy her did I say? Enjoy the Devil in the Flesh at once!* I know not how it was, but he would fain have been a Bed with her, but she not consenting on unlawful Terms, *(but sure all Terms are with her unlawful)* the Knight soon marry'd her, as if there were not hell enough in Matrimony, but he must wed the Devil too. The Knight a little after died, and left this Lady of his (whom I shall *Moorea*) an Estate of six thousand Pounds *per Ann*. Now this *Moorea* observed the joyous *Frankwit* with an eager Look, her Eyes seemed like Stars of the first Magnitude glaring in the Night; she greatly importuned him to discover the Occasion of his transport, but he denying it, (as 'tis the Humour of our Sex) made her the more Inquisitive; and being Jealous that it was from a Mistress, employ'd her Maid to steal it, and if she found it such, to bring it her: accordingly it succeeded, for *Frankwit* having drank hard with some of the Gentlemen of that Shire, found himself indisposed, and soon went to Bed, having put the Letter in his Pocket: The Maid therefore to *Moorea* contrived that all the other Servants should be out of the Way, that she might plausibly officiate in the Warming the Bed of the indisposed Lover, but likely, had it not been so, she had warmed it by his Intreaties in a more natural Manner; he being in Bed in an inner Room, she slips out the Letter from his Pocket, carries it to her Mistress to read, and so restores it whence she had it; in the Morning the poor Lover wakened in a violent Fever, burning with a Fire more hot than that of Love. In short, he continued Sick a considerable while, all which time the Lady *Moorea* constantly visited him, and he as unwillingly saw her (poor Gentleman) as he would have seen a Parson; for as the latter would have perswaded, so the former scared him to Repentance. In the mean while, during his sickness, several Letters were sent to him by his dear *Belvira*, and *Celesia* too, (then learning to write) had made a shift to give him a line or two in Postscript with her Cousin, but all was intercepted by the jealousy of the Black *Moorea*, black in her mind, and dark, as well as in her body. *Frankwit* too writ several Letters as he was able, complaining of her unkindness, those likewise were all stopt by the same Blackmoor Devil. At last, it happened that *Wildvill*, (who I told my Reader was *Frankwit's* friend) came to *London*, his Father likewise dead, and now Master of a very plentiful fortune, he resolves to marry, and paying a visit to *Belvira*, enquires of her concerning *Frankwit*, she all in mourning for the loss, told him his friend was dead. "Ah! *Wildvill*, he is dead," said she, "and died not mine, a Blackmoor Lady had bewitched him from me; I received a Letter lately which informed me all; there was no name subscribed to it, but it intimated, that it was written at the request of dying *Frankwit*." "Oh! I am sorry at my Soul," said *Wildvill*, "for I loved him with the best, the dearest friendship; no doubt then," rejoyned he, "'tis Witchcaft indeed that could make him false to you; what delight could he take in a Blackmoor Lady, tho' she had received him at once with a Soul as open as her longing arms, and with her Petticoat put off her modesty. Gods! How could he change a whole *Field Argent* into downright *Sables*." "'Twas done," returned *Celesia*, "with no small blot, I fancy, to the Female 'Scutcheon." In short, after some more discourse, but very sorrowful, *Wildvill* takes his leave, extreamly taken with the fair *Belvira*, more beauteous in her cloud of woe; he paid her afterwards frequent visits, and found her wonder for the odd inconstancy of *Frankwit*, greater than her sorrow, since he dy'd so unworthy of her. *Wildvill* attack'd her with all the force of vigorous love, and she (as she thought) fully convinc'd of *Frankwit's* death, urg'd by the fury and impatience of her new ardent Lover, soon surrender'd, and the day of their Nuptials now arriv'd, their hands were joyn'd. In the mean time *Frankwit* (for he still liv'd) knew nothing of the Injury the base *Moorea* practis'd, knew not that 'twas thro' her private order, that the fore-mention'd account of his falshood and his death was sent; but impatient to see his Dear *Belvira*, tho'yet extremely weak, rid post to *London*, and that very day arriv'd there, immediately after the Nuptials of his Mistress and his Friend were celebrated. I was at this time in *Cambridge*, and having some small acquaintance with this Blackmoor Lady, and sitting in her Room that evening, after *Frankwit's* departure thence, in *Moorea's* absence, saw inadvertently a bundle of Papers, which she had gathered up, as I suppose, to burn, since now they grew but useless, she having no farther Hopes of him: I fancy'd I knew the Hand, and thence my Curiosity only led me to see the Name, and finding *Belvira* subscrib'd, I began to guess there was some foul play in Hand. *Belvira* being my particularly intimate Acquaintance, I read one of them, and finding the Contents, convey'd them all secretly out with me, as I thought, in Point of Justice I was bound, and sent them to *Belvira* by that Night's Post; so that they came to her Hands soon after the Minute of her Marriage, with an Account how, and by what Means I came to light on them. No doubt but they exceedingly surpriz'd her: But Oh! Much more she grew amaz'd immediately after, to see the Poor, and now unhappy *Frankwit*, who privately had enquir'd for her below, being received as a Stranger, who said he had some urgent Business with her, in a back Chamber below Stairs. What Tongue, what Pen can express the mournful Sorrow of this Scene! At first they both stood Dumb, and almost Senseless; she took him for the Ghost of *Frankwit*; he looked so pale, new risen from his Sickness, he (for he had heard at his Entrance in the House, that his *Belvira* marry'd *Wildvill*) stood in Amaze, and like a Ghost indeed, wanted the Power to speak, till spoken to the first. At last, he draws his Sword, designing there to fall upon it in her Presence; she then imagining it his Ghost too sure, and come to kill her, shrieks out and Swoons; he ran immediately to her, and catch'd her in his Arms, and while he strove to revive and bring her to herself, tho' that he thought could never now be done, since she was marry'd. *Wildvill* missing his Bride, and hearing the loud Shriek, came running down, and entring the Room, sees his Bride lie clasp'd in *Frankwit's* Arms. "Ha! Traytor!" He cries out, drawing his Sword with an impatient Fury, "have you kept that Strumpet all this while, curst *Frankwit*, and now think fit to put your damn'd cast Mistress upon me: could not you forbear her neither ev'n on my Wedding Day? abominable Wretch!" Thus saying, he made a full Pass at *Frankwit*, and run him thro' the left Arm, and quite thro' the Body of the poor *Belvira*; that thrust immediately made her start, tho' *Frankwit's* Endeavours all before were useless. Strange! that her Death reviv'd her! For ah! she felt, that now she only liv'd to die! Striving thro' wild Amazement to run from such a Scene of Horror, as her Apprehensions shew'd her; down she dropt, and *Frankwit* seeing her fall, (all Friendship disannull'd by such a Chain of Injuries) Draws, fights with, and stabs his own lov'd *Wildvill*. Ah! Who can express the Horror and Distraction of this fatal Misunderstanding! The House was alarm'd, and in came poor *Celesia*, running in Confusion just as *Frankwit* was off'ring to kill himself, to die with a false Friend, and perjur'd Mistress, for he suppos'd them such. Poor *Celesia* now bemoan'd her unhappiness of sight, and wish'd she again were blind. *Wildvill* dy'd immediately, and *Belvira* only surviv'd him long enough to unfold all their most unhappy fate, desiring *Frankwit* with her dying breath, if ever he lov'd her, (and now she said that she deserv'd his love, since she had convinced him that she was not false) to marry her poor dear *Celesia*, and love her tenderly for her *Belvira's* sake; leaving her, being her nearest Relation, all her fortune, and he, much dearer than it all, to be added to her own; so joyning his and *Celesia's* Hands, she poured her last breath upon his Lips, and said, "Dear *Frankwit*, *Frankwit*, I die yours." With tears and wondrous sorrow he promis'd to obey her Will, and in some months after her interrment, he perform'd his promise.

NOTES

Even now, relatively little is known for certain of Aphra Behn (1640-89), probably the first professional woman writer in English literature. "I hope to establish that she was born in 1640," wrote Maureen Duffy in her seminal study *The Passionate Shepherdess* (London, 1977); and it is in similarly tentative terms that much surrounding her parentage and birth, the sojourn in Surinam on which she drew for *Oroonoko*, her spying activities (in the employ of Charles II) in the Netherlands in 1666-7, her imprisonment for debt, and much beside, is frequently and of necessity expressed in biographical accounts. What *is* certain, however, is that she first had a play performed in 1670 (*The Forced Marriage*), and that throughout the 1670s and 80s plays poured from her pen, and were joined by verse and prose. A friend of Etherege, Otway and Dryden, she was celebrated in her lifetime, and was buried in Westminster Abbey when she died on 16 April 1689.

For twentieth century purposes, Behn's name was importantly re-established by the Summers edition (see below), which drew upon invisible but significant input from Edmund Gosse, and then consolidated with an essay by Virginia Woolf in *A Room of One's Own* (1928). Identifying Behn as the first English woman to earn a living by her pen, Woolf, in praising her "vitality, humour and courage", nonetheless betrayed her own customary snobbery in describing these, in an allusion to Behn's presumably humble origins, as "plebeian virtues".

Behn's reputation today rests chiefly on her numerous plays, most particularly *The Rover* (1681), which has been successfully revived in recent years. But her prose, above all *Oroonoko* and *The Fair Jilt*, repays serious attention. Never as completely neglected as some polemicists would now have us believe, the fiction was handsomely presented in the seminal edition published in 1915 by Montague Summers, and to that edition, whatever its failings, all subsequent editors have in some degree been indebted. (A new complete edition is currently appearing under the editorship of Janet Todd.) Maureen Duffy's study referred to above can be recommended as a highly readable and soundly researched critical biography. In the notes that follow, words that can be found in any good dictionary are not glossed. *Ed.*

OROONOKO, OR THE ROYAL SLAVE

This novel (or romance, or, from its length, novella) was probably published c. 1678 and re-issued in the *Three Histories* of 1688. It was widely translated (e.g. into German in 1709, into French for the first of several times in 1745) and the 1696 stage adaptation by Thomas Southerne (1660–1746) commanded theatre interest throughout the following century.

Oroonoko is widely seen as the first sustained protest in English literature against the slave trade. Indeed, it goes further: Behn urges the superior moral virtue of the Africans and of the indigenous South American peoples, and shows their white oppressors as hypocritical and treacherous.

p. 9   *Surinam*: after inauspicious beginnings ending in massacre at the hands of the indigenous peoples, the English established the colony of Surinam, on the north coast of South America, in 1650. Under the terms of the Treaty of Breda (1667) it was exchanged with the Dutch for New York. For a long time the question of whether Aphra Behn herself ever set foot in Surinam was a matter of debate, but the issue is now settled, and there is strong evidence that she visited the colony in 1663.

p. 10   *the Indian Queen*: play by John Dryden and John Howard, first performed in 1663.

p. 13   *Coromantien*: also known as the Gold Coast, now Ghana.

p. 15   *the deplorable Death of our great Monarch*: Charles I, executed in 1649.

p. 34   *maugre*: despite.

p. 45   *Backearary*: slave-owner.

p. 49   *Shock-Dog*: a dog with long or shaggy hair.

p. 54   *my Father dy'd at Sea*: this is now accepted as biographical fact.

p. 54   *his late Majesty*: Charles II died in 1685.

p. 54   *parted so easily with it to the Dutch*: cf. note to p. 9.

p. 56   *Harry Martin*: Henry Marten (1602–80) was a follower of Oliver Cromwell (though they subsequently disagreed) and sat on the trial of Charles I.

p. 58   *Numb-Eel*: the electric eel.

p. 66   *Salvages*: i.e. savages.

p. 69   *Byam*: William Byam rose to become governor of the Surinam colony in 1663.

p. 72   *Colonel Martin ... my new Comedy*: George Marten, brother of Henry (cf. note to p. 56). The new comedy was *The Younger Brother*.

p. 74   *Newgate*: the old prison of the City of London and the County of Middlesex, located where the Old Bailey now stands.

p. 75   *Mobile*: mob.

THE FAIR JILT, OR THE HISTORY OF PRINCE TARQUIN AND MIRANDA

First published 17 April 1688 and re-issued the same year in the *Three Histories*.

Tarquin claimed to be of the line of the kings of Rome, though he was widely regarded as an impostor. (His name was hardly auspicious; in legend, Tarquin was not only the last king of the Romans, but it was the rape of Lucretia by the son of Lucius Tarquinius Superbus that led to the insurrection of Junius Brutus and the expulsion of the Tarquins from Rome.) Maureen Duffy (*The Passionate Shepherdess*, pp. 72–3) quotes the *London Gazette* of 28-31 May 1666 to this effect: "The

Prince Tarquino being condemned at Antwerp to be beheaded, for endeavouring the death of his sister-in-law: being on the scaffold, the executioner tied a handkerchief about his head and by great accident his blow lighted upon the knot, giving him only a slight wound. Upon which, the people being in a tumult, he was carried back to the Town-house, and is in hopes both of his pardon and his recovery." The next number of the *Gazette* reported that Tarquino "has since obtained his pardon from his Excellency the Marquis de Castel Rodrigo".

Behn's claim that her story is true, indeed an eye-witness account, has led to an amount of misconceived debate concerning the author's veracity; clearly it is her artistry that should interest us more.

p. 85   *Henry Pain*: Henry Neville Payne, Catholic playwright and "ardent partisan of James II [...] He is said to have been the chief instigator of the Montgomery plot in 1690, and whilst in Scotland was arrested. 10 and 11 December of that year he was severely tortured under a special order of William III, but nothing could be extracted from him. This is the last occasion on which torture was applied in Scotland." (Summers' note.) Payne died in 1710.

p. 87   *Scrutore*: i.e. escritoire, writing-desk.

p. 89   *Begines*: the order of the Beguines, established in the Low Countries in the 12th century, did not involve sisters in the taking of vows, and they were free to come and go and indeed to marry. (The name probably comes from Lambert de Bègue, a priest at Liège.)

p. 89   *Bando*: i.e. a bandeau binding a head-dress.

p. 92   *Cordeliers*: Franciscans.

p. 117 *Mittimus*: warrant.

p. 120 *Portugal Mat*: a mat of woven rushes.

p. 124 *Flambeaux*: here, not torches but torch-bearers.

THE HISTORY OF THE NUN, OR THE FAIR VOW-BREAKER

First published 1689. The novella was long shrouded in bibliographical mystery occasioned by confusion with both 'The Fair Jilt' and 'The Nun, or The Perjur'd Beauty', but the efforts of Edmund Gosse and the Belgian scholar Paul Hamelius resulted in the first reprinting of an authoritative text in the 1915 edition edited by Summers.

p. 139 *Toor*: parade.
p. 143 *Iper*: i.e. Ypres, in Flanders (Belgium).
p. 148 *Candia*: this town on Crete was besieged by the Turks in 1645 and finally taken by them in 1669. Cf. p. 181.
p. 176 *progging*: economizing.
p. 187 *Spahee*: a Turkish cavalryman.

THE ADVENTURE OF THE BLACK LADY

First published posthumously in 1698.

p. 204 *Overseers of the Poor*: officials who administered the Poor Law.

THE COURT OF THE KING OF BANTAM

First published posthumously in 1698.

p. 211 *chusing King and Queen*: it was a traditional custom to choose a "king" and "queen" to preside over Twelfth Night festivities.
p. 214 *Questions and Commands*: clearly a parlour or party game.
p. 215 *Statira ... Roxana*: the titular heroines of *The Rival Queens* (1677) by Nathaniel Lee (c. 1653–92).

271

p. 220 *Cully*: bogus.

p. 221 *A King and no King*: by Beaumont and Fletcher.

p. 223 *Morpheus*: the Greek god of dreams.

p. 224 *Chine*: saddle of mutton.

p. 224 *The London-Cuckolds*: play by Edward Ravenscroft, first performed in 1682. Until the mid-18th century it remained one of the most popular comedies on the English stage.

THE NUN, OR THE PERJUR'D BEAUTY

First published posthumously in 1698.

THE UNFORTUNATE BRIDE

First published posthumously in 1698. Frederick M. Link, who proves in his study *Aphra Behn* (New York, 1968) to be curiously out of sympathy with Behn's fiction, observes that the final scene is "as sentimental as it is unconvincing".

p. 255 *Pontick Ocean*: the Black Sea.